Maya Blake's hopes of becom... when she picked up her first ro... Little did she know her dream would come true! Does she still pinch herself every now and then to make sure it's not a dream? Yes, she does! Feel free to pinch her, too, via Twitter, Facebook or Goodreads! Happy reading!

Jackie Ashenden writes dark, emotional stories, with alpha heroes who've just got the world to their liking only to have it blown wide apart by their kick-ass heroines. She lives in Auckland, New Zealand, with her husband, the inimitable Dr Jax, two kids and two rats. When she's not torturing alpha males and their gutsy heroines she can be found drinking chocolate martinis, reading anything she can lay her hands on, wasting time on social media or being forced to go mountain biking with her husband. To keep up to date with Jackie's new releases and other news sign up to her newsletter at jackieashenden.com.

THE SICILIAN'S BANISHED BRIDE

MAYA BLAKE

THE MOST POWERFUL OF KINGS

JACKIE ASHENDEN

MILLS & BOON

First Published in Great Britain 2020
by Mills & Boon, an imprint of HarperCollins*Publishers*
1 London Bridge Street, London, SE1 9GF

The Sicilian's Banished Bride © 2020 Maya Blake

The Most Powerful of Kings © 2020 Jackie Ashenden

ISBN: 978-0-263-27832-3

MIX
Paper from
responsible sources
FSC® C007454

This book is produced from independently certified FSC™ paper
to ensure responsible forest management.
For more information visit www.harpercollins.co.uk/green.

Printed and bound in Spain
by CPI, Barcelona

THE SICILIAN'S BANISHED BRIDE

MAYA BLAKE

CHAPTER ONE

'HE'S YOURS, ROCCO. Find him...find him!'

The words pounded a relentless refrain in Rocco Vitelli's head as his Gulfstream sped him in the opposite direction towards a destination that had been nowhere on his itinerary when he'd woken up that morning.

The photograph in his hand shook and he tightened his grip.

Impossible.

His grandmother's words were simply...impossible.

Didn't they say everyone had a twin somewhere in the world? *Dio*, even that extrapolation was too far-fetched. This picture was of a child. He was a grown man of thirty-three. This child had nothing to do with him. Nothing...

'We'll be landing shortly, *signor*. Is there anything you require?' his attendant enquired.

Inform the pilot that I wish to change course immediately, he wanted to say. He held his tongue, his grandmother's pale face etched in anguish fresh in his mind.

Jaw clenching, he closed his fist over the picture, hiding it from sight. Unfortunately, Nonna's distressing words weren't so easy to dismiss.

'He's yours. Find him!'

Ridiculous. If he had a son, a flesh and blood extension of him somewhere in this world, he would know... wouldn't he?

A sudden wave of long-suppressed yearning swept through him, stealing his breath.

He would know. He was strict about taking precautions with his sexual partners. None of his liaisons in the recent past had lasted longer than a few weeks. And, by strict choice, none of them had been English.

He hadn't set foot in England in years and he hadn't taken an English lover since—

'*Signor?*'

He sighed. 'No, *grazie.*'

Just this once, he promised himself grimly. His grandmother rarely asked him for anything, not because he'd refuse, but because she insisted she needed nothing but the roof he'd provided over her head. After everything she'd sacrificed for him, running this fool's errand, even though it lodged a fist of remembered bitterness in his gut, was necessary if only to reassure her.

This visit would be short, however. Whoever this child was, Rocco intended his presence in its life to be very brief indeed.

'Has the driver been apprised of our destination?' he asked.

'*Sì, signor.* I emailed the details immediately after take-off.'

Satisfied, he nodded. Barring traffic, he should be back in the air within a few short hours. A quick detour via his Palermo villa to reassure Nonna there was no mysterious great-grandchild to be distressed about, and he could return to Abu Dhabi to oversee the final phase of the children's hospital his company was building.

Wheels touched down with barely a bump. Before it had rolled to a stop, he was moving towards the exit. His car waited on the tarmac and he slid into the back seat, grateful for its warm interior. It was early autumn, yet the temperature was near freezing.

Easing back in his seat, he glanced once more at the photo. The cherubic features, the strange, yet familiar blue eyes of the child sent another stab of deep yearning through him.

No. He wouldn't think of the past. Of *her.* The past was done, buried—

I don't want your baby!

He clenched his teeth against the chilling words slicing through his thoughts. Why were memories he'd successfully expunged for years resurfacing, today of all days?

Grimly, he shoved the photo into his breast pocket and turned his thoughts to his grandmother.

Her hysteria over the billboard picture she'd spotted on the way to morning mass was beyond his understanding. Nonna had collapsed on the pavement, much to the distress of her companion, and no amount of reassurance had soothed her except Rocco's promise, once he'd rushed to her side, that he would verify the child's identity immediately.

So here he was, on what could only be politely described as a wild goose chase. He stifled a dark curse and looked up at his driver's discreet cough.

'The news reports gridlocked traffic ahead, sir. I'll have to take a different route if you're to keep your schedule.'

Rocco's mood darkened further. With every fibre of his being, he wished himself elsewhere. But he'd made his grandmother a promise. He'd keep it, even if it meant being in the same country, breathing the same air as that... Jezebel.

He inhaled, brought his feelings under control.

'Take whatever route you must. But make sure it's quick.'

Mia Gallagher stole another indulgent caress of her sleeping son's soft cheek before stepping away with a wry smile. Nap time was fast becoming a battle of wills. At two and a half, Gianni was vigorously resisting taking his much-needed naps. This afternoon he'd hidden behind his bedroom door, unaware his chubby legs were clearly visible through the gap in the door frame. How he managed to keep so still at his age astounded her.

Her smile slipped.

She knew exactly how he came by that particular trait.

The man whose blood ran through her son's veins possessed that formidable knack, after all—

No, she wasn't going to think about him. Not now, not ever, if she could help it.

She shut the bedroom door with a sigh of relief. With an hour to herself before he woke, she had enough time to tackle the laundry and start dinner.

The sound of the doorbell as she approached her small living room made her heart sink.

Mrs Hart.

With her financial juggling getting trickier by the day and another of Gianni's photo shoots cancelled—the third one in two weeks—the last thing Mia needed was her neighbour's nosiness disguised as friendly concern. For a moment, she considered not answering.

The doorbell pealed again, followed by an insistent knock.

Mrs Hart had probably seen them return from the park. Mia had no choice but to answer or risk Gianni waking up.

She pulled open the door, a firm but polite excuse on her lips, only to take a horrified step back, her words choking in her throat as a painfully familiar figure filled the doorway.

Rocco reeled with the shock of coming face to face with the woman he'd banished from his life three years ago, even as the molten burn of instant lust thickened the blood roaring through his veins.

'Cosa è questo?' He wasn't sure whether he questioned his body's unwelcome reaction to her or the fact that someone in his security team had made a fatal blunder when he'd asked for the location of the child in the photo. Because this had to be an inexcusable, colossal error.

The breath he sucked in did nothing to provide clarity.

Someone's head…hell, several heads, would roll for delivering him to the last person on earth he wished to encounter; the one person he'd sworn never to even think of, ever again!

He conducted a swift scrutiny of Mia Gallagher and experienced a fresh jolt of shock.

Gone was the sleekly coiffed, elegant and voluptuous woman who'd graced his boardroom and bedroom for several months over three years ago. Gone were the thigh-skimming designer suits and the stunningly made-up face that had held him in thrall for far longer than he'd deemed wise, even then.

This woman looked pale and shadows lurked under her eyes, rendering the once vibrant depths a dull green. Her honey-blonde hair, scraped back in a utilitarian ponytail, lacked its former lustre. Her face was devoid of make-up, and her mouth, now hanging open, although still full and sensually curved, was bare of gloss.

His gaze lowered, and he frowned. She'd lost weight but, somehow, her breasts seemed fuller, heavier than he remembered. Lower still, her long legs were covered by pair of baggy shapeless jeans.

Altogether an unattractive package, and far removed from the sensual bombshell he'd lusted after...and nearly lost his mind over?

He jerked back at the hard, unexpected kick in his groin. *Don't even go there!*

His gaze flicked back to her face and Rocco forced himself to dismiss the twisting current of sexual tension that gripped him. What interested him was discovering who had brought him here, to this woman.

He reached for his phone, then paused when he glimpsed the look on her face. Surely that wasn't...panic?

'Of course.' Why hadn't he realised it before? There was no else involved. She'd orchestrated this meeting. And now, faced with his visible anger, she was panicking.

Dio, her audacity astounded him!

He watched her unease mount and almost felt sorry for her. She'd made a gross error of judgement; a far greater error than her betrayal three years ago.

By tricking him into coming here, wasting his time when he should be searching for the child in the photograph, she'd just reignited the fire of retribution he'd banked down all this time.

He inhaled an anticipatory breath, absently noting he was no longer as disgruntled by the weather as he'd been minutes ago.

'So, Mia, are you going to invite me in?'

In the tiny region of her mind not frozen in disbelief, Mia absorbed the deep smoothness of Rocco Vitelli's voice, the way its low timbre slid over her senses like warm, sun-kissed honey. But her shock soon dissipated, forcefully wrenched aside by a different set of terrifying emotions.

'You can't be here!'

Throwing her weight behind the door, she fought to slam it shut. It barely moved a few inches before one strong hand held it open, ridiculing her efforts.

'What's the meaning of this?'

His voice, alternately heard in her dreams and night-mares, but always with that smoky, gravelly Italian inflec-tion, caused tiny explosions along her nerve endings.

'I don't know what game you're playing, but you're not getting me into trouble by turning up on my doorstep.'

'Getting you into trouble? Shouldn't that be, "Ciao, Rocco. How have you been?" After all, you orchestrated this meeting.' With lithe grace, he entered, forcing her to abandon the door or risk collision with his hard, lean body.

Her heart hammered as she watched his tall, dark form fill her living room, her sanctuary.

Dear heaven, Rocco was here, in her home.

Tension gripped her throat, but she forced herself to

speak. 'I've no idea what you mean. But I want you to get out, Rocco. Mrs Hart, my neighbour, will testify that you turned up on my doorstep unannounced.' Through her window, she spotted his silver limo already attracting attention. Good. If, by some stroke of bad luck, Mrs Hart had vacated her normal window-seat vigil, she'd have other witnesses.

Twin brows the shade of raven's wings shot up. 'Testify? In trouble with the law again, *cara*? What on earth have you got yourself into this time?' He advanced as he spoke, intense dark blue eyes holding her prisoner until he stood close, way too close.

She stood her ground, refusing to retreat. 'What have I got myself into? Is that some sort of joke?'

He moved closer, the gleam in his eyes spiking her nervousness.

'You must be desperate if you're relying on neighbours to bail you out of whatever predicament you're in.' He paused a beat, eyes narrowed. 'Or is that why I'm here?'

His deeply masculine scent hit her nostrils, triggering memories she'd hoped never to recall. 'What do you mean, is that why you're here? This is my house. You've turned up unannounced. I want you to leave. Right now.'

He froze, as if captured in the frame of a lens.

No matter how many times she saw it happen, Rocco's ability to remain completely motionless fascinated her. She stared, much the same way she'd stood behind her son's door, staring, fascinated, less than ten minutes ago—

Gianni.

She closed her eyes. *Breathe, just breathe.*

This is just a nightmare. It'll be over in a few minutes.

'I detest games, *cara*.' Dark menace tinged his voice. 'You've lured me here, the least you can do is tell me why.'

Her eyes snapped open. '*Lured* you here? Are you mad?'

His face darkened. 'On the contrary, my mind has never

been clearer. Which member of my staff did you bribe this time to pull this stunt?'

She gasped. 'I beg your pardon?'

'Isn't that your *modus operandi*?' he continued in a low silky tone. 'Using members of my staff to lay your hands on property that's not yours? Who gave you my grandmother's itinerary? Or mine, for that matter? It's not my driver or my pilot. They've both been with me for years. I trust them both implicitly.'

Pain stung through her body. After what he'd put her through, she'd never dreamed she'd see Rocco again. Yet here he was, tall, dark, lethal, in her home, spouting the same accusations, intent on exacting more retribution.

Three years ago, she'd foolishly believed nothing could be worse than having all your wishes granted, only to have them snatched away in the cruellest way possible.

But nothing had compared with what he'd done after he'd ordered her out of his life. When he'd discovered she was daring to contact him, daring to make him change his mind about her, to hear her out. *Then*, the real retribution had been exacted. *Then*, she'd experienced the full might of Rocco Vitelli.

'I've no idea what you're talking about.' The words slipped past lips frozen with renewed pain at how this gorgeous, heartless man had caused her life to implode.

A grim smile curved his lips. 'Still wasting your breath on lies? Why am I surprised? After all, a leopard doesn't change its spots, does it, *cara*? Or are you more of a snake? Either way, a word of advice: next time you try to entice a man, dress appropriately for the occasion. Baggy jeans and a threadbare top aren't a turn-on.'

Hot, sharp anger shot through her. 'How dare you—'

'Save your protests and tell me why I'm really here.'

Tears prickled her eyes and she blinked furiously. 'No, I

will not save them. I told you then and I'm telling you now, I never stole from you!'

His lips curled. 'Then explain to me how the blueprints, locked in my safe on an encrypted flash drive, ended up in your possession? Or how the same firm who'd bid against Vitelli Construction ended up with copies of it right after your meeting with them?'

She angled her chin. 'I told you before, I've no idea.'

'And like I told you then, you are a liar.' Heavy scorn laced his words.

She'd imagined herself immune against this intense, searing ache. She was wrong. Renewed pain clenched her heart, squeezed until her breath cracked in her lungs. But damn it, she'd suffered enough. He'd humiliated her, dragged her name and reputation through court, and, worst of all, denied his unborn child. And now he'd turned up for what reason? To rub even more of his twisted brand of justice in her face?

Anger welled higher. 'I don't care what you think. What I want is for you to leave my house.' Thankfully, her voice emerged cold, steady. 'Now.'

Before Gianni woke up. Rocco might not care about his child, but Mia intended to keep the brutal truth of what his father had done to them from her son.

She shot a glance towards the stairs and prayed Gianni hadn't heard the raised voices. Sensing Rocco's incisive gaze on her, she quickly averted her eyes.

'Are you saying you didn't arrange this meeting?' Only his lips moved. The rest of him remained carved in stone.

The question was so ludicrous she would've laughed, had anxiety and the deep shame of unwanted, erotic heat not continued to surge like a rising tide inside her.

'I most certainly did not. If this is some sort of game, I don't appreciate it.' And if she received another intimidating letter from his lawyers, she'd fight it. There had to be

grounds against this sort of behaviour. A claim for harassment at the very least.

His gaze narrowed. 'Game? You think I would choose
to be anywhere near you?'

The stark disbelief in his tone grated. Loath to let him
see the devastation his words caused, she whirled and
headed for the farthest seat, which in the small space was
only a handful of steps away.

She longed to sink into the armchair that'd been her
grandmother's favourite seat, seek comfort from its familiar smell, but that would show weakness.

Instead, she sought refuge behind the chair, her hands
gripping the headrest. She was glad for its sturdiness when
her eyes settled more firmly on him.

Raw, devastating masculinity. Three years had only
added to the gravity of power that surrounded him like
an invisible cloak, made all the more distinguished by the
faintest sprinkle of grey in his otherwise jet-black hair. His
handmade Italian designer suit sat on broad shoulders in
perfect symmetry to his well-honed physique.

From stinging, unbidden memory, she knew his six-
foot-four frame carried not an ounce of spare flesh. Its
sleek, toned muscle, hard planes and smooth contours had
once held her fascination for embarrassingly long periods
of time.

But it was his face—the arrogant jut of nose, chiselled
cheekbones and square jaw sporting a day's stubble—that
repeatedly took her breath away. Deep-set blue eyes the
colour of a stormy summer night could capture a rapt audience, burn with ferocious passion or freeze with heart-
stopping cruelty.

Her gaze dropped to the curved sensuality of his lips
and an electrifying sizzle ignited deep in her belly. Dear
Lord, what those lips had done to her!

Lifting her gaze, she found him studying her as intensely as she studied him. She needed to get rid of him. Now!

'What you choose to do isn't my concern, Rocco. What I care about is that you're in my house, without my permission.'

Her grip tightened on the chair when his head cocked slightly. Laser-sharp eyes bored into her and, even from the across the room, their white-hot heat consumed her.

'Are you sure? You can barely breathe from your excitement, yet you expect me to believe that this…reunion wasn't planned?' His disbelief mocked her.

She should've been mortified by how accurately he'd read her. Yet all she felt was a shockingly visceral need; a need that whipped at her with unbelievable force. Swallowing hard, she tried for a careless shrug.

'Don't confuse anger with arousal, Rocco. I've always had my doubts about some of the people you employ. Someone has obviously made a mistake. Again.'

The last word hung between them. He acknowledged it with a cynical smile. 'You too were once my employee. Until you managed to successfully elevate your status.'

'Believe what you want. This—' she waved her hand between them '—wasn't my doing.'

He strolled to her, reached out and ran a long, graceful finger down her heated cheek. 'You were always very good at denial, weren't you, *tesoro*?' His thumb caressed her lower lip, his voice low, hypnotic.

Mia snatched in a fevered breath as delicious flames licked through her. His heated scent wrapped around her like a magician's spell and she fought to remain sane. She couldn't, *wouldn't*, let him drag her back to that dangerous, euphoric place where she'd lost more than just her power of speech. She had more important things to think about.

Like Gianni awakening with Rocco still in the house.

'This conversation is going nowhere. You've obviously

taken the wrong turn somewhere. Tell me where you wish to go and I'll happily point you in the right direction.'

He ignored her suggestion and continued his caress along her jaw, sparking a belly-clenching hunger that terrified her.

'You surprise me by maintaining the same tired line of defence. There was an appointment in your electronic diary both on your computer and your phone; a meeting took place during which you discussed confidential plans you were working on at Vitelli Construction. This was corroborated by more than one person.'

He was determined to drag her through their last, humiliating encounter, where he'd hurled soul-searing accusations at her. But short of throwing him out of her house—an impossibility given his sheer size—she had to get through this as quickly as possible.

'I never denied attending that meeting, but I thought I was acting in my capacity as your structural engineer.'

He cupped her chin and tilted her face to his. 'Yet you conveniently neglected to mention you'd passed on sensitive information regarding the Abu Dhabi project. And the fact that you'd accepted a job offer with a company in direct competition with mine.'

Mia gritted her teeth and breathed through her rising stress. 'I didn't divulge sensitive information. And the job was offered. Out of politeness I said I'd think about it. Besides, against Vitelli Construction, they would never have been serious competition.'

A superior smile curved his lips. 'I agree. That aspect of your betrayal was sorely misjudged and didn't cause me even a moment's discomfort.'

She sucked in an astonished breath. If Rocco hadn't condemned her for that... 'Then why—?'

His smile disappeared. The atmosphere turned from

darkly sensual to arctic in the space of a heartbeat. 'You dare to ask me *why*?'

Confused, she rubbed her temple. 'Correct me if I'm wrong, but you broke off our engagement, fired me and threw me out of the Milan headquarters because you thought I'd stolen your blueprints and given them to your competitor to secure myself a job.'

'I didn't think. I knew it for a fact.'

'So, if you cared so little about that, what exactly ended our relationship?'

He carried on regarding her, his expression cold, forbidding.

Rocco wasn't a man to be crossed. She knew this from painful experience. So why was she questioning him? Why not keep her mouth shut, let him leave? What did it matter that he'd ended their relationship two months before their wedding? What did it matter that it appeared the subject of the stolen blueprints wasn't the only thing that had blackened her in his eyes?

What he'd done afterwards was unforgivable. He'd ruined her life and dismissed his unborn child with heartless cruelty. Which was why she needed to tread carefully. For Gianni's sake, she couldn't end up in jail—

'Are you serious?' he bit out eventually.

Mia waved him away with fabricated flippancy. 'It doesn't matter—'

'Doesn't matter? Have you any idea what your betrayal did to my grandmother? Do you know the heartache you caused by telling her you had no intention of ever bearing my child?'

She gasped. 'But—'

'She was inconsolable for weeks!'

The ferocity of his tone dried her words.

Rocco's grandmother meant the world to him, which meant she'd become immediately important to Mia. It hadn't been difficult to see why Rocco worshipped the ground his *nonna* walked on. Her instant, unconditional affection had soothed the deep ache caused by the circumstances of her own mother's distance and indifference and the slow decline in her health Mia attributed to her lifelong bitterness and apathy.

'It was never my intention to upset her.'

Rocco inhaled deeply. 'I'll give you one last chance. Tell me why I'm here.'

'Perhaps your hearing is faulty, Rocco. I didn't summon you here. So why don't you tell me why *you are* here,' she tossed back, fighting rising panic.

He didn't answer. After several heartbeats, his gaze left hers to conduct a survey of the shabby clutter of the tiny room.

The furniture had seen better days, but wasn't threadbare. Her grandmother had taken pride in her home, unlike the tiny flat Mia had shared with her mother. *That* home had reeked of apathy, despair and bitterness, and it'd shown in everything from the dark curtains to the cold floors and the callous disregard Mia had endured. All because she'd deigned to be born.

Mia was a little ashamed to admit that, mingled with the guilt she'd felt at distancing herself from her mother's cold orbit at the first chance she got by taking a job first in London, and then in Italy, had been a tinge of relief.

But with every dispiriting visit and phone call in those intervening years before ill health had claimed her mother, Mia had been plagued with doubt as to her own worthiness. As to whether she would visit the same indifference and apathy on her future offspring.

It was why she'd been terrified of motherhood. Why she'd refused to even contemplate such a sacred and lifelong undertaking. How could she? When she had no clue what maternal love was? When she had no way of ascertaining whether her mother's bitterness had rubbed off on her and risked being transferred to her own child?

Of course, she'd had her answer the moment Gianni was placed in her arms.

Gianni.

Thoughts of her son grounded her in the present.

She watched Rocco inspect her house.

She'd taken down the framed pictures and boxed them away so she could repair the peeling paint, but her dwindling finances had stalled that project. Cheap rugs provided relief from the cold hardwood floors and a place for Gianni to play in front of the grated fire when the weather was too cold.

It took seconds for Rocco to take this all in, for his gaze to snap back to trap hers.

'You need money, *si*? Judging from the state of this place, you're short on cash.' His head snapped up. 'Are you sick?'

'No.'

Suspicion narrowing his eyes, he nudged a finger under her chin. 'But you need cash?'

Of course she needed cash. Thanks to his effective blacklisting, she'd been forced to give up her much-cherished career. Any other means of earning a living while caring for Gianni was virtually non-existent and the last of her savings was almost gone. But she'd crawl on hot coals to hell before she admitted it to the man responsible for ripping her life apart.

Her hands tightened on the chair. 'I need nothing from you. Except for you to leave my house.' Before she did the unthinkable, like give in to the need to touch him.

Go. Please, just go.

Finally, he dropped his hand. She immediately berated herself for wishing it back.

'I'm beginning to think this has been an…unfortunate mistake.'

She exhaled in relief. 'Can I trust that it won't happen again?' As long as there were no repercussions, she would be grateful.

Icy disdain tightened his face as he turned away. 'I dismissed you from my life long ago. Believe that I've no wish to set eyes on you again.'

'Trust me, I feel the same.' Her voice emerged with a calm she didn't feel. Inside, she wanted to scream. She clamped her mouth together as tears threatened, stung into being by his harsh words.

Blinking furiously, she watched him leave from behind the solid safety of her chair, even now unable to stop herself from feasting hungry eyes on his broad back, recalling the warmth of his skin under her searching caress, the silky luxury of his hair she'd once loved to run her fingers through.

He paused at the door. 'I don't know who orchestrated this meeting, but I will get to the bottom of this incident. And whoever is responsible will pay.'

She managed a stiff smile, her muscles threatening to seize up from the rigid control she kept on them. 'You still haven't told me *why* you came here in the first place, but, since I'm not responsible, I don't much care. Goodbye, Rocco.'

She didn't move until the door shut behind him. Then, galvanised by sheer self-preservation, she rushed to the window to make sure he was really leaving.

His long limbs had already carried him to his car by the time she nudged aside the curtain.

Inexplicable longing battered her. Her heartbeat thundered as she acknowledged that this might be the last time she ever saw Rocco Vitelli.

Greedily, she drank him in: the way his hair lifted in

the cold breeze, the set of his strong, powerful shoulders as he hunched deeper into his jacket, even the hand he lifted to wave the driver away from opening his door caused her heartbeat to escalate until Mia feared it would burst out of her chest.

Dry-mouthed, she forced herself to turn away. Limbs shaking, she collapsed into the chair and buried her face in her hands, the reality of her lucky escape washing over her.

After several minutes of taking deep, careful breaths, she rose. A strong cup of tea would help get over the shock. That was all it was, she stressed to herself. Seeing Rocco again had shocked her.

Shocked and *excited* her. Reminded her how good they'd been together. In the boardroom. In bed. She closed her eyes in shame, sternly reminding herself of the consequences she'd suffered for once being a lust-sick fool. A stupid, besotted fool.

But she was over that. God, was she over it.

Nothing ripped off rose-tinted glasses quicker than finding out the man you loved saw you only as a brood mare. And a thief.

Realising she was standing in the middle of the room, wringing her hands, she abruptly stilled the movement. She would not let him affect her like this. Whatever ill wind had blown him here, he was gone.

Whirling, she started for the kitchen, then paused.

Something was wrong. With a start, she realised she hadn't heard Rocco's car leave.

The tiny cottage she'd inherited from her grandmother after her passing last year was on the outskirts of a Hampshire village. It was where she'd retreated to after barely surviving the tornado that was Rocco. It was located in a quiet cul-de-sac and at this time of day, before children returned from school, the place was so peaceful, she could normally hear even the quietest engine idling.

Dread crawling up her spine, she moved with leaden feet towards the window and nudged aside her curtain.

Rocco stood on the pavement, deep in conversation with Mrs Hart.

Mia's heart slammed in her chest, then jumped into her throat when Rocco's head jerked up.

No!

His gaze snapped to the window, snagging hers with the accuracy of a grappling hook. Even from that distance, the look in his eyes knocked the air from her lungs. Fingers frozen around a clump of curtain, she watched in dread as, without breaking eye contact, he retraced his steps down her flagstone path.

This time there was no knock.

He merely turned the handle and strode in. Straight to where she stood. Long, strong fingers pried the curtain from her hand, edged her away from the window.

He reached into his breast pocket.

Her palms grew damp with the rush of apprehension. 'No!' Dear God, not another ghastly letter. What would it demand of her this time? The very heart beating in her chest?

But what he extracted wasn't a letter. It was far too small, barely three inches wide, coloured and glossy.

Bewildered, she watched him pass a thumb over its surface, his gaze fixed on the image. His face was ashen, harsh pants rushing through his clenched teeth as he fought for breath.

Finally, his intense, almost unholy gaze speared hers.

'You wanted to know why I came here? Because Nonna is convinced there is a vital secret I need to uncover. Something that belongs to me. So I'm going to ask you once, Mia. Who is this child? Where is he and, more importantly, *what is he to me?*'

CHAPTER TWO

MIA REELED AS her heart kicked.

Was this some sort of sick, twisted new game? Was Rocco now colluding to make her appear unstable so he could take Gianni away from her?

Over my dead body!

She would go through every legal channel, sell every last possession she owned to pay for lawyers before she let that happen.

'Mia.' Her name, like his statement, was delivered with such care, such precision, that a cold slice of fear knifed through her thoughts.

'Are you serious?' she tossed back.

Rocco took a step forward, until there was less than a foot between them. She craned her neck to stare into his face and almost wished she hadn't.

This close to him, she could see every magnificent masculine feature, breathe in the scent of skin and cologne that was all Rocco, feel it attack her flailing senses from all sides. His eyes, cold, direct and hypnotising, blunted every last weapon she intended to use against him.

One long-fingered hand gripped her chin and Mia was again lost.

Three long years she'd dreamed of his touch. Against her will, in the cold of winter, the long, hot, lazy summer night, she'd yearned for these same fingers that had caressed her to ecstasy, touched her, teased her, made her cry out to join her soul with this man.

And now he was touching her again and she could hardly remain still for the surge of excitement that fizzed through her veins. She wanted to lean into his touch, press his fingers more deeply against her, imprint his skin on hers until she didn't know where he ended and she began.

'Answer me, Mia. Do you know this child?'

Mia jerked away, stung and ashamed.

What was she doing playing right into the hands of her enemy? Rocco no longer had sexual power over her, so why was she standing there, gazing up at him like…like…?

She took a hasty step back, tried to remain calm as her gaze dropped to the picture. A cherubic face smiled back at her with cheeky impertinence. The child's dark blue eyes twinkled with mirth and the mop of black curls danced in a slight breeze. She wanted to reach out and caress the slightly dimpled chin, which some day would deepen like his father's.

Did she know this child?

Of course she knew him.

She'd carried him in her womb for nine months, loved him with every fibre of her being long before he'd delivered the first of many vicious kicks inside her, and adored every strand of hair, every soft velvety inch of him from the moment he was placed in her arms.

'Of course I know him,' she replied, her voice strong and steady with the power of emotion she felt for her son.

Shock detonated in Rocco's eyes.

For a moment there, she'd almost given into the urge to deny knowledge of her own son to keep him safe. After all, Rocco had never met him, so he didn't know what Gianni looked like.

But her innate honesty and fierce pride as Gianni's mother had overridden that urge immediately. Besides, from the look in his eyes, Rocco had expected her to lie. After all, she was an expert at it, right? Well, wrong.

Gianni was her son, and she would do *anything* to protect him.

Rocco's already ashen pallor—from whatever Mrs Hart

had said to him—faded even more. Intrigued, she watched the picture waver as his hand trembled.

That in itself was so shocking, so out of character, her eyes flew to his. Rocco? Tremble? Never. Even in bed, in the throes of ecstasy, he'd trumpeted his dominance, much like a lion roaring in triumph.

'And how, exactly, do you know the child?' His voice tremored, his accent thickening on the hoarse whisper.

She gulped, tried to calm the near hysterical warning voice shrieking in her head—*he's playing games with you. Stop him at all costs.* 'You know very well how I know him. And stop calling him *the child*. His name is Gianni.'

He absorbed that with another round of jaw-gritting. 'How do you know him, Mia?'

'I don't appreciate whatever game you're playing, Rocco. Get out of my house. Right now, or I'll call the pol—'

He whirled away from her, clawing visibly trembling fingers through his hair. The action killed off her words long before he reversed direction, closed the gap between them and gripped her arms.

Desperately, she tried to wrest herself from his hold, to curb the sensation stealing through her senses, but he held her easily. And the sorry thing was, Mia didn't really want to fight the torrid sensation cascading through her. The intoxicating memory of how it'd felt to be held like this by Rocco.

'You will tell me what I want to know. Now.' Eyes as dark as a stormy sea threatened to flay her.

The command spurred her to do something other than languish in painful memories. 'No. Go to hell. I will not indulge in this stupid game with you.'

'According to Mrs Hart, he's asleep. His afternoon nap, am I right? Perhaps you'd like me to wait for him to wake? See for myself what you're hiding from me?'

The blood drained from her face. Rocco hadn't changed. If anything, the laser-sharp intellect that had seen him rise from a renowned architect to iconic innovator had been honed even sharper. With a few words, he'd whittled away her resistance.

'No, I think not,' he emphasised with calm incisiveness. 'Instead, you'll answer my question.'

'Why should I?' she croaked through lips tingling with a thousand firing nerves.

'Because I dropped everything to come here to find out and I will not be toyed with.'

Her fists slammed against his chest as anger fired up within her. 'Yet you're happy to do the same with other people? Does it give you a sick thrill to hold the power of life and death in your hands, Rocco?'

His lips twisted. 'You've developed quite a taste for melodrama since we last met, *cara*. But it's a taste I don't have the time or inclination to indulge in.'

She shivered at his chilling tone. 'Why now, Rocco? Do you have some sadistic urge to see how I live? See what you've reduced me to?'

He started to frown but she waved him away.

'Don't bother pretending. Thing is, I never took you for a sadist. More fool me, right? Because when it comes down to it, what had I really known about the man I was once engaged to marry?' Nothing because, in the end, the man she'd loved, the man who'd purportedly respected her intellect and creativity by day and whispered heated, magical promises to her as he'd worshipped her body with his own by night, had morphed into a snarling, heartless, vitriol-spewing monster.

A monster who was now asking her a question to which he already knew the answer!

He dropped his arms and paced the living room once

more, his expression bewildered. The action focused her gaze on his stunning, harsh beauty. Unforgiving blue eyes glowered at her, giving her no quarter from their lethal demand. Cheekbones seemingly fashioned from polished marble stood out in haughty relief; his dark stubbled jaw made her fingers tingle wildly.

'You're talking in riddles and my patience is running thin, Mia.'

She could verify that from the frantic pulse throbbing in his temple. 'Then you can leave the same way you came. The door is still open.'

Use it. Please, please leave.

'*Christo!* Answer me!' he barked.

'Why?'

He growled and uttered a single curse. It was a curse she'd heard him utter only once before, when it had seemed her begging and grovelling for a chance to explain had got too much for him to stomach three years ago. Then, he'd thrust her away from him and marched out, telling her in no uncertain terms that she had twenty minutes to pack her bags and clear out of his Palermo villa before his security detail gave her a firm hand.

Now those hands were braced on his hips, his eyes narrowed on her face. She forced herself not to cower as she witnessed his failing patience in the hectic colour slashing his contoured cheekbones.

Lifting her head, she glared right back. 'You know exactly who he is, Rocco. What I don't know is why you're pretending otherwise. You know Gianni's my son. Just as you know he's yours!'

Silence, thick and monumental, circled them, rising, whipping up her bewilderment until it threatened to choke her.

Rocco's hands dropped to his sides in shock. Then he

trembled. She had to hand it to him. His acting skills were impeccable. Oscar-worthy.

'You lie.' His voice was a strangled rasp, barely audible over her thundering heart. 'You lie,' he insisted, his voice growing deadlier with each word.

His skin was stretched taut over frozen features and his eyes—although they bored into hers—held the stunned glaze of disbelief and made her think he wasn't really seeing her.

'For goodness' sake. Why would I lie about something like this?' Something he already knew.

Her answer seemed to rouse him from some dark, unknown place. He focused on her, and the look in the stormy depths stilled her breath.

'This child is mine?'

Again the warning shrieked in her head. Rocco Vitelli was playing a very dangerous game with her; a game she had no way of winning unless she focused. To do that she needed to get away from him, put some space between herself and his heady, mind-altering proximity.

She took a step out of his immediate orbit. He didn't follow. Because he was too stunned?

Certainly the way his eyes had darkened, the way his hand wasn't quite steady when he raked through his dark hair again, implied he was.

But…why? He'd known about his child as soon as she'd found out she was pregnant with Gianni. And she'd kept him apprised of every single milestone in her early pregnancy in the hope that he'd come around, that he'd let her explain—again—her version of the events that had ended their engagement. Of course, in the end, that had backfired on her big time. Her life had been hurled into a hellish nightmare the likes of which she could never have imagined.

Rocco had seen to that.

Rocco, the same man who now stood before her, feigning aggrieved innocence.

She backed towards the door. With any luck, Mrs Hart would still be lurking outside, greedy for gossip. This time Mia didn't mind who saw her. She'd need witnesses who'd testify that she hadn't invited Rocco here. Mrs Hart would be perfect—

'I want to see him.'

The simple, hoarse words stopped her in her tracks.

She whirled to face him. 'No. What you need to do is leave my house.'

'You tell me I have a son, sleeping upstairs, a child I have never seen, and you expect me to leave?' His accent was even thicker, his voice rising with incredulity.

The injustice of the accusation stung deep. She abandoned her plan to seek witnesses and stalked back to him. 'And whose fault is that, Rocco? You had endless chances and chose not to take them. So don't you dare act as if any of this is my fault.'

'Not your fault? Who should I blame, then, *cara*, hmm?' The vibrant olive tinge to his skin hadn't quite returned, but his eyes were alive again, threatening to tear chunks out of her with each glance.

'I know it's very hard for you, but perhaps you could try pointing the finger at yourself? Instead of getting to know him, of taking the chance to be a part of your son's life, to watch him grow, you decided to punish an innocent child instead.' Her voice threatened to crack, but she swallowed away the pain. 'Well, you'll see him over my dead body!'

'*Maledizione!* From the melodramatic, you've now descended into the downright absurd. Punish an innocent child? If by that you mean depriving him of his right to know his father, then you should be pointing the finger at yourself. *Dio mio*, you sound delusional!'

Neon lights lit up in her head as her worst fears were

confirmed. 'Finally. I was wondering when you'd get round to making that accusation. You've changed, Rocco. You used to get to the point pretty much instantly. Now you go around the houses, and what for? Playing the puppet master is now your thing, is it?'

'*Che?* What in heaven's name are you talking about?' He shook his head, reached out and grasped her wrist. 'Something's not right with you. Since I got here, nothing you've said has made any sense.'

Mia couldn't stop the hysterical laughter that bubbled up in her throat or the cheap thrill it gave her when Rocco's frown intensified. Her laughter grew until warm tears streamed down her cheeks. 'You...you are really priceless, Rocco, you know that?'

His jaw tightened. 'Enough! I've had more than enough of your histrionics. I want to see the child, and I want to see him now.'

That dissolved the laughter instantly. Somewhere in her mind, she registered he still hadn't used Gianni's name, almost as if her son wasn't real to him. But if Rocco didn't want to acknowledge their child, why was he insisting on seeing him?

'Not until you tell me why. Why do you want to see him, Rocco? Why now?'

Rocco tried his damnedest to stop his senses spinning. To still for a moment so he could formulate one clear, coherent thought.

But the moment he focused on Mia, on the feisty woman whose pulse hammered beneath his hand, everything began to blur again.

Mia.

His child.

Here. Living in this sleepy village in the middle of Nowhere, England.

Mia, spouting some garbage about him ignoring his child, not taking the chance to know his own flesh and blood. The blur intensified, threatening to spin out of control. A door cracked open in his mind, throwing more light on the long-buried yearning he'd sealed drum-tight. Dreams of a family, of love, hope, everything that had callously been denied him, until Nonna had taken control, sacrificed everything for her grandson, shown him a different way, not knowing the scars were already too deep to heal—

He slammed the door shut, gritted his teeth and forced himself to focus.

How could Mia believe that he'd ignore his child's existence? When he'd made no secret of how much he'd wanted an heir. A fact she'd known but had had no intention of fulfilling with him when she'd rapturously accepted his proposal…

From what the neighbour had said, the child looked healthy and seemed well taken care of. *Seemed.* But who knew what went on behind closed doors?

Madre di Dio! He couldn't believe Nonna had been right. The sheer, fragile coincidence, the flimsiness of fate, of what he could've missed all his life, terrified him to his very soul. Made him want to curse. And punish.

What if his grandmother had taken another route to mass? What if she hadn't been paying attention to the electronic billboard on the side of the road?

The thought that he could've remained oblivious to his son's existence, his own flesh and blood, sent a renewed wave of anguish and anger through him. And all because of the selfishness of the woman in front of him.

What had she asked him? Why now?

As if he'd ever been given the chance before. He took a calming breath, stifling the urge to deliver a tiny dose of what he was going through.

As an only child, he had been so desperately lonely, what

with his parents' callous and blatant neglect, and Nonna working all hours to provide for him. At the age of ten, watching his grandmother scrimp and save to make ends meet, he'd vowed first to make enough money to see her in luxury in her old age, a vow he'd made come true hundreds of millions of times over. His second vow had been that no child of his—should he ever have them—would grow up experiencing the deep scars of neglect and cruel indifference. For Nonna's sake, he'd never ruled out marriage. But to do that he'd also vowed to find a suitable wife who would fulfil his strict parameters of care for his future children.

That particular goal had been elusive, and over the years it'd slowly eroded until he'd eventually given up any hope of ever fulfilling it.

Then he'd met Mia Gallagher. With her, he'd contemplated the rebirth of all his long-cherished but slowly abandoned goals. Or so he'd thought.

She'd led him on with promises of a future he'd all but encouraged Nonna to give up on. Right up to the weeks before he'd placed his wedding ring on her finger. Then he'd had the scales pulled viciously from his eyes.

Her lies he could tolerate, if not forgive. But this! Keeping his own flesh and blood from him?

'Are you insane to ask me why I want to know the existence of my own child? You think anything will come between me and my flesh and blood?' The ugly sneer he heard in his own voice made his anger rise. He never lost control like this. Never. But this woman had driven him to the very brink of sanity. Once three years ago. And now.

Her eyes had widened. Clear green eyes he'd once upon a time drowned in; eyes he'd seen fill with tears when he'd gone down on one knee in the presence of his beloved grandmother and proposed to her; eyes he'd watched darken in passion as she'd whispered how much she adored him, how he meant everything to her, how much she couldn't wait to join her life with his.

Of course, she'd had a different interpretation of just what she'd been hoping for from their union.

Clear, luminous, almond-shaped *deceptive* eyes. Eyes that held his without a hint of remorse even in the face of her barefaced lies. Add that slight tremble to her plump, kissable lips and any man was destined to believe every insincere word she uttered.

Any man but him. He'd taken her measure when she'd lied through her teeth even in the face of concrete evidence three years ago.

So why was he standing here, trying to reason with her? Could he even believe the child was his? Well, only one way to find out. He whirled away from her and stalked to the stairs. A house this small, it wouldn't be difficult to find the child.

An affronted gasp sounded behind him as she scrambled after him.

'Wait! Where do you think you're going?'

Good, that was the reaction he wanted. Maybe now she'd drop this crazy pretence and take him seriously.

His foot was on the second step when her small hands closed over his bicep. The kick of lust he'd felt earlier returned, sharper, deeper, awakening senses he'd thought long dead. His anger only escalated and he stiffened against the reaction, ready to pull away.

'Rocco, wait! You can't go up there!'

He glanced down into her heart-shaped face and read real terror there. *Dio!* Did she think he intended to harm the child?

Or was she reacting to something else? He stepped down quicker than he'd climbed.

'Why are you so afraid to let me see him? Is he unwell?

Is that why you've kept me in the dark about his existence? If so, know that nothing will—'

She jerked back with a frown. 'No, of course not. Gianni is a perfectly happy and healthy little boy,' she defended hotly.

Rocco let out the breath locked in his lungs and regained the step. '*Bene*, then nothing should prevent me from seeing him. Do you want to lead the way, or should I just wander from room to room until I find him?'

Stormy eyes snapped with dislike. 'I'd prefer neither option, quite frankly.'

He shrugged, then felt a mild sense of loss when the movement dislodged her hands. 'Fine. Stay here.' One way or the other he intended to see the child—*his son*. He'd already been denied his existence for over over two years.

Dio, two years! He forced himself to calm down and took the stairs three at a time. She scrambled up after him, but his eyes were glued to the door at the top of the stairs.

Was that where his son slept? A hot rush of air filled his lungs, leaving him faint by the time he reached the last step. Would there be an instant, instinctive bond, or would he, thanks to the actions of the slip of a woman behind him, have to get to know his own flesh and blood?

Rocco's heart hammered the way it never had before as he faced the door. Reaching out, he grasped the doorknob.

'That's not Gianni's room,' Mia's husky voice said from behind him.

He jerked back with a mixture of relief and trepidation. For in that instant, before his hand had closed over the knob, he'd felt as if, somehow, he'd failed his son. That by cutting Mia off so completely, maybe he'd somehow been to blame for not knowing of his son's existence.

Which was ridiculous, he reminded himself. He'd done nothing wrong. He'd thrown Mia out of his life because she'd turned out to be a thief and a liar. And while he

wouldn't have chosen such a person as the mother of his
child, the situation was what it was. But if the child behind
the next door was his, a fact an unknown instinct was warning him was so, he would move heaven and earth to make
up for the time he'd lost. Taking a deep, restorative breath,
he faced her. One look at his face, and she moved swiftly
along the short corridor.

She stopped in front of a door painted a bright yellow.
Stencils of racing cars and teddy bears danced on the frame
and a brightly coloured sign proclaimed it as Gianni's Kingdom. The smile that tugged at the corner of his mouth was
quickly suppressed beneath the torrent of emotion raging
through him.

With a beseeching look at him, Mia slowly opened the
door and tiptoed in.

Rocco stood on the threshold, knowing without a
shadow of a doubt his life was about to change for ever.
But he couldn't have turned back if his life depended on it.

He stepped into the room. The curtains, stencilled with
another racing-car theme, were drawn against the afternoon
sun, so at first he couldn't see the small lump burrowed
underneath a brightly coloured blanket.

Another step brought him closer to the cot.

A tremor went through him at his first glimpse of his
son.

Dark curls peeked out from the top of the blanket. Even
that small sight had the power to stop Rocco's breath. As
he watched, the boy stretched in his sleep, a slow, indulgent
movement that revealed the full impact of his perfect, innocent, heart-stoppingly beautiful face. A face that marked
him, without a shadow of a doubt, as a Vitelli.

A face that Rocco knew he would treasure for ever.

CHAPTER THREE

FOR THE SECOND time in the space of an hour, Mia watched, fascinated, as Rocco Vitelli froze into absolute stillness. Were it not for the pulse that raced in his neck, she would've believed he'd turned into one of the polished marble statues of his beloved Palermo.

Haltingly, she took another step closer and cast a frantic glance at him. His eyes were on Gianni, the feverish blue fastened with staggering intensity on her son.

Their son.

Gianni was lost in the land of slumber, the effects of swimming and running around in the park having taken their toll. Her gaze returned to Rocco and the resemblance between father and son hit her dead in the chest. Not having seen them this close before, she'd had no warning how strong the likeness was between them. Confronted with it now, there was no doubt.

Gianni had the beginnings of the strong Vitelli jaw, the dark slashed eyebrows and high cheekbones of his antecedents.

Beside her, Rocco drew in a shuddering breath. Slowly, his fist unclenched and reached towards his son. Long, strong fingers caressed one plump curl, which immediately clung into his touch. With trance-like movements, he sank down until his face was almost level with Gianni's through the slats in his cot.

'*Mio figlio,*' he breathed. My son.

Without warning, Gianni's eyes popped open.

Father and son stared at each other for one heart-stopping moment.

Mia forgot to breathe. Her nails dug into her fingers as her limbs froze.

Then just as abruptly, Gianni blinked, rolled onto his side and promptly went back to sleep.

Mia's breath shuddered out as Rocco surged to his feet. He seemed to have trouble breathing. He swallowed several times, his eyes still fixed on their sleeping son.

Then, utterly awestruck, her heart leaping into her throat, she watched a single tear roll down his cheek. With a shaky hand, he brushed it off his face. His massive shoulders heaved as he inhaled. Her own eyes prickled, and she bit her lip to stop the distressed sound in her throat from emerging. Before she could utter a word, he stepped back from the cot.

When he turned to face her, his face was clenched tight, but his eyes were ablaze with turbulent emotion.

'Downstairs. Now, *per favore*,' he bit out.

Without looking back at his son, Rocco left the room.

Mia took her time, composing herself while slowly tucking the blanket more securely around her son.

Downstairs, she found him once again pacing her living room in tight, tension-filled circles.

She wanted him out, as quickly as possible. But after what she'd witnessed upstairs, she wasn't so sure she could accuse him of playing games any longer. It was the same instinct that warned her not to break the silence. So she stood, one hand braced against the banister.

Eventually he stopped in front of the box on the floor, his eyes zeroing in on its contents. Bending his large frame, he plucked up a picture of Gianni, taken moments after his birth. He stared at it for endless moments. Then he brushed the surface with his thumb, much the same way he'd done with the picture in his pocket.

When his gaze snagged hers, it held a mixture of stark bleakness and eviscerating anger that had her clutching the banister tighter. 'Gianni's my son. You kept him from me. Why?'

The raw pain cracking his voice rendered Mia speechless as the depth of his anguish rocked her soul.

She opened her mouth but no words emerged.

He held out one hand to her in entreaty, further confounding her. '*Per favore*, tell me why,' he muttered in a ragged whisper.

Mia dragged in a desperate, bewildered breath. 'I didn't keep him from you, Rocco. You know I didn't. I—'

His hand slashed through the air. 'You keep insisting that I did. But I didn't know, Mia. I didn't know!' he roared.

'How on earth can you say that? How can you insist on calling me a liar at every turn but then tell me you didn't know you had a child? What's *really* going on, Rocco? You claim you weren't aware of Gianni's existence, so how come you have his picture and my address?'

She reeled as another bolt of pain slashed across his face.

'Nonna saw his picture on a billboard on the way to mass yesterday morning. According to her companion, she took one look at the picture and became so agitated she almost collapsed. My staff thought she'd lost her mind when she insisted the boy in the picture was my child. The doctor was called. She was so distressed she had to be sedated. But eventually, when she'd calmed enough, she called me, told me I had a son and I had to find him.'

Mia gasped. 'But how…how was she so sure?'

'There's a picture of me, almost identical to this one. Nonna wears it in the locket around her neck. It was the only proof she had that she hadn't lost her mind. Hell, even I didn't believe it at first. But she was adamant, almost to the point of hysteria, that I dropped everything and flew back from Abu Dhabi to see her.'

A memory resurfaced. 'I know that picture. She showed it to me once, but when she said it was of her *bambino*, I assumed it was your father. That was you?'

He gave a stiff nod.

'And so she called you, based on seeing Gianni's picture on a billboard?'

'*Sì.*' His hand clenched over the picture and swallowed hard before he looked up. 'And to think I almost dismissed her pleas. For as long as I live, I will owe her a priceless debt for insisting I come here. If she hadn't, I would still be in the dark about my son's existence.' He speared her with a look so unnerving, Mia's stomach twisted into thick knots. He tucked the picture away. 'Later, we will address the subject of why my son is posing in a children's catalogue. For now, I'm still waiting for an explanation.'

Mia's head throbbed from absorbing the information pelting her like icy rocks in a hailstorm. She wanted to let go of the banister, but she wasn't sure her legs would support her if she did. Rocco gave no quarter. He stood, hands on hips, tall and solid in front of her, waiting for answers.

But they were answers she knew he already had. There was no way he could not have known about Gianni. Hell, she still had the last letter from his lawyers cautioning her against asking for child support.

Confusion mingled with all the other emotions welling up inside her and she massaged her nape in the vain hope of easing her tense muscles and helping her think clearly. 'Help me out here, because I'm really confused. Did you have an accident recently? Or bump your head and develop amnesia? Because—'

His face darkened even further and with a frustrated growl he dropped the picture back in the box.

'Sorry, I had to ask. Because that would be the only reason why you would be asking me these questions.'

'*Santa cielo!*' He closed his eyes, took a calming breath, then spiked his fingers through his dark hair, ruffling the normally neat strands into further disarray. 'Fine. Let's just pretend I've been in an accident recently; that I have no memory of the last three years. What would've happened that I'd need to know?'

She licked dry lips and swallowed. 'Besides showing up here after making my life a living hell for three years, and then pretending you don't know anything about it? Well, for starters, you should know to be ashamed of yourself, but then you have no shame, do you? You only see things in black and white, with no tolerance for grey. You decided I was guilty of stealing and condemned me to pay for the rest of my life. My God, even if by some stretch of the imagination I would've been willing to forgive you for that, what you've done to my son I find very difficult to forgive and I will never forgive you for that, Rocco. Never—'

She was too busy venting long-suppressed emotions and shaking so hard with the pain that came with it that she didn't see him approach, didn't sense the danger signs until it was too late. Too late to stop him from grabbing her; from hauling her hard against his solid frame. To avert her head to avoid the emotional devastation of his lips as they seized hers, ground into hers, forced her shocked lips open to delve into her unguarded mouth. Her stunned senses grappled to find reason, to latch onto her fast-dwindling sanity, but the battle was lost under the attack of a deep, dark resurging hunger.

The hands she braced against his chest to push him away swiftly lost their fight as his tongue took control of hers. That first, singeing assault made her knees buckle. She would've landed in an ungainly heap had it not been for the strong arm around her waist. Within seconds, her hands were curling into his hair, renewing their acquaintance with the sleek short strands. She caressed his nape, his rough, stubbled jaw, the strong curve of his cheek as he continued to wreak havoc on her senses. Pleasure, potent and exquisite, flooded her veins, searing a demanding path straight to that secret, forgotten place between her legs.

In a split second, the direction of his intention changed. Instead of overpowering, he caressed, in place of forceful demand, his hand gentled as he moulded her to his rigid length. And that only sucked her deeper into the maelstrom of feeling this man always evoked within her.

His hand moved lower, brought her even closer to his body. Her gasp as she felt the force of his arousal was swallowed into the heat of their kiss. She groaned deep in her throat, wanting the feeling never to end. When he broke the kiss and moved to her neck, she closed her eyes and threw back her head to give him easy access.

His hard chuckle as his hot mouth teased her pulse made her melt inside. She gave up and shuddered against him as lust-filled gooseflesh raced over her skin. His chuckle turned into deep-throated laughter.

'Your neck is still as sensitive as ever, *cara mia*. It pleases me to know that at least that hasn't changed.'

Heat was instantly replaced by cold, cold ice. Dear God, had she lost her mind? She tried to wrench away. 'Damn you! Let me go!'

His grip loosened but he didn't raise his head from the exploration of her neck. In fact, he intensified his attack by passing a lazy tongue over her flesh before nipping it gently between his teeth. 'Why?' he rasped. 'So you can spout more mystifying garbage? No. This is so much better.' Raising his head, he conducted a searing survey over her face, down her neck, to her breasts.

Following his gaze, she saw her nipples had stiffened to painful attention beneath her thin sweater. Heat flamed up her face as he dipped his head and circled one damp tongue over the jersey-covered flesh. Mia was unable to stop the helpless jerk of her body. With a mocking smile, Rocco closed his mouth over his prize, teased the sensitive nub between his teeth until she gave a strangled cry. 'Indeed, I prefer to use the language of lust. At least our bodies don't lie, even after all these years.' Straightening up, he backed her against the banister, then moved closer still, imprinting the hard, lean tower of masculinity against her.

Fire threatened to melt the ice she'd fought hard to build around her emotions, even as she acknowledged that, when it came to Rocco, that task was an uphill battle. But she couldn't afford to let him do this to her. It was humiliating enough that she'd let herself drown in his kiss. Surrendering to his touch a second time was unthinkable. Especially given the devastation he'd wreaked on her life.

'Well, this body wants you as far from hers as possible,' she informed him coldly.

His lips twisted in a parody of a smile. 'Really? Then why does it curve around mine? Why are your arms clamped around my neck? Your hips undulating against mine with an urgent need for me to take you, right here, right now?' he asked huskily.

The heat that flooded up her face only made the scarlet haze rise again. 'I swear on everything I hold dear, if you call me a liar one more time, you'll regret it.'

'Since screaming and frightening my son is out of the question, and the phone is on the other side of the room, I'm curious to see what else you come up with.'

'For starters, my knee, between your legs. Would that get your attention?'

He let out a short bark of laughter. 'I'll give you some free advice, *amante*. Never let your opponent know your intention before you act,' he told her. But he made no move to protect himself.

And it galled her that he knew she wouldn't follow through; that when it came to the two of them, the only act that bordered on turbulent was the insane passion that threatened to rage out of control.

But she had to do something. She would surely lose her mind trapped against him like this, the heat of his body

flaming hers; the thick ride of his erection nestling so forcefully against her belly, reminding her with searing accuracy
how it had felt to have that power, that delirium-inducing
force inside her.

With increasing desperation, she threw caution to the
wind.

'Let me go. Or this time I will scream, and I don't care
if Gianni wakes up. Maybe it's time he met his monster
of a father.'

Her reckless accusation removed every last vestige of
laughter from his face. His features tightened into a dark,
taut mask and he stilled. But this time she knew he hadn't
turned to marble, because she felt the thunder-strong beat
of his heart kick up against her breast, felt the harsh exha-
lation of his breath against her face. And the arm he still
held around her waist tightened.

'Clarify that statement, if you please,' he demanded in
a deceptively soft tone. 'Why would my son perceive me
as a monster?'

Dropping her hands from his nape, she pushed hard
against his chest, but he didn't budge. He merely waited
out her feeble efforts until she was panting with frustration. When her gaze clashed with his, he raised one haughty
eyebrow.

'Damn you! Because you accused his mother of stalking you! You dragged her into court when she was three
months pregnant, exhibited every phone message, every
email, every letter she'd sent you, even photographs you'd
secretly taken of her as she waited for you in your office.
You admitted everything as evidence of her stalking and
then convinced the judge to slap a restraining order on her.
You didn't even turn up in court because your lawyers informed the judge you were in fear of your life from your
unborn child's mother and insisted she was to stay at least
five hundred feet from you at all times.' She stabbed a fin-

ger in his shoulder. 'Gianni should know that, because of you, his mother hasn't been able to work to provide for him, that all her friends and so-called colleagues would have nothing to do with her when she was branded the pregnant psycho stalker of the great Rocco Vitelli!'

Rocco let her go so abruptly, she stumbled wildly. The sturdy banister was once again her saviour when she fell against it. Chest heaving and struggling not to cry, she turned away from him and collapsed onto the last step.

Damn him.

Damn Rocco Vitelli to hell and back. Reliving her trauma of three years ago was the last thing she wanted to do, but, being who he was, Rocco had pushed and pushed until she'd broken, just as he'd done the last time.

Shame flooded her as she recalled how she'd begged and pleaded for him to take her back. For one month, she'd rung him every day, emailed him over a dozen times and in the end resorted to letters, which she'd pleaded with one staff member in his mail room to hand-deliver.

The messenger had assured her he'd delivered it, and she knew Rocco had received it because that last letter, where she'd begged him to take her back for the sake of their unborn child, had been one of the letters exhibited at the dreadful hearing. It had been read out loud in court, earning her a pity-filled look from the judge. But it hadn't stopped him from issuing the restraining order, banning her from ever contacting Rocco Vitelli, in person or via electronic channels, before strongly advising her to seek help for her *obsessive* condition.

She'd staggered from the courtroom, dazed, from the ashes her life had turned into seemingly overnight. She'd lost her temp job almost immediately and found out very soon that all other employment avenues were closed to her, the Vitelli name an iron-clad guarantee to overpower the name of Gallagher.

Thank God for her grandmother's unquestioning support when Mia had turned up on her doorstep, pregnant and broken.

Her painful introspection ceased when she opened her eyes and encountered designer-styled shoes planted in front of her. She looked up and up into Rocco's stony face. The grey pallor was back, tingeing his skin and making his eyes look gaunt. His mouth was set in a flat, immoveable line as his hands balled into fists at his sides.

'You have levelled one absurd accusation after another since I walked through this door today, Mia, but this…' he shook his head in stunned disbelief '…this outshines them all.' He retreated to the far end of the room, his broad shoulders stiff, as if trying to keep a tight rein on his control.

'I know we didn't part on the best of terms three years ago. I can understand that having the truth of your actions brought to light would've been upsetting for you, but this bizarre story you're concocting is beyond my understanding. I don't know what you mean to achieve by pursuing it—'

Astonishment lent strength to legs as she lurched upright. 'Wait a minute. Are you accusing me of making this up? Are you crazy?'

Rocco's head went up as if he'd been struck. 'On the contrary, I think you're the one who's impaired in some way.'

'Damn it, I am not making this up. You know I'm not!'

'Prove it. Show me some concrete evidence that my child is not in the care of a delusional excuse for a mother. Prove what you are saying or, so help me, I will take immediate steps to have him removed from your care.' He spoke in such a controlled, even tone and perversely that made Mia want to lash out at him even more.

Stark anger at his threat made her gasp in outrage. 'You

bastard! You utterly heartless bastard. Haven't you done enough?'

'Obviously not. I should have kept a closer watch on you after we parted. You're not the first aggrieved ex-lover to attempt to keep a father from his child.' His jaw clenched hard on the words.

Mia clenched her fists and tried to take a deep breath. With every bone in her body, she wanted to tell him for the hundredth time to go to hell.

But what good would that achieve? Rocco had already been here far too long. Gianni had been asleep far longer than normal, but he wouldn't be asleep for much longer. And whatever the cost, she had to make sure Rocco wasn't here when her son woke up.

'You want evidence? I'll show it to you. But first I want something from you.'

'I don't think—'

'I don't care what you think. You claim you don't know what I'm talking about. Fine. I'll prove what I'm saying. But first, I want your written assurance that your being here won't be held against me in any way.'

She saw his puzzled frown and pre-empted his objection. 'Please spare me another I-have-no-idea-what-you're-talking-about episode. If you want to see the evidence, then you'll agree.'

After a terse silence, he nodded. 'Very well.'

She stifled a sigh of relief. 'Secondly, once I show it to you, I want you to leave.'

Immediately he shook his head. 'That would be impossible.'

'Then you leave me no choice.'

Trying to hide her trembling, she crossed the room and picked up the phone.

'What do you think you're doing?'

'I have an intruder in my house. I'm phoning the police.'

He didn't so much as flinch at her threat. 'Don't be stupid. How do you think the police will react when they find out just how long the intruder has been here?'

'Then go! I don't want you here.' Tears threatened, joining all the tumultuous emotions raging through her. 'Please, just go.'

For a beat he stared at her. Examined her face with an intensity that shook her insides. Then, he jerked out a nod. '*Va bene.* You have my word. I will leave once you show me this evidence you have. But before you look so pleased, rest assured, I will be back tomorrow morning, when I expect to be properly introduced to my son. After that we will have a long talk.'

'There's nothing to talk about.' Her voice held a desperate edge she prayed he hadn't picked up on.

'Show me the evidence, Mia.'

'Then you'll go?'

He heaved a frustrated breath. '*Sì.*'

She walked over to the cabinet set against one side of the tiny room. Opening the first drawer, she took out a key, which she used to open the second drawer. She hated the way her hands trembled as she pulled out the file, hated the way pain ripped through her as she nudged closed the drawer and turned around. Most of all, she hated the way Rocco stared so intently, witnessing every emotion she struggled not to feel as he held out his hand calmly for the file.

Taking it without a word, he retreated and seated himself on her favourite chair—and earned himself another black mark.

She stood in front of the cabinet and watched him leaf slowly through the file. He thumbed through copies of the emails she'd sent in desperation after he'd refused to take her calls; through photos his investigators had taken of her outside his office, chasing down his car on the road that last morning when he'd taken his private elevator to the garage instead of the front lobby as she'd been led to believe. That day she'd spent six hours in his reception waiting for a chance to speak to him, only to glance up and see him outside, preparing to slide into his Ferrari.

That memory brought a fresh wave of humiliation.

'Haven't you seen enough?' She moved to take the file from him.

He looked up. 'These pictures, when were they taken?'

'When do you think?' He continued to stare at her. 'Oh, for goodness' sake. There's a date stamp on the back.'

He flipped a few over and stared at the dates. 'This is dated six weeks after we parted.'

So he remembered when he'd ended their engagement? Why wouldn't he? He'd documented her every move to use as evidence against her. 'We didn't part, Rocco. You threw me out of the Palermo villa and the Milan apartment.'

The brief flare of his patrician nostrils was the only indication that he'd heard her. 'You remained in Milan all that time?' He was frowning again.

'I remained in Milan for two months, as you well know.'

He didn't answer this time as he set down one photo and picked up another. After examining each one, he finally picked up the transcript. Again he took his time reading the two-double-sided court document that forbade her from ever contacting Rocco Vitelli or coming within speaking distance of him.

Finally, he closed the file and stood. His face had grown gaunt; his pallor even more ashen, as if he'd received the worst shock of his life. But with his back against the window, Mia couldn't be certain. What she could see was that he was staring at the file as if it were an alien being.

'Makes grim reading, doesn't it, seeing it all in black and white? Now that you've refreshed your memory, can you please go?'

He lifted his gaze to her and Mia bit back a gasp at the stark torment in the dark depths of his eyes. When he exhaled, it emerged a harsh, cracked sound.

'I have no idea who did this to you, Mia. But it wasn't me.'

CHAPTER FOUR

'EXCUSE ME?' MIA was sure her hearing was playing tricks on her.

'This—' Rocco lifted the file '—was not my doing.' His voice was as stark as the look in his eyes. With abrupt movements he slammed the file on the chair. 'I swear it.'

Light-headed with the rapid drain of blood from her head, she swayed against the cabinet. 'This is not your doing,' she echoed the words through numb lips. Her brain struggled even harder to grasp their meaning.

'No. It is not.' He advanced as he spoke until he stood right in front of her. Up close, she could see the terrible tension that gripped his face, held his body taut. 'If the evidence in that file is to be believed...' he paused at her outraged gasp '...then someone has perpetrated a terrible injustice on both of us.'

'Someone?' She'd found her voice, even though it emerged higher than she would have wished. 'You seriously expect me to believe that this had nothing to do with you? That someone *else* did this? How stupid do you think I am?'

He let out another harsh breath and grasped her arms. 'You need to calm down so we can talk about this rationally.'

'No!' She wrenched herself away from him. 'Enough. Please, enough. Whatever game you're playing, it's gone on long enough. You said you'd leave once I showed you the evidence. You've seen it. Now leave.' She was hanging by a thread, and she didn't know how much more she could take. Rushing to the door on unsteady feet, she reached for the doorknob.

'I understand you're emotional—'

She rounded on him. 'Of course I'm emotional. I'm

human, not a robot like you. I don't revel in mind games the way you do. At least have the decency not to insult my intelligence. You know every single shred of evidence in that file is the truth. The charges may have been trumped up, but it's based on the truth, or a twisted version of it. I sent you those emails. I made those phone calls. I camped outside your office for a chance to talk to you. For two months I tried to get you to talk to me, and I used every means available to me because I thought you had the right to know about your unborn child. But to use it against me that way? To accuse me of stalking?' She stopped to swallow a sob that threatened to escape. 'You disgust me, you know that?'

'*Basta!* If you would just calm down and think this through properly, you'll realise I speak the truth.'

'No. You listen to me for a change. I want you out of my house, and out of my life. Here, take the file with you. You can refresh your memory over a glass of Chianti. But know this. If you ever turn up on my doorstep again, I will take action against you for harassment.'

Her rant went unanswered as he slowly dug his hand into his breast pocket. 'Did you hear what I said?' she demanded, fighting a wave of hysteria that threatened to suck her under.

When his hand emerged, he held his passport. He turned to retrieve the file. 'Come here.' His terse command achieved the opposite. She held her ground and remained by the door. After a moment, he looked up. 'Mia, if you want this nightmare to end for both of us, indulge me for a moment. *Per favore.*'

Against her better judgement, she moved towards him, morbid curiosity biting into her. He had the file opened to where his statement was etched in grim black and white. Words like *dangerous*, *unhinged*, *obsessed* jumped out at her and she cringed as tears prickled behind her eyes.

Rocco flipped the statement to the last page. Opening his passport, he held it next to his signed statement. 'Do you see a difference?'

Blinking, she frowned. 'What am I supposed to be looking at?'

'Purportedly, I signed this statement, no? Look at the signature in my passport. Now look at the two signatures and tell me what you see.'

She looked closer. A tingle shot down her spine and a strange buzz started in her head as the pages blurred. Blinking hard, she stared, her eyes darting between the two documents. Slowly, the implications began to sink in.

She raised her gaze to him. 'Are…are you saying this is not your signature?'

He gave a grim nod. *'Io sono spiacente.'*

It took another few seconds for his meaning to sink in. She flew at him, landing blows everywhere she could reach. 'You're sorry?' she shrieked. 'For over three years I've lived in fear of being hauled off to jail on a whim, lived in fear of losing my child in case I somehow violate the terms of the restraining order…and all you can say is, you're sorry?' Tears streamed down her face as her emotions finally burst their bank.

Rocco didn't move. Not a muscle as her anger and despair ripped free. Finally, overcome by racking sobs, she collapsed against him. Then he caught her to him, holding her in his arms as she shuddered with emotional overload. Through her distress, she heard him murmur soft words in Italian, words meant to soothe, but that only made her cry harder as she continued to slam her fists against his arms, shoulders, anywhere she could reach, until she was drained and wretched.

It was only when her tears lessened to unladylike hiccups, that she heard it. The sound she should have been listening out for. The sound that should have been her first concern in all this madness.

The impatient wail that was Gianni's waking call.

She wrenched herself out of Rocco's arms and stumbled backwards. 'Go. Now!'

'*Cara*, you are not in a state to be left—'

'No, you said you would leave. You promised!'

'*Sì*, and I will, when you've calmed down.'

Gianni let out another plaintive cry. Torn between going to her son and making sure his father disappeared as quickly as he'd arrived, she paused. And nearly jumped out of her skin when the doorbell pealed. With a sharp cry, she whirled towards it. The hand that closed over her shoulder stopped her in her tracks.

'Go and get the boy. I will get the door.' Rocco's authoritative voice was couched in helpful charm. As much as she wanted to tell him to go to hell, Gianni's demand to be let out of his cot was getting to the stage where Mia knew that if she didn't get upstairs immediately, he'd attempt to climb out himself.

Reluctantly, she nodded, and, swallowing down the last of her hiccups, she headed for the stairs.

'Mia?'

She turned to find him behind her, pulling out a cotton square from his pocket, which he held out to her. 'Unless you want to upset our son, I suggest you try and remove some of the evidence of your distress.'

Belatedly, she lifted a hand to her face and realised her cheeks were still wet with her tears, not to mention her runny nose that must make her resemble a wet scarecrow. With a deep flush engulfing her face, she snatched the handkerchief, not bothering to murmur her thanks as she fled up the stairs.

She'd reached the top of the stairs when she heard Mrs Hart greeting Rocco as if they were old friends.

Pursing her lips at the further unwanted intrusion, she hurried down the hall and arrived in time to see Gianni swing one plump leg over the top of the cot, ready to escape his perceived prison.

She rushed to him and swung him into her arms. 'No, no, sweetheart. I told you, you mustn't do that.'

Hiding her face against his chubby neck, she hugged him close to her, all her anger and anxiety draining out of her to be replaced by the rush of love she felt for her little boy.

When he pulled at her hair and repeated her words— 'No, no, tweehar...'—her smile wobbled and she clutched him closer. He protested and began to squirm.

But knowing what faced her downstairs, Mia held on for a moment longer, selfishly basking in her son's innocence until he wriggled harder, eager to be set free.

'All right. But you know the drill. First a nappy change. Okay?'

Immediately he shook his head. 'No nappy.'

Her smile widened. 'Yes nappy, then you can play with your racing cars.'

It could've been the change in his normal routine or the instinctive warning that all was not right with his mother. But far from crowing with joy the way he normally did at the prospect of playing with his beloved racing cars instead of sitting in his high chair in the kitchen for his pre-dinner fruit plate, he regarded his mother solemnly for several seconds with a gaze so shrewd and reminiscent of his father's, Mia's heart twisted in pain.

Then a smile broke over his face. 'Racing car!'

'Yes, but first, nappy change.'

And then, please, God, let Rocco have disappeared quietly without making a fuss by the time she returned downstairs. The notion that she was grasping at straws stayed with her as she changed Gianni's nappy, but she refused to let go of the hope as she clutched her son—who in turn clutched one yellow and one red racing car in his fists—and made her way downstairs.

With each step she recalled her conversation with Rocco just before Gianni woke up. Was it true? Had someone instigated the accusations against her, dragged her to court under fabricated charges, all without Rocco knowing? That seemed too unthinkable, so impossible, that she couldn't begin to wrap her head around it. She paused as another, equally unthinkable, thought struck her.

If Rocco hadn't known of his son's existence, what would he do now that he knew? The image of his face when she accused him of knowing and deliberately ignoring Gianni's existence rose in her mind.

What had he said?

You think anything will come between me and my flesh and blood?

What did that mean? Her veins filled with ice as possible new interpretations tumbled through her mind. Did Rocco mean to take her son away from her? Somehow declare her an unfit mother and demand full custody and spirit her son away to Italy?

Suddenly desperate to know his intentions, she hitched Gianni securely onto her hip and clambered down the remaining stairs.

Only to find her prayers had been answered.

Her living room was empty.

After a rough night where tossing and turning had alternated with anxious pacing in the close confines of her bedroom, dawn came with Mia being no further enlightened as to Rocco's true intentions. Was he coming back? Or was he going to disappear just as quickly as he'd appeared, leaving her life in even deeper turmoil?

Somewhere in the long dark, daunting hours of the night, she'd realised that she'd been too distressed to question him further when he'd claimed he'd had nothing to do with the restraining order under whose shadow she'd lived for over three years. As the weak sunlight snuck around her curtains, she also realised she was still as in the dark about every charge thrown at her as she'd been when she'd demanded Rocco leave.

If *he* hadn't instigated those charges against her, who had? And to what end? It turned her blood cold at the thought of someone being so cruel, as to do that to her and her unborn child.

During her time in Italy, first as Rocco's structural engineer on his latest resort-building project, and later as his fiancée, she'd met countless people who inevitably passed through the life of an influential and powerful billionaire. Most had been pleasant, some not so much, but wracking her brain, as she'd done many times during the night, she'd come away with nothing but a throbbing headache.

Rocco's cousin Alessandro, and his wife, Allegra, had been cool and dismissive towards her when Rocco had moved her from his Milan apartment into the Palermo villa he shared with his *nonna* soon after their engagement. With Alessandro's departure for Brazil where, as Rocco's right-hand man, he'd been spearheading the push of Vitelli Construction into Latin America, their relationship had never truly blossomed. If Mia was honest, she'd never felt any genuine warmth from Alessandro, but she wouldn't have stooped so far as to accuse him of orchestrating such a hideous vendetta against her.

Which brought her to another dilemma. If the order and charges against her were bogus, trying to overturn them would involve hiring a lawyer or a private investigator to prove her innocence and that, of course, would cost money. Precious money she couldn't afford.

So she was back to square one. She had no means of

fighting the injustice done against her, no way of proving it unless she found the money from somewhere.

She was still burning millions of brain cells over the issue when her doorbell rang just after nine. Setting Gianni's breakfast of Marmite soldiers down in front of him, she brushed crumbs from her fingers and went to answer it.

Rocco stood on her doorstep, large, imposing and dangerously handsome, dressed from head to toe in black. Her stomach executed a perfect triple somersault, the blood rushing through her veins at the speed of light, both independent actions causing her a light-headedness that had her clinging to the doorknob for support.

He really had no right to look this good first thing in the morning, she thought bitterly, especially when she knew she looked far less than her best, her brief glimpse of herself in the bathroom mirror as she'd splashed water on her face having confirmed that fact.

'You look like you're going to a funeral. And did your hearing die along with your conscience? I distinctly recall asking you not to come back.' The words spilt from her lips before she could stop them but she refused to take them back, simply because she hated the way he made her heart beat twice as fast just with his presence; hated the way he made every cell in her body sing with life and her legs turn to jelly just by being there; she hated the way he seemed to glow with life when she felt worse than death. Most of all she hated the clamouring instinct that warned her he wasn't here to enquire about her health.

'Still get testy when you don't get enough sleep?' he countered smoothly, his lips twitching with amusement, before slipping his impressive bulk past her to enter her cottage.

'Whether I did or not is nothing to do with you,' she forced through clenched teeth only to grit them further when he sent her a mocking glance. 'What are you doing here anyway?' Conscious of Gianni in the next room, she tried for an even tone, even though she wanted to shriek the words at him.

'You really expect me to stay away after what I discovered yesterday?' he questioned, incredulous.

She turned to shut the door, taking a few precious moments to regroup. When she turned, he was facing her, his intense blue eyes narrowed as he raked her from head to toe. The scrutiny did nothing to ease the pounding in her chest or the sudden careening of butterflies in her stomach when his return gaze paused for an indecent amount of time on her breasts.

'I was hoping you'd respect my wishes, yes.' Her voice emerged shaky and slightly feeble. She cursed herself. And him. His ability to upset her equilibrium with just a look wasn't going down well in light of her tumultuous feelings this morning.

'Don't be so naïve, Mia. I have a son whose existence I've only just been made aware of. I intend to form a relationship with him. Unfortunately for you, no amount of wishing on your part will make that fact disappear. I've already informed Nonna that her suspicions were right.'

Where she'd failed miserably, his tone was smooth and even, moderated, she suspected, for the sake of Gianni, who was banging on his high chair in the kitchen.

As if pulled by a magnet, Rocco turned towards the sound.

'Wait,' she whispered urgently, although she knew she was only delaying the inevitable.

'No. I will not wait,' he sliced at her, his voice gruff with emotion.

She bit back a shocked gasp at the dark torment in his eyes when he speared her gaze with his.

'I've been kept in the dark for three years. Whoever is

at fault will pay for that, never doubt it, but I will not wait one second longer to meet my son.'

His long legs carried him to the kitchen in six easy strides. By the time Mia joined him, he was already kneeling in front of Gianni.

Once again father and son regarded each other with equal fascination. And once again, Mia's heart hammered until she was sure it would burst out of her chest.

'*Buongiorno*, Gianni. *Io sono papà*. I am your father.' The raw words, spoken with a tortured mixture of pride and pain, tore through Mia.

As if he understood the profound words, Gianni nodded. His lower lip pouted, then trembled. Rocco lifted a slightly trembling hand and touched his son's cheek. Gianni's pout deepened. Mia held her breath, ready to scoop up her child at the slightest sign of distress but, thankfully, no tears arrived. She stayed by the door, her heart in her throat.

Gently, Rocco moved his hand up and stroked Gianni's curls, all the while drinking in his features as if to imprint them on his brain. He whispered soft, incoherent words to his son, which must have soothed him, because gradually Gianni's pout retracted, to be replaced by curiosity. When Rocco's hand returned to his cheek, Gianni reciprocated the gesture by picking up a piece of toast and shoving it in his father's face.

Warm, hoarse laughter broke from Rocco's throat as he caught the food between his teeth and munched with relish. Breaking into a grin, Gianni picked up another piece and repeated the gesture.

Turning away from the heart-wrenching scene for fear that her son would witness her tears, she busied herself fetching his small pot of yoghurt from the fridge.

Behind her father and son deepened their instant bonding by murmuring adorable rubbish to each other. With every soft word uttered, every murmur of appreciation for what a clever child he was—it was amazing how quickly her understanding of Italian rushed back when it counted—her heart crumbled further.

A wave of shame washed over her as she admitted that some small part of her had hoped her Gianni would hate his father on sight. But really, would that have made things easier? Rocco was nothing if not a ruthless fighter. After all, weren't his sharp mind and extreme risk-taking in architecture what had made her seek out a job in his company fresh out of university? If he hadn't bonded instantly with his son, he wouldn't have given up. And a determined Rocco was a formidable force to be reckoned with. So perhaps it was easier this way.

She turned from the fridge to find him wiping the excess Marmite from his son's chin. Sensing her gaze, he glanced up.

Instantly his soft look disappeared. 'We need to talk.' He stood to tower over her, his even tone belying the piercing intent in his eyes.

There was no escaping the inevitable. 'I need to feed him his yoghurt.'

Her stalling tactic failed as he reached out a hand and smoothly relieved her of the small tub. 'I'll take care of it. You can use the time to pack a bag—'

She snatched in a shocked breath. 'Pack a bag? If you think I'm going anywhere with you, you need your head examined.' Realising her son was studying her with intense fascination, she struggled to smile through clenched teeth. 'We can talk here.'

When he reached out again, she tensed, afraid of what direct contact with his touch might do to her crumbling state of mind. But he merely reached past her to grab a plastic spoon off the counter. His eyes mocked her as he read her reaction.

'Easy, *cara*. You've developed a penchant for overreacting at the slightest opportunity—'

'Can you blame me? I've lived in fear of being imprisoned for the last three years!'

A spasm of some unknown emotion raced across his face but was gone too quickly for her to decipher, although the intensity in his face eased. 'I merely wanted you to pack a bag for Gianni since we'll be gone most of the day.'

She crossed her arms defensively. 'And where exactly are we going?'

'I delivered your file to my lawyers last night. They assure me that this is the first time they're aware of this document, which confirms my suspicion that the case against you is a fraudulent one.'

The mingled shock and relief that spiked through her lasted for a mere second but nevertheless it caused her to lose what little feeling she had in her legs. She started to sag against the sink.

Rocco's hands arrived at her waist, easily holding her up. 'Are you all right?'

She shook her head, wisely extricated herself from his hold, and cleared her throat before attempting to speak. Still her voice emerged as hollow as a discarded seashell. 'Are you saying that all this time, all the threats, the letters, my living in fear…were all for nothing?'

A grim look crossed Rocco's face as he returned to his task of spooning yoghurt into his son's waiting mouth. 'I have no doubt that whoever sent them meant for you to take them seriously.'

'But who would do that?' Sheer disbelief gave way to anger so deep she shook with it. Taking a deep breath, she struggled to hold herself together.

Rocco continued to feed Gianni, although his massive shoulders lifted in a shrug underneath the stretch of expensive black suit. 'I have a lot of enemies. Unfortunately, it goes with the territory where money and power are involved. Someone must have believed they could get to me through you. Or vice versa.'

His words made tears prickle and her laugh grated painfully in her own ears. 'But they couldn't have been more wrong, could they? You wanted nothing to do with me after your precious blueprints went missing and you were forced to halt construction of the Abu Dhabi project. In fact, I'm surprised you didn't think of this sort of punishment yourself.'

He stiffened as if a bolt of electricity had shot through him, but his face gave nothing away. With casual ease, he continued to feed his son until the pot was empty. Then he put it to one side and cleaned up the remnants of Gianni's breakfast as efficiently as if he'd been doing it since he was born.

As she watched him, the small part of Mia not reeling with shock and hurt found it hard to believe Rocco had only just met his son. And the realisation of how keenly and naturally Rocco had taken to fatherhood sent a spike of alarm through her, effectively blotting out the niggling that had started at the back of her mind.

Rocco picked up a red racing car off the counter and handed it to his son, brushing his hand affectionately through his hair before turning to her.

'The women I associate with are normally well aware of the terms of our association. Yours was the only alliance I had a little…difficulty with.'

Heat rushed up her face at the deliberate barb, but she forced her chin up. 'I'm sorry if I didn't just slink away quietly when accused of being a thief! I wouldn't have been able to live with myself if I hadn't tried to defend myself.'

'That's a very admirable quality, in the right circumstances. Unfortunately, when the weight of evidence is against you, sometimes it's better to make a quiet exit than to draw even more attention to yourself.'

'And be labelled a thief for the rest of my life? No one would've hired me. You certainly weren't inclined to give me a reference and you made sure I was blacklisted everywhere. So, tell me, where would that have left me?'

Narrowed eyes threatened to tear strips off her skin. 'Married to a billionaire, if you'd only kept your mouth shut and not further compromised your situation by revealing your true intentions before my wedding ring was on your finger. That way you'd have been set for life, wouldn't you?' His words were by no less deadly for their soft delivery.

Confusion caused her to frown. 'What are you talking about?' she demanded.

He ignored her question and glanced at his watch. 'We have an appointment with my lawyers at one o'clock. If we are to make it, I suggest you get a move on.'

The mercurial direction of the conversation was causing her head to spin. 'Your lawyers? Why would they want to meet with me?'

'This is now officially a fraud investigation. You need to provide a formal statement.' His eyes flicked to Gianni and the ruthless determination in their depths caused her heart to miss several beats.

'Why wasn't I consulted before you arranged any of this? You can't just blow into my life after making it a living hell and start making decisions without my consent. Besides, everything you need is in that file. That should be enough.' Her voice had been rising with her agitation and, belatedly, she noted Gianni staring at her, his lower lip beginning to tremble. She rushed forward and scooped him out of his chair. Murmuring soft words to him, she glared at Rocco over his head.

He leaned back against the small counter and crossed his legs at the ankles, but his easy stance didn't fool her for a second. 'Perhaps I was wrong, but I was under the impression that the chance to clear your name would please you, not cause you so much distress.'

'I'm not distressed! I'm angry,' she hissed at him. 'You can't just swoop in out of nowhere after three years and start laying down the law like some...like some...' The word she wanted to utter wouldn't have been suitable for her son's innocent ears, so she contented herself with an even more withering glare.

Rocco merely folded lean, muscled arms over his chest and regarded her steadily. 'So I take it you don't want to clear your name? That you'd rather live with this "obsessive stalker" label hanging over your head?'

She yearned to claw the mockery out of his eyes, pound her fists against his chest for taunting her into falling in with his plans. But with her son in her arms, she had to content herself with an even fiercer glare before, walking out of the kitchen, she placed Gianni on his play mat in front of the unlit fireplace.

Turning, she found Rocco directly behind her. Every essence of his masculine aura filling every angle of her vision so completely, she had to force herself to concentrate on what she'd been about to say.

'I hate you,' she husked out with as much feeling as she could muster without distressing her son.

His eyes glinted with dark amusement. 'I take it that's a yes, then?'

Her hands balled into fists. 'Of course I want to get to clear my name. That doesn't mean I'm willing to let you ride roughshod over me to do it.'

In a flash, his expression altered. His mouth softened into a sensual curve and his eyes blazed a long-forgotten hunger that made the muscles of her stomach dance crazily.

'I seem to recall there were two things that could hold your utter attention: sex and work. While I enjoyed our mental grappling in the boardroom, I found the bedroom games just as stimulating.' His hands slid over her waist to cup her bottom, bringing her into sharp contact with his groin and the masculine dominance of his erection. His mouth descended, a sensual promise that came to hover deliciously over her lips. 'In the bedroom we had perfect understanding, *cara*, and if that's the only way I can get your cooperation, and stop you spitting nails at me, then I'm willing to try it.'

'Don't go martyring yourself for my sake.' The sarcasm she aimed at him emerged high-pitched and desperately false.

He laughed low in his throat, the sound singing along her nerves in ways that did nothing to soothe her equilibrium.

'Trust me, it won't be a hardship at all. I told you last night, the body doesn't lie and right now mine is demanding that I be true to it in the most primal way.' One hand caressed its way up her side, sparking flash fires wherever he touched. When it curved beneath the soft swell of her breast, she knew she had to do something or risk dissolving into a heated puddle at his feet.

The hands she lifted to push him away with felt feeble. 'Aren't you forgetting something?'

He lifted winged brows, even as his mouth descended another tempting millimetre, his warm breath washing over her tingling lips, setting them on fire so she had to fight not to give into the temptation to lick moisture into them.

'You threw me out of your life three years ago. You warned me never to darken your door again, remember?' Her voice emerged husky, heavy with a need she was fighting desperately to deny.

'Not because I had grown tired of the exquisite pleasure I found in your body. In fact, that was the reason I swore never to set foot in England again.'

She was shocked by this stark admission; her eyes flew

to his. 'You couldn't trust yourself to be around me, despite labelling me as a thief?'

A grim smile twitched his lips. 'You see what the power of sex can do? Even in the midst of bitter disillusionment and betrayal, the body wants what it wants.' To demonstrate, he brought her closer still to his tight, masculine form so she could not fail to feel the evidence for herself.

'God, you make it sound so cheap and sordid!'

'Deny it if you must, but it's the truth.' This time his lips lowered enough to brush over hers.

The brief contact sent a wild shudder through her, the force of her own need stabbing her deep in the pelvis. A moan of pleasure escaped before she could stop it. When he lifted his head, she realised her hands had curled into his chest. She straightened them, but found she couldn't quite remove them from the heated, cotton-covered flesh.

'Don't do this, Rocco. If this is the example you're hoping to set your son, then I pray for his upbringing.'

If she'd meant the words to cause offence, she was disappointed. In true Latin style, he shrugged eloquently.

'It's right for him to learn that feelings should be expressed naturally. I don't want him to be brought up with the suppressing of feelings and stiff-upper-lip nonsense you English are so fond of. It's also good for him to see that his parents can express natural feelings towards one another.'

She knew he meant this as she'd witnessed, and envied, the open love and warmth he shared with his grandmother and cousins. But still, 'I wouldn't describe what I'm feeling for you right now as natural.'

Raising his head, he feathered a forefinger down her cheek, his lips curving with a hint of a smile she recalled as devastating when fully unfurled. 'Really? How would you describe it?'

'Murderous is a good start,' she forced out, despite the battle she fought against the urge to curl into his touch.

He tossed out another shrug, in no way disturbed by her answer. 'You're not the first to want my head on a platter.'

'You mean I'm not the first person to be falsely accused of stealing by you?'

Where the first reminder had failed miserably, this second reminder of why he'd thrown her out of his life succeeded. Like a switch, the heat was extinguished from his eyes. Mia should've been thankful that she'd achieved her aim, but all she felt was bereft when his arms fell from her. She cursed herself for her weakness. Why? After all he'd done to her, couldn't she summon enough willpower to resist him?

'Perhaps you're right. Some things should not be aired in front of my son.'

My son.

The fierce possession in his statement fired a warning in Mia's head. *He's my son too*, she wanted to rage at him, but Gianni had already been bombarded with too many emotions this morning and her normally chatty son was now gazing solemnly at his parents. It irked her that Rocco was right, that she hadn't considered her son's feelings before she'd let herself be dragged into a heated exchange in his presence.

But then he'd always had that effect on her, hadn't he? His lean, dark, heart-stopping good looks combined with that hard muscle-packed body had spelt trouble for her the first time she'd laid eyes on him two months into her employment with the London division of Vitelli Construction. But it was the deadly combination of that and his superior intellect that had tipped her over the edge of uncontrollable lust into full-blown infatuation.

And hadn't he fed into it? He'd lapped it up as if it were his due, taken everything she had to offer and more, until she'd felt herself disappearing into the giant, larger than life force that was Rocco Vitelli.

It enraged her now to think she'd come so close to giving up everything, every damn thing she'd worked so hard for, to please him. Only to find out the real reason for his proposal: first as a means of pleasing his grandmother, and then, provided nature took its course—and why shouldn't it, since Rocco Vitelli willed it?—as a breeding machine to carry on the Vitelli empire.

Of course, in the end it hadn't mattered because clever, quick-thinking and infinitely superior Rocco had got the boot in first and she'd been forced to give up everything anyway. The career she'd so carefully planned and proudly achieved *in spite* of her every misgiving, *in spite* of the very loud echoes about her unworthiness, had been ripped from her in the blink of an eye.

Except now he was dangling the carrot of getting her life back, to put the horror of the last three years behind her. Was she a fool to refuse this chance to finally move on with her life, to start providing for her son the way she'd been unable to do since he was born? She could wallow in bitterness for what had happened to her, or she could dust herself off, accept his offer of assistance and start reclaiming her life.

'How long will we be gone?' she asked, after taking a steadying breath.

The barest hint of tension eased from his frame. A minuscule signal that he wasn't blasé about all this. For some absurd reason, it eased Mia's knotted insides.

'If everything goes according to plan, the business side of things should be concluded in a few hours,' he replied.

By teatime she could be free of the nightmare that'd been hanging over her for three long years.

Of course, it wasn't till much later that the full meaning of his words truly sank in.

CHAPTER FIVE

ROCCO'S GAZE TRACKED Mia as she walked away from him.

Last night he'd barely slept. Finding out you had a son and discovering the nefarious circumstances that had kept his birth from you had a way of depriving a man of sleep in a way the strongest caffeine or most challenging boardroom negotiations could not achieve. Anger, shock and a sense of profound loss had all wrestled for equal chunks of him.

But in the end, steely resolution had won out.

He had a son. And he intended to claim him, by any means possible.

He walked over and crouched down in front of Gianni, his heart once again overwhelmed by the miracle in front of him. Plump hands lifted up the red racing car to him. He accepted it, swallowing the lump in his throat before settling himself on the floor in front of him.

He had a son who had surpassed all goals to become his number one priority. And for now he had to recognise that mother and son came as a package, which meant any plans he had for Gianni would have to include Mia. He'd known what he needed to do even before he'd picked up the phone to confirm the news to Nonna.

His grandmother's sobs of happiness had brought a brief smile to his own lips and alleviated any guilt he felt about what he had to do to secure his place in his son's life.

The Mia he knew had always been feisty, fighting her corner, whether in the boardroom or against his absolute possession of her in the bedroom, so he had a fight on his hands to convince Mia to fall in with his plans.

And in light of what she'd been through—an ordeal that would've cowed most people but evidently not Mia, since she'd remained impressively, admirably spirited—he had to tread carefully. But, ultimately, he was determined to win.

First, he would restore all that had been ripped away from her three years ago. As she'd proved with resounding success to him, money and privilege were a potent aphrodisiac, dispensing with even the staunchest of beliefs. All he had to do was set her dreams in front of her to have her.

Fate, if you believed in that sort of thing, had taken care of her one objection to their previous relationship. She'd been willing to enjoy the influence and power his position brought, but not the child she'd known he'd ultimately wanted.

What had pained him most then and continued to disillusion him now was that she'd been so engrossed in trying to clear her name, so intent on salvaging her career, she'd brushed aside his shocked demand.

His lips thinned in memory of their confrontation that last morning.

Of course, I didn't want to have your child!

The words still had the power to freeze his insides, the callous words raw and bruisingly bracing in ways he'd never imagined possible.

So why had she gone ahead with the pregnancy?

Had she had a change of heart the moment she'd known she was carrying his child? Or had she needed convincing? How had she coped with the pregnancy itself? With firm resolution, he pushed away the questions. He was burning to know the answers but the reality of his son made them less urgent. The promise he'd made to Nonna had been fulfilled, even without him realising it.

And now he'd been blessed with this gift, he intended to hang onto it with both hands.

Mia stood in front of her wardrobe, eyeing its meagre contents with increasing anxiety. Although why she should be anxious about meeting a bunch of lawyers, she had no idea. Surely she should be celebrating the fact that her name was about to be cleared? She could finally move on with her life and take proper care of her son without having to worry. So why was she stressing over what to wear?

Biting her lip, she acknowledged her anxiety stemmed from another source. Rocco hadn't mentioned his plans concerning Gianni. And after witnessing the depths of Rocco's emotions both yesterday and this morning, and the instant bond between father and son, she'd be naïve to think Rocco wouldn't demand some sort of contact with Gianni.

The thought of being parted from her son for even a minute tore her insides to shreds.

Maybe she was jumping the gun, she mused impatiently as she whipped the only decent outfit—a knee-length navy-blue dress with a crossover bodice that had seen better days—off the hanger. The soft jersey material would have to do the job of keeping her warm, especially since she'd been putting off buying tights until the weather got really cold. She located her black-heeled pumps at the back of the wardrobe, slipped them on and took a few experimental steps to the window and back. Having lived in flats and trainers since Gianni's birth, the last thing she wanted to do was to topple over in her three-inch heels with her son in her arms.

Confident she could carry it off without coming across like a limping ostrich, she brushed her hair, smoothed on a trace of gloss and re-hung the clothes she'd strewn on the bed. Checking her appearance one last time, she slipped into Gianni's room and picked up the bag she'd packed for him.

The sound of laughter reached her ears as she descended the stairs.

The first thing she saw was Rocco's legs splayed out, followed by powerful thighs, lean tapered hips and impressive torso, on which lay her son, giggling uncontrollably at the faces his father, sprawled out on her living room floor, was pulling.

It took several moments for them to realise they had an audience, and several more for the humour to be wiped from Rocco's eyes. In those moments, she was reminded of when they'd been together, sharing a joke, or laughing for no reason, simply because she was happy.

The painful reminder delivered a punch so forceful to her midsection, she struggled to catch her breath.

'I… I'm ready,' she said, her voice scratchy with torn emotions.

She wanted to hate Rocco, she really did. But now she was presented with the picture of an indulgent father and content son, her heart flipped in a way that sent huge alarm bells through her brain.

Her heart took a further hammering when he sat up easily, one strong arm secure around his son as he rose fluidly to his feet and raked a tidying hand through his hair, looking sexily and sinfully dishevelled as he stared down at her.

'Ah. Your mamma has decided to grace us with her presence.' Dark blue eyes gleamed as they raked her form, lingering over her cleavage and hips in ways that made her hot all over.

Gianni beamed his approval. 'Mummy…lovely,' he said.

Setting down the bag before it fell from her suddenly clammy fingers, she reached for Gianni. 'I changed him just before breakfast so he doesn't need changing. I'll just put his sweater on and we can be on our way.'

Rocco handed him over, but his gaze stayed on hers for a charged second, sending spikes of heat through her and bringing thoughts of their earlier conversation flooding through her. She felt his gaze on her as she carried Gianni over to the sofa, sat him down and pulled his sweater over the long sleeve T-shirt and jeans he wore.

When she looked up, Rocco had the door open and the case in his hand. 'I'll take him so you can lock up.'

Unused to having another adult presence in Gianni's life since her grandmother's death, and feeling bereft at being relieved of him so quickly, she hesitated.

Rocco's eyes narrowed and the last of the warmth left his face. 'I'm not going to spirit him away the second your back is turned, if that's what you think.'

But that was just the problem. She had no idea what to think, since she had no idea what role he intended to play in his son's life. Biting her lips over her jumbled emotions, she handed Gianni to him, fished her keys out of her bag and locked the door behind her.

She approached the car in time to see him settle Gianni into a brand-new car seat. Seeing her surprise, he raised his brows in query.

'Did you think I would forget such an important safety issue?' he drawled.

If she was honest, yes, although now she thought of it, she realised Rocco, with his menagerie of nieces and nephews produced by his extended family, had more experience with children than she'd ever had, and the thought caused her even more worry.

Sliding into the silver Bentley to sit opposite her son, she felt unmoored, as if her life were spiralling out of her control, which was ridiculous. All he'd done was buy her son a car seat. Nothing wildly strange about that, she assured herself.

'I flew in by helicopter this morning, but as I wasn't sure how Gianni would react to the flight, I suggest we travel by road.'

Gianni would've probably loved it, but since *she* hadn't been keen on Rocco's helicopter rides during the times she'd had to accompany him on site visits, she nodded. 'It's probably best.'

She crossed her legs and immediately uncrossed them when her calf brushed the warm material of his trousers. Heat, delicious and stinging, raced along her skin, tightening her nipples into painful points. The immediacy of the reaction sent a gasp flying from her lips. And the thought that she had to endure almost two hours of Rocco's dark, masculine presence sent a moan chasing after it.

'I would ask you what is wrong, *cara*, but I already know. I felt it too.' Molten eyes the colour of a storm-tossed sea speared her with flames of desire.

She swallowed hard. 'Whatever I feel…whatever you feel, this is going nowhere,' she warned, more to herself, she suspected, than to him.

His eyes dropped to her mouth, lingered for tense, dangerous seconds, before arriving back to hers. 'We shall see.'

The words sounded so very much like a challenge, Mia swallowed again. Her gaze fell on her son and she breathed a sigh of relief. While Gianni was in the car with them, Rocco would not try anything.

Would he?

She cast him a furtive glance and caught his gaze on her face. Reading her features clearly, he smiled. It was a wholly untamed, deeply devastating smile that reeked of masculine arrogance.

Colour shot up her face, but she raised her chin and stared him down. After several seconds he turned his gaze on Gianni.

For several miles he entertained Gianni, leaving Mia to suffer his more than occasional, seemingly innocent contact every time he adjusted his large frame. And with each brush of body against hers, she experienced a bone-deep tingle that reignited primal sensations and a fierce yearning to pull closer to the powerful, masculine temptation that was Rocco.

Instead, she forced her hands to stayed curled in her

lap, her attention on the grey motorway that whizzed past her window.

'Grazie.' The pull of his scrutiny, accompanied by the solemnly uttered word, drew her attention. She turned to see his gaze shift from his dozing son's smooth, innocent face to hers. As much as she tried not to be affected by the hypnotic gleam in their stormy depths, several missed heartbeats told her she hadn't been successful.

'For what?' she asked with genuine puzzlement.

'For naming Gianni after my grandfather. He's an exceptional boy. Nonna will be so proud.' There was a discernible vein of pride in his voice coupled with a fierce possessiveness.

She couldn't help the blush that suffused her face, and nor could she pull her gaze from his compelling eyes that made deadly promises she knew he wouldn't deliver, no matter how difficult. God, hadn't she learned her lesson?

Pushing down her despair, she answered with a thin shrug. 'I know how much your grandmother misses your grandfather, even after all these years. I... I hoped this might in some way help her cope with her loss.'

Rocco's grandfather had died very young from a sudden heart attack, when Rocco was only nine. His grandmother had never remarried and had chosen instead to bring up her orphaned grandchild by herself, working her fingers to the bone to provide for him.

Rocco's eyes narrowed on her, a small amount of surprise and a healthy dose of suspicion in his gaze. 'And how do you know this?'

'Caterina told me how your grandfather died, and how she knew from the first time she met him that he was the only man for her.' Mia also remembered how her heart had sung at the time because she'd believed she had same in Giovanni Vitelli's grandson.

How wrong she'd been!

Puzzlement replaced the suspicion in Rocco's eyes, prompting her to ask, 'What?'

'I did not know you had such intimate conversations with my grandmother.' His frown evidenced his obvious displeasure at the knowledge and Mia couldn't defend herself against the barb of hurt that pierced her.

To hide it, she lifted her chin. 'There were a lot of things you didn't bother to find out about me, Rocco, starting with the misconception that I was a thief.'

His jaw immediately tightened, an accurate sign that her barb had hit home. 'The evidence against you was real. I had proof. My competitors came into possession of the blueprints the same day you attended the meeting. A source confirmed you were in possession of it when you arrived.'

'That's a lie!' For the millionth time, Mia wracked her brain for why someone had concocted such a web of lies against her, but she came up empty. She shook her head to clear the memories and to think straight beneath the intensity of Rocco's condemning scrutiny. 'The only thing I had in my possession when I arrived for that meeting was my briefcase containing my laptop and portfolio. And as far as I know, toying with looking and being offered a job isn't a crime.'

'But you didn't tell me you were looking for a job. You hid it from me until I confronted you with it.'

Mia inhaled slowly as remembered regret flooded her. Looking for another job had been the last thing she'd wanted, but with the Vitelli Construction office grapevine blazing with speculation as to how she'd landed the job working with Rocco, she'd known to preserve her professional integrity she either had to find another position or end her relationship with Rocco. The latter had been out of the question, of course.

The job offer with Rocco's competitor had been, seemingly out of the blue, and a step down for her, but she hadn't dismissed it out of hand. The knowledge that Rocco would dislike the idea even more was why she'd kept the offer under wraps.

She sighed. 'I'd meant to tell you.'

'Really? When?' he sliced at her, derision rife in his tone. 'As you were walking out the door to my competition?'

'When I was sure I even wanted the job. Things were happening so fast. We were newly engaged and the Abu Dhabi project was about to take off and—'

'So you thought the best way forward was to give the opposition a lending hand?'

'No! If you must know, my professionalism was being called into question because…because we were involved. It didn't matter that we were engaged. Everyone thought I landed my position because I was bedding the boss. My degrees and hard work didn't count for anything, not when I apparently only needed to bat my eyelashes to get a promotion.' Humiliating heat suffused her face at the admission and the memory of the whispering campaign she'd tried to overlook, but which had become unbearable in the end. Unable to bear the force of his stare, she turned her head, only to have her move thwarted when strong fingers cupped her jaw and reversed her retreat.

His eyes had narrowed into icy slits. 'Who called your conduct into question?'

'It doesn't matter who.' The past was the past. The last thing she was going to do was name Rocco's cousin Alessandro as the prime culprit in her harassment and character assassination whenever the chance had arisen.

Alessandro Vitelli had pretended to be cordial with her in Rocco's presence, but hadn't bothered to hide his contempt when they had been alone.

The one time she'd confronted him and attempted to ascertain why he despised her so much, he'd implied it was all in her head. And had actually laughed at her.

Mia had tried to put that unpleasant episode behind her.

She'd seen the way Rocco fiercely protected his family, especially his grandmother. He wouldn't have welcomed her pointing fingers then and she had nothing to gain by pointing fingers now. 'You were so convinced I was in the wrong when you acted as judge, jury and executioner, and doled out your punishment. Why do you want to know anyway? Because there's a possibility you might have been wrong?' she threw at him, and added a sweet smile. 'If that's the case, then maybe I should leave you to wallow in your guilt.'

To say her response had annoyed him was an understatement. The hand that left her jaw to curve around her nape tightened only a split second before he yanked her close.

Her breath fled her lungs as the hands she threw up connected with hard muscles flexing beneath the expensive cotton of his shirt. Heat flared within her, igniting sensation along nerve endings now straining with acute excitement.

'Wh-what are you doing?' she gasped as he hauled her into his lap.

'Reminding myself that there must have been something besides your abrasive tongue I found so appealing about you three years ago.' His mouth hovered over hers, the hiss of his words landing like explosive little kisses on her lips.

With a desperate gasp, she parted them to suck in oxygen and trembled violently when a primitive growl echoed from his throat. One hand slid down her back to cup her behind, exerting pressure to bring her even closer.

'You…we can't—'

'I assure you, Mia, we can, and I fully intend to.'

His mouth breached that last centimetre, searing her own with a burning fire that immediately overwhelmed, consumed her so every thought, every single objection flew straight out of her head.

Salvation came in the form of a loud snuffle as Gianni stirred in his sleep.

Beneath her, Rocco stiffened at the sound, then dropped his forehead to hers with a muted groan. 'I now know what parents mean when they bemoan their children killing their sex lives.' Warm self-derision invited her to share the joke.

'You can rest easy, Rocco. We don't have a sex life to bemoan. Hell, after we meet with your lawyers and get this straightened out, we don't even need to be in the same vicinity unless strictly necessary.'

Her voice was reassuringly firm and even, her spine straight.

But inside, Mia was trembling. Crumbling beneath the brooding, enigmatic look he sent her. Because that look was ten times more potent than the one he'd delivered that chilling day in his office when he'd annihilated her.

And as the limo sped towards London, her instincts shrieked that they were far from done. That she was nowhere near being free of Rocco Vitelli.

CHAPTER SIX

THE OFFICES OF ROCCO's lawyers were located exactly where Mia suspected they would be—slap bang in the middle of the Square Mile ensconced behind its towers of steel and glass.

Sharply suited professionals moved around with brisk efficiency. Within minutes, they were whisked skyward and into a sleek conference room. Gianni took it all in his stride, his eyes wide as he looked around him. His usually effervescent questions had quietened down, perhaps instinctively sensing the momentous occasion. Or it might have been the firm hold his father had on him, the awe with which her son looked up at his father as they were ushered into the conference room.

Mia didn't want to speculate any more than her wild imagination was already hammering at her. Rocco hadn't spoken to her since her tight announcement in the car following their horrid little entanglement. His calculating gaze had settled on her more than a few times though, enough to heighten the sense of unsettling dread bubbling beneath her skin. She refused to engage in whatever he was plotting behind those sharply intelligent eyes.

A few short hours. That was all she needed to hold it together before she could be back in Hampshire with her son. All further dealings after today would be through lawyers she could employ once she was back on her feet.

The door opened, and a stream of lawyers entered. It was easy to distinguish between the Italian contingent and their English counterparts. The Italians were more flamboyantly dressed, their bespoke Milan suits shrieking their Latin flair, while their English colleagues were a little more conservative, although both could not have been mistaken for anything other than the sharp pool of sharks Rocco retained.

Conservative greetings were exchanged, and Mia watched them align themselves across the conference table.

They were barely settled when Rocco leaned forward, his eyes fixed on the senior partner. 'Do you have answers for me?'

The older gentleman, with greying hair and rimless glasses, nodded. 'Our investigators are still working through how this debacle came to be but my team has been able to confirm that your earlier suspicions were right. The documentation is all fraudulent.'

A tight knot unfurled in Mia's belly, her breath expelling sharply. After years of living under the strain of persecution, she couldn't believe how completely she'd been duped. But the utmost emotion rolling through her was relief.

Slowly, though, bitterness followed. Things had gone seriously wrong but it still couldn't be denied that Rocco had cut her completely out of his life, not bothering to answer any of her emails long before this fraudulent court case had been brought.

'How?' she blurted, her voice thick with emotion she couldn't contain. 'How could this have been done without you or Rocco knowing?' Deep down she suspected she knew. Only someone with a vindictive agenda and in a position of trust could've done this. Someone with the backing of Vitelli billions.

The English lawyer turned to her. 'That was what we were hoping you would be able to shed some light on, Miss Gallagher.'

She frowned. 'Me?'

Another lawyer, this one an Italian, leaned forward. 'You attended the court, *sì*?' he asked, his accent thick as he peered at her.

She gritted her teeth, choosing not to rise to the clear

scepticism in his tone. 'If you are in any way insinuating that I knew all of this was some huge set-up, you couldn't be more wrong.'

'The lawyers for the claimant are a small firm, we have discovered. Little more than a father and son outfit. The father, the one who dealt specifically with your case, is no longer practising. In fact he has fallen ill and is not in a position to testify to many of these allegations.'

Dismay hollowed her stomach. 'And his son?'

'Claims to have no knowledge of this affair.'

'That's terribly convenient, isn't it?' she snapped.

The lawyers exchanged glances. It was clear to Mia they had been thinking the same thing. *About her.*

She slapped her hands on the table. 'What exactly is going on here? I came here to clear my name. And you started off this meeting by confirming that these allegations are bogus. So why do I feel I'm still under suspicion?' She turned towards Rocco as she asked the last question. He was staring at her, narrow-eyed and speculative again. 'Rocco? What is this?'

He shrugged. 'We're all trying to find answers, *cara.*'

She hated that he used that soft endearment. It was dangerous and misleading. Hypnotic in a way that swayed her into overlooking the sharp eyes still brimming with suspicion. 'Well, I'm sorry, but I don't have any,' she remarked, bitter memory cutting sharply through her. 'I got the summons and I turned up at court and grasped enough to understand that I was being accused of harassing and stalking you.' Past hurt seared her insides but she refused to let it affect her. She needed to hold it together just enough to finish this and be gone. 'The lawyer I hired confirmed it too. You were clearly stated as the plaintiff. So this is all on you. It's your business to find out.'

'But you do know something, don't you?' Rocco said it again softly, his eyes boring into her.

'I'm not going to keep speculating. I've told you everything I know.'

'But not everything you *suspect*,' he pressed.

She kept her mouth mutinously shut.

His gaze remained on her face, probing beneath her skin for another minute before he faced his lawyers. 'Someone impersonated me and pulled this off without any of you knowing. I'm beginning to wonder why I keep you on retainer if this is the level of service I receive.'

Half a dozen lawyers shuffled their papers and twitched in their seats. Eventually the senior partner spoke. 'While we don't wish to speculate, Mr Vitelli, we all agree that it could only have been someone close to you, someone who was sure they could carry this out without suspicion.' A few glances settled on her.

Mia stiffened, ready to launch another defence but Rocco beat her to it. 'Someone close to me?' he echoed, his face taut.

The lawyer shifted in his seat before nodding. 'Your investigators have been in touch with your IT department. It seems there's evidence of deleted emails and possible tampering with your server. We think that the only person who could have done that may have been your assistant.'

Rocco's jaw clenched. 'My assistant has been with me since the very beginning. I trust him with my life. It's not him. Look for a different culprit.'

Gianpaolo, Rocco's assistant, had come straight from university into his role. Even Mia knew he would cut off his own arm before he betrayed Rocco. Just as she knew Rocco's implicit trust in his assistant, where he'd had none for her, bruised deep.

Silence descended on the table, only disturbed when Gianni rose from his seat, reaching for the pen in front of Rocco. He'd been well-behaved thus far but Mia knew restlessness was about to set in with a vengeance. 'Are we done here? I need to tend to my son.'

'Pardon me, Miss Gallagher, I have one question. It may be a little bit indelicate, but it needs to be asked. Did you make any enemies while you were working at Vitelli Construction?'

She barely stopped herself from glancing at Rocco, the man who'd made himself public and private enemy number one the moment she'd attended an meeting with his competitor, then compounded her sins by informing him she wasn't ready to start a family on his schedule. She bit her tongue, a part of her unwilling to antagonise the situation and a part of her wanting to state blatantly that he was the only nemesis she could think of.

But then he wasn't the only one, was he?

Alessandro Vitelli had made it his life's mission to make hers miserable the moment she'd set foot in Vitelli Construction. Could she say it now? It had been established that she had been duped. Wasn't that enough?

'If you know who it is, Mia, spit it out,' Rocco said tightly, his face taut as he stared at her.

She inhaled slowly, her instinct screaming at her to keep the information to herself. But at the same time she wanted the truth of her suspicions explored. Deep down she knew she couldn't rest until she discovered who had done this to her. 'The only person I can think of is your cousin Alessandro.'

The first expression of shock was Rocco's sharp intake of breath. Then the Italian contingent exchanged glances before their faces tightened.

Mia held herself tight. 'What? You asked me a question and I'm sorry if you don't like the answer.'

'You happened to pick the only person who wouldn't be able to corroborate your statement. A little curious, don't you think?' Rocco replied. If he had been tense a moment ago, he was downright rigid now.

'What are you talking about? Why wouldn't he?'

Brackets formed around his lips as he tightened them, staring at her for another tense moment before he rasped, 'You know exactly what I mean. You accuse a dead man incapable of telling his part of whatever story you're concocting.'

A cold rush of dread unravelled through her. Partly because she was receiving evidence that Rocco didn't truly believe her. The other was at the news he'd just delivered. 'Alessandro is dead?' she whispered.

Again his lips flattened. 'His car crash was sensationalised by the papers.' His tone of voice suggested that she should know.

'I don't keep abreast of news headlines. Especially foreign ones. I'm too busy looking after my son.'

'The TV and newspapers carried the story for days. It would have been impossible to miss.'

'Well, I'm telling you it is possible because I missed it. The question remains do you believe me or do you think I'm making this up as well?'

'What reason would he have to do this?' Rocco asked stiffly.

She forced a shrug. 'That's what you have to find out for yourself.'

His nostrils flared, a very Latin, very emotive expression that sent a shiver down her spine.

'So we have a perpetrator who is no longer with us and a co-conspirator lawyer who is unable to testify as to his role in this?' He gave a thin smile.

She answered with one of her own. 'Life has a funny way of unravelling, doesn't it?'

His narrowed gaze raked her face before he turned his attention back to his lawyers. 'We keep investigating. We don't stop searching until we know the facts for certain. Is that understood?'

Brisk nods accompanied verbal assurances.

Rocco rose, leaned down to place a gentle hand on Gianni's head, attracting his son's attention from the picture he'd been drawing on the piece of paper.

Gianni looked set to protest at the interruption. Anticipating it, Rocco murmured in his ear. With a pleased grin, Gianni grabbed the paper and pen and jumped to his feet. Without addressing his lawyers again, Rocco strode after his son, leaving Mia to follow.

In the lift, Gianni chatted on, negating the need for his parents to converse. But the look Rocco pinned on her announced loud and clear that the conversation was far from over. Mia dragged her gaze from his, so overwrought by the events of the last hour that, once they were in the car, it took a while to notice that the driver was heading back out of London.

She turned to Rocco, who was staring at her, one finger dragging slowly across his lower lip in that contemplative way she knew all too well.

The question she'd intended to ask about where they were going dried in her throat. 'When did he die?'

He exhaled heavily. 'Almost eighteen months ago,' he replied.

'Was he…is his family okay?'

'He was alone in the car, if that's what you're asking. Allegra and the kids were at home in Palermo.'

'Where did it happen?'

'He was on a business trip to Brazil when it happened. He lost control of his sports car.'

Her heart twisted. 'I… I'm sorry for your loss. I know you two were close.'

He nodded briefly, his eyes flashing with something akin to pain before he expunged it. 'You really expect me to believe Alessandro did this to you? What would have been his motive?' The questions were sharp, rife with suspicion.

She shrugged. 'He didn't like me, Rocco. And that's not a frivolous or desperate observation I'm casting around because I've no one else to pin this on, if you think that's what I'm trying to do. Alessandro actively despised me for whatever reason. He didn't want me in the company and he certainly didn't want me to marry into the illustrious Vitelli family.'

His features darkened, thunder rolling across his forehead as he stared at her. 'We were together for two years. You never bothered to tell me any of this?'

Again she shrugged. 'Maybe I was trying to spare your feelings. Or maybe I was misguided enough to think I might be able to win him over eventually with my sparkling personality. What does it matter? You'll only make up your mind one way or the other, won't you? Why am I even wasting my breath with this?'

'Because you spoke his name in the boardroom. And I'd like to think that you wouldn't speak so ill of the dead.'

Frustration rushed through her. 'We're simply going around in circles. Until we know exactly who did this, there's no point speculating, is there? So can we be done for now?' She stared at the window and then returned her attention to him. 'Where are we going?'

'To my house in Knightsbridge.'

Her eyes widened in surprise. 'I didn't know you had a house in England.'

A brittle smile ghosted his lips then just as quickly disappeared. 'It was meant to be a surprise wedding gift. For you.'

Her heart lurched. She steeled herself against it, determined not to dwell on silly might-have-beens. 'Why did you keep it?'

He gave a careless shrug. 'I leave my real estate portfolio to my advisors. If it'd been prudent for them to dispose of it, they would've, I'm sure.'

The dismissive comment was meant to sting. And it did. Mia steeled herself harder. 'Well, I thought I'll be returning to Hampshire.'

His gaze flicked to Gianni. 'You think our son will appreciate being cooped up in the car for another several hours?'

She answered reluctantly. 'No. Frankly, I'm surprised he's been this calm.'

'*Bene*, we'll stop in Knightsbridge. I've arranged for us to have lunch. We have further things to discuss before any of this is resolved.'

'Like what?'

He raised an eyebrow. 'Have you forgotten there is still the matter of your employment to discuss?'

'My employment?' she echoed, disregarding the electric cluster that formed in her stomach. 'If you think I'm taking a job with you, you are very much mistaken.'

Hard amusement lit his eyes. 'Perhaps you should wait until it's offered before you refuse.'

She shook her head, unwilling to even accommodate the idea. Her last mistake of mixing business with pleasure had ended disastrously. So much so even the idea of just business with Rocco was unfathomable to her. 'My future employment is none of your business. All I want is for my name to be cleared so I can get on with my life.'

'And we will discuss how to facilitate that during lunch.'

She knew she was being manipulated but, short of insisting on being returned home, she had no choice.

'We'll come with you. But I'm catching the train this afternoon, once we're done.' She didn't intend to stay in Rocco's company any longer than was necessary.

'We'll see,' he said, another enigmatic smile ghosting his lips before he turned his attention to his phone.

For the rest of the journey, Rocco conducted several conversations in rapid-fire Italian, which she wasn't quick enough to grasp save for establishing they were all business calls.

Twenty-five minutes later they pulled up in front of a stunning house in a tree-lined avenue in Knightsbridge. Mia was vaguely cognisant of house prices, enough to know that the dwelling they stopped in front of was well into double figures in millions.

It was set over three stories with a grey slate roof, the pristine white exterior gleaming with a rarefied air of class and timeless elegance that the whole neighbourhood clung to.

Confronted by the heavy white oak door, Mia was suddenly reluctant to enter. She didn't want to know what her life might have been like if Rocco, and circumstances, hadn't worked against her.

If she hadn't taken that meeting.

If someone, likely Alessandro, hadn't perpetrated such cruelty on her.

If she hadn't asked Rocco about his London property ten minutes ago!

But she couldn't change any of it. So she sucked in a breath, and entered the house that Rocco claimed would've been hers had they married. All the while conscious of his sharp, unwavering scrutiny.

As she'd suspected, the interior was breathtaking.

Polished marble floors gleamed, reflecting lofty ceilings and crown mouldings. Stunning chandeliers and strategically placed lights spotlighted tasteful *objets d'art* in the entry hallway.

In the living room, bespoke white furniture with warm accessories were arranged just the way she would have done it, given the chance. But it was the white grand piano taking up pride of place at the far side of the room, with a wall of paintings behind it, that stopped Mia in her tracks.

She knew each painting by heart, having rhapsodised over her favourite English painter to Rocco over many stimulating art and cultural conversations. Just as she'd expressed the desire to learn to play piano at some distant point in her future.

She whirled towards him and encountered his expectant, *mocking* expression. Her lips moved, but no words emerged.

Asking him if he'd deliberately brought her here to rub her face in what she could've been would only invite further hurt. Not to mention be far too revealing.

'Nothing to say?' he invited when a terse minute passed.

She turned away without answering, her gaze rushing over the rest of the space, awed but not surprised that Rocco's steel trap of a mind had stored away bits and pieces of her dream home wish list and effortlessly replicated it.

Sternly, she pulled her gaze from admiring the beautiful interior; reminded herself that she wasn't here to gawp at the stunning paintings or the interior design plucked straight from her heart. She was here to finalise the next step of her life. A life that had been cruelly and ruthlessly halted by this man, who now leaned against the doorway, gazing at her as if he owned every cell in her body.

'Shall we get on with this?'

'So impatient,' he commented, a smirk playing around his lips. 'You haven't even mentioned what you think of the house.'

Her shoulder felt leaden as she shrugged. 'It'll make a gorgeous home for someone once you get bored of it, I'm sure.'

His mocking expression evaporated and his jaw clenched once but Mia didn't congratulate herself on landing the blow. Not when her insides were clenched tight with the need to hold herself together.

'Perhaps I'll hang onto it, set down roots for Gianni. He's half English, after all,' he drawled.

'Are we really discussing real estate? I would've thought you'd be upset by the events of the last few hours.'

He lifted one masculine shoulder, drawing her attention to the sheer breadth and magnificence of his towering body. 'I'm learning not to sweat the details. My investigators will uncover the truth in due time.'

'You're just prepared to shrug it off until it all comes together for you?'

'What's the point of stressing about it? Like you're so eager to, we need to get on with other discussions. But first things first.' He strolled over to a console table, lifted the phone and spoke in Italian. Almost immediately, Mia heard the click of approaching footsteps.

The middle-aged woman who entered the room was conservatively dressed, and pleasant-looking. She greeted Rocco before glancing at her.

'This is my Mrs Simpson, my housekeeper,' Rocco introduced. 'She's already prepared Gianni's lunch.'

The older woman smiled at Mia. 'I have three grandchildren of my own so I know just what a two-year-old likes to eat. It's all set up in the kitchen. If you don't mind him coming with me?'

To respond any other way would have been discourteous. So Mia nodded. 'Thank you. If you need me, I'll be...' She paused, glancing at Rocco.

'We'll be in the dining room, having our own lunch. But Gianni is going to be a good boy for Mrs Simpson, aren't you, *mio figlio*?'

Gianni, who had looked up from his drawing with interest when the housekeeper entered, nodded at his father. She'd been concerned about how her son would take to having a male figure in his life. Judging from the look that passed between father and son, he was coping brilliantly.

A part of her wanted to be disappointed but it was a small, selfish part that she managed to smother as Mrs Simpson and Gianni walked away, hand in hand.

'He's only going to the other room, Mia, not Outer Mongolia,' Rocco quipped.

She sent him a sharp look. 'I'm not used to other people taking care of him, okay?'

He regarded her steadily. 'I'm becoming aware of that. I recall you disliked talking about your family. Do I assume hiding away in your little village was by choice?'

'If by choice you mean was I alone once my grandmother passed away soon after Gianni was born, then yes.'

His eyes shadowed. 'Were you close?'

A swell of sadness filled her heart. 'Close enough to make me regret not spending more time with her,' she said before she could trap the revealing words.

'Meaning?' Rocco pressed.

'Meaning we all have regrets. Less time with my grandmother is one of mine.'

His gaze probed. Deep. Making his next words unexpected. *'Le mie condoglianze.'*

Condolences.

'Thank you.'

He nodded. 'But things are going to change. You know that, don't you?'

She raised her chin, unwilling to divulge that she suspected the very same thing. 'Do I?'

'Sì, cara,' he said far too softly, ambling to a halt in front of her. For an eternity, he stared down at her, then lifted a finger and traced it down her cheek. 'For starters, you are no longer alone.'

The words echoed through her, sinking into unguarded spaces inside her, awing and terrifying in equal measure. She tried to read his face, but Rocco gave nothing away.

'Come.' He held out his hand, his command softer but imperious.

The urge to take his proffered hand was far too tempting. So she refused it, and walked past him. Only to stop when she got to the door, having no clue where the dining room was. Still she forced herself not to look at him, not to be overwhelmed all over again by the ever-morphing Rocco, who seemed to have changed from ruthless strategist in the car to something bordering on…charming?

'This way,' he said when he joined her, directing her down a short hallway and into another opulently appointed room with a long, antique dining table she was willing to bet had belonged to a prince or a lofty aristocrat once upon its lifetime.

At the top of the table, an elaborate setting for two was arranged with gleaming silver and crystal ware.

Rocco pulled out a chair, saw her seated and took his own seat. In silence, he uncovered dishes and served her before indicating the wine resting in the sterling silver ice bucket.

'Would you like some wine? Or are you…?' He paused, an almost bashful look on his face as his gaze dropped to her chest. 'You are not still breastfeeding, are you?' he asked, his voice curiously husky.

She spluttered, an unwilling laugh rising in her throat before she could stop it. 'Gianni's two and half years old, Rocco.'

His gaze lingered for another heated second on her breasts before he shrugged, a wry smile curving his lips. 'I'm still learning, *cara*. So is that a yes to wine?' he drawled.

She needed to keep a clear head for what was coming. But what harm would a small, confidence-bolstering glass do? 'A small one, thanks.'

He poured a half-glass for her and then filled his. The

first bite of poached salmon was heavenly, but anxiety over the upcoming discussion eventually killed her enjoyment of the meal. After a few minutes of pushing it around her plate, she looked up, noting that Rocco was equally uninterested in his food.

Almost in accordance, they gave up pretence of eating and sat back. When the silence stretched, she folded her napkin and dropped it next to her plate. 'We need to discuss next steps.'

'Agreed.'

'So?' she pressed when he didn't elaborate.

'So, you're not returning to Hampshire, Mia.'

'Maybe not right this minute, but I'm definitely…' She stopped when he gave a brisk shake of his head.

'No. To get what you want you need to give me what I want and neither of those scenarios involve you returning to the back end of nowhere. I think we need to agree on that before we go forward.'

CHAPTER SEVEN

ONCE UPON A time when she'd dreamed of being exonerated of these fraudulent charges, she'd imagined a scene when Rocco would grovel at her feet, beg her forgiveness for all the wrong perpetrated against her. Over time that dream had morphed, reality throwing harsh light on that fairy tale, reminding her of the ruthless being she was spinning whimsical webs around.

In the much more realistic scenario, Rocco had perhaps thrown a brusque apology her way for the treatment she'd suffered, perhaps even tossing lawyers at her, tasked with providing adequate compensation to ensure she kept her mouth shut, but ultimately Rocco had walked away, shrugging his mile-wide shoulders as if nothing besides a pesky irritation had occurred.

Nowhere in those scenarios had she accommodated sitting down to lunch as a prelude to negotiating a deal with him. 'You want me to give you more than I already have? You don't think what you've put me through is enough?'

For one blazing second, raw emotion flashed across his face. 'What was done to you was deplorable, regardless of who perpetrated it. For that you have my regret. *Mi dispiace.*' He spread his hands in a typically Latin gesture she couldn't help but follow before she could rein in her composure.

He was sorry.

It wasn't the grovelling she'd dreamed of, but it was… enough to ease something inside her.

'You will get the chance to name your price and necessary reparations will be made.'

That soft place hardened, ejecting a bitter snort. 'This all sounds like a business transaction to you, doesn't it?'

Another flash of emotion threw doubt on her assertion. 'You forget that I suffered by this course of action too,' he said, his voice a rough rasp.

Her heart lurched for a foolish moment, before she registered that he was talking about Gianni. Not her.

Never her.

'If you would hear me out, perhaps my solution might salve your feelings of…hurt?'

'Nothing will repair what I've endured. Right now, I just want move on. Forget it, and *you*, ever happened.'

His eyes roved lazily over her face, clocking her agitated breathing before he leaned forward. 'It was never going to be as simple as stating your case, wrapping this up, and walking away, Mia. Surely you knew that?'

'You keep implying that I owe you something. Let's get things straight between us. I owe you nothing.'

He eased back in his chair, but Mia wasn't fooled for a moment. Tension coiled within him, the barely bridled domination emanating from him all but screaming at her that he intended to win this argument. Whatever it might be.

'What about Gianni, Mia? You told me three years ago that you didn't intend to have children. So you'll excuse me if I find all of this new, devoted-to-motherhood part of you a little bit surprising?'

She gasped, felt the blood drain from her head as she stared at him. 'You think I'm faking it?'

'Are you?'

'How dare you!' She whirled around, heading blindly for the door with one intention in mind—to claim her child and leave this place.

'What do you think you're doing?'

'Whatever the hell I want. And right now the thing I want the most in this world is to never see your face again. I'm going to get my son and we're leaving.'

'Calm yourself, Mia. You really want Gianni to see you in this state?'

She reversed direction, her emotions boiling as she faced him. 'You're unbelievable, do you know that? Now you're accusing me of upsetting my son?'

He spread his arms again, his eyes narrowing as he approached. 'Don't put words in my mouth, *cara*. From what I've seen so far, you're devoted to our child.'

Again, his unexpected words weakened the hard knot in her chest. But she knew better than to trust it. 'Thank you, but I sense a *but* in there.'

'But this display of...emotion serves no purpose. Like I said before, you have cared for Gianni alone but it doesn't need to be the case going forward. You can deal with me now or you can deal with my lawyers before you reach the home you are so determined to run back to. Which is it to be?'

She inhaled sharply, surprised at herself for momentarily forgetting the depths Rocco could sink to to achieve what he wanted. 'You haven't changed even a little bit, have you?'

His resolve was a hard, unshakeable mask. 'I discover a son I never knew existed and you expect me to do what exactly, Mia? Go back to Palermo and forget all about him? Or were you hoping I'd sit back and let you dictate terms? When have you known me to be that...*unaffected* when it comes to something I truly want?' he asked, his voice deceptive lazily.

Since the question was rhetorical, and since the throb of something in his tone tossed her back to another time frame, when that something he'd wanted was *her*, she kept her answer locked in her throat.

While the net tightened around her, dragging her towards a precarious destination she didn't want to go. Still, she managed to raise her chin, look him square in the eyes. 'I'll give you ten minutes to hear you out. But I won't be railroaded into anything, just so we're clear,' she stated, pleased when her voice came out even, without hinting at the hysteria bubbling beneath her skin. 'What do you want? Specifically?'

He didn't answer immediately. He stared at her, gauging the emotions she was grappling with before his gaze sauntered down her body to her toes. The return was slow and hot, setting off fireworks she didn't want to acknowledge. 'A few things come to mind. But for now, specifically, my presence in my son's life. And I suspect the way to achieve that is to give you what you most want.'

What she most wanted was to remove herself from his orbit. To stop the fizzle of giddy static from lighting her veins every time her eyes met his. Every time she breathed him in. 'And what do you think that is?'

'Why, a return to the career status you enjoyed before our parting, of course. Am I wrong?' he enquired, a knowing gleam in his eyes she wanted to erase but knew she couldn't. Because she *did* want back what she'd lost.

'I'll get it back. But it'll be on my own, with no handout from you, thank you very much. If you think that's some sort of carrot to dangle to get what you want, then the answer is no. My son isn't some bartering chip for you to trade,' she stated.

'So much righteous pride,' he drawled. 'Are you sure you're wise to dismiss my help?'

'Help? When it comes with an endless amount of strings? No, thanks,' she reiterated. The voice that urged her to stop talking grew louder. Even if she intended to reclaim her life by herself, did she want to brazenly antagonise him? She'd been out of the workforce for the better part of three years. Did she really want to start at the bottom of the pile again when a few words from Rocco could pave the way for a decent enough re-entry, enabling her to look after herself and Gianni? Wasn't it the least he owed her?

As if he knew the direction of her thoughts, he stepped closer, bringing the full force of his aura and the temptation of his body within mouth-watering reach. 'Is that your definitive answer, then, *cara*? Your decision-making used to be so prudent and pragmatic. It was one of the things I admired about you. Have you grown rusty or are you simply disregarding what your brain is telling you simply to continue tussling with me?'

She wanted to protest, toss out some clever answer that would put him in his place once and for all, but the voice urging caution held her tongue for the moment.

He continued, his voice turning lower and deeper, almost seductive as he laid his plans before her. 'Let me tell you what my intentions are while you think about the wisdom of contemptuously dismissing me out of hand. I'm not sure whether you've kept up with Vitelli Construction's progress in the last few years?' One eyebrow tilted, as he waited a beat for her to answer. When she didn't give him the satisfaction of confessing the secret compulsion she'd had of tracking his company's stellar progress over the years, he carried on.

'Our Middle East expansion has now reached eight countries. The workforce is five times the size of what it was when you were last with me. Before his passing, Alessandro also expanded the Latin American arm. Eventually, should you wish it, you can take a pick of where you wish to base yourself.'

Her heart jumped, a treacherous little action she condemned. Because she didn't want to be seduced by what he was offering. Didn't want to be tempted by memories of working alongside him, basking in the glow of his intelligent mind and the thrill of knowing she was working for the best of the best, her career poised to soar as a result of her hard work.

She managed to throttle down the unwelcome excitement, and clinically sieved through his words. 'Eventually,' she echoed. 'What exactly do you mean by *eventually*?'

Incisive eyes rested on her face, dropped down to her mouth before rising to meet her gaze. He shrugged, walked past her to shut the doors of the dining room. Foreboding rained icy shivers down her spine, but she clenched her fist, forced herself to hold her ground as he sauntered back towards her. 'I'm assuming you wish to be where our son is, don't you?'

She frowned. 'Is that even a serious question? Of course I do.'

He nodded, as if she had given him the exact answer he wanted. 'Then we're agreed.'

Her ire and confusion intensified. 'What exactly are we agreed on?'

'That where I am, you will be. With our son. To start off with, that place will be in Palermo. For the next six months at least. Perhaps even a year. Depending on Nonna's health issues and how quickly she recovers.'

She spluttered, unsure which outrage to address first. 'You think I'm coming to Italy to live with you? Why on earth would I do that?'

When you threw me out. When for weeks every street I walked in Palermo reminded me of you and what I'd lost.

His steady regard didn't falter. 'What other solution do you propose? That I commute every other day to your little Hampshire hamlet? With Nonna living in a faceless motel somewhere close by, perhaps?'

'Where you or your grandmother live has nothing to do with me. I'm not going anywhere with you. Let's make that absolutely clear.'

'Then how do you propose we raise our son together?' he delivered with a deceptively silky voice.

Raise our son together.

Against her better judgement, those four words sent a

treacherous rush through her. Reminded her of everything she'd yearned for when she'd tried to give him the news of her pregnancy. A chance to raise their child together. A chance to rewrite her own history through Gianni. To give him what her own mother had failed to give her.

A relationship with her father. For her son not to be tormented as she had been with questions about the man whose name appeared on her birth certificate but who she'd never clapped eyes on because her mother refused point-blank to discuss him, save for the fact that he was a mistake that should never have happened.

Much like Mia had been to her.

As if he knew how much the words affected her, Rocco strode closer, his eyes not leaving her face. 'Tell me about your father, Mia.'

She stiffened, more against the anguish of discussing the man she didn't know than by Rocco's question. 'Why?'

'Because, as we're both discovering, we were engaged for a time over three years ago, but clearly didn't know a few important details about one another.'

'And why do you think that is?'

He shrugged. 'Perhaps we thought we'd have time to uncover what needed uncovering.'

'Do you think so? Or were we too afraid to find out we wouldn't like what we discovered beneath the surface so avoided it?'

It was his turn to stiffen. 'Perhaps. So, let's be brave now. Let's stop the speculation,' he said, cleverly tossing the ball back in her court.

Her father.

Her answer was simple. And soul-destroying. 'I don't know a thing about him because I've never met him. My mother refused to tell me who he was or what happened between them. Other than he was a mistake she'd rather forget ever existed.'

Mia knew by revealing that, she was exposing her jugular. Or at the very least, giving him ammunition for his argument. But Rocco's gaze gentled, his breath slowly releasing as he absorbed her words. 'You may think it a bad thing that your mother withheld details from you. But perhaps she was protecting you. Maybe you were better off remaining oblivious.'

Memories of her mother's bitterness whenever Mia had asked about her father made her think otherwise. 'Would you have let it go were you in my shoes?'

His lips curved in a rueful smile. '*Assolutamente no.* Even if it meant discovering that one's parents were far... worth revering.'

Her eyes widened, the notion that Rocco was offering her a brief glimpse behind his private, emotional veil stopping her breath.

They regarded each other for an endless stretch before, with a conscious shuttering of his emotions, he continued, 'Despite opposing forces, circumstance has brought my son and I together. I don't intend to squander that chance.'

Still a little shaken and more than curious at his revelation, she took a moment to gather her wits. 'I didn't intend to throw Gianni into the deep end of the relationship-with-family pool by uprooting him to Italy.'

'And *I* will not be sidelined to part-time parenthood. Gianni is mine. You will give me the chance to get to know him as I haven't been able since his birth.'

'And what I want and what's best for Gianni doesn't matter?'

The shrewd gleam in his eyes said he had the answer to that too. 'You disagree that what's best for Gianni is to be with both his mother *and* father?'

'Of course not,' she bristled.

'Then it helps immensely that I know *you* love Italy. Almost as much as I do.'

She had, once upon a time. Had uprooted her life for him and blissfully contemplated becoming an Italian citizen after they were married without a single regret. She'd never really got around to learning Italian because their work had been based mostly in the Middle East, but she'd loved everything about Italy and had looked forward to spending the rest of her life there with him. How stupid she'd been. And now he was proposing she go back to where he had dismantled her whole life?

No way was that happening.

'That was a long time ago. I've made a life for myself and Gianni in England and I intend to keep on living here.'

'Answer me this, Mia. Why did you go to the trouble to contact me three years ago if you didn't want me to play a part in our child's life?' he asked 'Was it because you didn't want to revisit what happened to you with your own father on our son?'

A cold, heavy stone settled in her belly. And she couldn't even blame him for cleverly using her history against her. Because it was the truth.

Her own loneliness and abandonment issues had been acute and painful, a past she carried with her as a reminder to not let her own child endure the pain she'd suffered. And yes, she had hoped in some secret part of her that Rocco, learning of the child she carried, would rethink his absolute rejection of her, let her back into his life.

But that was before the scales had fallen from her eyes. That was before she'd fathomed the depths of his ruthlessness. Who was to say that this wasn't another calculated scheme on his part to lure her into his web?

'Well?' he pushed.

She looked deeper into his eyes, unable to remain unaffected by the turbulent gleam that suggested this was important to him. 'For good or ill, I believe every child has the right to know his parents.' Before the turbulence turned into triumph, she rushed on, 'But expecting me to blithely step back in time and pick up where we left off...' She tailed off when his eyes conducted that heated exploration again, stripping her of every ounce of composure.

'Perhaps not pick up exactly where we left off, but I don't see why some things can't go back to the way they were.'

'Whatever you're implying, I suggest you stop.' She'd intended to snap her response. Only it emerged uneven, detonated by that vicious thrill of excitement that simply refused to die. The memory of the torrid kiss in the car kept pushing to the front of her thoughts, reminding her of his skill as a lover, the insatiable depths of his passion, and her eager acceptance of everything he had to give.

Heat bloomed in her belly as he watched her with that knowing look. The one that mocked her every attempt at keeping cool, calm and collected.

'You can have your old position back,' he murmured, his voice deep and low and tempting enough to make her believe he was the devil himself, handing Eve the doomed apple.

Her heart lurched, thumping hard against her ribs.

He waited, watchful, taunting her with the knowledge that she was tempted. Oh, so tempted. She knew he wanted her to ask which position he was referring to, the subtle double entendre simply waiting to catch her out.

After a moment, where she battled against the drowning sensation, he added, 'Think of how much easier your life would be if you had it all back. How difficult things could get if you have to start from scratch. Is that what you really want, Mia?' he taunted softly, dangerously.

'Is that what this all boils down to? You threatening to withhold restoring my reputation if I don't agree to come to Palermo?'

His jaw gritted for a moment. 'You were an asset in my company before you decided to defect. Provided your skills haven't grown rusty, I could use someone with your expertise.'

'I didn't defect,' she snapped.

He didn't acknowledge her denial with so much as a blink. 'I don't need to threaten you. Contingent upon a few things, you can have your old position back.' He snapped his fingers. 'Just like that.'

'Contingent upon what?'

'The only reason I'll let you back is if you agree that you and I will be working very closely together. Where I can keep an eye on you. You will not be left to your own devices.'

'Next you'll be suggesting I wear an ankle monitor like a common criminal.'

His lips twisted with genuine amusement. 'Not an offer I'd have thought of myself. Thanks for the suggestion but maybe not. I don't think it's a good look for Vitelli Construction.'

'You find all of this funny, do you?'

A layer of humour left his face. 'I'm attempting to repair the damage done to you by giving you back everything you lost with all its advantages, and more. I suggest you stop fighting me on every angle before I withdraw the offer.'

She lifted her chin, snatching in short breaths so she wouldn't breathe in his intoxicating scent. 'You've listed what you think I want but have *you* stopped to ask yourself whether you want this? You've known Gianni for a mere twenty-four hours. How do I know you won't get bored a month from now?'

Affront, and some dark, anguished shadow she couldn't quite name, drenched his features. 'Because he's not some accessory I intend to toy with and toss away when the novelty wears off. Make no mistake, Mia. I want my son. And I mean full access. I want him embraced by his family, in Italy, where he belongs. For my grandmother not to fret over it and further damage her health. What I want is for those things to happen immediately and to stay that way for as long as possible until I deem it otherwise.'

She tilted her head, attempting to emulate his earlier humour. 'Are you sure you wouldn't prefer the ankle monitor? Because that sounds suspiciously like a prison sentence to me.'

He didn't return her amusement. 'Hardly, *cara*. I'm offering you everything you claimed you wanted when we were together three years ago. All I need from you is your agreement to live under my roof.'

'Live under your roof?' she echoed.

He stepped closer, until every corner of her vision was filled with him, her every sense infused with that illicit thrill he never failed to evoke in her, even when she knew deep in her bones that this kind of exposure was detrimental to her sanity. 'Not just live under my roof, *cara*. You will do all the above, after you take my name. In short, Mia, I want you to marry me. Accept my marriage proposal or there is no deal.'

CHAPTER EIGHT

ROCCO WASN'T SURE whether to be insulted or amused when a look of horror chased across her face.

'You want me to…to *marry* you?'

'*Sì.*'

She grew paler, and the last trace of amusement departed.

Watching closely, he could've sworn she swayed beneath the heavy demand of his words. For a single, unbridled moment, Rocco wanted her to exhibit more emotion, perhaps something resembling the naked rapture that'd accompanied her ecstatic *yes* when he'd asked this very same question three years ago. Even the somewhat unnerving *happy tears* he'd dabbed away then, he would've tolerated now.

Anything but the pale apprehension she was showing so far.

'Absolutely not.'

'Which part of it do you disagree with, considering it was what you agreed to three years ago, minus the blessing of our son, of course?'

'Oh, but you forget, I wasn't in the position where I knew your true colours, was I? That enlightening moment came later. Thankfully before I made the mistake you're suggesting I make again.'

A hard stone settled in his stomach. 'You believe marriage to me would've been a mistake?'

'When you're so quick to believe the worst about me? Yes!'

He dragged in a slow breath, attempting to calm the frenzied emotion that threatened to spin out of control whenever he was within arm's reach of this woman. 'Let's spell things out between us, then, so there's no misunderstanding this time around. This isn't a love match or some lofty declaration of devotion. This is simply a transaction. You regain your position in my company. I get my son under my roof and my grandmother's health and well-being ensured.'

'And if I say no?'

'What is so wrong with attempting to strive for better where our son is concerned, Mia?'

'I...what?'

'Trust your instincts. Do you believe Gianni will come to any harm by being under my care?'

Her lashes swept down, veiling her expression from him. He shoved his hands in his pockets to prevent him from cupping her chin, tilting her gaze to his so he could read what she was hiding from him. 'No,' she murmured after an eternity.

His breath expelled in relief. 'Then, is what I'm proposing so bad?' he attempted to reason, although a very primitive, very masculine part of him simply wanted to throw her over his shoulder, find a dark cave to seal them both in to hash this out.

He clenched his gut against the sensation. It wasn't one he particularly liked about himself but...hadn't he experienced this...primitive possessiveness with Mia from the very time he'd spotted her? This need for exclusivity with her where he'd neither cared nor accommodated that in any of his previous liaisons?

'Mia?' His voice was hoarser, sharper than he'd intended.

She startled, looked into his eyes and he realised, just like yesterday, she'd been equally caught up in carnal memory. A little too pleased with that knowledge, he raised an eyebrow, watched her flush before she averted her gaze.

'Don't overthink this. You, me and Gianni. Together.

We all get what we want. You also make an old woman you claimed to like immeasurably happy. Is that so bad?'

Her soft lips twisted. 'You appeal to my better nature in the same breath you insult me. I never *claimed* to like your grandmother. I did.'

'Then why break her heart by denying her whatever time she has left with her great-grandchild?'

She paled again and he felt another bite of guilt. 'Whatever time she has left? Is she…ill?'

'I told you she collapsed when she saw Gianni's billboard. She hadn't been too well before that. Her doctors think it's her heart.'

She bit her lip, drawing Rocco's attention to the plump curve he longed to taste one more time. And several times after that. 'This is emotional blackmail.'

He firmed his resolve. 'It's the plain truth. I won't allow her to suffer further. Not if I can help it.'

Her gaze shifted to the door. 'I need time…to think.'

'What's there to think about? Don't you want your *career* back?' He couldn't stop himself from sneering the word. From emphasising the only thing she'd cared about when she was with him. 'You could be at your old desk in Milan as early as Monday morning.'

She inhaled sharply. 'You think that's all that matters to me. It's not. Not now I've Gianni to think about. We've never been apart and… I…'

'My grandmother and every member of my household will be devoted to his care when you're at work. Since Alessandro passed, Allegra and her children have moved into the villa. Gianni won't lack for anything.'

Another shadow passed across her face. 'Allegra and her children live with you?'

He nodded, eyes narrowed at her carefully neutral tone. 'Is that a problem?'

Long lashes swept down again. 'No, of course not. Besides, it's your house.'

'It'll be *our* house, when you accept my proposal.'

She swallowed, her eyes still not meeting his. Rocco wanted to ask why she was refusing him when most women within his social circle would turn cartwheels at the thought of bagging a man of his stature.

'Why marriage? It's not like you need a shotgun wedding to protect my honour or anything like that. Besides, you're already listed on Gianni's birth certificate as his father. Isn't that enough?'

He finally gave into the insane urge and closed the gap between them. He slid his hand along her jaw to cup her nape. He revelled in the slight shiver that raked her frame. 'It wasn't enough for you, Mia, and it's most definitely not enough for me. My parents abandoned me when I was a child. Had it not been for Nonna's unflinching intervention, who knows where I would've ended up? She gave up a better life for me. She almost lost everything in the process. I won't deny her this. Most importantly, I won't deny myself.'

The depth of the words he hadn't spoken to anyone else spilling from his lips shocked him. Perhaps he wanted to reach someone who didn't exist. The woman he'd thought shared his values when he'd placed his ring on her finger three years ago. Whatever. They were said and he couldn't take them back. Nor could he look away from the wide-eyed shock in her own eyes as she stared up him.

They stayed locked in that revealing little bubble. Not breathing. Not speaking. The only movement his thumb slowly tracing back and forth across her lower lip.

But eventually, that seemingly unquenching well of lust swelled, ebbing and flowing in stronger waves that threatened to consume them. A soft sound, which he deciphered as a moan a few seconds later, rippled the air between them.

As he'd yearned her to, she swayed into him, her lips

parting, her warm breath caressing his thumb, sending a stronger wave of electricity through his body.

Rocco leaned down, unable to stem the tide consuming him.

A hair's breadth away from tasting temptation, she swayed in the other direction, snatching in an audible breath as she ripped herself from his hold.

'Like I said, I...need to think. I'm going to see Gianni.'

Without stopping for his response or to ask for directions, she flung her lithe, tempting body towards the door, leaving him standing there, a deep throb in his groin and the unsettling dread that he was falling under her spell... again...building in his chest.

For the second time in her life, Rocco Vitelli had proposed to her.

Only this time she wasn't the wide-eyed innocent who'd believed a candlelit dinner and a husky, accented proposal in a flower-decked courtyard of his Palermo villa was the start to her happy ever after.

Perhaps she should be grateful he'd spelled out exactly what his intentions were. Which were all about him and his grandmother and zilch to do with her emotional needs.

Not that she wanted him to cater to *any* need. Certainly not that insistent need that was making its presence felt as she attempted to smile for Gianni's sake, despite the fact that he was barely paying attention to her.

The housekeeper had found him a box of toys—apparently left over from her grandchildren's visit—and Gianni, content from a spaghetti lunch, was fully engrossed in it. Free from Rocco's presence, she had time to think.

Marriage. To Rocco.

For Gianni's sake.

Wasn't that what she'd wanted three years ago, even in her darkest moments when she'd feared she and Rocco might not settle their differences? For her child not to be denied its parent, the way she'd been?

So why did she feel this void inside her, as if something was missing? Besides a relationship with Gianni, Rocco was offering her career back. Another chance to fulfil the promise of both a profession *and* family, the way her mother had never been able to do.

For as long as she could remember, her mother's bitterness at what she'd deemed her unfulfilled potential at a career had been blamed on Mia. It was the reason she'd resisted the urge to jump straight into a family with Rocco when they'd first got engaged, despite the subtle pressures.

Fate—and a particularly heated bout of lovemaking where she couldn't remember whether they'd used protection or not—had found a way to settle things once and for all.

She had a son she'd never known she could love this much.

Rocco had the son and heir that he'd not so secretly craved. His grandmother had the offspring from her only grandchild. In essence, everyone would get what they desired if she married Rocco.

So what was stopping her?

Because you want more. She hid a grimace as the answer echoed in her heart.

No, she couldn't want more because more was *dangerous.*

My parents abandoned me when I was a child...

Mia's gaze swung to her son; she watched his profile, a younger version who would one day grow into the same formidable man his father was.

Could she deny him a chance to grow under his father's care?

No, she couldn't. She knew first-hand the anguish that would bring.

But marriage?

Her fingers shook, and she folded her arms to hide the trembling. It didn't mean anything, she assured herself. She would merely be another occupant underneath the roof of the sprawling villa in Palermo where Rocco lived with his grandmother.

Her lips twisted.

Most likely Rocco wouldn't even notice her presence, as absorbed as he'd become in his son in so short a time. Again that hollow inside her shifted, widened. Much as she wanted to dismiss it, Mia knew it wasn't that easy.

Once upon a time Rocco Vitelli had been the centre of her world.

Goodness, she'd even fancied herself in love with him. And, as evidenced, he still had sexual appeal she couldn't easily evade. But *she had* resisted him...

As she watched her son, her resolve slowly hardened.

She could do this.

That sexual weakness had been a temporary aberration, thrown up by the unsettling reality of coming face to face with Rocco after all this time. There were more important things to focus on. Gianni's emotional well-being. Her career.

And when the appropriate time passed, she would be free. She slowly breathed out. This was her decision, and she would make it work. Retracing her steps from where she'd paced to the window to stare out into the vast manicured garden, which seemed almost too good to be true in a property in Central London, she stopped beside her son.

Unable to stop herself from touching him, she ruffled Gianni's hair.

He looked up, a smile breaking on his face as he held up a toy. A red racing car. Mia smiled back, her heart filling with love all over again. If anything good came out of this, she prayed, let it be that Gianni would receive everything she'd been denied. To not experience the isolation she'd been forced to endure in her own childhood with a mother who'd laid all her hardships at her daughter's feet.

No matter how much she wanted to keep her son to herself, she knew that he would benefit from getting to know the Italian side of his family.

But before she gave an inch of ground to Rocco, she needed to put in a few contingencies.

She played with Gianni for another half-hour and then left him with the housekeeper and returned to the living room.

Rocco wasn't there.

About to go in search of him, she turned down the hallway.

She saw him coming down the stairs, a pillar of vitality and rugged handsomeness that stopped her dead in her tracks. Heat rose in her belly, and within seconds engulfed her whole body. He'd changed from the bespoke suit he'd worn earlier into a pair of stylish trousers and a polo shirt.

His hair was sexily dishevelled, as if he'd run his fingers through it repeatedly. Her fingers tingled, the urge to do the same overwhelming her for a shocking second before she wrestled the feeling under control. She might have had that liberty in the past, but no more. From here on out everything needed to be clinically platonic. She firmed lips that had parted at the sight of him, locking her knees as hawk-like eyes latched onto her.

She held her breath, delaying breathing him in as he stopped before her.

'Are you lost on the way somewhere or were you looking for me?' he drawled, sinful lips curved in amusement.

'We need to talk.'

One eyebrow rose. 'You've come to a decision so soon? I imagined I would be strung along for several hours, possibly a day at least.'

She shrugged. 'There's no point in delaying for the sake of theatrics. I've made up my mind.'

He regarded her steadily for a few tight seconds, his own breath seemingly held as he tried to read her. Then he nodded briskly. 'Come into my office. You can tell me what you've decided.'

He walked away, leaving her to follow.

His office was a masculine space, floor-to-ceiling book-cases interspersed with paintings and sculptures Rocco collected from far-flung places, turning the space from a simple office into a cultural and architectural masterpiece.

Mia wanted to stop and admire each piece of art, ea-gerly enquire of its provenance. Ask if their shared love of books had initiated this magnificent creation in the house he claimed he'd designed for her. She held her tongue. Be-cause this wasn't three years ago. She might have given her body and what she thought was her heart to him a long time ago, but they were now strangers. Evidenced by the look on his face as he perched on the corner of his desk, arms folded, and regarded her with cool expectancy.

'Tell me then, *cara*, what have you decided?'

She held the decision tightly in her chest, debating the wisdom of her answer for one final second. But really, she had very little alternative.

She would do anything for her son. And denying him a bond with his father was unfathomable to her.

So, with her fingers bunched and her heart banging against her ribs, she announced her decision. 'I will marry you.'

A different sort of tension seized his frame, his nostrils flaring in the throbbing silence that followed. 'Repeat it for me, *cara*. Just so we're both clear that—'

'Don't pretend you didn't hear me. I said I will marry you,' she repeated, her voice firmer, resolute. 'But before you go crowing about getting your way, I have a few stipulations of my own.'

His breath eased out of him, his stance growing deceptively relaxed as he rested his hand next to his taut thigh. 'Of course you do. Perhaps I should be glad we're both laying all our cards on the table?'

'You should. I'm assuming we will be staying at the villa in Palermo?'

He nodded. 'When we're in Sicily, yes. But the villa in Rome and the apartment in Milan are still available should we need them when we're on business.'

She licked her lip, suddenly reticent about her demand. 'And…the Palermo villa…it's the same villa you owned when… I mean three years ago?'

'Sì,' he replied, his voice low and silky smooth despite the speculation narrowing his eyes.

Mia nodded, a little bit of the tension easing out of her. 'My stipulation is for separate sleeping quarters. I'm assuming you're still using the north wing, so I'll take the guest quarters in the east wing.'

He shook his head. 'That won't work. The east wing is currently occupied by Allegra and her children. And the west is still occupied by my grandmother. Unless you wish me to throw one of them out…' His voice trailed mockingly.

'Of course, I don't want that,' she said even while her stomach dipped alarmingly.

She'd wanted her living quarters to be as far away from Rocco as possible but even her first stipulation looked as if it was to be denied. 'We'll have to come up with something suitable, then.'

He rose from the desk, sauntering towards her with a gleam in his eyes that made her hackles rise. 'You agree to marry me in one breath then seem desperate to be as far away from me as possible in the next. Anyone would think you were running scared of something.'

She forced her gaze to stay on his. 'I don't care what you think. I just want my privacy.'

His eyes narrowed. 'Wanting privacy is one thing. Removing yourself so far away from me that it raises questions is quite another. Do you trust yourself so little?' he taunted.

'It's you I don't trust.'

He stiffened, his jaw clenching a moment before he spoke. '*You* don't trust *me*?' His voice was infinitely mocking, covered in ice. 'Pray tell, what have I done to deserve that distrust?'

'You really expect me to answer that? After throwing me to the wolves the very first chance you got?'

'I did nothing you didn't deserve.'

It was a testament to how unguarded she was around him that pain glanced through her midriff. 'One day, Rocco, I swear you'll regret what you did to me. If you don't, then you'll just confirm how heartless you've shown yourself to be since you threw me out.'

For the briefest nanosecond, she fooled herself into thinking she saw regret in his eyes. But then he shrugged.

'I've been called worse, *cara*. As to your request, if you feel that strongly about it, the adjoining suite to mine is still available.' He lifted his hand and ran a lazy finger down her cheek, leaving a trail of fireworks beneath her skin. 'It's yours to decorate to your heart's content until such time as you get over your false indignation. Then you'll know where to find me.'

She took a step back, removing herself from his charged orbit. 'That's not going to happen. Because my second stipulation is that you won't touch me again. Ever. If you want this marriage to happen, then you'll agree that it'll happen without any further physical advances from you.'

His eyes narrowed, and his hands dropped down to his sides. 'I seem to recall that you've come willingly into my arms each time.'

Heat surged into her face, his low, thickly accented words sending flames of shame and lust through her. Memories. 'They were temporary aberrations that will never occur again.'

'Never say never,' he drawled, a tight little smile lifting the corners of his mouth. 'And be careful what challenges you issue, Mia. You know how very hard it is for me to resist them.'

She remembered all too well. Didn't he pursue her relentlessly for three months before she agreed to go out to dinner with him?

She'd got the job at Vitelli Construction after a gruelling set of interviews and she'd accepted with the sole aim of furthering her career and a determination to do nothing to jeopardise it.

The reminder of what her mother had endured as a single parent with zero career prospects, the accusations levelled at Mia for the simple fact of her existence, was the reason she'd vowed to herself at an early age never to fall under the spell of a man to the exclusion of all else.

But Rocco had very quickly consumed all her senses, his business acumen and his personal sexual charisma overcoming her every resistance. Those warnings had proved correct eventually. She'd lived in bliss for months, fooled herself into believing she was the exception to the rule. That she could have it all.

The reality check had been harsh and devastating. Within weeks she'd lost everything, save the new life she'd carried in her womb. She couldn't forget that abject lesson. 'So are we agreed?'

'Agreed that the physical side of this agreement will remain off the table until you come crawling to me?' he mocked.

'I won't. But if that's what will make you agree, then yes.'

His smile was pure shark, making her nape tingle alarmingly again. 'Of course, *cara*. If you insist.'

Refusing to rise to the bait he was setting, she turned
to leave.

'That's it?' he enquired, sounding a little stunned.

She shrugged. 'What else is there? You wanted me to
make a decision. I have. Now Gianni and I are going home.'

He was shaking his head even before she'd finished
speaking. 'No, Mia. You are going nowhere. In anticipation of your agreeable answer, I took the liberty of getting my people to apply for a special licence. You will stay
here with Gianni, and we will fly to Sicily in the morning.
Preparations are already under way for us to be married.'

It was her turn to be stunned. 'How is that even possible? You've only known about Gianni's existence for a
little over a day.'

'That should tell you how much I want him in my life.
You've said yes so what's the point in delaying?'

The sensation of the ground shifting beneath her intensified. 'The point is that I have things to do.'

'Things like?'

'Like…sorting out my home. My life!'

He tossed her argument away with a very Latin gesture.
'My people will take care of that.'

'Take care of it how?' she asked, but she knew.

It was with the same head-spinning efficiency that he'd
first relocated her into his life the moment she'd accepted
his proposal three years ago. As a renowned architect,
Rocco had exceptional focus and organisational skill that
seemed almost godlike at times. His ability to create magic
within a vacuum had inspired a following long before he'd
reached his thirties, and the list of clients waiting for his
creations across the world inflated his ego and multiplied
his power. So why did he continually leave her slack-jawed
by his ability to pull off something so simple as disman-

tling her life and rearranging it into his in the space of a day? How was she even surprised that he'd calculated the move a dozen steps ahead?

'Gianni doesn't have a passport,' she blurted, digging in as the ground gave way beneath her.

'That too will be arranged,' Rocco announced. 'Any other objections?'

A dozen easily rose to mind, but she knew that he would bat them all away with calm efficiency. And as he'd stated, she'd agreed to marry him. There was no sense in prevaricating.

'No. Looks like you're a few steps ahead of me. Congratulations.' Again she turned to leave.

'One more thing. I'd very much like to know why my son ended up on a billboard.'

She'd wondered when he'd bring it up again, wondered whether he'd condemn her for it, but his expression only held keen curiosity. 'Because it was a way to pass time.' And a way to earn money, which had been secondary but also welcome. Of course, she didn't tell Rocco that. She still had a little bit of pride left. 'And before you object to it, you should know, we worked with a very child-friendly agency and he was recruited by one of the mothers in the mother and baby group. There was nothing underhanded about it.'

'Did Gianni enjoy it?' he asked, stunning her all over again. From his reaction before, she'd been prepared for his condemnation.

Her insides unknotted enough to trigger a smile as she answered. 'He was the centre of attention, so of course he loved every minute of it.'

Her heart raced when one corner of his mouth lifted. '*Bene.* I'm thankful for the course of action that brought him into my life, but, besides the security risk, I'm also selfish and possessive about my son. So shall we agree to end the contract with the agency?'

She didn't owe him any explanation. That was why she didn't tell him that it'd only been a temporary thing. And of course, he was right. Now that Gianni had been claimed as Rocco's son, his father's wealth and influence meant his privacy and security were paramount. 'Fine. Are there any other edicts you wish to throw around?'

'You haven't lost your fierce spirit, *cara*. That's good to see. I have a feeling you'll need it in the weeks and months to come.'

'Is that a threat?' she asked sharply.

His smile widened, its pulse-racing effect making her clench her thighs tighter. 'No, *cara mia*, it's quite the opposite. Call it anticipation. Butting heads with me always turned you on. Seems you haven't lost that urge.'

Feeling another wave of heat invade her belly, she took a hurried step towards the door. 'I really don't know what you're talking about. Now if you'll excuse me, I'll go and inform Gianni that we're staying.'

He nodded. 'Has your email address changed?'

'Why?' she asked warily.

'To enable my team to liaise with you about packing up your house.'

Dear God, it was all going so fast. She raised a hand to her temple and massaged it, hoping to stop the dizziness assailing her. 'I have a say in something, then, do I?'

Displeasure etched into his face. 'I'm not a complete tyrant, Mia,' he murmured.

You could've fooled me, she wanted to blurt. But she'd exhibited far too many weaknesses around him. 'It hasn't changed,' she murmured.

'Good,' he said abruptly, then, with another penetrative look, he turned away and sauntered back to his desk.

Mia left, reeling from the breakneck speed of events. Needing his grounding presence, she went in search of Gianni. She found him in the garden, exploring the profusion of flowers being tended to by the housekeeper. As if sensing she wanted to be alone with him, the housekeeper discreetly absented herself, leaving Mia to bask in her son's unabashed delight as he dug through dirt.

Hearing a plane flying overhead, Gianni excitedly pointed to it.

Unbidden, a lump formed in her throat. Tomorrow, her son would be taking his first trip on a plane. She stopped herself from telling him just yet. It wouldn't stop the freight-train momentum of what was happening, of course, but she needed a little more time where she could pretend everything was normal.

Eventually, when his exploration tired him out, Gianni crawled into her arms. She carried him inside, and, at the housekeeper's direction, headed upstairs to the guest suite.

Just like everywhere else in the house, it was opulently decorated. Thick luxurious carpeting muffled her footsteps as she made her way to an equally breathtaking bathroom. Every amenity had been provided, making her task of giving Gianni a quick bath an even more pleasant experience. After changing him into the lounge clothes she'd packed, she settled him into the multi-pillowed bed. She was barely a few pages into his favourite bedtime story before he fell asleep.

She was tempted to join him but the thought of Rocco coming in search of her made her reluctantly leave the room. Tentatively she made her way downstairs, only to discover that Rocco had left the house, with instructions for Mrs Simpson to feed her and a message to say he would see her in the morning.

Mia barely tasted her meal. For the life of her, she couldn't stop her mind from dwelling on where Rocco had gone. Which brought her to another matter she couldn't seem to stop her brain from dissecting.

Was Rocco seeking anyone? If so, how would it play out

once they were married? He was a virile and passionate
man, one who didn't apologise about indulging his needs.
And since she'd effectively closed the door to anything
physical between them, did that mean he'd cater to those
needs elsewhere?

The bite of jealousy seared so deep, it killed the dregs
of her appetite. What he did in his private life didn't...
shouldn't matter to her. Just as she had asked for her privacy, she would turn a blind eye to his. Wouldn't she? But
how would that affect Gianni? Realising she'd left one vital
subject unexplored, she pushed her plate away.

Did she really have it in her to permit him to have liaisons with other women while married to her? The question
kept her tossing and turning through the night, making her
increasingly agitated and annoyed with herself for her inability to dismiss it.

This was a marriage in name only for the sake of their
son. Surely what Rocco did outside ensuring Gianni's care
and well-being was none of her business?

After repeating that hollow-sounding statement to herself a few hundred times, she finally got to sleep, only to
awaken what felt like a handful of hours later to bright
sunshine. Momentarily disoriented, she rose and rushed to
Gianni's room, to find his room empty and a young girl,
who introduced herself as Mrs Simpson's niece, making his
bed. After she smilingly informed her Gianni was downstairs with his father, Mia returned to her room. As much
as she wanted to storm downstairs and ensure her son was
fine, she knew she needed a little grounding time. Plus a
quick look in the mirror cheerily announced the effects of
her restless night.

After a quick shower she donned the dress she'd worn
yesterday and went downstairs to find Gianni and Rocco
tucking into their breakfast. She stopped at the sight of
them, her heart flipping over at the similarity between the

two. They remained oblivious to her for a few seconds, giving her a chance to absorb their interaction.

Gianni was regaling his father with a rambling tale while attempting to stuff miniature pancakes and fruit into his mouth. Rocco was smiling, his attention rapt on his son's face.

An instant later he looked up, his hawk-like eyes locking on her. '*Buongiorno.* Are you going to join us?'

Gianni looked her way and broke into a wide smile. 'Mummy!'

Her heart filling, she approached him and dropped a kiss on his head. Taking the seat next to her son, she glanced at Rocco. 'Why didn't you wake me when he woke up?'

'We have a busy day today. I felt an extra hour or two in bed wouldn't do you harm.'

'Busy day?' she echoed as she helped herself to coffee. Rocco pushed a platter of pastries towards her. 'I thought your little minions had everything covered?' she asked, a little bitterly.

'We aren't just flying home to Palermo. When we get there you have event planners ready to liaise with you regarding the wedding. You are planning on being involved, aren't you?' he drawled.

That ground-shifting sensation returned. 'Is there any reason why we need to rush into this so soon? Can't we wait a few months?'

His eyes flicked to his son. When they returned to hers, their ferocity was intensified. 'I like to strike while the iron is hot, *cara*.' His voice was deceptively soft, for Gianni's sake, she suspected. 'And because I'd prefer my son in the rightful place that has been denied him since his birth.'

'Are you sure that's not your Sicilian machismo talking?'

He shrugged. 'Perhaps so. But I still want what I want. And I won't be denied.'

Before she could respond, a bell sounded. He tossed his napkin down, ruffled his son's hair before rising to his feet.

'That'll be my lawyer now. Finish your breakfast and join me in the study. There are some papers to sign.'

Mia blindly reached for her coffee cup, reassuring herself that it didn't matter in the long run when she married him. It was going to happen anyway, so why not get it out of the way?

She ate her breakfast, then fed Gianni the last pieces of fruit. As if by telepathy, Mrs Simpson appeared. Reluctantly, Mia handed her son over, and made her way to Rocco's study.

The same Italian lawyer who'd questioned her at the meeting yesterday greeted her neutrally, before producing papers the moment she settled in the chair in front of Rocco's desk.

The twenty-page document was meticulous, outlining in stark detail everything she'd agreed with Rocco. In return for marriage, she would get her previous position in his company back. The marriage would be mutually dissolved once his grandmother's health was improved or at such time as Gianni wasn't adversely affected by a divorce between them.

Mia moved on, her stomach twisting weirdly every time she read the word *divorce*.

She froze when she saw the sums detailed for her in settlement for her future divorce. She looked up at him. 'I don't want your money,' she said, her voice sharp and uneven.

Rocco's lawyer's eyes widened. He opened his mouth to speak but Rocco waved him away. 'You will take it nonetheless or there's no deal.'

She tossed the papers on the desk. 'Then there is no deal,' she stated firmly.

This time it was Rocco's eyes that widened. 'You feel so strongly about it?'

'I don't want *gold-digger* added to my list of apparent sins. I earn my own salary and when we're no longer together I'll look after my son with my own money. You can keep yours. Those are my terms, Rocco. Take it or leave it.'

His eyes narrowed into slits, his lips a flat line of displeasure. Before he could launch a counterargument, Mia reached across the table, took his fancy fountain pen, and drew a line through the offensive clause. After printing her initials next to it, she carried on reading, aware of the tense silence surrounding her. When she was done, and happy with the custody clause, which was most important to her, she signed the document and set the pen down.

Defiantly she stared at him.

Keen speculation gleamed in his eyes as he slowly reached for the contract. That gaze rested on her for endless minutes before he signed his name next to hers. Once the lawyer had witnessed it, he departed.

'If that was some ploy to make me think—'

'I don't really care what you think, Rocco. Not any more. Gianni's the only one I care about.'

A shadow crossed his face, a mix of speculation and suspicion. Unwilling to linger and be drawn into another charged argument with him, she left the room, went into the suite she'd slept in last night and gathered her things.

Five hours later—after a fifteen-minute video conference with expert relocators who had miraculously packed up her whole house and assured her her possessions were secure until she needed them—Mia struggled to keep an excited Gianni contained as they arrived at the private strip in North London. She explained to him what was happening as his father held him and, although she wasn't sure whether he'd fully grasped the unfolding events, he babbled excitedly as he was escorted in his father's arms up the short flight of stairs into the plane.

Once they were airborne, Rocco excused himself and

occupied himself with business calls for most of the three-hour journey. He returned to where she sat with Gianni a few minutes before they landed, buckling himself into the seat next to his son.

Then he speared her with dark eyes. 'Your performance is about to begin, *cara*, so I suggest you compose yourself and stop shooting those dagger eyes at me.'

She inhaled sharply. 'My...what performance?'

'I've just been informed that my grandmother's meeting us at the airstrip. She couldn't wait to meet her great-grandchild. So prepare yourself.'

That was all the warning she received before she was flung into high drama that made her wish she'd taken another day, week or year to agree to this devil's bargain with Rocco.

Because it wasn't just his grandmother—leaning heavily on a walking stick beside the gleaming black limo—who waited for them when they stepped out of the plane.

Allegra Vitelli, Alessandro's very young, very designer-clad widow stood right beside her, one arm curled around the old woman's arm in comfort, while the disdainful glare she'd perfectly copied from her husband blazed from the eyes fixed squarely on Mia.

CHAPTER NINE

THE OVERFLOW OF emotion the moment Caterina Vitelli clapped eyes on her great-grandchild left a lump wedged in Mia's throat for a solid hour. She'd been prepared to defend herself and her child from even the merest hint of censure, direct or implied, but all they'd received since the swift journey from private airstrip to sprawling Palermo villa was unabashed joy, first from Rocco's *nonna*, then the household in general. Even the staff displayed wide smiles and open arms at being introduced to Gianni.

Mia's fingers tightened around the excellent glass of limoncello made with authentic Sicilian lemons they'd been served as part of what was turning out to be a lengthy celebration of welcome for the newest member of the Vitelli family.

For his part, Gianni was lapping up the attention.

A shame Mia couldn't relax long enough to even take a full breath. As she'd suspected, her child was being absorbed a little too eagerly into the family that had been denied him and was in the process of being spoiled rotten before her very eyes.

No, she had nothing to worry about in that department. But as one hour grew into two, Mia quickly realised she had everything to worry about in the form of the very carefully hidden contempt emanating from Rocco's cousin-in-law.

As if summoned by her thoughts, Allegra slid into the seat next to Mia. 'I haven't had the chance to add my welcome to everyone else's,' she said, her voice a sultry just-above-a-whisper murmur that Mia was sure she cultivated just so her companions would lean in to hear her.

She'd witnessed its effect many times when she'd been

with Rocco. Not that Allegra needed it. She was the sort of stunning, statuesque beauty that stopped most men in their tracks.

'I could hardly believe it when Rocco informed us of the news,' she continued, chocolate-brown eyes sizing Mia up as she took a delicate sip of her sparkling mineral water. 'In fact, I'm still finding it difficult to wrap my head around it.'

Mia's spine tensed. 'I'm sure it all seems surreal to the outsider.' Hell, she was grappling with the fact that she was back here, in the majestic villa poised on a hillside in Palermo, the place she'd dreamed of spending the rest of her life.

A tight smile curved Allegra's plump lips. '*Sì*, you're right. But I'm not an outsider, of course. I, like everyone else, found it immensely distressing that your child's existence was hidden from us.'

Your child. The stress on the word matched the suspicion in the young woman's eyes.

'It wasn't by design. At least not mine anyway,' Mia responded, her voice a little sharper than she'd intended.

She grimaced inwardly when Allegra's eyes widened, sharp speculation gleaming in the depths. 'How very intriguing. What do you mean?'

Mia pressed her lips together. 'It's nothing that should concern you, I'm sure.'

Her gaze grew sharper, attaining malice that made the hairs on Mia's nape tingle. 'Oh, but everything to do with my family concerns me, Mia. I've learned to keep my loved ones closer, since the tragedy of my loss. I'm sure you understand.'

The lump in her throat dropped to form a rock in her belly. Was she being warned? 'What's that supposed to mean?'

Allegra smiled but never replied. Probably because Rocco arrived beside Mia in the moment, his incisive eyes latching onto her. But more than likely, Allegra had learned the art of subtle torture from her late husband.

Either way, she rose, swayed close to Rocco and laid a hand on his arm. 'Mia and I were getting reacquainted. It's good to see her looking so…well, again, *sì, caro*?' She flashed another sultry smile at Rocco before glancing down at Mia. '*Mi scusi, per favore*, I must go and check that the staff have done as I asked regarding preparing your suite, Mia.' With that, she set her glass down and strode off, her hips swaying with unapologetic femininity, leaving behind the unfailing declaration that she was the one in charge of the household.

'Is something wrong?' Rocco enquired after a tense beat.

'Why should it be?' Mia demanded tightly, unable for the life of her to breathe around the knot growing in her belly.

'Because you look like you're about to break that glass in two.'

She forced her fingers to relax. 'Can you blame me? This was never going to be a walk in the park.'

'Only if you don't allow it. Or am I misremembering that you thrive at the deep end?'

She bit back a snort of disbelief. 'We're not in the boardroom, Rocco.'

'No, we're not. And as far as I can see, you've been welcomed with open arms. So I ask again, is something bothering you?'

Mia looked towards the doors through which Allegra had departed, wondering if she was over-exaggerating what she'd sensed from the woman. She bit her lip and shook her head. 'No. Everything's fine. But I think I need to rescue your grandmother from Gianni's exuberance before he wears her out. He'll be a nightmare to settle down if he gets too overexcited.'

Her announcement was overly loud, she realised a second later.

A throb of silence went through the room. Then Caterina smiled. '*Certo*, Mia. Perhaps once you're settled in, you can let me know his habits? I would not like to upset his routine too much.'

Touched by the ease with which her request was granted, Mia relaxed. 'He's been resisting his naps lately, but normally he sleeps for an hour or so mid-afternoon, then has his supper at six. We...we can join you when it's time for his supper, if you want?'

Her hesitant proffer was greeted with a warm smile. 'I would like that very much, *ragazza dolce. Ciao, bambino*,' she said to Gianni, who responded with a smile, albeit one worn around the edges.

Perhaps he was as overwhelmed as her because he didn't protest as Mia placed him in his bed ten minutes later.

'You have made my grandmother very happy,' Rocco rasped as they left a sleeping Gianni in the bedroom decorated with his favourite racing-car theme. Just how Rocco had managed to pull this off within twenty-four hours made her head spin.

'That was the plan, wasn't it?' she said, then immediately felt rotten. 'I... I didn't mean it like that.'

'Didn't you?' His voice was tight with displeasure, his hand frozen on the double doors that led to his private wing of the villa.

'No, I didn't. I just...' She shook her head.

'What is it, Mia? Are you going to spit out whatever's on your mind now or ambush me with it in another boardroom three years from now?'

She gasped. 'Excuse me?'

'I'm talking about your suspicions about Alessandro. And why you never told me.'

She rushed after him when he threw the doors open and

walked into his private living room. From memory, she knew hers was the mirror image of the large, opulently decorated room, complete with the obligatory bust of some important Roman figure, a Renaissance painting or three, and the very best of mod cons. Heck, even the walls were lined in silk in Rocco's world. 'You're throwing the fact that I tried to spare your feelings regarding your cousin in my face?'

'Spare my feelings?' he asked, his voice chillingly amused. He continued through his living room into hers, then into the bedroom, which had been redecorated since the last time she was here. Where there'd been pleasant pastel colours before, the room was now wall-to-wall virginal white from ceiling to carpet. Mia was wondering if this was Allegra's doing when Rocco added, 'I'm hardly a wallflower, *cara*.'

God, she remembered that all too well. 'Fine, if I'd come to you three years ago and told you your cousin was making my life a living hell behind your back, what would you have said?'

Without missing a beat, Rocco replied, 'I would've demanded an explanation from him.'

'Just like that? And if he'd denied it?'

'You're so sure he would've?'

'I don't know. But I didn't want to risk it!'

His face darkened. 'You didn't want to hurt my feelings or didn't want to risk not being believed? Which was it, Mia?'

'Either. Both.' She rubbed her throbbing temples. 'I'm not sure exactly what you want from me but it's a waste of both our time to second-guess the past. We are where we are.'

'*Sì*, we are.'

The change in his voice sent a different sensation charging through her body. That latent passion covered by the thinnest veneer of civility was rumbling again, like the not so dormant volcano this part of the world was known for. A single glance showed the innate sensuality was rousing, an uncoiling beast ready to strike.

For the first time, Mia became vividly aware of her surroundings. The vast queen-sized bed a few feet away. The wide, sumptuous chaise longue, which seemed entirely adequate for a torrid tryst set before the perfect backdrop of French doors and the ocean beyond. The ankle-deep carpet beneath her feet.

Even the thought that Allegra might have picked every item in this room didn't stop flames from invading her belly, her nipples from tightening to painful buds as lust roared to life within her.

'There's one more thing we never got around to discussing yesterday,' Rocco rasped, sauntering towards her.

To step back would've exhibited weakness, to look away, the same. She did neither, even though she felt the ground tilt beneath her when he slid his hand over her nape, then up through her hair.

'What…what is it?'

'I allowed your wish to have separate suites. But outside this room we present a united front. No one, especially my grandmother, will know that our marriage isn't…for the lack of a better word, completely *fulfilled*.'

'Which means what, exactly? That I should pretend to be infatuated with you?'

A glint lit his eyes, wholly enigmatic enough to send frissons of excitement-tinged alarm through her. 'I wouldn't be so insensitive as to ask you for a performance you can't pull off. Attempting to withstand being in the same room without wishing for the ankle monitor you referred to should suffice.'

She hated herself for the searing bruise in the region

of her heart at his rancour. 'I think I can bring myself to do that.'

His eyes narrowed a touch, then his gaze dropped to her mouth. 'Just so we're clear, that may include physical gestures,' he rasped.

'Because you don't wish to throw your virile masculinity into question?' she taunted, despite every instinct warning her it was unwise to remain this close. To not protest the slow, hypnotic circles he was drawing on her skin.

'We both know I have no qualms in that regard. But just say the word, and I'll happily demonstrate.'

'No, thank you,' she said, cringing when her voice all but wobbled.

He leaned in closer. 'Are you quite sure?'

Mia cast around frantically for something to dilute this thickening fog of lust threatening to consume her. 'What about Allegra?'

He frowned. 'What about her?'

'Did we need to run our performances past her too? Because she seems to be running things around here.'

He shrugged. 'Allegra likes to feel needed. She never expected to be widowed at this stage in her life. She's doing what she needs to cope.'

Is that all? she wanted to ask. But she held the question in, part of her feeling ungracious at suspecting the woman's motives. 'Fine. Is that all?'

The question wasn't framed in a provocative way. But still it seemed to spark something to life. Something that needed very little in the way of kindling to come alive.

The very air seemed to consume her, even while giving her sustenance. She was aware her breath had shortened, her heart jackhammering in her chest. From the way Rocco's lips parted, the way his nostrils flared, he felt it too.

'Mia…' His voice was thick, throbbing with arousal.

One that ricocheted through her with such ferocity, she nearly gasped.

Resist.

She jerked away, uncaring if the move was seen as weakness. 'I'm tired. I'd like you to leave, please.'

For a moment, he remained exactly where he was. Contemplating. Probing. And she feared he would call her bluff. Dare her to deny the dark magic spinning around them. Trouble was, she wasn't sure she would've been capable of it. She could barely recall her own name as it was.

Slowly, his hand slid from her nape. But he didn't remove his touch. Not until he'd drawn his thumb across her lower lip, something he'd loved doing years ago. A gesture perfectly aimed to remind her how the physical side of things had been between them.

'I'll leave you be, for now, *tesoro*. But *this* isn't going to go away just because you wish it to.'

'Then I'll simply file it under "the nuisance to be tolerated".'

He had the audacity to laugh. A wickedly husky, dark-as-sin laugh that stroked her in all the right places. 'And I'll enjoy watching you try.' His hand *finally* dropped. And she refused to admit she missed his touch as he strode to his suite. 'You know how to contact the staff if you need anything. Dinner is still served at eight. Nonna normally eats earlier but she's joining us tonight after we put Gianni to bed. We will give her the happy news of our impending wedding together then.'

Rocco didn't relish living in the state of perpetual anxiety. And yet he couldn't offload the sensation. But he absolutely refused to glance at his watch. He'd already done so at one minute past eight. That felt like…a lifetime ago.

'What is it, *tesoro*? You're acting like one of those feral cats that patrol the streets of Palermo at night.'

He would've been amused, and slightly disturbed at being referred to in such unpalatable terms by his grandmother, had his nerves not been so displeasingly frayed.

Mia was late.

She was never late. Or at least she'd never been tardy, either fashionably or otherwise, to an event when they'd been together. But then hadn't it been proven that he barely knew the woman he'd been about to marry?

She walked in a minute later, and he actively despised himself for the relief that oozed through him.

'I'm sorry I'm late. I decided to look in on Gianni.'

'Is he okay?' Nonna asked.

Mia smiled. 'He's fine. Wide awake when he should be asleep, but fine. I got pulled into reading him a story.'

He rose from his chair at the dining table and pulled out hers. 'That's good to know. I was beginning to worry you'd wandered into the sea.'

Mia stiffened. Nonna sent him a sharp look. Rocco hid a grimace, aware things were getting out of hand. Again.

Just as he knew the solution. An unbreakable commitment to secure his son in his life. For starters. Only once he knew Gianni was going nowhere would he be able to rest.

But that wasn't all, was it?

These fevered little incidents with Mia needed to be culled. One way or the other. And her wild accusations regarding Alessandro disproved sooner rather than later. His cousin had been hard-working, ambitious and fully dedicated to him and Vitelli Construction. The idea that he could've mistreated Mia, in any way, was deplorable to him.

And yet as he resumed his seat he couldn't halt the niggle of doubt that'd been resurfacing since Mia's declaration in his lawyers' boardroom.

Alessandro's not-quite-so-offhand musing over if Rocco was rushing his relationship with Mia.

Alessandro's questioning Mia's credentials as an engineer.

He'd also noticed that when his cousin had been around, he'd demanded more of Mia than any of Rocco's junior engineers.

As if he'd wanted to see her fail?

He frowned inwardly, allowing Mia and Nonna to converse as he delved deeper into his memory. Looking out for his cousin and ultimate boss was one thing, but would Alessandro have deliberately kept him from his own child?

He shook his head, unable to fathom Sandro's reasoning for it. *If* he was guilty. The verdict was still out and he wouldn't rush to condemn his cousin until the evidence was before him.

'Caro? Che cos'è?'

He refocused at his grandmother's concerned expression. Mia, too, was staring at him but with less concern and more…indifference. That look grated. Resembled much too closely the one he'd seen on his father's face as a child. His mother's preoccupation with his father to the exclusion of her own son. Their callous dismissal of his very existence until their deaths and the realisation that he would never even know whether he'd ever been wanted. Whether he'd mattered in any way to them or merely been a biological accident they'd been saddled with.

He'd moved heaven and earth not to be irrelevant to anyone. That Mia would dare rake that particular wound—

'Perhaps we should leave him alone. It looks like he wants a meditative dinner rather than to be bothered playing host, eh, Caterina?'

The little challenging spark eased his tension, scorching away that unfortunate moment of self-pity. She wasn't indifferent to him. Hell, he'd stake his substantial fortune that it was the opposite. Still, there was a purpose to this evening beside breaking bread with the woman who'd betrayed him.

That urge to get beneath her skin sharpened. Without second thought, he reached for her hand, felt her tense at his hold and hid a smile. No, Mia was far from indifferent.

'I wasn't distracted, *cara*. Merely contemplating whether to deliver our news before or after we eat. And I've decided there's no time like the present, *sì*?' He raised her hand, brushed his lips over her knuckles. Relaxed even further when she trembled. Of course, confirming she wasn't indifferent to him returned him to that state of arousal he couldn't seem to halt whenever he was in her presence.

But that too would be handled.

'*Che notizie hai?*' his grandmother probed, momentarily forgetting that Mia wasn't fluent in Italian.

He switched his gaze to Mia, deliberately locking gazes with her as he kissed her knuckles again. Her breath shivered out, her expression giving her away. 'Mia and I are getting married, Nonna. And since so much time has been wasted, we've decided to wed immediately.'

His grandmother's reaction was gratifyingly warming. Rocco even managed to tolerate her tears and frequent bouts of excitement as the meal progressed. He barely tasted it, his gaze recurrently drawn to a solemn Mia.

Eventually, Nonna noticed too. 'You are happy about this, Mia?' she asked.

To her credit, Mia scrounged up a genuine smile. 'Yes, I am. But I wish I had more time to prepare though.'

He stiffened, but Nonna came to his aid, brushing away Mia's concern. 'Rocco is right. No need to delay this if it is what you both want. Plus you're wedding a powerful man. No reason why you shouldn't use his connections to ease your way in this process. I will of course help in any way I can.'

'*Grazie*, Nonna. As long as you don't wear yourself out.'

She waved him away. 'It was a little incident, nothing more. *Mio pronipote*, Gianni, has given me a new lease of life. Now, Mia, tell me everything you require and I will make a list. We will start early tomorrow morning.'

Rocco sat back, satisfaction easing through him as one box was successfully ticked in securing everything that was his. He was confident the rest would fall into place just as easily.

No alternative outcome was permitted.

Nine days after her arrival in Palermo, Mia stood outside the ancient double doors of a duomo a few streets from Rocco's villa. In terms of size, the cathedral wasn't large, but in grandeur stakes it dripped with history and prestige, from its golden, eleventh-century basilica to the carefully preserved mosaics, magnificent stone arches and Corinthian columns. It was also Caterina Vitelli's local church where she attended mass twice a week.

Mia's hand trembled and she couldn't quite catch her breath. While she wanted to blame the tight cinch of the corseted wedding dress, she knew it had nothing to do with the gown's design—which was a rich cream silk lace, sweeping, with a train stunning enough to render her breathless—and everything to do with the butterflies that had invaded her stomach when she'd awakened the morning after their arrival to Caterina's arm-long to-do list, and the reality that this wedding was happening.

Rocco, during their one and only discussion of the wedding, had acceded to her wish to keep it small. But Mia had quickly found out that *small* in Vitelli terms meant a few dozen people, because, while Rocco was Caterina's only grandchild, his grandfather had several siblings who'd generated a plethora of second and third cousins, most of whom were currently employed by Vitelli Construction. *All* of whom were eager to remain in Rocco's favour by honouring his invitation to attend his wedding.

One person in particular had been conspicuously absent in the last week though.

Allegra.

Apparently, she was visiting her parents in Northern Sicily with her children. The news had brought more relief than Mia was willing to admit. Nevertheless, over the past few days she'd grasped just how deep Allegra's influence went in Rocco's household. Each morning, there were fresh flowers delivered to every room in the villa as per Allegra's instructions. And Mia had discovered that most decisions concerning the running of the villa were approved or vetoed by Allegra.

Mia tried to tell herself she didn't care. But it grated to discover she couldn't request Gianni's favourite pasta be added to the shopping list without seeking approval from Allegra Vitelli.

'Mummy?'

She started and looked down to find Gianni staring up at her, impatience etched on his face. She'd given him the choice of standing next to his father beside the altar or walking down the aisle with her and her heart had turned over with joy when he'd chosen to walk with her. In his miniature version of Rocco's grey morning suit, with his hair neatly combed, he was too adorable for words.

'Shall we go in?' She infused lightness into her voice.

He nodded eagerly, tugging at her hand.

She took comfort in his innocent touch, a mountain of reassurance in his unabashed stride as he urged her through the doors and down the wide aisle. Soft, indulgent gasps accompanied what was most people's first sighting of her son, but it did nothing to ease her nerves as those gazes swept up to probe her because the most probing was Rocco's.

Even from the distance between them, she felt its power, its laser-like, unwavering focus. It drew her like a magnet, propelling her forward until she was beside him.

Vaguely, she sensed Gianni being ushered away by his great-grandmother.

Then Rocco was taking her hand, firm and implacable, and turning her to face the priest.

The ceremony was shockingly quick, the words barely sinking in before she felt the soul-shaking finality of his ring sliding onto her finger.

She shivered; her fingers trembled wildly.

Rocco's grip tightened, his nostrils flaring in that possessive, definitive way that spelled that he'd well and truly captured her. Then he clasped her shoulders, tugged her to him. When their lips were a breath apart, he held her there, locked in his arms and by his gaze.

'You're mine now, *cara*,' he breathed, his voice low and for her ears only. 'Now show the world you're ecstatic about it.'

It took a moment to realise he was leaving the option to *her*. To buck tradition and initiate their wedding kiss. It was a clear challenge, a push for her to play her part.

Perhaps it was simply because this man drove her to dangerous extremes. Or perhaps because he expected her to refuse. It might have had something to do with not wanting to invite speculation from the dozens of Vitellis holding their collective breaths.

Whatever it was, she refused to back away from it.

So she curled her hands beneath his silk lapel, slowly slid her hands up to lock around his nape. Then rising on tiptoe, she pressed her lips to his.

It was meant to be brief, to the point.

It turned out to be anything but. The moment her lips touched his, Rocco took over. The alpha male who couldn't cede control for longer than two seconds, he slanted his lips across hers and deepened the kiss, his tongue gliding between her lips to stroke hers.

The cheer of the crowd fell away, the rush of blood in her ears drowning out everything save the riot of sensation pummelling her. Time ceased to register. By the time Rocco ended the kiss they were both breathing hard, his eyes dark and stormy as he stared at her.

It might have started off as a way to make a point. But it ended with her recognising that she'd only weakened the armour she should've been fortifying around him.

That thought triggered mild panic as Rocco escorted her down the aisle and out into the waiting limo. As had been prearranged, Gianni would ride with his grandmother and her retinue in another limo, leaving Mia alone with Rocco.

She watched him reach into his breast pocket as the car left the church to head back to the villa. When she realised what he was holding out to her, her lips fell open in shock.

She stared at the flawless, square-cut diamond engagement ring that had adorned her finger for many months before she'd realised she was living in a dream world. 'You kept it?'

He shrugged. 'I was tempted to throw it into Mount Etna at one point, but luckily I resisted that particular melodramatic gesture.'

Because he couldn't be bothered? 'Why? I'd have thought you'd be eager to be rid of it.'

His lips twisted. 'Perhaps I needed the reminder? Or more likely, whoever was tasked with removing your belongings thought it prudent for it to find its way to my bank vault. Which is where it's been all this time. Don't overthink it, Mia. You picked it. It's yours again now.'

He caught her fingers with his and slid the ring next to her wedding band. As if designed for the sole purpose of complementing one another, the rings fitted together perfectly. If he'd been anyone else, she'd have asked whether he'd intended it that way. But as he'd said, he'd barely given the ring, and her, a second thought until now.

She tugged her hand away and balled her fist, to hide its trembling and to hold emotions determined to overflow locked inside, while he sat back, his eyes resting on the rings for a moment before rising to her face.

'I take it from that smug expression that I've passed another one of your tests?' she asked.

'The one at the altar you passed with flying colours. For a moment there, even I was convinced we were an ecstatically married couple, crazily lusting after one another. So you see, *cara*, your transition back into my life is going to be less fraught than you think. And speaking of transition…'

The pause was deliberate. A predator taunting its prey. She knew it but still couldn't help herself. 'Yes?'

'We have an opportunity to kill two birds with one stone.'

She shook her head. 'I don't follow.'

'Nonna tells me you're struggling on where to settle on for our honeymoon.'

'I thought it better to appear indecisive than to burst her bubble by telling her we weren't going on honeymoon.'

A wicked smile curved the lips she could still taste on hers, causing her fist to spasm harder. 'Oh, but we've come this far, *amante*. We can't turn back now.'

Her heart did that crazy cartwheel again. 'What's that supposed to mean?'

'It means, as of two days ago, I've officially signed on to build a performing arts centre in Macau. You'll accompany me when I visit the site. Nonna can be rest assured our marriage is off to a great start while she babysits Gianni. And you can dip your toes back into your precious career.'

'You expect me to leave Gianni behind?' she asked in surprise.

'We'll only be gone a few days. Besides, I don't think Gianni and Nonna are ready to be parted from one another so soon.'

It was true that her son and his great-grandmother had fallen head over heels for one another. But Mia had never been parted from him. 'I thought the whole idea behind this was so *you* would also get to know him, not swan off at the first opportunity?'

His face tightened. 'Like most working parents I accept it's impossible to spend every waking moment with my child. How were you proposing to accomplish work and motherhood?'

She opened her mouth but no words emerged.

He sighed. 'I don't intend us to make a habit of it, Mia. And I will miss him too.'

She knew she needed to keep her guard up, but his words weirdly appeased her. She locked eyes with him for several heartbeats before she nodded. But when he reached out for her, she startled. His jaw clenched.

'We've arrived back home, *tesoro*. And we have a considerable audience watching our every move, so I suggest you put your game face back on.'

Her game face stayed all throughout the small but elaborate reception in the villa's lavish gold-themed ballroom—because Vitellis didn't do things by half measures. Through a stream of cousins, uncles and aunts whose names all blended into one after the first dozen. Through a first dance with Rocco while a renowned concert pianist serenaded them, when he held her far too close, murmured thickly, 'I think it would remiss of me not to mention you look breathtaking, *mia moglie*,' then delivered that wicked smile telling her he knew his effect on her. Through another dance where Gianni joined them, held between them as they swayed on the dance floor and Mia fought a different emotion, one that threatened to rip her heart in two because of secret yearn-

ings she could never reveal. A yearning for these circumstances to be different. For them to be enjoying their son
as a true married couple, with no signed agreements or re-
straints or bartering between them.

A dream that was destined to be unfulfilled.

'Mummy, Papà, dance!' Gianni cried.

Mia realised she'd stopped moving. As had Rocco. That
they were locked in place staring at one another, with their
guests looking on. She blinked, hastily erasing whatever
emotion was laid bare on her face before she gave herself
away. Then spent what was left of the reception wondering
what Rocco had seen to make that contemplative gleam in
his eyes flare for a pulse-racing, untamed second.

A handful of hours later, she drew in another half-breath,
this one of relief as she bent over Gianni's bed to brush a
goodnight kiss on his cheek.

'*Bella*, Mummy,' he murmured sleepily, stroking a
chubby hand over the lace sleeve of her wedding dress.

For some reason, the words brought a tear to her eye. Or
perhaps it was hearing him utter the Italian word. It wasn't
his first. All week, he'd been repeating words Rocco had
taught him. 'Thank you, my darling.'

'I see you're relentless with that charm offensive, *mio
figlio*,' Rocco's deep voice murmured amusedly as he appeared beside her. 'But it's time to sleep now. *Dormi bene,
caro*.' He leaned down and dropped a kiss on his son's head.

Another tear rose in Mia's eyes. She stepped back, blinking them away. Then she hurried from the room.

A few yards from her suite, she heard Rocco's footsteps behind her. She quickened her strides, eager to flee
from him and from the cornucopia of sensation cascading
through her.

Of course, he wasn't going to let her get away that easily.
He'd sensed weakness in that moment on the dance floor.
And, like a typical alpha warrior, was out to capitalise on it.

She threw open the doors to her bedroom, then turned, forced herself to stand her ground when all she wanted to do was back away, flee from that ferocious intent in his eyes. 'Did you want something?'

He smiled, lazily reached for his tie and tugged it off. He was the epitome of virile masculinity and suave assurance, and her already shortened breath strangled to nothing. 'I want a great many things, *tesoro mio*, but I suspect you might be more in need than I.'

'I haven't the faintest idea what you mean.'

He sauntered towards her, slowly winding the tie around his fingers before slipping it into his pocket. Then he nudged his chin at her dress. 'Your stylists helped you into that sensational contraption but I'm wondering how you intend to get yourself out of it,' he drawled.

Mia bit her inner lip. The corset was knotted in a profusion of ribbons at the back. It would take a contortionist act to free herself from it without help. But she didn't need the kind of help her husband was offering. Not when she didn't trust him. Or herself.

Rocco stopped in front of her. 'No need for such turmoil, Mia. All I'm offering is my assistance.'

A tight little laugh escaped her. 'Next you'll be asking me to believe in fairy tales where the big, bad wolf is just a friendly tomcat.'

He gave a throaty laugh. 'The only parallel to be drawn is that red *is* my favourite colour. But you're thankfully far from a guileless innocent, *bella mia*. And I have no wish to devour you.' He reached out, dragged a finger down her cheek to her throat, his touch testing her pulse. 'Not immediately anyway,' he added, a throb of unmistakable arousal in his voice.

'Rocco…'

He snatched her close, wrapping his arms around her waist. 'Give in to me, Mia,' he muttered thickly, his mouth trailing the sensitive skin of her neck, leaving a trail of gooseflesh all over her body.

'No.' The denial was weak, barely audible. So she tried again. 'That's…that's not what we agreed.'

Another kiss lingered on her racing pulse. 'The beauty of being adults gifted with reasoning and willpower is that we can change our minds. Renegotiate. You want me. And I need you.'

He pressed her closer so there was no mistaking the depth of his thick, powerful need. A helpless moan ripped free from her throat, ferocious desire mounting inside her.

'Are you going to deny this? Deny *us*?' he rasped fiercely.

Mia shook her head, more to rid herself of the fog overwhelming her than in answer. Vaguely, she felt his busy hands at her waist.

'Then kiss me, *amante*,' Rocco muttered, drawing back a fraction and holding himself temptingly just out of reach, just as he had at the altar.

And just as before, need shamed her resistance to smithereens, triggering a wild clamour that had her fisting his lapels and yanking his head down, her lips already parting as he hungrily bore down on her, accepting her greedy invitation to fling them both into madness.

And, oh, what sublime madness it was!

Mia couldn't get enough of his taste, of the thick arms that dragged her closer until they were plastered together from chest to thighs. Couldn't get enough of the rough sounds he made as he savoured her, his hands gripping her hips for a moment before he lifted her off her feet.

Her senses and body went into free fall when Rocco tossed her on the bed. He bore down on her, swallowing her cry of surprise with another torrid kiss that had her free falling all over again. Her fingers speared through his hair, gripping him tight to deepen the kiss. She moaned again when he wrapped an arm around her waist and rolled them over. Splayed on top of him, she felt a sense of feminine power and desire smash through her. She broke the kiss, awed and overwhelmed as their gazes locked. The surreal connection that had existed between them from the moment they laid eyes on each other returned in full force. Without conscious thought, she moved, dragging her heated centre over his erection.

Rocco groaned, gripping her hips to deepen the contact. *'Mia dea...'*

My goddess.

He'd used to call her that. She'd used to love it.

In the past. Before her life had detonated.

What was she doing?

Before she could course-correct, he spun them around again, resuming his dominant position and crumbling her resistance. This time, his hands wreaked deeper havoc, reaching beneath the silk and chiffon to brand her skin. Mia felt him tug at her underwear. Then he was parting her thighs, sinking to his knees beside the bed.

Mia cried out in stunned pleasure as his hot, expert lips delivered a carnal, soul-searing kiss. 'Rocco!'

He didn't respond. He was too busy throwing her legs over his shoulders, parting her wider in order to drive her deeper into insanity. Mia was aware of the sounds emitting from her throat. Of her heart attempting to bang itself out of her ribs. Then, as he pleasured her with supreme expertise, she felt stars dancing at the edges of her vision. Right before she screamed in sublime release.

When she came to, he was kissing her fingers, her wrist, the oversensitive skin of her inner elbow. When he reached her shoulder, he murmured in her ear. 'Tell me I can have you, Mia.'

She opened drowsy eyes, stared at the stucco ceiling of her suite.

What was she doing?

The question came again. Starker than before. Reminding her how dangerously close she was getting to losing herself again.

'No. You can't.'

He reared up, mild shock tightening his features. His eyes blazed holy hell for a second. Then he launched himself off the bed. He dragged rough fingers through his hair, paced to the window and back. Then he speared her with an intense glance.

'You win this round, *dea*. But remember that ultimately I play to win. Make me suffer and I might just let you beg me for a victory.'

With that, he sauntered off, leaving her wound tight as a drum despite the fact that at some point Rocco had achieved his purpose, loosened her corset and set her free from her wedding dress.

CHAPTER TEN

SAYING A TEMPORARY goodbye to Gianni was heart-wrenching. It didn't help that he was completely oblivious, happily learning an Italian nursery rhyme as he perched on his great-grandmother's lap. Beside Caterina, Allegra's twin seven-year-old boys sat, playing on their tablets.

Mia was aware of Rocco's tense presence behind her. And of Allegra—who looked more as if she'd fresh returned from a luxury spa than from a family visit—lounging beside the massive mosaic-laid fireplace, her sharp eyes boring into Mia. She'd been surprised by the other woman's appearance at the breakfast table this morning, had known something was up with her when she'd proceeded to ignore Mia and converse in Italian with Rocco and Caterina.

But Mia had ignored her, preoccupied with the scene from last night that'd kept her awake long into the night. As she caressed Gianni's hair one last time, the morning sun glinted off her rings, as if she needed the reminder that the man prowling behind her was her husband.

The husband she'd displeased with her withdrawal last night. One who was still pissed off, if the turbulent look he'd levelled on her when she'd entered the dining room this morning was any indication.

'We're going to be late, Mia,' he growled, earning himself a sharp look from Caterina.

Mia rose, studiously avoiding him as she crossed the vast *salon* to retrieve her bag.

But contrary to hurrying her out, Rocco took her place, sinking low until he was eye-level with his son. She couldn't quite make out the words he murmured so she wandered out into the hallway, fighting back the stupid tears that threatened.

She swiped at her eyes, just as Allegra materialised beside her. Mia steeled herself to meet her chilling eyes. 'You think you're so clever, don't you?' Allegra hissed.

Mia stiffened in shock. 'Excuse me?'

'Making accusation about my poor Alessandro?'

Mia suppressed a gasp. 'How…? Who told you that?'

Allegra's face tightened. 'So it's true! You think you can take what's mine and soil my Sandro's memory in the process?'

'*What's yours?* What are you talking about?'

The other woman flicked a sideways glance at Rocco, long enough to ensure he was still occupied with Gianni, then stepped closer to Mia. 'I never thought he would be foolish enough to go through with this…*farsa*! But that was my mistake. One I intend to correct.'

'Do…do you mean my marriage?'

'There is no marriage, is there? Not when you didn't even spend your wedding night together,' she crowed.

Mia felt her face redden with humiliating heat. She didn't know how Allegra knew but she wasn't going to lower herself by asking.

'If you know what's best for you, you'll crawl back where you came from.'

Anger rippled up Mia's spine. 'Careful who you threaten, Allegra. You may have had your little reign here, but I'm effectively mistress of this house now. Which means I can kick you out like that.' She snapped her fingers in front of her face.

Allegra paled. Just as Rocco walked into the hallway. His eyes narrowed. 'Are you ready to leave, Mia?'

'Of course…*caro*.' She infused false warmth into her voice, her eyes still locked with Allegra's. The other woman's expression wavered, a flicker of fear in her eyes before it hardened again.

But when she turned to Rocco, she was soft and pliable, her sinuous body swaying as she pressed a hand to his chest, dropped a lingering kiss on his cheek and murmured in Italian.

Rocco gave a brisk nod, then catching Mia's elbow, he led her outside to the waiting car.

The first ten minutes passed in tense silence as she fought the burning sensation in her chest.

'Did you sleep well, *cara*?' he asked, his tone mocking the endearment the same way she had minutes ago.

'What do you care?' she snapped.

One eyebrow elevated. Then his mouth twitched. 'Shall I conclude that you didn't in fact sleep at all? That you're afflicted with the same discomfort I was?'

'Even if I believe you were in any way afflicted, you seem well on your way to resolving it.'

He frowned. *'Che cosa?'*

'I'm talking about Allegra. With her hands all over you. And you lapping it up.'

His eyes widened a fraction, then his smile returned. Wider. Deeper. 'Are you jealous, *amante mia*?'

Yes, she was. Wildly. Disturbingly.

'No. I'd just rather not be forced to endure the spectacle.'

'Rest easy. I have no interest in Allegra. I have no interest in any other woman except the one I married.'

She turned sceptical eyes at him. Then scepticism turned into shock as she read the veracity of the statement in his eyes. 'I…'

He made a very Latin gesture with his hand. 'You have locked us into this, Mia. I'll give you some time to get us out of it. But I won't wait for ever.'

'Wh-what does that mean?'

'It means I won't tolerate indifference, pretended or otherwise.' His tone was harsh, ringing with a deeper meaning that made her heart trip over. 'Deny this…*impazzata*

between us all you like. But don't expect me to follow suit.
I told you last night, I will win in the end.'

The warning was still ringing in her ears when they
pulled up to the private hangar in Boccadifalco Airport.
She'd been on the Vitelli corporate jet before and had always been overawed by the experience.

This time, however, preoccupied both by the little incident with Allegra and by Rocco's comments, and the fact
that he seemed intent to delve straight into business, Mia
had very little time to gawp at her opulent surroundings
before they were taking off.

Soon after that, he turned to her.

'I have the blueprints of the project with me. I'd like your
take on it. Shall we?'

She nodded, a thrill bursting to life in her chest as she
followed him to the middle part of the plane, where a large
conference table and equipment had been set up for business. When she'd first met Rocco, and they'd travelled on
his plane, she'd been concerned about the impact private jet
travel was having on the environment. When she'd voiced
her concern, he'd enlightened her as to the rigorous steps he
took to offset his carbon footprint. And she soon discovered
that every Vitelli Construction project was undertaken with
materials that minimised its impact on the environment. It
was one of the many reasons she'd loved working for him.

Within seconds of Rocco spreading out the blueprints of
the proposed new performance arts building she saw that
this was equally eco-friendly. In fact it was the most advanced ecological building she'd ever seen. Both in design
and in implementation it was simply breathtaking.

After several minutes of absorbing the beauty and symmetry of his creation, she looked up from the blueprint to
find Rocco's intent gaze on her, eyebrows raised. 'Initial
thoughts?'

'It's…breathtaking.'

His eyes stayed on her for another moment before he gave a brisk nod. *'Grazie.'* The word was terse.

She sighed. 'I mean it, Rocco. This is magnificent.' The structure was designed to resemble a delicate brush stroke, poised towards an easel. The 'easel' was to be the main facility with the brush stroke containing everything from galleries to auditoriums, restaurants and a techno park for interactive play.

'It may be bold and innovative, but I need a structural engineer to show me how I can pull it off without it falling to the ground,' he mused.

She nodded, her eyes moving over the blueprint. 'I can give you an initial assessment once I see a feasibility report on the land and specifications of the actual materials we're using.'

Rocco handed her his tablet. 'The full report is on there.'

Their fingers brushed as she took the tablet from him. They both froze.

Rocco moved away first, firing questions at her as they examined the blueprints closer. He was halfway through another question when his phone rang.

'I need to take this.'

He moved away, and, eager to get started, she pulled up the two-hundred-page report. She was so absorbed she didn't notice he'd finished his phone call and was sitting across from her, intently watching her until she looked up.

Mia caught a naked expression of hunger on his face before he schooled his features, and other bout of heat flamed through her belly.

I won't tolerate indifference, pretended or otherwise.

His words returned to her, impacting deeper than she wanted them to. Had he been referring to his parents? She wanted to ask but wasn't she the one reinforcing the wall between them? What right did she have to personal details?

The plane banked slightly and again sunlight glinted

off her rings. She stared down at her finger, wondering for the second time in a very short time if this was some sort of message. She wasn't one for flights of fancy, but since Rocco seemed intent on renegotiating their deal, was she foolish to dismiss it out of hand? Again she looked up at him, watched his eyes travel from her face to the rings and back again.

'Something on your mind?' he rasped.

She opened her mouth to say *no* but the word stuck in her throat.

What was she doing? She'd been married barely a day and already she was doubting herself? She pushed her thoughts away and glanced down at the report.

'The land is a little more waterlogged than I anticipated. You'll need more substantial reinforcement of the foundation to support the building. And the soil is also porous, so you'll require specially treated steel. I'll be able to give you a better assessment once we're onsite,' she said, striving for a no-nonsense tone.

A flash of disappointment crossed his face.

Had he been hoping that she would delve into the personal? With everything still so strained between them?

His expression neutralised, the moment passing. They discussed the Macau project in further detail, then moved to other projects he was working on around the world. Each one was a stunning work of art and she eagerly absorbed every detail.

Oh, how she had missed this. As much as she loved being a mother to Gianni, her work life had sustained her spirit, her contribution to transforming Rocco's vision from mere steel and bricks and mortar into beautiful works of art fulfilling in the extreme.

She barely felt time speed by but five hours later, when they reluctantly broke for lunch, Rocco tossed her an amused half-smile. 'You're enjoying yourself,' he observed, his gaze raking her face.

She shrugged. 'I can't deny that I've missed this.'

'Working with me?'

'Working at all. But since you're the only one I've really worked for, yes.'

Slowly, the amusement drained from his eyes. 'Then why did you do it?'

Mia stared back at him, praying he would read the truth in her words. 'I didn't.'

For what felt like a lifetime he simply stared at her.

'Do you believe me?' she pushed.

'Is it important to you that I do?' he parried, his voice thick with emotion she couldn't quite name.

She wanted to toss out a flippant answer to show she didn't care one way or another. But she did care. Perhaps much more than was wise. 'Yes, it is.'

'Then I will,' he stated equally simply. Starkly.

Her breath caught. 'Just like that?'

'The stalking case against you is fraudulent by all indication. It's reasonable to assume whoever went to the trouble set you up for the blueprints too. I don't need hard facts to tell me that. And in the grand scheme of things, no harm was caused by my opponents getting hold of those blueprints. They didn't have the expertise to pull out such a structure in a desert environment like Abu Dhabi. And once it became known that they were trying to pass off my work as their own, their reputation took an irreparable dent. If you want me to believe that you didn't betray me, then I will be prepared to put it behind us.'

A lump rose in her throat, despite the fact that he hadn't given her the ringing endorsement of belief she'd sought. He was merely giving her the benefit of the doubt.

'What about Alessandro?' she blurted.

His features closed up, not before she spotted a shadow

of doubt flash across his face. 'I will not rush to judgement until I have irrefutable evidence before me.'

She shouldn't have been hurt, of course. Still, her heart squeezed painfully. 'Very well.' She pushed her plate away, her appetite gone.

About to reach for the tablet to resume reading the reports on his various projects, she stopped when he brushed his fingers across her knuckles. 'It's time to take a break. If we don't want to battle jet lag when we land it might be a good idea to catch a few hours of sleep.'

Immediately her pulse leapt, her blood heating as memories from last night flooded her. 'I…okay, but not just yet. I want to finish this.' She indicated the report.

He stayed seated for a beat, then nodded. *'Bene.'*

Mia wasn't sure exactly what came over her, causing her to blurt, 'Why did you tell Allegra?'

He frowned. 'Why did I tell Allegra what?'

She exhaled. 'You said you didn't want to jump to conclusions or speak ill of the dead, but you told her that I suspected Alessandro was behind what happened to me.'

His frown intensified. 'Besides my lawyers, I haven't spoken to anyone about this.'

'Well, she knows. She accused me of sullying her husband's memory.'

'When?' he asked sharply.

'This morning. In the hallway, before we left,' she answered.

Fury blazed in his eyes for a few seconds as he wrestled down his emotion. Without another word to her, he rose and strode out, leaving her staring after him in confusion.

If he hadn't told Allegra, then who had?

Without a forthcoming answer, she refocused on the reports. It took precious few minutes for her to fully absorb what she was reading. By the time she was done, her neck was stiff and her back ached.

She'd barely managed to sleep last night, and her body was reacting to the adrenaline of re-immersing herself in her work. Shutting down the tablet, she made her way to the back of the plane where the master bedroom and bathroom were located. After using the washroom, she entered the bedroom.

Thick gold covers gleamed invitingly, sunlight slanting through half-pulled shades bathing the room in warm, enticing light. Unable to resist, she perched on the bed, kicked off her shoes and flexed her feet. Grabbing one corner of the spread, she tugged it down and slid between the sheets.

She meant to shut her eyes for ten minutes, fifteen max. When she blinked awake, the sun was setting and semi-darkness shrouded the room. But even in the dimness she knew she wasn't alone. She turned her head to see the dark figure heading towards the door.

'Rocco?'

He froze then turned around. 'We're not landing for another couple of hours. Go back to sleep. I only came to check on you.'

She sat up, relaxed against the pillows. 'Did you manage to get some sleep?'

In the darkness she saw his teeth flash a wry smile. 'At the risk of sounding like a broken record, sleeping comfortably when you're around has become impossible.'

She frowned. 'I really affect you that much?'

Again he smiled as he slowly walked towards her. Mia couldn't help but greedily absorb every animalistic movement of his streamlined body. She shivered at the intensity in the eyes that stared down at her when he reached the bed.

'You create a deep impact on me, *cara*. I've stopped bothering trying to deny it.' The words were thick, gruff, the hands shoved into his pockets attesting to the knife-edged control he balanced on.

Just like last night, feminine power resurged, sweeping through her veins like sweet, irresistible nectar.

'I believe it's why I reacted so strongly to the unfortunate incident three years ago,' he elaborated tightly.

'We're reducing it to one unfortunate incident, are we?' she asked.

One broad shoulder lifted in a shrug, drawing her attention to the fact that he'd discarded his suit jacket at some point and rolled up the shirt sleeves. 'I'm not interested in the past. Not any more. I wish to look to the future. And that future requires that we address this thing between us. I fear I will be intolerable if I keep losing sleep over you.'

She clamoured for outrage, but only ended up with breathless anticipation. 'That sounds suspiciously like another threat. I suggest you try harder to get some sleep. Perhaps you'll be less disagreeable.'

She started to turn away, but he placed a hand on her shoulder. 'Wait.'

Her eyes flew to his, connecting with the tempest raging in his eyes. 'If we can't indulge in one way, I'd very much like something else from you.'

'What makes you think—?'

She stopped when he placed a finger over her lips.

'Per favore,' he breathed.

Several heartbeats ticked by, all crammed with the urge to say no. But his gruff plea wrapped itself around her heart, and, as foolish as it was to let it affect her, Mia found herself nodding.

He didn't voice his request straight away. Instead, his hand moved from her shoulder, down her side to her flat belly, his gaze dropping to track his slow journey. 'Tell me about the pregnancy.'

Shock held her still. 'Why?'

His eyes rose to spear hers. 'My seed grew inside you,

and you bore my son. Whatever went before and whatever comes after, it won't change the fact that the birth of my son is an experience I regret not sharing,' he said in a thick, charged undertone.

Having seen for herself how enamoured he was with Gianni, his pain touched her. Regardless of who was to blame for their circumstances, she believed Rocco would've liked to know about his unborn child.

Swallowing the lump in her throat, she let the memories flood in. 'I heard his heartbeat for the first time at nine weeks.' She smiled, her heart brimming with love. 'It was loud and strong. Funnily enough, it also made the atrocious morning sickness bearable. Be thankful you missed that part.'

Rocco gave a pinched smile and sank onto the bed next to her. 'On the contrary, I'm not thankful I missed any of it…but go on,' he urged huskily.

'Everything went smoothly after that.' Mia's gaze dropped to the handbag sitting on the floor.

Rocco's gaze followed, his eyes sharpening. 'What?'

'I have a picture of the ultrasound if you want—'

'*Sì*. I want. Very much,' he insisted.

She reached for her bag, taking out her purse and the celluloid frame she kept within.

Rocco took it from her, his gaze absorbing every inch of the black and white image. Perhaps it was the naked emotion in his face that prompted her next action. Reaching once more into her bag, she took out her phone, flicked through the photos.

He took the phone from her, flicking back and forth through the images taken by her grandmother in her cottage garden when Mia was in late pregnancy. Wearing a yellow sundress with her hair long and flowing, she was the epitome of barefoot and very pregnant.

After an age, Rocco swallowed thickly. '*Dios mio, eri*

squisito. I would've given much to see you for myself like this. So ripe, so beautiful with my child.' His gaze lifted from the phone to her face. 'You cared for him in the midst of uncertainty and strife. For that, you have my thanks, Mia.'

His words triggered a shiver from temple to toe, in the process flattening her tongue to the roof of her mouth. Speechless, she watched him reach out and turn on the bedside lamp. She had nowhere to hide, but her body didn't seem interested in heeding her commands to move. So she lay there, her fists bunched in the bed covers.

Then, almost of their own accord, they slowly drew back.

Rocco inhaled sharply, his sizzling gaze scouring her body before coming back to rest on her face. 'Sleep will be the last thing we'll be doing if I get into that bed with you, Mia,' he growled.

'I know.'

Eyes locked on her, he toed off his shoes, then started to unbutton his shirt.

Mia swallowed, her senses jumping in a wild dance as she watched him shrug off his shirt to reveal washboard abs.

Dear God, he was glorious.

He paused with his hand on his belt, his eyes narrowing enquiringly on her face.

Her breath shivered out, ending in the low moan. And then she was rising, boldly placing her hands over his, brushing them away to take hold of his belt. Fingers trembling wildly, she eased it free, then slipped it through the hoops.

Rocco's breath hitched as her fingers grazed his thick erection. Hers followed suit at the realisation that she'd stepped on a roller coaster that would only have one heady, thrilling end.

Or a new beginning?

She pushed the thought away, too afraid to contemplate the future. She was living in the moment. Whatever happened afterwards, she would deal with that too.

'Do you intend to torture me to death with the slow teasing, *amante*?'

She looked up into his tense face, then looked down and realised that her fingers were frozen on the button of his trousers. Catching her lower lip between her teeth, she slowly eased it free, then drew down his zip. He gave a tortured moan, his hands jerking out to rest on her shoulders before sliding into her hair to grip a handful.

'Have your fun, *tesoro*, but do it quickly before one of us expires.'

She summoned a smile, caressing him with a light dance of fingers over his erection. 'Hmm, I'm almost tempted to see who wins this battle of wills.'

'Keep challenging me and we will find out,' he responded thickly.

Then in typical alpha fashion, he hooked his fingers into his waistband and dragged both boxers and trousers down. He straightened, his body on full, unapologetically masculine display as he stared down at her.

Swallowing, Mia looked down, her senses tripping over each other as she stared as his manhood—beautifully sculpted, virile and infinitely tempting. She couldn't help herself. She grasped him, then brought him to her lips. Another tortured groan ripped from his throat as she covered him with her mouth.

He allowed the caress for only a handful of seconds before he drew her back. 'Enough.'

Then he went on the attack, efficiently undressing her until she was equally nude.

Just like last night, he picked her up and tossed her back

onto the bed. Without giving her a chance to recover, he prowled over her and settled himself between her thighs.

Rocco took her mouth in a hot, torrid kiss, delving deep and tasting her with the boldness that robbed her of what little breath she had. She clung to him, her fingers digging into his shoulders as she drowned in desire. They rolled from one end of the bed to the other, almost animalistic in their desire to extract maximum pleasure from touch and taste and the heady scent of their coming together.

Eventually, driven to the edge of madness, she broke free of the kiss. 'Please, Rocco, I need you.'

Her words triggered something inside him. Blindly he reached for the bedside table, pulled the drawer open and extracted a condom.

Rising onto his knees, he tore the packet open and slipped it on.

He was back, his fingers spearing into her hair as he angled her face up to his. Eyes locked on hers, he slid inside her. For five full seconds, Mia trembled, unable to stop the unrelenting tides of pleasure sweeping through her as he buried himself fully inside her. '*Dio mio*, you feel incredible,' he rasped.

She had no words to reciprocate. She could only moan in sublime delight as he began to thrust inside her. With each stroke, she grew wilder, clawing at him the same way sensations clawed beneath her skin, attempting to reinvent her very being.

Dear God, her memory had failed her. Because this was so much more sublime than she recalled. More soul-stirring.

From being on the edge of control when she was undressing him, Rocco seemed to have regained his willpower over his body. Repeatedly, he drove her to the brink of release only to slow down, fuse his lips to hers and patiently wait for the tide to recede before enacting the dark magic all over again.

Mia was sure she drew blood from clawing at his back, her throat raw from screaming her pleasure.

'I told you I would make you beg, didn't I?' Rocco muttered throatily when he had her poised on yet another peak.

'Yes,' she accepted. 'Please,' she begged. 'You win. Please.'

He held still, his lips a whisper from hers. 'This changes things between us. You know that, don't you, *mio moglie*?' he pressed, taking full advantage.

She didn't care. She was going out of her mind with this madness. 'Yes,' she cried.

'Just so we're clear,' he murmured, after pressing another hot kiss to her lips. 'No more separate bedrooms, *sì*?'

Mia groaned her acquiescence, her fingers digging into his back, her knees wrapped around his thick thighs as she ground herself into him. 'No more separate bedrooms,' she gasped.

Triumph flashed over his face. In the next breath, his control snapped. His thrusts intensified, his face a harsh, beautiful mask of desire as he finally gave them both what they needed. Mia tumbled first, unheeding where she landed as she dived headlong into the most earth-shattering climax she had ever experienced. But through the fog of her bliss, she heard Rocco give a rough shout as he found his own release.

Sweaty, hearts racing, they collapsed into each other's arms and he rolled them sideways. He brushed his lips over her temple as they fought to regain their breaths.

Mia knew she needed to move, establish some much-needed distance, but for the life of her couldn't find the energy. When Rocco rolled onto his back and pulled her over him, she went willingly, her head resting on his chest as he toyed with her hair.

'I suppose you'd like me to do the honourable thing and

restate my request now that I am not holding an orgasm over your head?'

She closed her eyes, revelling in the rumble of his voice beneath her cheek before raising her head to look him in the eyes. 'Do you feel like doing the honourable thing?' she asked, half teasing.

He raised an eyebrow and then shrugged. 'That depends.'

'On what?'

'On whether your answer will still be yes.'

Her senses screamed at her to be circumspect, to take a moment to reconsider what she'd readily surrendered moments ago. But she knew she was only fooling herself. She could only fight this powerful chemistry with Rocco for so long. At least on the physical side they were both equally bound by this spell. She wasn't fooling herself into thinking there were emotions involved. For as long as this chemistry raged between them, why not indulge?

'Contrary to what you accused me of last night, I'm not indifferent to the physical side of our relationship.'

An expression crossed his face, part triumph, part bewilderment. He didn't answer immediately, just continued to toy with her hair for another minute before he nodded. 'Then we are in agreement.'

She should've done the sensible thing then, just enjoyed the tension-free moment. Or, even better, encouraged him to sleep, thereby granting her some thinking room.

But Mia found questions crowding her brain and she let the first one slip out before she could stop herself. 'Is that what your parents did? Hurt you with their indifference?'

He stiffened beneath her, his face locking in a formidable rejection of her attempt to probe. 'What does it matter?'

'You seem hung up on it, that's why.'

His lips twisted. 'Aren't we all hung up on something?'

'I want to know, Rocco.'

His eyes narrowed into icy slits. 'Why? So you can tick a little feasibility box about me in your head?'

Her heart squeezed, mocking every intention to stay neutral. There was nothing neutral about what she felt about Rocco. Never had been. 'Don't do that.'

His nostrils flared, but he didn't respond. Not for the longest time.

When he looked down from the ceiling, his eyes were bleak pools of bruised hurt she'd never witnessed before. Her breath caught but she forced herself to remain still, not to offer comfort yet in case he withdrew.

'My grandfather left a sizeable inheritance when he died. With careful planning, my grandmother could've lived comfortably for the rest of her life. But my father coerced her into handing it over, with promises that he could double it. Within a year, he'd driven Nonna to the poverty line.

'Then he became obsessed with chasing what he had lost. He played the same game with my mother, frittered away her inheritance as well. The cycle just kept on repeating itself. Unfortunately for them, I came along.' His voice throbbed with bitterness but he clenched his jaw and continued. 'An inconvenience they tolerated up until the burden of having a child grew too much for them. They dumped me with Nonna and I hardly saw them more than a few times a month. When I saw them, my father would regale me with how busy he was. How he was taking over the world and how he would get back everything he had lost. Nowhere in that narrative did I feature. I remember wondering why he was bothering with me when clearly he didn't give a damn about me. Why he was torturing us with visits when it was clear he always wanted to be somewhere else, anywhere else but wherever I was.'

'Rocco...'

He shrugged away her sympathy. 'They died when I was seven. I remember that day clearly. The authorities arrived at Nonna's doorstep and I immediately knew. I told myself I didn't care.'

'But you did.'

He stiffened again, his gaze shifting away from hers to rest on the ceiling, but his fingers didn't stop playing with her hair. 'It doesn't matter.'

'Of course it does. Your feelings matter. You expected them to care for you.'

'Nonna provided me with everything I needed. More than.'

'But Nonna wasn't your parents. They brought you into this world. It's different, I'm sure, if you didn't know your parent at all, but to have them there right in front of you and still feel alone, unwanted or irrelevant hurts. Believe me, I know.'

His gaze dropped, latching onto her, compelling her own pain from where she had buried it deep.

'I don't know which is worse—having a full-time parent right in front of you who blames you for their every misfortune or having one who is occasionally present but distant.'

'Your mother.'

She gave a painful nod.

'Tell me.'

She shrugged. 'She got pregnant with me when she was starting out in her career. She wanted to be a nurse. But she was a young, single mother with no income to speak of. So she settled for…less. And she…hated me for it.'

Rocco frowned. 'Where was your grandmother in this picture?'

'Sidelined. For whatever reason, my mother refused all help. They fell out over my upbringing and never really healed their relationship. She seemed determined to lay all the blame on the timing of my arrival rather than…' She stopped, fresh anguish flaying her.

'Was that why you didn't want children?'

She tensed. 'It was why I wanted *to wait* to have children. I never *didn't* want children, Rocco. It was simply a matter of timing.'

Silence pulsed in the room, then he cursed under his breath. 'None of that matters any longer, *si*?' he said gruffly.

Something weighty shifted inside her. 'No. The moment he was born, Gianni became my everything,' she whispered.

They both stopped, absorbed the wonder of their child. From the first, she'd vowed to be a better parent. The way her mother had never been. The way she'd always yearned for.

'He makes me want to do things differently,' Rocco said gruffly, echoing her thought so succinctly her heart flipped over again.

Dear God, what was happening to her?

A lump rose in her throat and to combat the emotion, she simply nodded.

Then the plane lurched.

Rocco rolled them over and braced himself on his elbows. He stared down at her, but something told Mia the little heart-to-heart was gone. Certainly, the look in his eyes was no longer bitter, bewildered, or holding that hint of vulnerability she'd spotted as he'd spoken about his parents.

He was back in alpha-male mode, in control of everything around him. Of *her*. 'By my reckoning we land in about half an hour. This give us just enough time.'

'Enough time for what?'

He smiled, a wickedly male smile that reignited the fire in her belly. 'Let me show you.'

And he did, wringing cries from her throat as the plane started its descent. After another bout of lovemaking, they only had time for a quick shower before the plane landed.

Mia slipped into business mode as if she'd never left her role at Vitelli Construction.

The visit to the building site went off without a hitch, her initial assessments confirmed once she'd walked the ground for herself. The proposal to commence work in four months' time was signed off. Then she and Rocco headed back to their hotel.

The next three days flew by in a flurry of meetings, dinners with Macau city officials and clients. And to top each night off, mind-melting sex with Rocco. Private video-conferencing sessions with Gianni arranged by Rocco made the searing ache of missing him a little easier to bear.

They were preparing to go out to dinner with another set of clients the night before they were due to leave when Rocco excused himself to take a phone call.

Mia nodded distractedly, her gaze on her reflection in the mirror. Specifically, her dress.

The selection of outfits that had arrived from the exclusive boutique attached to the hotel, courtesy of Rocco's insistence, had been hard to choose from, each garment a little more perfect than the last.

She'd eventually settled on a sleeveless dark lilac silk sheath. But what struck her more wasn't the flawless design of the dress, but the renewed glow to her skin, the fuller curve of her hips and the vitality in her cheeks and eyes.

Observing the changes had quietly shocked her. Had it only been two weeks since Rocco charged back into her life? She'd changed inside and out, a realisation that triggered mild panic.

As she had been terrified of that first day, everything was moving too fast. But then hadn't it always with Rocco? Life with him was like a roller-coaster ride that could either stop at any minute or spin faster until you grew too dizzy to recognise your surroundings.

Was that what she wanted in the long term? She'd already abandoned her one stipulation not to share his bed. And how long would that even last?

Unable to face the questions darting through her brain, she turned away, slid her feet into designer heels that came with the dress and caught up her clutch. Leaving the bedroom of the presidential suite where they were staying, she spotted Rocco pacing the balcony. His phone was glued to his ear—a not unnatural occurrence since their arrival, but even from the distance, she sensed his tension. The sound of her clicking heels on the immaculate hardwood floor caused him to whirl around.

Laser eyes latched onto her, tracking her. When she reached the French doors, he ended the call and strode towards her.

'Is everything okay?' she asked.

'Ovviamente.' Despite his assurance, she couldn't mistake the terseness in his voice or his tense frame as he held out his arm to her. 'Shall we?'

She slid her arm through his, allowing him to lead her into the private lift and then downstairs to the restaurant where they were meeting their clients.

Rocco slid effortlessly into host mode. But throughout dinner, she caught his gaze returning to her repeatedly, the expression in his eyes unreadable. Her unease heightened as the dinner drew to a close.

Knowing she wouldn't be able to rest until she got to the bottom of what was threatening their albeit new but shaky status, she smiled at the client as coffee was cleared away, ready to make her excuses. But it turned out Rocco had other ideas.

'I'm eager to show Mia a slice of night life before we leave Macau. Would you care to join us?'

Mia barely managed to keep the astonishment off her face. 'You are?'

On previous nights, Rocco had bristled with impatience to get her back to their suite, barely waiting for the door to shut behind them before divesting her of her clothes.

Rocco smiled her way but it didn't cause quiet chaos in her. Probably because the smile didn't reach his eyes. 'We leave tomorrow, *cara*. We've done nothing but work for the past three days. I think you deserve to see something of Macau. After all, we have to report to Nonna when we get back, don't we?'

Of course. She'd forgotten that this was supposed to be a purported honeymoon as well as a business trip. Sure, the intimacy side of things had been thoroughly fulfilled, but she could hardly cite that, or recite the particulars of blueprints and steel samples when asked about her honeymoon, could she?

She let herself be ushered out of the restaurant and into a gleaming limo. Easy conversation flowed as they were driven into the heart of Asia's gaming capital. They alighted in front of a towering hotel, one of the many that had helped earn Macau the title of Vegas of the East.

A personal welcome from the owner of the hotel and the presentation of a huge pile of chips later, Rocco took over the blackjack table in the VIP section of the casino.

Mia tried not to gape in alarm as thousands of dollars changed hands at the careless throw of a dice. She would've been sickened by the sight but her husband defied the odds and, even in a game of chance, repeatedly emerged the winner. A performance that garnered a small crowd he seemed oblivious to, one possessive arm clasping her to him and the other tossing dice with reckless abandonment.

It was only when he caught her trying to suppress a yawn for the dozenth time that Rocco finally stepped back from the table and brushed a kiss across her temple.

'I think my lucky charm is done for the night,' he drawled.

Amidst good-humoured laughter, he took a hand, pressed a kiss to her knuckles.

Questions still teemed in her mind as they re-entered the

limo, but this time, with just the two of them riding back to their hotel, Rocco had other ideas. The moment the doors locked behind them, he dragged her into his lap, sealing his lips to hers before she could utter a word.

As if he was on a mission, he didn't relent, drugging her with his kisses and greedy, fevered touch until they drew up in front of the hotel. Then he proceeded to slay her with passion, sweeping her off her feet, the moment they entered their suite.

An hour later, too exhausted to speak, think or even breathe properly, she fell into a blissful sleep.

Rocco stared down at his wife, guilt eating at him as he watched her sleep.

The phone call he'd received from his lawyers just before they left for dinner still sent shock waves through his system.

Alessandro had orchestrated everything.

His cousin had systematically and cruelly worked to hide the existence of his son from him, while attempting to bury Mia in a fraudulent claim.

Rocco could barely fathom it, had been reeling all through dinner at the thought that his own flesh and blood had gone to such deplorable lengths.

For what?

Power?

Had he not given Alessandro every opportunity? How had he found Mia so threatening that he had done this? Questions chased through his mind until they drove him out of bed.

Pacing the living room, he grappled with another decision.

He couldn't tell her.

Not yet. He'd only just managed to secure his position in her life. Discovering what Alessandro had done to her, to their son, might tip the scales into him losing everything. Everything he hadn't even known existed two weeks ago. He couldn't let that happen.

When the time was right, he would reveal everything to her. But not just yet.

More than discovering how much he'd missed the physical aspect of his relationship with Mia was the reminder of how much he'd missed her brilliant mind and her ability to see his work in a new light. Within three short days, she'd impressed his clients and team, both effusive with the compliments of her.

Far from having grown rusty, she'd delved back into a career that should never have been disrupted with an enthusiasm Rocco was nowhere near ready to lose.

'All I want is for my name to be cleared so I can get on with my life.'

Her words echoed in his head but he ruthlessly dismissed them.

He couldn't let that happen. Perhaps he was being underhanded and would pay when the time came, but that was a problem for another day. Hopefully a day when he'd reinforced the foundation beneath his feet with time and the promise of...

Of what?

A better future?

Why not?

His son was happy. Nonna was happy.

And he...was he happy?

Rocco couldn't deny that he derived a wealth of satisfaction from having Mia back in his life and in his bed. So...*sì*, perhaps he was happy. Thanks to his parents, he only had a barometer of what dysfunction looked like. Only time would tell how it all shaped up and, *accidenti*, he was going to take that time.

He crossed the living room to the liquor cabinet, and,

despite it being the early hours of the morning, poured a cognac before returning to the bedroom. He slid in beside his wife, gratified when she rolled over and slipped effortlessly into his arms.

This was where she belonged.

This was where he would keep her. And when the time was right, he would come clean.

CHAPTER ELEVEN

MIA STARED AROUND HER, the overload of glitz and glamour triggering a mild headache.

Monaco during Formula One weekend wasn't the arena for the faint-hearted. The billionaires per square metre was eye-watering. And with her husband easily part of the exalted club, the level of sycophancy was almost nauseating.

Of course she would endure it all, and more, to keep basking in the smile that was plastered on Gianni's face.

Her son had been beside himself when his father had announced at the breakfast table that, as part of his—week-long and counting—birthday celebrations, he'd been granted VIP status to the renowned Paddock Club in Monte Carlo.

But then in the months since his father entered his life, Gianni had been beside himself with joy on most days. True to his vow to be a different father than his parents had been to him, Rocco showered his son with his attention, their mutual love of fast cars only cementing their strong bond.

'Papà, look!' Gianni pointed to another sports car from his perch on his father's shoulders, his eyes goggling in his chubby face.

'I see, *mio figlio*, I see,' Rocco responded with a grin, slanting a smile at Mia that, right on cue, set off fireworks in her belly.

She'd believed that the time before Rocco had cut her off from his life three years ago had been the most sublime of her life. She'd been wrong.

On the morning of their departure from Macau, she'd woken to a seemingly changed man. In all the right ways. Power and prestige had been a given in a life with Rocco. But the attention he'd showered on her and Gianni, the steps he'd taken to ensure her transition back into Vitelli Construction and the corner office that had come with her return to work had been mind-boggling. She'd quickly returned to being a valued member of his team. And best of all, oversea trips without Gianni had become a thing of the past.

To say her life had done a complete one-eighty was an understatement.

The only fly in her ointment was the delay in figuring out just who had tanked her life three years ago. And, for a man who demanded answers in every corner of his life, Rocco's seemingly relaxed stance in getting to the bottom of it didn't sit well with her.

Although…could she really blame him? Would she be in a hurry to discover if her own flesh and blood had betrayed him the way she still suspected Alessandro had if she were in Rocco's shoes?

Most likely not.

Nevertheless, the need for closure had been eating at her the last few weeks. Their conversation on the plane to Macau replayed frequently in her head. As much as she wanted him to believe her, Rocco had stated plainly that he wouldn't do so without solid evidence.

And more and more, Mia had felt as if without that, her life was on hold.

'Papà?'

'Sì, caro?'

'Can I have that racing car?' Gianni pointed predictably at a bright red sports car with Ferrari emblazoned on the side.

'Not that exact one, but maybe we can—'

She cleared her throat, shooting Rocco a pointed look. His grin widened, and her heart did that crazy thing again.

'We will discuss it when you're older, mio figlio.'

'Much, much older. Like when you're in your eighties,' she said under her breath, earning herself a low laugh from Rocco.

It was getting ridiculous how she'd begun to live for that laugh. For those smiles. Hell, how she'd begun to live for him full stop.

She didn't need to search deep to know that she had far surpassed the infatuation she'd felt for him three years ago.

Hell, who was she kidding? She'd fallen in love with Rocco somewhere over the Indian Ocean on the way back from Macau. So why did that make her heart twist each time she examined it?

Because she had no clue what he felt for her. He was seemingly content with their life together. The sex was beyond world-class. Gianni was thriving. Caterina's health had improved dramatically over the past few months.

And yet, every now and then she caught that tension within Rocco. And for the life of her she couldn't put her finger on it.

Her thoughts were still darting about when they eventually made their way to the VIP lounge. While Rocco and Gianni remained at the balcony to watch the race get under way, Mia made her way to a quiet corner of the lounge with her glass of mineral water.

From there, she watched, half bemused, as several women attempted to approach Rocco and were coolly rebuffed. Little did they know that no one came between Rocco Vitelli and his son. Did that commitment extend unconditionally to her? Or was she living on borrowed time until the verdict proved her guilt or innocence?

Unable to stew in the questions that had been plaguing her for weeks, Mia rose and made her way to the ladies' room. Exiting the cubicle, she stumbled to a halt when her gaze clashed with none other than Allegra Vitelli's.

Mia had been shocked when, on her return from Macau,

she had been informed that Allegra had moved out. Rocco had seemed completely unconcerned by the development and, for a second, she'd wondered whether he'd orchestrated it.

She hadn't questioned it, had even been secretly relieved to be free of the woman who now glared at her with seething venom.

'I thought that was you, practising your…what do you call it?…chapel mouse stance up there in the VIP lounge.'

'It's *church* mouse, and you should've stopped by to say hello. I don't bite,' Mia replied as she walked calmly to the sink, washed her hands and reapplied her lip gloss.

The other woman's fury visibly grew. 'I don't exchange pleasantries with peasants,' she spat out, her eyes glittering like crystals.

'Well, then, don't let me stop you from leaving me alone.'

'Trust me I will, right after I set you straight on a few things.'

'Such as?'

'Did you not wonder why I left Palermo so suddenly?'

Of course she had, but Mia wasn't about to give her the satisfaction of confirming it so she busied herself fixing her hair.

'Not going to ask? Don't worry, I'm feeling generous. You see, for starters, your husband paid me a lot of money. Three million euros, to be exact.'

Mia's heart hammered in her ears. 'What for?'

'To buy my silence. But you see, I no longer need Vitelli money.' She flashed a diamond the size of a small country at Mia, her scarlet lips parting in a smug smile. 'I'm engaged to a charming French count and in the process of moving to France. So really, I've nothing left to lose any more.'

'What does that mean?' Mia asked, her stomach dipping wildly in alarm because all of a sudden she was one hundred per cent sure she didn't want to hear what the woman was dying to spill.

'It means you deserve to know the secret your husband is keeping from you. And you deserve to hurt the way your little reappearing act hurt me.'

'I'm not aware I did anything of the—'

'Oh, please, spare me the wide-eyed innocent act. You went digging in business that should've died with my Alessandro. And you turned up with your Poor Little Destitute act and stole Rocco from me.'

Mia gasped. 'You're deluded!'

Allegra shrugged. 'Perhaps. I'll never know now, will I?'

Mia bit her lip, but the question tumbled out anyway. 'What was the pay-off for?'

The cruel smile returned. 'To keep his little discovery a secret, of course. I heard the rumours and did a little digging of my own. So what if Alessandro took steps to keep Rocco from making a mistake with you? You were clearly sleeping your way to power. The child you claimed was Rocco's could've been another man's.'

Shards of ice pierced Mia's heart. 'You really think you can justify your husband destroying my life? So what, he could land a better position at Vitelli Construction? I wasn't his competition!'

'Not yet, but you had Rocco's ear.'

'And that terrified him so much he committed fraud?'

Allegra's face twisted. 'He did what he had to to protect his position and his family. You would do the same.'

'No, I wouldn't. And what exactly do you hope to gain by telling me this if not to see another family destroyed?'

Her eyes blazed with triumph before she shrugged coolly. 'We all deserve to know who we lie down with. Your *husband* has been content to withhold this from you for weeks now. Maybe you should think about that?'

With that, she sailed out, head held high, blissfully un-caring that she, like her late husband, had shattered Mia's life.

For a second time.

Mia barely recalled making her way out of the ladies' room and out of the Paddock Club. Only had a vague mem-ory of typing a hurried text to Rocco, informing him she'd returned to the hotel.

In the hotel room, she kicked off her shoes and paced, the ever-expanding pain in her heart demanding action. Rocco had known she was innocent all along and hadn't told her.

Why?

As if summoned by the single question blazing in her head, the suite door opened and Rocco walked in.

Gianni wasn't with him.

He pre-empted her question. 'Sophia took him to get a *gelato*.' His voice was heavy, his eyes intensely watchful. Sophia was part of the Palermo villa staff, who it turned out was specialising in childcare. A month ago, she'd been officially hired as Gianni's nanny.

'You know.'

He gave a single, jerky nod. 'I ran into Allegra. Or I should say, she ran into me. On purpose. Mia—'

'Why?'

He didn't answer immediately. He paced before her, dragging his fingers repeatedly through his hair until it was a dishevelled mess. Not that it reduced his hotness by even an iota. Damn him.

'You told me, repeatedly, that you wanted to put this be-hind you and move on with your life.'

'And you found that objectionable?'

He shook his head. 'No, I didn't. Only that I couldn't… take the risk that you'd move on…without me.' The words seemed ripped from his throat, but Mia wasn't in the mood to accommodate his discomfort.

She laughed. 'So you withheld the truth? Made me live with this hanging over my head?'

He paced to the window, whirled about and returned to stand in front of her. 'What would you have done if I'd told you on our last night in Macau?'

She gasped. 'That's how long you've known?'

He grimaced. Then nodded. *'Sì.'*

Shock threatened to weaken her knees. She sank into one of the many chairs littering the room. 'I don't know what I would've done. And I'll never know because you didn't tell me. You made me think that I had to prove myself to you. That I had to jump through hoops to earn your trust again.'

'No, it wasn't like that. I just didn't want to lose you!'

Her heart leapt, then dipped almost immediately. 'You didn't want to lose access to your son, you mean?'

'Don't tell me what I mean. You were what preoccupied my mind, not Gianni. You were the one I was afraid to lose. You are the one who has become as vital to me as breathing.'

She held up her hand, stopping the torrent of words. 'You know what, I don't believe you. Because you said it yourself, you play to win. Always. Finding out Alessandro did this to me put you in a position of weakness. So you withheld it from me. It's that simple.'

'Finding out my own flesh and blood did such a horrible thing to *us both* made me ashamed,' he bit out. 'He smiled to my face and stabbed me in the back. He did worse to you and, for that, I'm sorry, Mia. *Sono così dispiaciuto,*' he muttered thickly, taking a step towards her.

Again she held up her hand. Because something inside her was crumbling. And she couldn't afford to let it. 'Don't.'

For the first time in her life, she spotted naked fear on

Rocco's face. He hid it well. In the bunching of his fists before clasping them behind his back. In the measured breaths he attempted to take while his gaze remained glued to her face. In the restraint he showed when she started to back away from him.

'Where are you going?' he finally jerked out when she grasped the door handle.

She stopped but didn't turn around. 'I've lived in fear for over three years. You can live with not knowing how this is going to turn out. See how you like it.'

He was in hell. Not just any hell. The special kind of hell reserved for *bastardi* like him who believed they could control the outcome of any event. He'd known the moment Allegra approached him with that cat-with-cream look on her face that his sin was coming home to roost.

He'd lied to the woman he'd never forgotten, the woman who owned his heart. All so he could hang onto her for much longer than he deserved. Just so he could try this *contentment* on for size when all along he'd known it was much more? That he simply couldn't live without her because he was nothing without her.

The next hour passed in excruciating torture, each second feeling like his last.

Rocco wanted to honour her wish to stay away, but what if each moment put her farther out of his reach? He'd never been one to sit and wait for things to come to him.

So, he wasn't surprised when his feet propelled him out of the door.

She was sitting with her back against the wall next to the lift, her head bowed. Rocco froze in place as she slowly lifted her head and speared him with eyes filled with pain and censure.

'You handled this badly, Rocco. So very badly.'

'*Sì*, I know.'

Tears filmed her stunning green eyes and he wanted to claw his own heart out. 'You hurt me. So much.'

Regret and fear shook through him. He swallowed both down. Everything was on the line. And now, more than ever, he needed to play to win. Deciding to risk it, he strode to her, scooped her up in his arms and returned to the suite.

And when she jerked herself out of his hold, he set her free. 'I swear on my life that I will never hurt you again.'

She shook her head, placing the length of the living room between them. 'I don't want that sort of promise. You can't guarantee that if you don't trust me.'

'I can and I do. Even at that first meeting in London, things Alessandro had said and done niggled at me. I didn't want to believe it. But on the plane when you asked me to believe you about the blueprints, I knew you were innocent of this too. But…we'd been barely been married for a day. We were so new. And what I felt for you overwhelmed me. All of this is no excuse, *amante*. But all I ask is that you give me chance to make things right.'

She brushed at a tear, and he felt it to his soul.

Dio mio, what had he done?

'How?'

'Whatever hoops you choose, I will jump through them. All I ask is that you don't leave me.'

'What if that's exactly what I want?'

He locked his knees to stop from reaching for her. 'Is that what you want? Truly?'

She didn't reply. But he spotted her fingers caressing her ring. Wild hope flared in his chest.

'What I want is…impossible.'

He shook his head. 'Nothing is impossible. Name it, *amore*. Speak the words and it will be yours.'

Her lips firmed for a long moment. 'I can't,' she whispered.

'Then let me speak them for you. You want to be loved—

ti amo tanto. You deserve to be adored—you are my heart itself. I had no blueprint for love, *mio prezioso.* Not until you spread your love all over me and showed me just how sublime it could be. Even then, I remained blind. But I'm not blind any more, Mia. I might fail sometimes, but I will never fail at loving you.'

'Oh, Rocco.' Her voice broke, and, *sì,* he was *un bastardo,* because it was the most beautiful sound he'd ever heard.

Unable to stand the distance between them, he crossed the room and reclaimed her. To his eternal gratitude, she wrapped her arms around his neck.

They kissed long and hard and desperately, until she broke free. 'I'm going to hold you to that promise. You know that, don't you?' she whispered.

'I would expect nothing less, *amore mio.*'

Then, simply because he believed he would expire if he didn't kiss her again, he did.

But again, she broke free. He groaned, laid his forehead against hers, and just rejoiced in having her. His wife. His heart. In his arms.

'Shall we go and find our son?'

Rocco shook his head. 'Not until I've shown his mother just how much I love her.'

Her smile was wide, stunning enough to snatch the breath from his lungs. 'I'm not going to stop you.'

He swung her into his arms and strode for the master suite. As he walked across the threshold, she laid her hand over his heart. 'Rocco?'

'Yes, my heart?'

'Just so we're even... I love you too.'

EPILOGUE

Five years later

THE CLICK OF the camera's shutter roused Mia from a drowsy sun-drenched nap. Even before she opened her eyes, her lips were twitching with a reluctant smile.

'I should start charging you royalties for all these pictures you keep taking of me.'

Her teasing admonishing didn't detract her husband one iota. The moment she opened her eyes, he zoomed in, taking another lightning-fast series of pictures.

Only when he was satisfied did he lower the high-powered camera. 'Name your price and I will gladly pay it, *amore*,' he murmured, his avid gaze trailing adoringly from her unfettered hair, make-up-free face, and down her body to her belly, where Mia knew he would linger for hours if she permitted him.

At nearly eight months pregnant with their third child, she had very little inclination to do much besides laze about waiting for their baby's arrival. A situation Rocco took full advantage of, memorialising each moment of their summer break, including this private beach picnic at their Palermo villa.

He leaned down, dropped a kiss on her forehead, then traced a few more down to the corner of her mouth. There he paused, his gaze intense as he whispered, 'Call me primitive if you will, but I find you even more beautiful like this, with our child growing healthy and content, inside you.' His voice had grown steadily gruff and the kiss that followed lingered until she reluctantly pulled away, glancing over his shoulder towards the beach.

'Keep going and you'll scandalise the children.'

Rocco grimaced, then followed her gaze to where eight-year-old Gianni was patiently showing his three-year-old sister, Luciana, how to build a sandcastle. 'I will contain myself, for the *bambinis*' sake,' he grumbled.

Mia laughed. As if on cue, both children looked up and grinned. And, of course, Rocco raised his camera and snapped several photos.

She sighed in contentment, resting her hand on her belly as she mused in wonder over the last five years.

Save for a few bumps in the road, marriage to Rocco so far had been beyond blissful. The only trying period had been when Allegra's engagement had hit the rocks and she'd decided to sell Vitelli secrets to a tabloid magazine, fabricating a story about Mia's alleged clashes with her late husband causing her being disowned by the Vitellis.

Rocco, adamant about protecting Mia's honour, had given a TV interview, setting the record straight. And, before the whole world, had issued a heartfelt apology to Mia.

She hadn't even known she needed that last selfless act until Rocco had offered it, making their bond even stronger.

Her smile widened when Rocco rested his hand over hers, love blazing from his eyes when their baby kicked in response.

'No more pictures, please. Just sit with me,' she said.

He raised their linked hands and kissed her fingers. 'Anything for you, *il mio cuore*.'

Perhaps it was the hormones. Or perhaps it was the sheer happiness that often felt too big to be contained in her heart, but Mia felt tears prickle her eyes. 'You did it, Rocco.'

He glanced at her, one brow rising in the sexy, arrogant way that stole her breath. 'Did what?'

'You've kept your promise. Every day you make me feel worthy. That I matter. That our children matter. You've made us the centre of your world, and I adore you for it.'

He inhaled, heavily and shakily, his eyes growing suspiciously misty as he smiled down at her. 'I vowed to you that I would, did I not? I intend to keep that promise. In this life and in the next. Because, you see, it's quite simple, *amore mio*. You are my everything.'

* * * * *

For the 300

CHAPTER ONE

ANNA FLEETWOOD STOOD by the window in the great medieval fortress that was the royal palace of Axios, staring down at the little city nestled at the foot of the mountains below, the white stone buildings glowing in the sun, the windows glittering.

Itheus. Capital city of Axios, a small, but pretty kingdom just over Greece's northern border.

She would have liked to do a few tourist-type things, since this was her first time out of England and away from the convent she'd grown up in, but unfortunately she wasn't here to play the tourist.

She was here to meet King Adonis Nikolaides, the Lion of Axios.

She took a breath, trying to resist the urge to rub her sweaty palms down her plain grey dress.

Of course she wasn't nervous. He was only a king. No big deal.

Anna turned from the window.

The big room she stood in was the king's receiving room, with walls of undressed stone and a stone floor. Some attempts at lightening the austerity had been made with a few silk rugs, a couple of ancient-looking tapestries depicting battle scenes, and an incongruous spray of orchids on a side table near the huge fireplace.

But even the bright sun pouring through the window couldn't soften the hard, very masculine energy of the room—of the entire palace, truth be told—and she was beginning to see why the Mother Superior of her convent had asked her to come to Axios.

The king needed someone to be a companion for his young daughter and, as the king's godmother, the Reverend Mother had decided to undertake finding someone herself. She'd consequently decided that Anna was perfect for the job, despite Anna's clear lack of anything resembling experience with either teaching or children. Anna had tried to argue, of course, but the Reverend Mother wouldn't listen. And somehow a meeting was arranged, and Anna found herself on a flight to Axios, a thick guidebook—the Reverend Mother eschewed technology—her only reading material.

Anna wandered over to one of the tapestries and examined it. It was very old, depicting a gory battle scene with people getting their heads lopped off with broad swords, and arrows embedding themselves in heads through visors of helmets.

She wondered which particular battle this one depicted, since the history of Axios seemed to be nothing but nonstop wars and skirmishes. An austere, military culture, according to the guidebook. Just like its king, by all accounts.

Anna squinted at the figure standing in the middle of the battle scene: a giant warrior wearing one of those ancient Greek horsehair helmets, his huge arms raised above his head, a massive sword held between them. Another warrior lay at his feet, hands lifted, either trying to stop an attack or beg for mercy, it wasn't clear.

What was clear was that there would be no mercy coming from the giant warrior.

A shiver of foreboding snaked down Anna's spine, which she ignored. How silly. It was just a tapestry.

She leaned forward for a closer examination—and maybe to prove to herself that the shiver had been an aberration—then wrinkled her nose. It was musty.

'Something about our history you don't approve of?' a voice said from behind her, deep and harsh, like a glacier scraping over stone.

Anna's heart leapt into her mouth and she froze, a primitive, animal part of her sensing threat. Had she done something wrong? Was she not supposed to be here? Had she touched something she shouldn't have? She hadn't heard anyone come in…

There was silence behind her.

She took a breath, her heart thumping, and turned around.

A bolt of pure, instinctive fear shot through her, because somehow the huge warrior on the tapestry had come to life and was standing a few feet away from her by the door.

He was a giant of a man, standing at over six feet four at least, with the kind of wide, heavily muscled shoulders and broad chest that she'd always imagined Atlas possessing, strong enough to carry the entire world on his back. His waist was narrow, his legs long and solid and powerful; he looked as if he could complete two marathons in a row without even breaking a sweat.

His features were roughly carved with a brutal, masculine kind of handsomeness: strong jaw, a blade of a nose, closely cropped black hair, straight dark brows, deep-set, piercing eyes the blue of a cold winter sky. And he radiated authority and power the way the sun radiated heat. It was almost a physical force, making her want to go to her knees and pray before him as she did before the altar in church.

The king.

Of course it was the king. She'd read up on him in the guidebook and it had to be said that the pictures of him, grim-faced and utterly impassive, looking as if he hadn't ever smiled one day in his life, didn't do him justice. They didn't capture that aura of power.

He looked as if he'd been born wearing a crown.

Her mouth had dried and her palms had got even sweatier, and she was a little appalled at herself and her ridiculous burst of fear. Because, though he might look as if he was more suited to the battlefield on the tapestry behind her than he was to a throne room, he wasn't going to do anything to her.

She bobbed a graceless curtsey. 'Um, sorry, Your Majesty. I was just admiring the…um…tapestry.'

He said nothing, his granite features utterly expressionless, his blue eyes glacial. He wore a conventional yet immaculately tailored suit of charcoal-grey wool, black business shirt and a tie of dull gold silk.

How strange. She'd been positive it was armour he'd been wearing when she'd first looked at him.

Don't get carried away.

No, of course not. She was flighty and prone to an overactive imagination, as the Reverend Mother had always said in kind yet slightly disappointed tones, and she needed to work on controlling her impulses and passions, since those only led to trouble.

Then again, it had been years since she'd been that young, wild girl who used to sing too loudly in the choir, talk too much at mealtimes, accidentally knock over the communion wine, and get grass stains on her habit.

She'd made a decision a year ago that it was a life of contemplation and prayer that she wanted, and had asked the Reverend Mother to approve her taking her vows.

The Reverend Mother had had other plans for her, however, such as a visit to Axios and 'some time away in the secular world', before making her final decision.

Anna had been frustrated because she didn't need 'time in the secular world' but, since she couldn't take her vows without the Reverend Mother's approval, she'd had no choice but to do what she was told.

Which meant comporting herself as befitted a nun rather than an untried novice.

'Anna Fleetwood, I presume?' the king said.

Anna inclined her head. 'Yes, Your Majesty.'

He eyed her dispassionately for a second then raised a hand, indicating one of the armchairs near the couch. 'Please, sit.'

She supposed the 'please' was for form's sake, since it didn't sound like a request. More like an order.

She'd never been particularly obedient—something else that concerned the Reverend Mother—but she went without even her usual irritation at being told what to do, moving over to the armchair the king had indicated.

It was a heavy piece of furniture, covered in dark leather and not particularly comfortable. Anna perched on the edge of the seat, clasping her hands together in her lap, watching as the king went to the couch and sat down. For all his height and muscular size, he moved with a kind of lethal, animal grace that she found oddly mesmerising.

The Lion of Axios, that was what they called him, and that was what he reminded her of: a great, predatory beast.

Which makes you a gazelle.

Anna didn't much like that comparison. She didn't want to get eaten and she didn't want to be hunted. What she wanted was to do the job the Reverend Mother had assigned her and then return to England to take her vows. Easy.

'So, Sister,' the king said in his deep, harsh voice, his English perfect and uninflected. 'I assume the Reverend

Mother told you what is required for the position you'll be taking?'

Actually, the Reverend Mother had been frustratingly opaque about it, merely assuring Anna that she would be perfect for the position no matter her inexperience and that the king—or more probably one of his staff members— would give her all the details.

But, on arrival at the palace, no one had given her any details. She had simply been ushered straight into the receiving room to wait for the king without a word.

Nervousness fluttered in her gut.

She hadn't much experience with men, still less with men who looked like him, and none at all when it came to royalty. And he was so very royal and so very…male.

He made her uncomfortable.

'A little,' Anna said, forcing the feeling away. 'The Reverend Mother mentioned teaching the princess.' And then, because she was incurably honest and wanted him to know, she added, 'I should warn you, Your Majesty, that I don't have any teaching experience. Or any experience with children at all, in fact.'

The king said nothing, merely looked at her, and Anna tried to stop herself fidgeting under the weight of that icy blue gaze.

'The position doesn't involve teaching,' he said after a long moment. 'The princess already has a tutor. I require a more…steadying influence.'

Anna frowned. 'Excuse me, Your Majesty? I'm not quite sure—'

He lifted a hand. 'You may address me as sire if it's easier.'

'Very well, sire,' she said. 'And, please, call me Anna.' She didn't much care for being called Sister quite yet, not when she hadn't taken her vows.

'Noted.' He leaned back on the couch, the slight movement making her aware of his long, powerful body, a very physical awareness she'd never experienced with another person before. 'You weren't quite sure of what?'

'What you meant by a "steadying influence".'

'Ah.' He shifted again, very slightly, and again her attention was drawn to the pull of fabric across his broad shoulders and powerful thighs.

Which was strange. Why on earth was she staring at his body? She might not have had much to do with men, it was true, but it wasn't as if she hadn't seen a man before.

Not a man like this one, you haven't.

'Ione's behaviour is an issue,' the king said without preamble. 'She is a loud, boisterous child, which is not becoming in the heir to the throne. I believe she needs to start learning how to manage herself and her emotions, and, since I do not have the time for it, help is required from an outside source.'

Anna ignored her own odd reaction to him and frowned. Surely, all children were boisterous? Then again, who was she to question a king's parenting decisions?

'I see. And is there anything in particular you'd like me to do?'

'You will be issued with a list of acceptable activities, as well as some rules concerning Ione, her behaviour, and what is permitted and what is not. You will also be assigned a room here in the palace for your personal use.'

Well, that didn't sound...onerous.

Anna opened her mouth to tell him it sounded fine, but before she could he said, 'The Reverend Mother heard that I was looking for a companion for my daughter and chose you specifically for this task.' He paused, his gaze raking over her in a way that made Anna distinctly uncomfortable for reasons she couldn't put her finger on. 'Any idea as to why that might be?'

She felt her cheeks heat. 'No.'

One of the king's black brows arrowed skyward. 'No? No idea at all?'

'I… No. I'm not sure.' Her poise, already shaky, began to slip. Because she really had no idea at all why the Reverend Mother had chosen her. She'd been called into her study and given the task, and the Reverend Mother hadn't explained. And Anna hadn't questioned it, too busy trying to prove her obedience.

She had nothing to be ashamed of, so why was she blushing?

'No,' she said more levelly and with greater confidence. 'She didn't tell me and I didn't ask. It wasn't my place. I do as she tells me.'

'I see.' The king's voice was very deep and glazed with ice. 'So nothing at all to do with seducing me into making you my queen?'

The nun's pretty grey eyes went very, very wide.

'I beg your pardon?' she exclaimed, in tones of complete astonishment.

Adonis wasn't a man who repeated himself and he didn't now. He simply stared at her, scanning and assessing her threat level the way he did with everyone he met.

Except the nun—or novice really—didn't pose much of a threat. She wore a plain and unflattering grey dress, her long, pale gold hair coiled in a loose bun at her nape, and she was round and very soft-looking. Her face was pretty, heart-shaped, with a firm chin and those wide eyes the colour of morning fog. Her mouth was a problem, though, full and red and…biteable.

Not that he would be doing any biting. She was a rabbit

who'd wandered into a wolf's den, or perhaps even a quail. Soft and round and far too innocent.

Luckily for her this particular wolf wasn't hungry and hadn't been for years, and even if he had been, he wouldn't have chosen such easy prey.

It was very clear that she had no idea what her interfering Reverend Mother had done. But he did. The Reverend Mother June was his godmother and had been sending him letters ever since his wife had died five years earlier. She'd said they were to 'comfort him in his time of need'. But Adonis didn't need comforting and he didn't need his godmother recommending various women to him as prospects for his next queen. He got far too much of that from his own royal council and their insistence that he take a wife; he didn't need it from one elderly English nun.

Unfortunately, it seemed as if said nun had ignored his gentle but firm commands to mind her own business and had sent him this pretty woman instead.

It was irritating and he was tempted to send her straight back to where she had come from, but if he didn't even grant her an audience, the Reverend Mother would no doubt only send him another sacrificial lamb and he really didn't want an endless procession of novices turning up at his front door.

And there *was* the issue of his daughter, who did, in fact, need a civilising influence.

He opened his mouth to ask her another question about her supposed purpose here when the doors suddenly burst open and a hellion in a blue dress with a plastic breastplate worn over the top, a helmet pressed down over her red curls, and waving a plastic sword came tumbling in.

She screeched to a halt beside the couch, waved the sword threateningly and shouted in Axian, 'Don't move or I'll cut your heads off. Right now!'

The nun's mouth dropped open as she stared at Princess Ione, Lioness of Axios and first in line to the throne.

'Ione,' Adonis growled. 'English, please. And where are your manners?'

His daughter whirled, took in his face, and the sword drooped. 'Sorry, Papa,' she said, switching languages effortlessly and looking contrite. Then she threw her weapon down, came over to the couch, and without even asking climbed into his lap and held a finger up in front of his face. 'My finger hurts. Can you kiss it better?'

She had begun to do this more and more whenever she was in his presence. Reach for his hand. Throw her arms around him. Beg to be picked up. Cry when he told her no and then shout that she hated him, not caring who might be around to note her behaviour.

It was unacceptable. A king was always under threat from enemies and anyone close to him could be a target to be used against him. So he tried to make sure that no one got too close. That had been relatively simple to achieve; he had no close friends anyway and no confidants. No one he trusted. He even kept his younger brother, Prince Xerxes, at arm's length.

Unfortunately, his daughter was too young to understand why this was necessary and why *her* father wasn't the same as other people's, and as she'd grown older she had become needier, and more demanding of him. She wouldn't do what she was told, was wilfully disobedient, had screaming tantrums loud enough to wake the dead, and he'd been forced to come to the conclusion that she needed taking in hand.

He'd hoped not to use the methods his own father had used on him, since they were a blunt instrument at best, and Ione was still too young for that anyway. He'd opted for a...gentler way. A meek, obedient nun, for example.

Whatever the case, Ione needed to learn control, how

to detach herself from her emotions, because a monarch could not be ruled by their heart.

He had learned. So could she.

He ignored her finger just as he ignored the urge to kiss it better. Those fatherly impulses were strong, but he was stronger.

'You cannot sit on me, Ione,' Adonis said, gently putting his daughter back on her feet again. 'How many times must I tell you?'

Ione's jaw got that pugnacious look, which usually heralded a tantrum, so he distracted her. 'This lady is Sister Anna. She might be here to be your friend.'

The tactic worked. Ione forgot her finger and looked over at the little nun. 'Her? But she doesn't even have a sword,' she said, somewhat disdainfully.

At that point, the nun seemed to break out of her paralysis and smiled.

And Adonis felt something inside him flicker, like a spark in a cold, dead hearth.

Because that smile was breathtaking. It lit up her face, turning it from pretty to stunning in seconds flat, those fog-grey eyes glittering with silver fire.

It felt as if the sun had come into the room.

'Hello,' the nun said to his daughter. 'You can call me Anna, if you like. What's your name?'

'Princess Ione,' Ione answered regally.

'What a pretty name. I heard you were a lioness.' The nun leaned forward slightly. 'Can you roar?'

'Yes!' Ione said, suddenly animated. 'Would you like to hear it?'

'Oh, yes, please.'

Ione roared obligingly and very, very loudly.

The nun clapped her hands and looked delighted. 'What a magnificent roar.'

'Ione,' Adonis said firmly, deciding to cut short this particular meeting. 'Please go and find Hesta. Miss Angela will be waiting for you in the schoolroom.'

Hesta was one of Ione's guards and probably responsible for his daughter's sudden interest in weapons. Adonis was not opposed to it, but Ione was still struggling with reading and that, surely, was more important.

'But—' Ione began.

'Now,' Adonis said.

His daughter made a grumpy sound and went disconsolately out through the door.

The nun was still smiling that radiant smile and he had the strangest urge to lift his hands to it, as if it were a fire he could warm himself in front of.

'She's delightful,' the nun said.

'She's a terror,' he disagreed.

Her smile became warmer, the sun shining directly on him. 'I know you wanted to kiss her finger. I hope you didn't stop for my benefit.'

And the spark in the cold, dead hearth of his heart glowed again. He crushed it. No fires could be lit in that fireplace. The only passion a king was permitted was for his country. It was something his father had often said and Adonis agreed.

'You didn't answer my question,' he said expressionlessly.

Sister Anna's lovely smile faltered, and the sun dimmed, as though it went behind a cloud. 'Which particular question?'

'I think you know what I'm talking about.' It was perhaps foolish to push for an answer when it was obvious that she had no idea about the Reverend Mother's real agenda.

Still. He wanted to hear the answer.

She looked away, smoothing her grey dress with her

hands. 'The Reverend Mother said nothing to me about… well, you know. She only said something about a tutor for the princess and that I would be a good fit for the position.' A flush stained her cheekbones, her fingers fussing with the hem of her dress.

It seemed she was uncomfortable with the turn of the conversation, which perversely only made him want to continue it. He couldn't fathom why. He had a great many other things to do that were much more important than making a pretty nun blush.

'I see.' He should end this conversation and dismiss her, yet he didn't. 'So nothing at all about the best way to seduce me, then?'

She flushed an even deeper shade of pink, her fingers furiously pleating the hem of her skirt.

It was wrong of him to tease a woman this innocent. That was more his brother's mode of behaviour—though, now Xerxes had married, he didn't do that so much any more. But the prince was more handsome and possessed far more charm than Adonis ever had. He was…fun. Adonis had never seen the point of fun.

Annoyed with himself, he was about to end the conversation, when suddenly the little nun met his gaze, her eyes full of what looked like temper. 'No, Your Majesty,' she said flatly. 'The Reverend Mother said nothing about seduction and it would be highly improper of her to do so even if she had.' She gave him a severe look. 'Why on earth would you think that's what I'm here for?'

Adonis stared at her in surprise. He was the king. Everyone was afraid of him and he didn't mind that. His entire purpose was to protect his country and put its interests first. He didn't need to be loved or even liked; what he needed was to be obeyed, and if respect didn't make that happen, then he'd settle for fear. He wasn't fussy.

But right now there was neither respect nor fear in the little nun's disconcertingly direct gaze, only offended dignity and outrage.

Another man might have apologised. But kings never apologised and neither did Adonis. In fact, far from prompting shame, the expression on her face instead ignited a small, electric jolt of sensation centred in much lower, baser parts of his body.

'Then what are you here for?' he asked, before he could stop himself.

The little nun drew herself up in her chair, lifting that determined and very firm chin. 'I'm here to help you with the princess,' she said with dignity. 'Just like the Reverend Mother ordered me to.'

'And do you do everything you're ordered to do?'

'Of course.' Her hands rearranged themselves in her lap. 'I shall be taking my vows soon and proving my obedience is one of the tasks I need to undertake before the Reverend Mother gives her approval.'

You could show her how to be obedient.

The thought was instinctive and so unexpected he sat there for a minute in shock at his own response.

He was a man who was in complete control of himself and his environment. A man who didn't suffer from sparks in the dead area of his chest where his heart should be. Or flickers of sexual interest in small, innocent creatures such as the one sitting opposite him. He had his hungers, but they were entirely physical and when his body needed a release he dealt with it either himself, or with a couple of very discreet, experienced women who were happy to see him when he needed them, and just as happy to say goodbye when he left.

So he didn't know why this particular woman, this very innocent *nun,* was making him feel things he did not want to feel. In fact, why she should make him feel anything at all was beyond him.

Detachment was the key to being an effective protector and defender of his country, and so he didn't let anything touch him. His father, King Xenophon, had been a hard and brutal teacher on that specific point, but Adonis had learned. He might once have raged against his father's methods, yet in the end he'd come to see the importance of it.

He felt nothing. And one little novice nun wasn't going to change that.

Ignoring the flickers of interest from his baser self, Adonis said curtly, 'Then you can prove yourself obedient by obeying my order to leave Axios.'

This time it was her turn to stare at him in surprise. 'Excuse me, Your Majesty? Did you—'

'Are you deaf?' he interrupted, suddenly irritated almost into anger at himself and this whole ridiculous situation. 'You will leave Axios by tomorrow morning. Am I clear?'

Shock rippled over her face, swiftly followed by another deep flush.

'I'm sorry if I caused offence, sire.' The spark of anger had vanished from her voice, leaving nothing but contrition. 'I spoke out of turn.'

She was absolutely genuine, of that there was no doubt. And if he'd been a man who felt normal human emotion, he might have felt sorry for her.

But he wasn't and he didn't.

Instead, he pushed himself to his feet. 'Tomorrow morning,' he said flatly.

Then he turned on his heel and left the room.

CHAPTER TWO

ANNA PACED AROUND the little guest room she'd been shown to after her failed audience with the king, anger churning in her gut.

She hated him. He was cold, rude, arrogant, autocratic. And, even though he might have looked as if he was going to kiss his adorable little daughter's finger, he hadn't. Certainly, he had no business accusing her of being here only to seduce him. What absolute rot. She was a novice nun, not a pretty socialite or member of the aristocracy trying for a good marriage.

She wanted to take her vows, not…seduce men.

It was absurd that he'd even considered it. Though now she was curious as to why he'd even think that in the first place. Perhaps the Reverend Mother had sent other novices to him. She hadn't heard of any, though, and anyway, why would the Reverend Mother send her if that was the case?

Sister Caroline was much lovelier than she was and Sister Maria was more refined. There was nothing about Anna to recommend her to a king.

She came to a stop near the door and glared at it.

Now she was to be sent home for absolutely no reason that she could see. Why? Did he not believe her when she said she'd obeyed the Reverend Mother? Or had he been offended by her outburst?

A trickle of shame slid slowly down her back.

She shouldn't have let her annoyance at him get the better of her, especially given it was his daughter's behaviour that he wanted her help with. Not exactly the best example to set. She'd only been shocked by his accusation and offended, if the truth be told. She wasn't a seductress in any way, shape or form.

And you definitely did not think about what it might be like to seduce him...

Anna whirled away from the door, going over to the heavy wooden bed. Her battered suitcase sat on the thick white linen quilt and she flung it open, digging pointlessly around inside it.

No, she hadn't thought about seducing him. She was a novice wanting to take her vows and she'd eschewed earthly pleasures. Not that she had any experience with said earthly pleasures, and not that she'd ever wanted to.

She knew about sex from a biological point of view and had sneaked a few romances from some of the other novices, so she'd learned about passion too. But that hadn't been enough to make her think she wanted a man in her life.

The Reverend Mother had mentioned following a vocation and Anna had decided that her vocation lay in the convent.

She'd grown up with the sisters, having been taken in as a baby after her mother had given birth to her before promptly disappearing. A year earlier Anna had tracked her down, wanting to find out her own history, and initially her mother had been receptive to the emails Anna had sent. Then, inexplicably, had cut off all contact, mentioning another family and a life she didn't want disrupted.

Not so inexplicably.

Perhaps if Anna hadn't indulged her temper and been

impatient when her mother had mentioned old memories being stirred up, that contact wouldn't have been cut off.

But it was too late now. She'd got angry and her mother hadn't contacted her again, and now Anna had added forgiveness to the list of virtues she needed to practise.

It was fine. Her mother had found the contact too difficult, and she was totally within her rights not to want to continue it. Anna didn't need her acceptance to find a home, anyway. She'd found her place with the sisters and that was where she was going to stay.

And she definitely wasn't going to be leaving that for a mere man.

No matter how interesting the man?

Anna shut her case firmly. There were no interesting men. And that included the arrogant, rude king with the ridiculous Christian name.

It felt grossly unfair that he was going to send her away without a reason. What would she tell the Reverend Mother? It had been her rudeness that had caused her dismissal in all likelihood, which wouldn't go down at all well. Especially when everyone knew what a temper she had.

Perhaps the Reverend Mother would even decide not to approve Anna taking her vows, which would be…

A cold feeling twisted in her gut. She would be cast out into the world to find her own way, with no friends and no family. Locked out of the only home she'd ever known.

She couldn't let that happen, she just couldn't. Which meant she'd have to go to this king and ask him for a reason for her dismissal. She deserved that much, didn't she? After coming all the way here? And if she knew the reason, then perhaps she could convince him to let her stay.

Anna stalked over to the door and pulled it open, glancing down the stone corridor. The palace was medieval, with high, vaulted ceilings and narrow stone hallways. There were lights, but it was a place that brought to mind flickering sconces and rushes on the floor, with lots of hounds and burly men in armour milling around.

She walked quickly, confident she'd find someone who'd point her in the right direction. Palaces were generally full of people, after all. They'd no doubt forbid her to see the king, since she supposed a nobody like her wouldn't be granted a second audience. Nevertheless, she was prepared to stand her ground. Even five minutes of his time for an explanation would be enough.

A few palace staff were around, but none of them were forthcoming about where the king was—understandably— but after she'd smiled winningly at one stern-faced guard he mentioned that the king was having some 'sparring' time in the gym.

Anna thanked him and went off down another corridor, pausing to ask another guard where the gym was. It was in a different wing of the palace, involving more corridors and a lot of stairs, and when she got to the doors she was stymied by a couple of guards who scanned her suspiciously.

However, she must have looked unthreatening, because after she gave them both another of those winning smiles and played the nun card one of them agreed to take her into the gym to request a personal audience.

The gym turned out to be a huge stone hall, with state-of-the-art exercise machines and weight benches down one end and a big open space covered by a mat near by. Right in front of her, though, was a boxing ring.

Several people stood around it, leaning on the ropes and watching the two men in the middle of the ring. One was a powerful-looking guard.

The other was the king.

Back in the receiving room, he'd been a still presence, projecting a cold, dominant authority. And apart from that one instant when she thought he might have kissed Ione's finger, there had been no warmth to him. Almost nothing human. As if he was a god to be worshipped, not a man to relate to.

But not here.

Now that he was stripped to the waist, wearing black and gold boxing shorts, boxing gloves on his hands, and circling his opponent, that cold authority was gone. There was nothing but the lethal intent and aggression of a large and very hungry predator.

His olive skin glistened, outlining every single hard, carved muscle of his arms and torso; he looked as if he'd been chiselled out of solid rock. He moved so fluidly, all deadly athletic grace that was mesmerising to watch, and, as he circled around, Anna noticed that he had a tattoo inked across the top of his powerful back: a crowned and prowling lion.

Someone made a soft sound and it couldn't have been her, absolutely not.

She abhorred violence.

Yet she couldn't take her eyes off the king.

Heat rushed into her face and she knew she'd gone scarlet, but she still couldn't look away. The lights of the gym glistened on his skin, and she followed every flex and release of those powerful muscles.

She'd never thought of a man being beautiful before, and when she'd first seen him in the receiving room all she'd been conscious of was his authority and power. But she was thinking it now.

Here, like this, all deadly grace and honed aggression, he was beautiful.

She started towards him, barely conscious of moving, but then the guard beside her said gruffly, 'Stay here, Sister. I'll speak to His Majesty.'

So she paused, her heart thumping as the guard approached the boxing ring. One of the men standing by the ropes held up a hand and the guard stopped.

For a second no one moved, and Anna discovered she was holding her breath.

Then the king abruptly burst into motion: a pivot, a turn, ducking under his opponent's guard, drawing his right fist back and slamming it hard into the other man's jaw. The man dropped like a stone.

Everyone watching cheered while the king went down on one knee beside his opponent's recumbent body and issued a sharp order. One of the watching men jumped into the ring, checking over the stunned man, who finally groaned. The king offered him a hand and pulled him to his feet. The king said something and the man grinned.

Anna's heartbeat was so loud she was certain the entire gym could hear it, and there was a fluttery feeling in her stomach, something like nervousness yet not. It was more similar to excitement, though that was strange, because why would she get excited about a boxing match?

The guard approached the ring and the king put his gloved hands on the ropes, leaning down as the guard said something to him. Then his head came up and he looked straight at Anna.

Electric-blue eyes pierced her right through.

She couldn't breathe. All the air had somehow vanished from her lungs, from the entire room, the sound of her heartbeat the only thing she could hear.

The king straightened, still staring at her. 'Out,' he said. And instantly everyone headed towards the doors.

Anna made as if to go too, in instinctive obedience.

'Not you, Sister,' the king said.

Anna froze.

'Come here,' he ordered as the last person left the gym.

She didn't want to. Something instinctive and very female told her that getting close to him would be a bad idea. But she couldn't disobey a king's command and, since she was the one who'd requested this meeting, she forced herself to move, walking slowly over the stone floor to the ring.

He leaned on the ropes, the lines of abs, biceps and sinews flexing, watching her every step of the way, making her feel like a mouse creeping closer to a huge, hungry cat.

She resented it. Being meek was yet another lesson the Reverend Mother wanted her to learn, a lesson Anna had always struggled with. Yet she tried to think of that lesson now as she went over to the king, her head bowed, resisting the urge to meet his gaze in instinctive rebellion.

He said nothing as she reached the ropes, and she suspected that silence might be a deliberate tactic of his to make people feel uncomfortable.

If so, it certainly wasn't going to work with her.

Despite her best intentions, Anna raised her head, meeting that intense blue gaze.

The force of his will almost flattened her.

'Was I not clear?' the king said finally, in his deep, harsh voice. 'Do you want me to tell you again that I wish you to return to England? I hope not. I'm not accustomed to repeating myself.'

Annoyance arrowed down her spine, and before she could stop herself she'd snapped, 'And I'm not accustomed to being sent away without an explanation like a naughty child.'

A crashing silence fell.

Anna's cheeks, already hot, felt as if they were going to burst into flames.

You idiot. He's the king. You can't snap at him like that.

Slowly, he pushed himself away from the ropes, straightening to his full, impressive height, making her feel very, very small.

'Come here,' he ordered.

Obviously he meant, come into the ring.

Briefly, Anna entertained a fantasy of ignoring him, turning her back and walking out. But that wouldn't get her the explanation she wanted and it certainly wouldn't endear her to the Reverend Mother, so she shoved the fantasy away, found the steps that led to the ring, and tried to get over the ropes in a dignified way. Naturally she failed, ending up clambering awkwardly between them while the king watched her, his arms crossed over his muscled chest.

She was blushing furiously and feeling like an idiot by the time she approached him, both of which made her temper crackle and spit like oil poured into a hot frying pan.

Not good, Anna. Not good.

She had to get herself under control. Especially if she wanted an explanation as to why he was dismissing her, and most especially if she wanted him to change his mind. Because if he needed someone to improve his daughter's behaviour, he was hardly likely to choose a woman who couldn't even manage her own.

She had to set an example.

So she tried to swallow the hot words on her tongue, and tried to project obedience, meekness, and humility as she gave him a curtsey. 'Your Majesty.'

The king's brutal features betrayed nothing. Instead he held out one gloved hand imperiously, palm up. 'Undo the tie, if you please.'

She blinked, realising that he meant the tie of his boxing glove and that of course he couldn't do it himself. But it wasn't until she took a step forward to untie it for him that she understood her mistake.

He was very close, his magnificently muscled and very

bare chest inches away. His olive skin was sheened with perspiration and he smelled of clean male sweat and something sharp and fresh like the sea. It was a very masculine scent and she didn't know why she liked it, but she did.

Her hands shook as she pulled at the tie, the heat coming off him so at odds with the cold air of authority he projected. It disturbed her on some deep level, making her very aware of his height and his power, and how much smaller she was, how vulnerable.

She didn't like it, and yet part of her did. Very much. Which didn't make any sense. What was wrong with her? Why did she suddenly feel like this?

'You have a temper, Sister,' the king said.

Anna, bent over his glove, kept her attention on what she was doing, trying determinedly to ignore his physical presence and its effect on her heartbeat.

You're attracted to him. Not a mystery.

But that was ridiculous. She'd never been attracted to any other man before, so why this one? It was a very bad idea. Especially given who this particular man was.

'I…apologise, Your Majesty,' she said, not feeling particularly apologetic as she tugged on the tie, which appeared to be knotted. 'I spoke out of turn.'

'Yes.' His voice was a deep, vibrating rumble she almost felt in her chest. 'You did. The Reverend Mother chose poorly in sending you. How can you manage my daughter when you cannot even manage yourself?'

It was exactly what she'd been thinking herself, the censure in his tone making her feel as if she were twelve again, hauled into the Reverend Mother's office for yet another transgression, the weight of guilt falling on her at the look of gentle disappointment on the Reverend Mother's face. *'Why can't you be good, Anna? I know you have it in you.'*

And her wondering if she really did have it in her, thinking that maybe she was just born bad...

Anger churned inside her at the memories. Anger at herself and her own behaviour, as well as her lack of control over it. She was supposed to be better. She *had* to be better.

'I'm sorry,' she repeated, tugging harder on the glove, the tie finally coming loose. 'It won't happen again.'

'That's twice now, in the space of a few hours.'

Anna pulled at the ties holding the glove closed with slightly more force than necessary, not trusting herself to speak, because he wasn't wrong. She *had* snapped at him twice. Him. A king.

'I said I was sorry, sire.' She tried to put every ounce of effort she could into sounding as if she meant it, but she had a suspicion that it only sounded sulky.

'Are you?' He lifted the glove and jerked it off his hand with his teeth, discarding it on the floor of the ring. 'You don't look very sorry to me.'

That flutter deep inside her sparked to life again and she couldn't for the life of her imagine why. Because he was standing there, huge and muscular, intensely masculine, power in every line of him, a very clear and physical threat. And she should be afraid of him, or at least intimidated, yet she wasn't.

Deciding that honesty was the best policy and, since she couldn't pretend, she said, 'You're right. I'm not sorry. I'm angry. I don't like being accused of seducing men I've never even met before.' She lifted her chin. 'Need I remind you that I am a novice, who'll be taking her vows imminently?'

Something glittered in the ice of his blue eyes.

'Not quite as biddable as you would appear, are you?' His intent stare made the fire in her cheeks burn hot. 'Is that why you forced your way in here? To chastise me?'

'I didn't force my way in and no, I'm not here to ch-

chastise you.' She wasn't sure why she stumbled over the word, yet charged on anyway. 'I only wanted a reason for you sending me away. The Reverend Mother will be very upset with me if I come back only a day or two after being sent here, and she'll want to know why.'

He lifted one powerful shoulder and glanced away, pulling on the tie of his other glove. 'That's not my problem.'

Anna was suddenly very tempted to kick this irritating king in the shins. 'Actually, sire, it's very much your problem. Especially since I came here in good faith.'

This time the ice in his eyes had melted, blue sparks flicking in the depths. 'Then perhaps you should talk to my dear godmother about meddling in affairs that don't concern her.'

'What affairs?'

'She wants me to remarry.' He bared his teeth in what looked like a smile but was far too feral to be one. 'And, since I have rebuffed her every suggestion, she's now taking the direct approach. With you.'

Anna blinked, the words not making any sense. 'Me?'

'Yes, you.' The king tore the other glove off and cast it on the floor, flexing one strong, long-fingered hand. 'You're round and soft and sweet. Just the kind of woman who would appeal to me.'

She stared, conscious that she was gaping at him yet unable to stop herself.

His gaze became electric. 'Perhaps you should try some seduction, little nun. We wouldn't want to upset the Reverend Mother, now, would we?'

Adonis knew he shouldn't have said it, but the adrenaline high from the workout he'd just had was still coursing through him, and there was something about Sister Anna

Fleetwood that got under his skin, that made those flickers of interest he'd felt earlier flare into sparks.

Sparks that could become flames if you're not careful.

But he was always careful. Yet there she was, after elbowing her way into his private workout space, looking up at him all shocked, her cheeks flushed, her gaze gone silvery as it dropped to his chest then back up to his face again, telegraphing loud and clear that she was not as nunlike as she made out.

Innocent, yes.

Immune to him, no.

It was a dangerous thing for him to notice, especially after one of his regular workouts, where he burned off excess anger and aggression in the boxing ring. And most especially when the adrenaline rush made him more susceptible than he'd normally be to physical chemistry.

Which meant he shouldn't be goading her.

Another, more experienced, woman would understand what was going on, but it was plain the nun did not.

'Wh-what do you mean?' she stammered, making that even more obvious.

What are you doing? Since when do you let innocents like this one get to you?

He never did. Sophia, his late, long-suffering wife, hadn't been an innocent and he'd thought she'd known exactly what she was getting into when she married him. He'd told her from the outset that their marriage would be one of necessity only, that love would not be part of it, and she'd assured him that, as she didn't love him, she didn't need it. But then she *had* fallen in love with him, and had been unhappy and hurt when she hadn't got love in return. He didn't want to put another woman through that. He had his heir already, and, now that his brother was married and producing children of his own, Adonis didn't need another wife.

A lover was a different matter, but he wouldn't choose someone like Anna Fleetwood to be his lover anyway. She was too young, too innocent, too soft. She was also a novice nun and under the protection of his godmother, which made her untouchable.

'Never mind,' he said curtly, turning away and stalking over to where his trainer had left a towel hanging over the ropes. He picked it up and used it to wipe his face, before draping it over the back of his neck. 'I don't care what you tell the Reverend Mother when you get back to England. Tell her anything you like.' He paused and turned around to face her. 'But you will be going.'

He couldn't have her here, not when it was plain she was going to be completely unsuitable for Ione anyway. He'd been hoping for meek, biddable, and self-contained, a good example for his daughter to follow, not argumentative, rebellious, and emotionally volatile.

Plus, he didn't want the Reverend Mother thinking she could keep sending him women on the off-chance he'd want to make one of them his wife. He'd already told her he wasn't going to marry again, so why she thought she could change his mind, he had no idea.

The nun frowned, her arms crossed over what he couldn't help but notice were full, generous breasts. Her cheeks were still bright red and her gaze kept dropping to his chest. It made her frown even more ferocious.

'I assure you, Your Majesty, that you are in no danger of being s-seduced by me,' she said very firmly. 'I have no interest in that…kind of thing.'

The way she was staring at him would seem to indicate otherwise, but he couldn't afford to be thinking about that either. What he should be thinking about was perhaps sending a message to Susannah, an American woman he sometimes spent time with, and working out any physical urges with her. She didn't require anything but sex, at least.

'Glad to hear it,' he growled. 'But I'm not changing my mind.'

'What about your daughter?' she shot back, undeterred. 'Who will help you with her? It's clear you do need some-one.'

'And you think you're the best person to curtail my daughter's behaviour?' He raised an eyebrow. 'After your own ill-considered outbursts?

She flushed. 'I know it may not seem like it, but I can manage myself. Or is there something else about me that offends you?'

Sneaky little nun. Not only had she lost any respect she might have had for his position, but she was also poking at him in a way she definitely shouldn't. A way that might prompt him to tell her explicitly what offended him about her. Or perhaps even show her...

No. Control yourself.

He gripped the ends of the towel in his hands, forcing down the burn of adrenaline. 'Are you sure you want me to do that? You might not like what I have to say.'

She gave him a challenging look. 'Give me two weeks, Your Majesty. Two weeks to prove that I'm the best per-son for the job. And if your daughter's behaviour hasn't improved I'll leave, just like you told me to.'

His instinct was to refuse, because once he gave an order he never rescinded it. Then again, his daughter needed someone, and urgently. And insisting on Anna's leaving would be tantamount to admitting that she had got to him, and he couldn't do that either.

She was one little nun. How could a nun—a novice nun at that—have any effect on the years of detachment he'd perfected? She couldn't, so why not let her stay for two weeks? It wasn't long. Enough time to test whether or not she had what it took to manage Ione and her demanding behaviour.

Sister Anna certainly had a few issues with authority that he didn't approve of, then again she was here already, and finding someone else would take time. If nothing else, he could use it as a chance to prove that she meant absolutely nothing to him.

He eyed her, not agreeing just yet. 'Is taking your vows really worth crossing swords with me, little nun?'

Why are you thinking about her vows?

He had no idea.

She lifted one fair brow. 'I don't know. What's wearing a crown worth to you?'

A fair comment, and clearly time to leave.

'Very well,' he said. 'I shall expect a report every evening on Ione's progress and if her behaviour hasn't improved in two weeks' time then you're going back to England with no argument.' He fixed her with a very level stare. 'Is that clear?'

'Yes, sire,' she said meekly enough.

But he didn't miss the tiny spark that lit in her eyes.

He pretended not to notice.

CHAPTER THREE

ANNA BENT OVER her suitcase and dug through the limited items of clothing she'd brought with her, though what she was looking for she didn't know. She hadn't packed much, since she didn't have much and clothing had never been important to her, so why she wished she had something more than a couple of plain dresses in her suitcase, she couldn't fathom.

Tonight was her first meeting with the king to give her report on Ione and she wanted to wear something…different. For inexplicable reasons.

Perhaps it was nerves. She desperately hadn't wanted to return to England and him granting her two weeks to make some difference to Ione's behaviour had been a concession she hadn't been expecting. She'd argued for it, of course, but he'd been so adamant it had felt like hurling herself at a stone wall and expecting it to break.

Snapping at him had been a mistake, but all that seduction talk had irritated her.

It wasn't irritation you were feeling.

Anna scowled at the contents of her suitcase, not liking that thought one bit. She'd tried to ignore her own physical reaction to him, to ignore that he was half-naked, but then he'd started talking about how the Reverend Mother was meddling in his affairs—affairs apparently including her being sent to seduce him.

'You're round and soft and sweet. Just the kind of woman who would appeal to me.'

Heat crept through her, the way it had done all day whenever she'd thought of him saying those words, which she'd tried very hard *not* to do. Because they made her feel... strange.

He'd called her round, but it was obvious he hadn't meant it in a bad way. In fact, the opposite. *Just the kind of woman who would appeal to me...*

She felt even stranger when she thought about that; appealing to him had never occurred to her. In fact, appealing to anyone at all had never occurred to her. The sisters always discouraged such vanity. Some of the younger ones had giggled a bit over one of the better-looking priests, but Anna herself had never thought about men or her own desirability. Once or twice she'd wondered whether she might like a husband and a family, but then had dismissed the idea. Romantic relationships had seemed fraught and dangerous to her, while the relationships she had with the sisters at the convent were much less complicated. There were clear rules for behaviour and you didn't have to fit yourself around another person's needs and wants.

It was less exciting maybe, but at least life at the convent was a known quantity. At least, she fitted there better than she fitted anywhere else.

You still liked the fact that you appealed to him.

Anna scowled and pulled a dress out from the depths of her case. It was fancier than her other dresses, in a silky ice-blue fabric with a demure scooped neckline and capped sleeves. The colour was pretty on her—or at least that was what Sister Mary Alice had told her, and Sister Mary Alice was known to have good taste.

She didn't like that she appealed to him. Not at all. Round and soft and sweet, indeed. It made her sound pathetic and ineffectual and she didn't much appreciate that. Nor did she appreciate that the Reverend Mother had perhaps had an ulterior motive for sending her here, either. Certainly, she'd never mentioned seduction to Anna.

Not that she should be concerning herself with such things. The Reverend Mother clearly had a purpose in sending her here and it wasn't up to Anna to wonder at it. She had to trust that the Reverend Mother knew what she was doing.

Still, as she put the dress on, Anna found herself glancing in the full-length mirror at the foot of the bed and noticing that her breasts and hips and thighs were all soft and gently rounded.

Just the kind of woman who would appeal to me...

She pulled down the dress hurriedly and smoothed the fabric, ignoring the unexpected glow of warmth inside her. No, she didn't want to like that she appealed to him. Because, no matter what either the king or the Reverend Mother thought, she was here for Ione. And to show her obedience so she could take her vows.

Two weeks he'd allowed her. Two weeks to prove herself and hopefully not get sent home. It wasn't much time in which to gain the trust of a child, let alone modify her own behaviour.

She'd made a start, though. Since she didn't know Ione and Ione didn't know her, Anna had decided to spend a couple of days on some getting-to-know-you activities. Today Anna had chosen drawing in the library for a nice, quiet activity that would allow some space to talk.

However, Ione hadn't been very interested in drawing— or, at least, not until Anna had had a brainwave and, remembering the girl's sword of the day before, had suggested drawing a knight fighting a dragon. That had gone very well until Ione had insisted on performing said fight and had knocked over a lamp that had been sitting on the table.

The little girl was a live wire, reminding Anna uncomfortably of herself when she'd been that age. It also made her wonder if some of the girl's boisterousness came from a lack of attention. She remembered feeling alone, as if she didn't fit in. There had been other children in the foster home run by the nuns and she'd made a few friends, but they never stayed very long, many of the other children having found homes.

But not Anna. No one had wanted to adopt her. And no wonder, since she'd always been over-loud, over-eager, over-friendly. Like a puppy, one of the sisters had said.

Perhaps that was the issue with Ione. Perhaps the little girl was lonely. It was something to raise with the king anyway.

She was sticking another pin into her bun when there was a knock on her door from a guard waiting outside to escort her to the king for her meeting.

Anna hadn't seen him since the day before, and as she followed the guard down the echoing stone corridors of the palace her pulse started to gather speed and her palms got sweaty, nervousness gathering inside her. All she could think about was him in the ring, moving fluidly around his opponent, the flex and release of hard muscle beneath olive skin, the way he'd stared at her, blue eyes piercing her…

Silly. She was silly. She wasn't a lovesick teenage girl and he wasn't a handsome teenage boy. He was a king, for goodness' sake.

The guard stopped in front of a heavy wooden door and Anna tried to moisten her dry mouth as he knocked and waited for admittance. The king's harsh voice called for them to enter, and then the door opened and she was ushered inside.

It was a large room with a stone floor and once again, like the whole palace, it seemed, the walls were of bare stone. Heavy wooden bookshelves stood against them, stacked with expensive-looking leather-bound books, while a massive wooden desk sat under one window. There was also a cavernous fireplace—unlit—with yet more heavy furniture in the form of a couch and an armchair arranged around it. Lamps were positioned at strategic points, giving the room a soft, diffused light, the bare stone softened with silk rugs on the floor and yet more dusty tapestries on the walls. The only concession to modernity seemed to be the sleek, paper-thin computer screen that sat on top of the huge desk.

The king himself was sitting behind the desk, looking at said screen, and for a second he looked so incongruous that Anna could only stare. She could imagine him on the battlefield wielding a sword, had literally seen him in the boxing ring throwing punches. But for some reason his sitting at a desk, frowning ferociously at a computer screen like an office worker, seemed...wrong somehow.

Then again, he sat in his office chair as if it were a throne, his authority and power a physical force radiating from him. His white business shirt was undone at the throat, the sleeves rolled up on his sinewy forearms, exposing his olive skin, and if he looked like anything at all, it was a *Fortune 500* CEO hard at work.

He didn't glance up as she entered the room and she was left to stand there awkwardly as the guard withdrew, closing the door behind him. The king frowned at the computer then hit a few keys, giving no hint that he was aware of her, which annoyed her intensely.

How did he do that? How did he make her feel as if she

were once again the disobedient child sent to the Reverend Mother for punishment? She resented it, especially now that she was a grown woman and had left the disobedient child in her behind a long time ago.

Have you, though?

Anna bit her lip, forcing that thought away. True, she hadn't exactly been a model of good behaviour since she arrived in Axios, but she had far more control over herself than she had used to. Plus, she'd learned from her mistakes. She wouldn't let her irritation or impatience get to her. She would be calm and poised and obedient.

She managed to stand there without fidgeting for what she was sure was a good ten minutes before he finally looked up from the screen. She'd braced herself, yet still the impact of his sharp, cold gaze was enough to make her catch her breath.

'You may approach,' he said curtly.

Anna went over to the desk and stopped in front of it, clasping her hands together in front of her. He'd focused on her very intently, and she found herself blushing again.

You appeal to him.

Oh, but she didn't want that in her head, not with him staring at her like that, making a deep part of her shiver. And it definitely wasn't because she was cold.

He said nothing and the tension that she'd felt the day before in the gym coiled around them. It made her uncomfortable, so she opened her mouth to say something, anything, but he forestalled her.

'My daughter broke a lamp in the library today.' His blue gaze was so sharp it was a wonder he hadn't drawn blood. 'You wouldn't happen to know anything about that, would you?'

Anna took a slow, silent breath. She'd known that would

get back to him and she'd hoped it wouldn't annoy him. Sadly, that didn't seem to be the case.

'Oh, yes,' she said. 'I was, of course, going to mention that.'

'Were you indeed? Explain.'

There was a hard note in his harsh voice that made her bristle and she wasn't sure what it was about this man that got under her skin so badly, because it didn't make any sense. She behaved herself with the Reverend Mother and the other sisters; what was it about this king that made her want to push back at him?

'I thought it would be a good idea if we got to know each other first,' she said, holding on to her poise. 'So we did some drawing in the library. She wasn't much interested until I suggested she draw a knight fighting a dragon. And then she decided to re-enact it and, well…she got a little carried away.'

The king's expression could have been carved out of granite. 'You're supposed to manage her behaviour.'

Anna tried to ignore her irritation at his curt manner. She didn't expect him to be friendly—it was clear from the two times she'd been in his presence before that friendly was the last thing he was—but he didn't need to be quite so rude.

'It's the first day,' she said, attempting calm. 'I needed to get to know her and she needed to get to know me.'

He said nothing, his gaze sharp as a knife.

'She's high-spirited,' Anna felt compelled to add. 'And if you ask me, she's probably also a little neglected.'

Instantly, the king's demeanour changed, the lines of his face hardening even more, his big, powerful body tensing. Deep in his icy blue eyes, real anger glowed.

'Be careful.' His deep voice vibrated with an edge of warning. 'Be very careful what you say about my daughter.'

Anna flushed, realising belatedly how she'd sounded. 'I

don't mean she's neglected physically,' she said hurriedly. 'What I meant was that she might be acting up to get attention.'

The king's expression didn't soften. 'And you came to this conclusion how? Based on what? Your thorough and extensive knowledge of my daughter?'

Sarcasm edged every word, making her flush even deeper. She was digging herself a hole, and if she wasn't careful it would get so deep she wouldn't be able to climb out of it.

And then he'll send you home.

No. That was not going to happen.

She met his gaze with equanimity. 'No. Based on my own experience as a very lonely child.'

Adonis didn't want to ask her. He wasn't interested in her or her childhood. But she was standing in front of his desk, wearing a sweet little dress of pale blue that wasn't at all like the plain grey dress of the day before. The colour was lovely on her, highlighting her creamy skin and giving her grey eyes a blue tinge. But that wasn't the worst part. The worst part was that, though the dress had a very demure neckline, it hugged the curves of her breasts and moulded deliciously to her hips, before flaring outward in a silky-looking skirt. It was a cheap dress, yet it also highlighted the fact that this little nun had the most beautiful, womanly body.

Not that it was merely her body he found appealing. If only it had been, because then he wouldn't have had any issues. Lust could be controlled easily enough. No, it was the intriguing fire in her that added to his fascination. The hint of a rebellious spirit. It shouldn't attract him, since it was the antithesis of what he believed in himself, but he'd always liked a strong woman. And, for all that she seemed so sweet and innocent, there was more backbone to her than he'd first thought.

She definitely wasn't a quail or a rabbit, which made her a problem.

Ever since yesterday, when she'd demanded that he change his mind about sending her away, he hadn't been able to get her out of his head. All he'd thought about was that spark in her eyes as she'd snapped at him, the flush to her cheeks as he'd talked about seduction. The way she hadn't been able to stop looking at his body…

It had been inconvenient. He'd tried to busy himself with other things, but she'd remained stuck in his thoughts like a song that kept playing over and over again. He hadn't had a woman occupy so much of his thinking before and it was clear he was going to have to take steps to resolve the issue.

Perhaps telling her to meet with you every night was a mistake.

Perhaps, but the thought of not being able to stand even ten minutes of her company without being bothered was ludicrous.

Yet he was bothered now, irritated by his body's response to her and annoyed by her suggestion that Ione had been neglected. He shouldn't let either of those things touch him, but they did.

Ione was *not* neglected. She had everything a child could possibly need, and if she was acting up to get attention, then she needed to learn that was not acceptable. Immediately.

Adonis stared hard at the woman standing on the other side of his desk. A lonely childhood… He didn't care. His mother had been killed at the hands of enemies of the crown when he was seven, causing his father to start down the road of teaching Adonis about the importance of detachment. Lessons that had involved making him listen to his little brother's torture.

It had been a hard childhood but a necessary one. Loneliness, in comparison, was a walk in the park.

'Is that so?' he said, which wasn't what he'd meant to say at all.

'Yes.' She lifted her determined chin as if she was facing him down over something that really mattered instead of something as insignificant as a childhood long gone. 'My mother gave me up when I was a baby and I was brought up in a foster home run by the nuns. They weren't cruel or abusive, but they weren't exactly warm either. And they didn't much approve of high spirits or emotional outbursts.'

She said it very matter-of-factly, though there was a faint note of something else in her voice, something he couldn't immediately identify.

He sat back in his chair slowly, looking at her. He didn't care. He wasn't interested. Yet somehow his mind started down a track he didn't want it to, wondering how she'd come to be at the convent and whether she was a woman looking for an escape from modern life or following a family tradition. But neither of those things apparently; she said she'd been given up for fostering…

His detachment was perfect. His emotions were completely under his control. If he didn't want to feel anything, he didn't, and so there should have been no reason for a strange, unidentified feeling to coil in his chest. No reason for questions to suddenly occur to him, such as why she hadn't been wanted, and whether she'd been adopted at last. But no, she hadn't been adopted. If she'd been brought up by the nuns and was hoping to take her vows, then it was likely she'd remained in the foster home…

Why are you thinking these things?

It was a good question, especially when it made the unidentified sensation in his chest coil tighter.

He ignored it, annoyed at being made to feel anything at all. 'And? You have a point to this?'

'Of course I have a point.' She frowned. 'I don't give people I don't know well personal information about my childhood for the fun of it.'

You have offended her.

So? What did it matter? He didn't care about his own feelings, still less other people's. A king was supposed to rule with his head, not his heart.

Then again, offending people needlessly wasn't diplomatic. Perhaps he should have got Xerxes to handle these interviews, since his brother was a lot more charming than he was.

If you can't deal with one small novice, perhaps your detachment isn't as perfect as you thought.

A cold sensation wound through him. No, he would not accept that. His father's lessons had been brutal ones, but he'd learned them. Emotions in a ruler were a threat and one he couldn't afford.

He had to do better.

'Continue.' He made an effort to keep the harshness of his temper from his voice.

She gave him a suspicious look then went on, 'As I was saying, the nuns were distant and not particularly loving, and I felt lonely. As a consequence, I got into trouble quite a lot, since being disobedient got me more attention than sticking to the rules.'

That was probably the least surprising thing she'd said all evening. Especially given that rebellious spark that showed in her eyes. In fact, he could just imagine her in a strict foster home, racing around with flushed cheeks and a loud voice, arguing with the nuns and perhaps stamping her foot...

Warmth curled through him, a warmth he didn't recognise. The same kind of warmth that had touched him when she'd smiled at him the day before. A spark flickering in the dead hearth of his heart.

He let it die. 'So you're saying my daughter is acting up to get attention?'

'Yes, that's exactly what I'm saying.'

'An interesting theory, but you're wrong.' He sat forward again, glancing down at the screen so he wouldn't have to look at her face, wouldn't feel the tug of curiosity that pulled at him, making him want to ask her more about how the nuns had treated her, why she'd felt so lonely, and more about the ways in which she'd been disobedient.

You could get her to be disobedient. Very disobedient...

'My daughter gets plenty of attention,' he went on, shoving that particular thought aside. 'She has many people who give her nothing but attention day in and day out. She's—'

'I believe she needs attention from you.'

Adonis blinked at his computer screen. This was the second time in as many days that she'd interrupted him.

Then what she'd actually said penetrated.

Attention from him.

You can't give it.

No. At least not the kind of attention he thought Anna probably meant. He was not that kind of father. He was a king first and foremost, and everything else came second. Even his daughter. Already, he'd noticed that Ione was too much like he had been as a child. Wild and rowdy and demanding, her emotions all over the place, and he knew where that led. He had to make sure she didn't make the same mistakes he had.

Attention wouldn't cure that, only discipline could.

Adonis pushed his chair back and stood up, staring down at the little nun on the other side of his desk, knowing he was being deliberately intimidating and not caring.

He would not have his decisions questioned, and certainly not by her. If she needed a lesson in respect, he would deliver one.

Her eyes widened as he stood, but she didn't lower her gaze. Didn't lower that insolent little chin either. She stood her ground, watching him as he stalked around the side of his desk, coming over to her and staring down at her from his far greater height.

'I suggest, Sister Anna, that you remember your place.' He didn't bother to soften his voice this time. 'If I wanted your opinions on how I parent my child then I would ask for them. But I do not. Seeing as how you are a childless, sheltered nun, I fail to see why you would think your opinions should matter to anyone at all.'

A dull flush crept over her cheeks, her lovely mouth hardening, the pulse at the base of her throat beating fast. He thought she might turn around and run away weeping, since that had been his late wife's response when he'd had occasion to lay down the law. Sophia had never been able to handle his coldness.

But Anna didn't burst into tears or run away. It was likely he'd hurt her, and if so then good, because she had to understand who she was dealing with. But he was also sure that the spark of pure silver that lit up in her gaze wasn't only hurt. It was temper as well.

Dangerous.

No, it wasn't dangerous. He wasn't in the gym now; this was his office and he was in perfect control of himself, regardless of their chemistry.

She opened her mouth as if to speak, then shut it again, her hands at her sides and clenched into fists. It was clear that she was struggling with her temper. Taking a deep breath, the fabric of her dress pulling tight across those lovely breasts, she said, 'I'm not questioning your parenting decisions, and I'm sorry if it came across as if I were. But you wanted me to report every evening on the progress Ione is making and so here I am, giving you a report.'

Interesting that she'd managed to keep herself under control. Perversely, it made him want to push her harder, to test her mettle. She smelled of lavender, a prosaic, homey kind of scent, with something a little sweeter and muskier beneath it, and he found he didn't have it in him to step away just yet.

'A report is a factual account of the day's events, not your very under-qualified opinion,' he said implacably, watching the temper ebbing and flowing across her pretty face.

The spark in her eyes glowed hotter. 'I'm well aware of my lack of qualifications. You don't need to remind me. But I only want to do what's right for your daughter.'

She should back down, she really should. There could be no good outcome from standing up to him like this.

But you like it.

A part of him did. A part of him liked how she didn't back away, fascinated by the stubborn lift of her chin and the spark in her eyes.

He'd once felt things the way she did, deeply and passionately. But it was so long ago now, he barely remembered it.

'I know what's right for my daughter.' He held her gaze. 'Because I'm her father. You're a person she spent a couple of hours with and that's all.'

The flush in her cheeks became scarlet. 'You wanted me to help her and that's exactly what I'm doing. It's not my fault you don't like what I'm telling you.'

He shouldn't get any closer, but somehow he'd taken another step forward anyway, close enough to feel the heat her curvy little body was throwing out, see the lighter flecks in her eyes, making it seem as if they were shimmering.

Was she deliberately inciting him? It certainly felt like it. He'd told her to give him some respect twice now, and yet here she was, still talking back, having not listened to a thing he said. She hadn't learned her lesson. She hadn't learned it at all.

Why do you care whether she learns it or not? Isn't your control supposed to be perfect?

It was. But his patience wasn't limitless and everyone had a line. And she was innocent. She wouldn't understand what this kind of pushing did to a man like him. The man behind the king.

He hadn't thought of that man for a long, long time. He thought he'd crushed the remaining shreds of him the day Xerxes had been banished from Axios, the last vestiges of the selfish, out-of-control child he'd once been, who hadn't listened to what his father was trying to teach him. The rebellious teenager whose refusal to learn had got his brother hurt.

There shouldn't have been anything left of that man at all now.

Apparently, though, he was wrong. The man wasn't as dead as he'd first thought. He was still there and hungry for what he couldn't ever allow himself to have.

A pretty, sweet, innocent woman.

Then again, she wasn't so sweet, was she? She had a bite to her and he liked that. He liked that far too much.

'You'd better be careful what you say to me,' he murmured. 'I like a fight, little nun. And if you challenge me, I will answer it.'

Her jaw tightened. She looked furious. 'I'm just trying to—'

But Adonis had had enough. He lifted a hand and laid

his finger across that pretty mouth. 'The hole you're in is getting deeper by the second. I suggest you stop digging.'

Her lips were soft against his skin and very warm, and her eyes had widened. It was a mistake to touch her and he knew that, but she wasn't listening to him and he had to get her to stop somehow.

Better a finger over her lips than his own mouth, which was what he wanted to put there.

Shock flickered over her face, the pulse at the base of her throat beating even faster.

He took his finger away, the warmth of her mouth lingering on his skin. 'Have you finished?'

'Yes.' Her voice was thick and slightly unsteady.

'Then you may go.'

Her throat moved and for a second she stared at him as if she'd never seen him before in her entire life. Then she turned abruptly and walked to the door, flung it open, and went out.

And he was not disappointed about that. Not disappointed at all.

CHAPTER FOUR

ANNA PULLED THE ice-blue dress over her head again and smoothed it down once more. Then she took a breath and tried to calm herself. Her heartbeat was thumping loudly in her ears and the nervous flutter in her gut that happened whenever she thought of the king was fluttering even harder.

She didn't want to check her appearance in the mirror, because she wasn't supposed to care what she looked like. It wasn't supposed to matter that she was wearing the same dress for the second night in a row. Her clothing was unimportant.

What was important was that the afternoon she'd spent with Ione had gone well—or, at least, nothing had ended up being broken. She'd asked Ione to take her on a tour of the palace, chatting to the little girl as they went, and it soon became obvious that Ione worshipped her father. It was all 'Papa said this' and 'Papa said that'. But it was also plain that Papa was always very busy and didn't spend much time with his daughter.

Anna understood—a king was very busy. But she did wonder why it was that he couldn't take a couple of moments out of his day to chat to her, hug her, give her some praise, because it was clear that Ione was crying out for it.

She was a bright, sparky, emotional kid who was plainly

lonely. And Anna knew how that felt. How it was possible to be surrounded by people all the time and yet still feel as if you were on your own.

It didn't help that after a bit of investigation, Anna discovered that the little girl had no friends her own age. Puzzled, she'd questioned the nanny about it, and the nanny had explained that the lack of friends was a security issue. Ione was the king's only heir and he protected her zealously.

The thought of Ione's loneliness made Anna's own heart sore and it cemented her decision to do what she could to help the little girl.

She thought about taking Ione into Itheus for ice cream, but after looking at the list of things she wasn't permitted to do, Anna soon realised that the princess wasn't allowed out of the palace without a contingent of guards in attendance, which severely limited her plans.

In fact, there seemed to be many things Ione wasn't permitted to do and Anna couldn't help wondering if those rules were all really necessary. She was such a sparky, intelligent kid and it was likely some of her behavioural issues weren't all to do with loneliness, but had a bit of boredom mixed in there as well.

Anna touched her hair nervously. Given how the king had reacted the night before, she was reluctant to bring these issues to his attention, but if she didn't speak up for Ione, then who would?

'I know what's right for Ione. I'm her father. You're a person she spent a couple of hours with, nothing more...'

A flare of volatile anger licked up inside her, but she fought it down. She couldn't lose her temper again the way she had the day before. She couldn't let the king get to her, no matter how rude or dismissive he was. She'd overstepped the mark and badly and he'd...

The memory of his finger on her mouth washed over

her, the heat of his skin like a brand, and even now, nearly a whole day later, she could still feel the imprint of it against her lips. She'd never been touched by a man before anywhere, let alone on her mouth, and, since she had no idea how to handle it, she'd solved the issue by not thinking about it at all.

Except she couldn't help but think of it now, of him standing so close, towering like a mountain over her. She'd never been that close to a man before either and maybe she should have been afraid, because he'd made her suddenly aware of how much bigger he was than her and how much more powerful. Yet it hadn't been fear that had gripped her but anger. She'd been furious at him for dismissing her and what she had to say as if it didn't matter. As if he hadn't been the one to order her to report to him every night on his daughter's progress.

She might have been the one insisting on staying in Axios, but he'd wanted her to help with his daughter's behaviour and so she would. It was important. And spending more time with Ione only made her realise just how important.

The king had certain…thoughts about his role as a father, clearly, which being a king exacerbated. He certainly didn't like being told he was neglectful—which she hadn't meant at all—but she seemed to have hit a nerve when she'd mentioned that perhaps what Ione needed was his attention.

She'd have to go carefully and stay calm if she was going to tackle this.

And definitely do not think about him touching your mouth.

No, most especially not that.

The guard knocked on schedule and Anna gave her dress one last smooth down before following him along the echoing palace corridors to the king's office once again.

This time the king was in a meeting and Anna had to wait in the corridor outside until finally a group of people came out of the room, talking amongst themselves.

The king was standing in the middle of the room, looking down at a piece of paper he held in one hand and frowning at it. He wore plain, dark grey suit trousers and a dark blue shirt open at the neck, and again the sleeves were rolled up.

His roughly handsome blunt features were set in their usual granite lines, betraying absolutely nothing, and his posture was imposing, those broad shoulders giving no sign of weariness. Yet…she couldn't shake the impression that he was…tired somehow.

Perhaps she didn't need to bring her thoughts about Ione to him tonight. Perhaps she should just give him what he'd requested—a factual account of events—and leave it at that.

'Enter,' he said, not looking up as she came into the room.

The guard closed the door and silence descended as the king continued to read whatever was on that piece of paper.

Anna looked around, noticing that on the low table near the couch some refreshments had been laid out. Cheeses and olives and various different breads. A bottle of white wine, condensation beading the green glass, was standing next to the food, along with some glasses. It all looked untouched; obviously the meeting had been a serious one with no time for relaxation.

Without thinking, she went over to the coffee table, poured out a glass of the wine and came over to where he stood.

'Here,' she said, holding out the glass to him. 'You look like you could do with this.'

He looked up, surprise crossing his features as he glanced at the wine in her hand then back at her again. For a second she thought he might refuse, but then he reached for the glass and took it from her. 'Thank you.' His blue gaze was customarily sharp and cold, and she felt again the burn of his touch on her lips, sensitising her mouth and making her breath catch.

No, she shouldn't be thinking of that. Shouldn't be thinking about what he'd meant when he'd told her how he liked a fight. How if she challenged him he'd accept it. What would it mean to fight him? She didn't imagine he meant actual fighting and, given that there had been something flickering in the depths of his icy blue gaze, he'd probably meant...

You know what it means.

Heat stole through her and her skin prickled. She shouldn't be thinking about this, about *any* of this. She was here for Ione, first of all, and to do her duty to the Reverend Mother, second. She couldn't allow herself to be sidetracked by inappropriate thoughts.

'What was that for?' the king asked.

'The wine?' She lifted a shoulder. 'You looked like you needed it.'

His gaze narrowed, but he didn't say anything else, raising the glass to his lips and taking a sip. 'Your report, please.'

It looked as if he was in no mood for chit-chat, which was fine. It was probably a good idea not to spend too much time in his company anyway.

Anna straightened and gave him a brief rundown on what she and Ione had done. 'Nothing got broken today at least,' she said as she finished up. 'And tomorrow I'd like to take her into Itheus for some ice cream and maybe a visit to a playground.'

'I see.' The king looked down at his paper again, sipping absently at his glass of wine.

Anna briefly tossed up whether to mention she wanted

to take Ione without her usual phalanx of guards or whether to tackle that issue tomorrow. Then again, if she wanted to take Ione without the guards, she'd need the king's approval and she might not be able to get it in time if she waited. She might as well ask him now, while he was here.

'I was thinking,' she began hesitantly, 'that it would be good to take her without a guard detail. Or at least not one so large.'

The king didn't even look up. 'No.'

Anna was conscious of the kick of her temper and firmed her grip on it. 'It wouldn't be for long,' she tried again. 'Just for an hour—'

'What part of no don't you understand?' He looked up from his paper, an icy glitter in his eyes. 'Ione will go nowhere without her guards.'

Last night his curt dismissal had irritated her unreasonably. Tonight though, for some reason, it didn't annoy her quite as much and she wasn't sure why. Perhaps it was because she sensed that there was something deeper going on here. He was tired, she knew that, and she could also sense his distraction. He clearly had a lot on his mind.

He was so hard and so powerful and so cold, and it was easy to assume that as a king he was somehow superhuman. He certainly looked it. Yet he wasn't. He was just a man, just a human being as she was.

'Is something wrong?' she asked before she could think better of it.

Surprise flickered across his features and then was gone. 'No. What makes you say that?'

'You just look…tired.'

He said nothing for a moment, then abruptly turned and went over to his desk, putting the wine and the paper he'd been holding down on it. 'It's none of your concern. Is that all?'

His posture was very tense and she had the strangest impulse to go over to him and put a hand on his back, to ease the stiffness from him. It was very odd to feel such sympathy for him. Especially considering how arrogant and autocratic he was towards her.

Clasping her hands together instead, she said, 'No, not quite all. I didn't mean to take Ione without any guards at all. Perhaps just Hesta and one other. And the rest could—'

'Why?' he interrupted yet again, turning and pinning her in place with his cold blue stare. 'What is this insistence on taking her out of the palace?'

Irritation prickled over her skin at his tone, but she tried to stay calm. 'I thought she might like a change of scene.' And then, with sudden inspiration, added, 'She will be ruling this country at some point, so it might be interesting for her to see a bit more of the town at least, and the people who live there.'

He stared at her. 'Why do you want to leave her guard detail behind?'

'Because it's difficult to have a normal outing to get ice cream and perhaps play at a playground when you have a whole troop of guards following you around.'

'What do you mean, a normal outing?'

Anna took a breath. She would have to go carefully here. 'Ione is very…restricted. She spends all her time at the palace with a lot of adults. I thought she might like to spend some time doing things an ordinary child might enjoy. Ice cream, for example. Playing with children her own age…' Anna trailed off as the expression on the king's face turned forbidding.

'If you want ice cream, I'll have it organised,' he said flatly. 'And there are plenty of places in the palace she can play. She doesn't need to go to Itheus to do it.'

The prickle of irritation became more insistent. 'So, you

don't let her go anywhere without her guards? Is that what you're saying?'

'She is the heir to the throne,' his gaze was wintry, 'as well as my daughter, and no, she doesn't go anywhere without her guards.'

'Like I've already said, I don't mean to go without any guards at all. But perhaps only—'

'No.'

The word was iron, with no room for argument, and it annoyed her. She understood that he wanted to look out for Ione's safety, but such a restricted childhood could end up being smothering, and limiting, as she knew herself.

She wanted to argue, but that hadn't ended well the night before and it probably wouldn't end well tonight either, and so she bit back her protest. 'Very well, Your Majesty,' she said instead, trying not to let her annoyance colour her voice.

Silence fell, the look on his face impenetrable.

'You're very annoyed with me,' he said, and it wasn't a question.

'No, of course I'm not—'

'You are. Don't deny it.'

Anna bit her lip. 'Very well, I am.'

'Yet you're not arguing with me.'

'Because you told me not to. Remember?'

Something leapt in his gaze, something hot beneath all that ice, and again she was conscious of him the way she'd been conscious of him the night before. Of how tall he was and how broad. How the fabric of his shirt pulled over the hard muscles of his chest and how the colour deepened the blue of his eyes. Of his warm, musky scent, filtered with a freshness that reminded her of sunlight and salt and the ocean, and which she found almost unbearably attractive.

He was so cold and hard and distant, and yet right now he seemed almost…touchable.

A shiver wound its way down her spine and it wasn't fear or dread or foreboding or cold. It was much worse than that. It was excitement.

Slowly, the king leaned back against his desk, the tension that had been in his posture dissipating. He put the heels of his hands on the desktop, strong fingers gripping the edge, his intense stare unwavering.

'I remember.' His voice had lowered, become impossibly deeper. 'Are you wanting that fight, little nun? Is that why you're looking at me that way?'

Her cheeks were hot, a forbidden, wicked heat winding its way through her. 'I'm not looking at you in any way,' she said, her voice sounding distant even to her own ears.

He tilted his head, the glitter in his eyes no longer so icy. 'Are you not? Because that blush in your cheeks would seem to say otherwise.'

Her eyes widened, her hands half rising as if to touch those pretty red cheeks of hers, before dropping back down to her sides. She was in that blue dress again and, since she'd also worn it the night before, it was probably because she didn't have another. It was an issue. Mainly due to the fact that she looked so sweet and delectable in it.

She would look even sweeter and more delectable out of it.

His thoughts were very much out of line tonight and he should be reining them in. But right in this moment, he couldn't bring himself to do it.

All day something had been eating away at him—a kind of impatience. He wasn't sure where it had come from, since impatience was another thing he didn't feel in the normal scheme of things, so he'd tried not to pay attention

to it. But it had tugged at him, making it difficult to concentrate on his duties, which was a serious issue. Ruling
his country required his full attention and he could not afford to be distracted.

It had got exponentially worse in the meeting he'd just
had with his councillors. He hadn't been able to focus and
he'd felt tired, along with the unfamiliar need to get up and
pace, to shake off the tension somehow. It was mystifying.
He'd never been bored or uninterested at a meeting before,
but he'd been both tonight, sitting there, irritated, wanting
them gone so he could…

He hadn't been sure what. Go down to the gym and do
a few rounds with the punching bag. Do some lengths of
the pool. Run on the treadmill. Do something hard and
physical to get rid of whatever this feeling was the way he
normally did.

Then his councillors had gone and she had come into
the room, and it had all become very, very clear to him.
His tiredness had dropped away and along with it the impatience, and he realised that she'd been the one he'd been
waiting for the whole time. Waiting for evening to come,
waiting to hear her report on his daughter. Waiting so he
could match wits with her, waiting to get her all pink and
furious and watch her eyes spark with silver fire.

It was disturbing. His entire life was crafted specifically to have no such needs. No such…attachments. No
one whose company he looked forward to being in, no one
he enjoyed talking with. He would allow himself nothing
that would distract him from the duty he'd been born for—
that of ruling a country. Axios came first and foremost,
and always would. He'd betrayed it once before because
he'd put someone else above it, and he wouldn't willingly
do so again.

One little novice nun should not have the power to distract him so badly.

Despite his determination not to, he'd been very angry about that, not helped by her insistence that she take Ione out of the palace, a suggestion he'd refused point blank. Ione could go nowhere without her entire guard detail because her safety was paramount, and most especially if it involved going down into the city. Ice cream and playgrounds were also indulgent and he didn't like the thought of that either.

His refusal to even entertain the idea should have signalled the end of the meeting and then he should have sent Anna away. But he hadn't sent her away. Because she was standing there, all scarlet-cheeked and angry, that silver fire glittering in her eyes, making a very male satisfaction coil tightly inside him.

He wasn't impatient or tense any longer. He wanted to push her further, make her even more furious, see what she'd do, and that was very, *very* wrong of him. The king should send her away and put her from his mind, but the man refused. The man wanted her to stay. The man hadn't indulged himself in anything quite as sweet and innocent as she was, perhaps ever, and he wanted to hold on to this moment for as long as he possibly could.

Or hold on to her.

Yes, he did want to hold on to her. His hands itched to get rid of the cheap fabric of her dress and touch her silky skin, trace her softly rounded curves. Watch her eyes darken with desire, teach her exactly how good that beautiful body of hers could make her feel.

He gripped hard to the edge of the desk he leaned against. The man might want those things, but it was the king who remained in charge and it was the king who would continue to do so. He wouldn't touch her, no matter how much his body demanded otherwise.

Flirting with her would be a test of his control, but perhaps his control could do with a test. It had been a long time since he'd felt the need to, after all.

'I don't know what you're talking about,' the little nun said, all flushed dignity and poise.

He almost smiled. 'Then why are you blushing?'

Her mouth firmed. 'If you're talking about last night when you touched me, then of course I'm going to blush. You shouldn't have done that.'

'No,' he agreed. 'I shouldn't. And maybe I should send you away before I do it again.'

Her eyes widened and she didn't move. And for a moment the tension between them pulled tight, a humming vibration that set all his nerves alight.

It had been too long since he'd felt an attraction like this, far too long. And yes, he should send her away, but what harm would it do if he indulged himself for a moment or two? It was only physical chemistry, nothing more.

Good God, if he could send his own brother into exile for ten years without a break in his heartbeat, then he could withstand the temptation of one small nun.

Are you sure about that?

Of course he was sure. Once, he might have been drawn to her rebellious spirit, his innate protectiveness might have been touched by her innocence and vulnerability. But not now. He was protective still, but that didn't focus on a person these days. It extended to an entire country.

It had taken more than his mother's death to teach him that lesson—he'd been a recalcitrant student—but he'd learned in the end.

'I don't understand,' she said, breaking the tense silence. She was standing very straight, her back flat, her chin lifted.

'I think you do.' He held her shocked gaze with his. 'You might be innocent, but you're not completely unworldly.'

The expression on her face shifted. 'I see. Is this something to do with the Reverend Mother sending me to you for seduction?'

She said the words with no hint of a stutter, but her hands had clenched tightly at her sides. Was it fear? Had he frightened her? Then again, he knew what fear looked like; he saw it in the eyes of people who faced him every day, and there was nothing of fear in hers. Only the flickering, leaping silver flame of her temper.

'She's very interested in my emotional welfare,' he said. 'She thinks I should marry again and has been suggesting eligible women as potential wives to me for months. And then you arrive, all innocent and sweet and unsuspecting. I knew what she was doing even if you didn't.'

She frowned. 'I'm not innocent and I'm certainly not sweet, so could you please stop saying that I am?'

Physical desire shifted and turned inside him. He wanted to push himself away from his desk and go to her, stand very close and look down into her silvery eyes, watch them darken. To see what would happen if he put himself within reach. Would she touch him? Would she have the courage? Perhaps he should find out.

'You're both of those things, little nun. Because if you weren't, you wouldn't be blushing quite so hard right now.'

She stared at him and he could feel that humming tension between them ratchet higher. He shouldn't be provoking her, yet he couldn't bring himself to send her away.

Suddenly she moved, coming right up to stand in front of him, and even though he was leaning back against his desk, he still had to look down at her.

Her gaze was very level, but her cheeks were bright red, her hands in fists. 'I'm not here to seduce you, Your

Majesty,' she said flatly, 'whatever you or the Reverend Mother might think. So if that's what you're worried about, you needn't be.'

She smelled of that sexy combination of lavender and musk, and he could see that the blush had crept down her neck, disappearing beneath the demure neckline of her dress. How far did it go? All the way over those pretty breasts?

He shouldn't be curious. He shouldn't want to know.

The pulse at the base of her throat was beating very fast and her breathing had quickened. Not fear, no. She wasn't afraid, of that he was certain.

'I'm not worried, believe me,' he said, and then, because he couldn't help it, he added, 'But aren't you curious? Aren't you curious to see whether or not you could seduce me? How you, an innocent novice nun, could seduce a king?'

Her mouth opened, then shut again. Her knuckles were white as her hands clenched tighter, and he wasn't sure whether it was because she was holding herself back or whether she was angered by his suggestion.

It was a mistake to have said that and he knew it, but he wanted to see what she would do, and besides, it had been a while since he'd indulged in flirtation.

You want her to do more than flirt. You want her to touch you.

The thought wound seductively through his head. He couldn't deny that he did want that. But still, she was an innocent and under his protection, not to mention one of his own godmother's novices. She was also employed by him. All very good reasons why he shouldn't be encouraging her…

'No,' she said tightly. 'I'm not interested.'

Except her gaze didn't move from his, as if she was mesmerised.

'Perhaps you're not.' Why was he so tense? Holding himself so still? It was almost as if he didn't trust himself to move. 'Or perhaps you're just scared.'

'I'm not scared either.' She drew herself up even straighter. 'And you should stop manipulating me.'

Of course she saw through him. She wasn't stupid.

'Am I manipulating you? Or are you letting me?' He tightened his grip on the edge of the desk. 'Maybe I should dismiss you, little nun. Put us both out of our misery.'

It would have been better for her if she'd nodded her head and said nothing. If she'd waited for him to dismiss her. But she didn't. Instead, her gaze searched his. 'What misery?'

'The misery of wanting to touch a woman I shouldn't.' He regretted it as soon as the words left his mouth, because he never explained himself to anyone and he didn't know why he was doing so now. Not that he planned on doing anything about it, but still.

Then again, it was too late to take it back now. She knew.

'Oh.' She blinked as if in shock, the light catching the soft gold of her lashes.

'You're surprised?' His own heartbeat started to accelerate, a dark, intense hunger collecting inside him. 'What about? I did tell you that you appealed to me.'

'I know, but...' She stopped, taking a ragged-sounding breath, staring hard at him. 'No one has ever said things like that to me before.'

Of course they wouldn't have. In a convent she would have been kept away from such concerns.

'Does it shock you?' He shifted, noting how she tracked the movement, like a prey animal watching a predator. Except this particular prey animal looked just as hungry as the predator himself.

The Reverend Mother would be appalled.

She would. But only if he did something about it, and

he wasn't going to. They were only talking and talking wouldn't hurt. Neither would a bit of honesty. The king was still entirely in control.

'No,' she said slowly, as if she'd only just decided. 'No, it doesn't.'

'It should. I'm not the right man for someone like you.'

If you really thought that, she wouldn't still be standing here.

No, she definitely wouldn't.

'Someone like me,' she echoed, her forehead creasing. 'What does that mean?'

'Isn't it obvious? You've been brought up by nuns and you're intending to take your vows. You're inexperienced. Innocent. Sweet. Kind. And I am none of those things.'

She frowned. 'Just because I've been living in a convent doesn't mean I don't know anything about…s-sex.'

The way she stumbled over the word went straight to his groin, making the hungry thing inside him growl. Making him want to cross the space between them, rip away that dress, and show her exactly what she didn't know about sex.

Enough. Finish playing with her and send her away.

Yes, that was exactly what he should do. This had gone on long enough and, though his control was excellent, it was not limitless. It was time to call a halt before he did something he'd regret.

'If you can't even say the word without stuttering then you really don't know,' he said, pushing himself away from the desk and straightening. 'It's time to go, Sister Anna. I would leave now, while you can.'

CHAPTER FIVE

THE HEAT IN the king's piercing blue eyes was still there, but the aching, breathless tension that had stretched between them, that had surrounded his taut, powerful figure as he'd leaned against the desk, was starting to drain away.

Anna knew she should be glad of it, but she wasn't.

Every nerve-ending in her body had seemed to come awake as he stared at her, as he talked about seduction and sex, and about wanting to touch her.

He'd mentioned before that she appealed to him, but not quite in so blatant a fashion. And it made her feel hot, turning the flutter inside her into an electric, thrilling excitement. Making her wonder whether a novice nun, with no experience whatsoever of men, really could seduce a cold, hard king.

She shouldn't be thinking such things. And if she'd really been the good, obedient servant of God she was trying to be, then she'd have told him in no uncertain terms not to speak to her like that. Then she'd have turned and walked out.

Yet she'd done none of those things. She'd found her gaze pinned by the electric blue of his, her awareness stretching out, taking in every inch of his muscular figure and how he leaned against the desk, the sinews in his forearms corded, the fabric of his trousers stretched over powerful thighs.

His shirt was open at the throat and her mouth had gone dry for some inexplicable reason at the sight of his bare olive skin and the strong, steady beat of his pulse.

She was attracted to him; she was aware of that now in a way she hadn't been before. She was thinking forbidden thoughts. Such as how he didn't seem cold now or distant, but hot and so very close. What would happen if she got closer? What would he do? He'd told her he couldn't touch her, and all the reasons he'd listed were very good reasons.

But what about her? She shouldn't touch him, of course she shouldn't. He was a king and she was only a novice, not even a nun. He was also the father of her charge, which made him her boss.

But if what he said was true about the Reverend Mother, then perhaps seducing him is part of your brief.

The thought was so sharp and burning it seared itself into her brain.

He perhaps couldn't touch her, but she could touch him, couldn't she? It might even be what the Reverend Mother wanted her to do. Of course, the Reverend Mother would never have said such a thing out loud, if what he'd said about her was true...

These are all justifications. You just want to touch him.

Her breath came faster now, her skin sensitised. She knew nothing very much about sex, still less about men, but yes, it was true. She did want to touch him. She very much did not want to be dismissed.

'But,' she began huskily, 'I don't want to leave.'

He was very still, a great stone carving of a warrior with burning sapphires for eyes. 'Perhaps you didn't understand me.' His deep, harsh voice sounded rough, as if he was talking through a mouthful of gravel. 'Would you like me to be clearer?'

'No, I understood.' She'd taken a step before she was even conscious of doing so. 'I just don't want to go.'

His gaze turned hot and that tension was back again, like a wire stretched to vibrating point between them. 'And yet I suggest that you do.'

'A suggestion isn't an order.' She took another slow step, her heartbeat sounding louder in her head. 'And I'm not very good at taking orders either.'

'What are you thinking, little nun?' His voice was even deeper, a growl.

'I'm thinking, what if it was true?' Another step took her to stand right in front of him, her head tipping back so she could meet his searing blue gaze. 'What if a novice really could seduce a king?'

Then, before she could think better of it, she put her hand out and laid her palm on his chest.

The look in his eyes flared with a heat that took her breath away. Or maybe it was the heat of his body that did that, seeping through the cotton of his shirt and into her palm, making her feel as if she'd put her hand against a hot stove.

She'd never touched a man before. Were they all this hot or was it just him? And were they all this hard? Because he certainly was. He was hard as iron, but warm, like living rock.

All the air had escaped her lungs and what little there was around her all smelled like him, salt and sunlight and a musky, masculine scent that set her heart racing.

'You really shouldn't do that.' His voice was so deep she could feel the vibration of it against her palm.

She searched his blunt, handsome face, noting the muscle that leapt in the side of his jaw and the tightness around his eyes and mouth. He was so powerful, so in control, and yet he didn't look that way now. He looked pushed to the edge. Was that her affecting him so badly? Did she, with her lack of experience and lack of knowledge, really have power over him in this way?

The idea fascinated her. She'd always been at everyone else's beck and call, the foster child taken in and cared for not by choice, but by necessity. Her place at the convent had always felt as though it had to be earned by being quiet and good and obedient. It wasn't hers by right or birth. Even leaving the convent and coming to Axios had been at the Reverend Mother's behest. And she was only staying on his sufferance.

He had the power, yet right now, with her hand on his chest, it felt as if she had some too. A different kind of power, but power all the same.

She liked it. She wanted more.

'Why not?' she asked, her voice sounding even huskier. 'You said you couldn't touch me, but you didn't say anything about me touching you.'

His blue gaze was so hot, spearing her right through. 'And what do you think is going to happen? That I'm just going to stand here and let you touch me? And what about after that? Do you think I'll wait until you've finished and then let you walk away?'

Something trembled deep inside her. No, she hadn't thought about any of those things. She'd just…touched him, responding to an urge she hadn't been able to deny or contain.

'I don't know.' She swallowed, the heat of his body burning into her. 'I haven't done this before.'

'I know you haven't. Which is why I suggested that you leave, because if you'd thought it through, you'd never have touched me.'

The trembling inside her got deeper, wider, and it wasn't

fear. She wasn't afraid of him in the slightest; no, it was something else entirely.

'Why?' she asked. 'What would you do?'

He was very still for a second. Then he said, 'This.'

And before she could move, he reached out and pushed the fingers of one hand into her hair, then bent his head and covered her mouth with his.

She'd never been kissed before. Never had another person's mouth on hers. There had been the brief, dry blessings on her forehead from the nuns, but nothing more. She'd never had heat, the firm press of warm lips on hers, never had anyone cradle the back of her head the way he was doing now, so very gently. As if he was holding something precious.

Her eyes pricked in a sudden rush of hot tears. Because she would have said that before this moment she'd never imagined being kissed. That she didn't want to be and never had. But that was a lie.

Everything she'd told herself was a complete and utter lie.

She *did* want it. And she *had* imagined it. But she'd told herself it wasn't something she could ever have so she'd shoved those thoughts away hard and pretended that such a thing had never occurred to her. Except now he was here and his mouth was on hers and the kiss was consuming her, making her aware of everything she'd never had, everything she told herself wasn't permitted.

And she wanted it. She wanted it *all*.

She put both hands on his chest, taking his heat and hard strength for herself, then she rose up on her toes, opening her mouth to him. He tasted hot, but with a cool bite from the wine he'd been drinking, and it was delicious. She wanted to drink from him.

A soft moan escaped her as the kiss deepened and he

began to explore her mouth with his tongue and his teeth, tasting her as she was tasting him, sipping gently from her, giving her gentle nips, testing her with his tongue.

Her fingers closed, gripping the warm cotton of his shirt, even as she felt his hand close around her hair as if in answer. The tug on it felt so good, small bolts of sensation that made her breath catch—what little breath she had left. Which wasn't much. He was taking it all, but she didn't care. She'd give it all to him. Everything he wanted, she would give.

It felt as if she'd been waiting for this moment, for him, her entire life.

'Little nun,' he whispered roughly against her mouth. 'Anna. We must stop.'

No, she didn't want to stop. She wanted to keep going, to have him kissing her, holding her, to have the extraordinary heat and hard press of his body against hers for as long as she could stand it. To have the sense of loneliness that had always dogged her become muted and dull beneath his astonishing kiss.

She clung on, seeking his mouth, trying to follow him as he lifted his head, only to be brought up short by the grip he had on her hair.

The blue of his eyes was electric, blazing with heat, but there was only iron in his voice when he spoke. 'We have to stop. We can't do this.'

'Why not?' Her voice was husky and a little raw, and she couldn't make her hands work, her fingers keeping their grip on his shirt.

The flame in his eyes burned everywhere it touched. 'So many reasons.'

'I don't care.' Her throat closed. She didn't want to give him up. Didn't want to lose this sense of connection, this feeling of closeness with another person. No, not just with another person, with him. 'Please, sire.'

'Anna...'

'I want you.' She couldn't hide her desperation. Didn't want to hide it from him. She wanted him to know what this meant to her. 'Please. I need...this. I need you.'

The blunt lines of his face were no longer expressionless but taut and sharp. As sharp as the blue of his eyes, relentless and fierce. 'You don't know what you're asking for.'

'Then show me.' She leaned into him, finally releasing the hold she had on his shirt, spreading her hands out on the hard warmth of his chest, pressing into it, loving the feel of him under her palms. 'Please, sire.'

He muttered a curse under his breath, a rough sound that echoed through her. His body tensed, his muscles tight, and she wanted to run her hands over him, to soothe him. Did he have anyone to do that for him? Did he have anyone to ease that tension? That tiredness she'd seen in him... Did he have anyone who gave him pleasure?

He probably has hundreds of women, you fool. He's a king. He could have anyone he wanted.

Yes, but he wasn't with just anyone now. He was with her. And it was her hair he had his hand in, her hands on his chest. And it was her he was looking at.

'You're a virgin,' he said. 'You'll be taking your vows. You're under my protection. Taking you like this, now, would be a violation of all those things.'

'I don't care.' And she meant it. She couldn't bear the thought of him letting her go and stepping away. All his heat withdrawing and all his strength, like a tide going out, leaving her high and dry. And lonely. Always lonely. 'I want you so much.' Her throat closed with the force of her emotion and she tried to swallow it down, realising belatedly that perhaps revealing herself so openly was a bad idea.

But perhaps he knew anyway, because his other hand cupped her cheek. For all his massive strength he was gentle, his big palm so warm and reassuring that she wanted to weep. 'Anna.' He said her name huskily, the sound of it whispering over her, the expression on his face softening just a fraction. 'You will care. When it's over, you'll care very much.'

Her heart felt full, pushing against her ribs, each beat painful. 'Don't tell me how I'm going to feel. You don't know. I've never had this before. Never felt it before. And yes, I'll be taking my vows, but I don't need to be a virgin to take them.'

Some emotion she didn't understand flickered over his face. 'And how will you feel afterwards? When I pretend it never happened? That none of this did? When you go back to being my daughter's companion and a trainee nun? Because that's what will happen. You can't be my lover, not openly, not given my position, and that's to protect both of our reputations. I will not acknowledge you as anything more than my daughter's companion and one of my godmother's charges. My job is to protect people and that includes you.'

She understood and it all made perfect sense. Of course he wouldn't be able to acknowledge her, just as she wouldn't be able to acknowledge him. He had a position to protect just as she did, and a country to lead.

'I understand,' she said thickly. 'I really do.'

'Do you?' His voice had become harsh. 'I have a duty to my country. If word got out that we were lovers, it would reflect very badly on both of us. I cannot be seen as a man who took advantage of someone weaker and more vulnerable, and that's how people would view it. And those that don't would look at you with suspicion. They would view you as a gold-digger or worse.'

She took a little breath as the implications sank in, because no, she hadn't thought of any of that. But again, it made sense. And it did nothing to calm either the desperation or the hunger inside her.

Except…he had much to lose. More than she did. If it got out that she'd had a king for a lover, the worst that would happen would be disappointment from the nuns and from the Reverend Mother. But for him, with a country to lead…

Her gut lurched. She couldn't ask it of him. It was wrong of her. She didn't care about the nuns' disappointment in her—they were always disappointed in her—not when all she could think about was him.

She swallowed the bitterness that collected in the back of her throat at the unfairness of it all. 'Okay. I wouldn't want to put you in a bad position. I'm sorry. I should have—'

His hand in her hair tightened, cutting her off, his blue eyes blazing. 'I didn't say no.'

Everything in her went still and quiet.

Keeping his gaze on hers, he lowered his hand from her cheek, dropping it down to the small of her back and settling it there, heavy and sure. Then he eased her closer, fitting every inch of her up against every inch of him.

The heat between them was searing, burning her, but she didn't want to pull away. No, she only wanted to get closer, press harder against him, take more, take it all… 'What are you doing?' she asked breathlessly. 'I thought you said—'

'I know I did. And all of that is true. I want you to understand the implications and the consequences.' He eased her even closer, so her hips were pressed to his and she could feel the long, hard ridge of his arousal. 'Because I want you, little nun. I want you very badly. And you need to decide if you still want to go through with this, because if you don't, you need to tell me now and tell me very clearly, so there can be no doubt.'

He felt so good, hard and hot, and so strong. She wanted to surround herself with that heat, with his power and strength, have him burn out the loneliness that sat inside her, melt the ice in the centre of her heart.

She understood the implications, and the consequences, and even though a part of her knew that she didn't, not really, she found she didn't care. She wanted him. She wanted this moment, because she knew she'd never have it again. If she turned her back and walked out of that door, she would lose something precious and she would never get it back.

So she didn't think and she didn't hesitate. She simply slid her hands up his broad chest and around his neck, rose up on her toes, and claimed his mouth, giving him her answer.

She tasted exactly the way he'd thought she would. No, better. If that was even possible. Sweet, like strawberries on a summer's day, or the fizz of very good champagne, the bubbles bursting on his tongue. Sweet, yes, but with the most delicious bite.

He shouldn't have kissed her, shouldn't have let her touch him. Because the moment she had, he knew he wouldn't be able to let her go. Definitely, he should have stopped himself from teasing her, taunting her, or daring her into challenging him.

But he'd never thought she would want him so badly, that she'd hold tight to him, her mouth hungry under his. He'd never expected that there would be tears in her eyes as he tried to put her from him, looking at him as if she were dying and he were her last chance of rescue. And he'd never realised that all of those things would get through his defences the way they had, making his control feel as tenuous as smoke, silently slipping through his fingers.

That could not be allowed. He had to get it back again and there was only one way to do that.

As if any of this is about your control. You just want her.

But he shoved those thoughts away. They didn't matter right now, because her mouth was on his and she tasted hot and it had been a long time, such a very long time, since he'd had a kiss this sweet. This tantalising and delicious.

Her body against his was soft and warm, a musky feminine scent winding around him and he was so hard he ached. He mostly preferred his women toned and athletic, because he was a hard man, and demanding. But she was all softness and womanly curves, and he wanted to sink into her, take all that sweetness for himself.

He pushed his fingers further into her hair, the little bun at her nape unwinding, spilling silk all over his skin as he held her steady to take the kiss deeper. She made another of those little throaty moans, pressing delicately against him as she tried to kiss him back. Her tongue was hesitant at first and then got bolder, exploring him as much as he was exploring her.

If he wasn't careful, this inexperienced, sheltered little nun would undo him.

He shifted, picking her up in his arms and carrying her over to the long leather couch. Then he sat down on it with her in his lap. Her hair was hanging down her back, pale as moonlight over her skin, and she kept trying to kiss him, her breathing out of control and ragged in the silence of the room.

He ran his hands down her back, soothing her at the same time as he found the zip on her dress and gently tugged it down. She sighed as the fabric loosened around her, her mouth on his becoming even more hungry, her hands going to the buttons on his shirt and fumbling with them. But he was faster, easing the material off her shoulders. Then he touched her, stroking his hands beneath her dress and over her skin, and yes, she was exactly as silky and soft as he'd expected. She gasped against his mouth, shuddering delightfully under his touch as he found the catch of her bra and undid it. A sigh escaped her and she gave a little moan as he trailed his fingers down the length of her spine. There was no hesitation to her, no alarm. It was as if she trusted him implicitly, and that made another unfamiliar sensation tighten in his chest.

You have been nothing but hard and rude to her. Yet she trusts you...

How strange that that should...affect him, especially when he accepted the trust of a nation as his due. But there was something about her that awoke the protector in him. Even though he didn't concern himself with other people's feelings, he wanted to keep her safe, to give her the pleasure she deserved. A pleasure to remember when she left.

Keep your distance.

Ah, but this was a single sexual encounter. Making sure it was good for one inexperienced nun wouldn't compromise that. He could afford to take care.

So he controlled the hunger in himself, put a leash on it. And he merely sat with her in his lap, kissing her lazily, stroking her back up and down, getting her used to his touch. She took what he gave her and then shifted, her hands moving again to his shirt and fumbling with the buttons once more.

It was difficult to hold back, to let her undo those buttons and just sit there as she uncovered him with shaking hands. But he didn't want to frighten her and, since he was the one with the better control, he let her set the pace initially. Plus, it felt almost too good when she finally managed to undo his shirt, to have her cool fingers on his skin, tracing the muscles of his chest and abdomen. She looked mesmerised by him and he let her touch, let her explore. But then she leaned forward and kissed his throat, her mouth hot, and the control he thought he had handled suddenly dissolved.

He shifted one hand into her hair and pulled her gently away. He had to redirect this otherwise it might be over before it even began.

'Lift your arms for me,' he ordered quietly.

She didn't hesitate, obeying without a word, allowing him to ease her dress up and over her head, taking her bra with it so she was sitting on him, facing him, naked but for a pair of white cotton briefs.

His breath caught. She was so lovely. Her hair was a skein of pale gold lying across one shoulder, her eyes darkening into tarnished silver. The flush that had tinged her cheeks did indeed go all the way down, across her neck and chest, over the most perfect round breasts he had ever seen, and sweet pink nipples, ready for his touch. She didn't cover herself and she didn't look shocked as he stared at her, only looked back at him as if she liked him looking at her as much as he liked looking.

He slid one hand to the small of her back, spreading his palm out, cradling her as he urged her forward once more, tasting the sweetness of her mouth. Then he eased his other hand to her hip, trailing his fingers up her silky warm skin, feeling her shiver, and he went higher and higher, until he found the curve of one full breast.

She gasped against his mouth, her body arching as he cupped her breast gently, then she moaned as he circled her nipple with his thumb, making her tremble.

'Oh…' The word was soft with wonderment and surprised delight. 'Oh…*sire*…'

'Call me by my name,' he murmured, rubbing his thumb over the sensitive tip of her breast, making her shudder yet again. 'I'm not a king right now.'

She sighed, arching into his hand, holding back nothing from him. 'Adonis…' His name sounded like a prayer, and he wanted to hear her say it again, so he ran his thumb over her nipple once more. And she obliged him, his name coming out sweetly husky.

The sound shivered through him and he couldn't remember the last time a woman had called him that, with no deference. Only a plea, a cry for more.

So he gave it to her, stroking her breast, toying gently with her nipple as he kissed her, exploring her mouth. And then, when she was panting, he eased her back across his arm and then it was his turn to put his lips to her throat, to taste the salty-sweet flavour of her skin.

She trembled, her pulse frantic against his tongue. But he held her still, going slowly as he trailed kisses over the delicate architecture of her collarbones, then further down, to the swell of those beautiful breasts, tracing the curves with his lips, before moving on to one hard nipple. He teased it, circling it with his tongue, which made her gasp his name yet again. Then he took it into his mouth, holding her as he sucked gently on it.

A moan escaped her, throaty and soft, and her hands lifted to his shoulders, gripping on to him. 'Adonis…oh… please…'

She smelled like sex and she tasted like heaven, and she was so warm, so soft and sweet. And he hadn't realised those were things he'd been craving, not until now.

His life was so very cold, nothing but hard edges and sharp decisions, and she felt like the antithesis of that. He wanted more, to spend longer tasting every inch of her delectable body, to take his time, because these moments they had together wouldn't last.

He could only give her now. But that was probably a good thing. Already he was so hard he ached, and the way she was giving herself to him, nothing held back and so trusting… It could become addictive if he let it.

So, you'd better not let it, had you?

Oh, he wouldn't, no fear of that. She might push his physical control, but that was all. She didn't affect any other part of him, least of all the distance he kept between himself and the world.

This was sex. Nothing more.

He switched his attention to her other breast, sliding one hand from her hip down to her thigh and stroking gently, before moving inward and up, then between.

She went very still as his fingers brushed over the damp fabric of her knickers, stroking the heat and softness behind the cotton, and he heard her breath escape in a wild rush.

'Oh, yes,' she gasped, her whole body suddenly shaking. 'Oh, yes, *please*…'

There was such delight in her voice and so much desperation that he tightened his arm around her, drawing her in close so her bare breasts were against his chest, her silky skin and hard little nipples rubbing against him. Then he stretched out his fingers between her thighs, stroking her over the material of her knickers, making her gasp and squirm and wriggle against him.

'Do you want more?' he demanded, his own voice so rough it didn't sound like his. 'Is that what you want? More of me touching you?'

'Yes,' she gasped. 'Please…yes…'

So he hooked one finger into the fabric and pulled it aside, baring her. Then he stroked his fingertips through the soft little nest of curls between her thighs, the folds of her sex hot and wet just for him.

She moaned, her hands gripping tight to his shoulders, as if she would fall if she let go, her breathing coming in short pants. Her hips twisted, following his hand as he caressed her, teasing and stroking the most sensitive parts of her.

He'd thought she might be modest or perhaps a little shy, but she wasn't. Like a person dying of heat exhaustion in the desert finally finding an oasis, she threw herself into it, clothes and all.

It was incredibly gratifying.

He found himself kissing her lovely mouth harder and with more demand despite the fact that he'd told himself he was going to take this slow. And then he was testing the entrance to her body gently, pushing one finger into her slickness, feeling the incredible heat of her sex close around him.

She shuddered like a tree in a hurricane, her mouth turning as hungry and as demanding as he was, her hips shifting on his lap as if she was trying to find some relief. But there would be no relief for her. None but what he gave her.

'Adonis,' she said hoarsely, her fingers digging hard into his shoulders. 'Please… I need… I can't…'

He wanted to push her down onto the couch cushions, take her hard and immediately. But she wasn't experienced and this was new to her, and he didn't like the thought of taking her roughly, with no niceties at all. He wanted this to be good for her. He wanted her to remember it. Remember him.

Why should you care about that?

He didn't know. She wasn't a politician or one of his council. Not one of his generals or a fellow head of state. She was only one little nun with whom he happened to have some chemistry and there was no need at all for her to remember him.

But he wanted her to.

She was shaking in his arms now, moaning against his mouth, so he kept his hand between her thighs, his finger sliding in a rhythm that made her shake even harder. Then he pressed down on the most sensitive part of her with his thumb, just a small brush.

And he held her as she convulsed against him, a cry of pleasure escaping as the orgasm washed over her.

He let her sit there for a moment, running one hand absently up and down her back to ease her down, barely aware he was even doing it. It was painful having her in his lap because he was so hard. But he didn't move. There was something sweet about holding her in his arms, about the way she turned her hot face into his neck, her breath warm on his skin.

Then quite suddenly she sat up, her silvery eyes staring fixedly at him, a crease between her fair brows. She didn't seem concerned that she was sitting there basically naked while he was mostly fully dressed.

'Please tell me there's more,' she said, her voice scratchy.

And he found himself smiling, predatory and hungry.

'Oh, yes,' he murmured, impatient now. 'There's more.' Then he moved, taking her down onto the couch beneath him. 'There's a lot more.'

CHAPTER SIX

ANNA FELT AS if she was outside herself. As if she'd changed in some way, become someone else. Someone who didn't have to be quiet and good. Someone who didn't have to make sure she was grateful all the time for any scrap of attention that came her way.

She'd become a woman made entirely out of heat and sensation, a wanton who demanded attention and got it. Who demanded pleasure and got it.

Who had the entire focus of the most beautiful, most exciting, most powerful man in the world centred on her and her pleasure.

She lay on the couch, the leather cool against her back, with Adonis's big, hard body stretched above her, and there was nowhere on earth she wanted to be right now other than where she was, beneath him.

She'd had no conception of what sex could be like. What touch could mean. Had no idea that she wouldn't feel shy and she wouldn't feel modest when he took her dress off. When he touched her breasts or the place where she was most needy, between her thighs. All she'd been conscious of was how intense the sensations were, how incredible it felt when he touched her. When that piercing blue gaze raked over her. And it wasn't cold any more, but blazing hot, electric.

And it was she who'd done that to him. It was she who'd melted the ice. No one special, no one all that different. Just a girl nobody had wanted.

But he wanted her. This king.

Except she couldn't see the icy, controlled king any more. The man above her was hungry and powerful, and as predatory as the lion he wore on his back. A man who had that intense, laser focus centred only on one thing—her.

There was more, of course there was more. And when he came to his knees between her thighs and pulled off her knickers, all she felt was relief. Because the need inside her was building again. He'd quenched it before, with his magic hands and his hot mouth, but just looking at him, just imagining what was going to happen, had the breath catching in her throat and desire sharpening between her thighs.

But not only her own pleasure. She was hungry to touch him too. Hungry to give him the same pleasure he was giving her, to share with him what she was feeling.

He was so cold. A mountain made of ice and stone, towering over the rest of the world. Powerful and remote, and very dangerous. Yet alone. She could sense that in him, because it was that loneliness that lay at the heart of her too. Whether he knew it or not, whether he was even aware of it, he felt it, because the evidence was there in the hunger in his eyes. As if he recognised the heat inside of her and wanted it for himself.

A mountain was lonely. A mountain was on its own.

She stared up at him as he looked down at her, his hungry gaze following the line of her naked body, zeroing in between her thighs.

Did he have anyone to keep him company? Did he have anyone at all who wanted to climb to the peak and sit beside him in the cold? Or was he a peak too dangerous to scale?

There were avalanches and storms, fissures and crevasses. You could get hurt so very easily climbing a peak like that one and maybe that was how he liked it. Maybe he didn't want anyone near. Maybe he was happy being remote.

Her heart squeezed unexpectedly tight at the thought. No, it wasn't true. It wasn't. She would see that there was heat at the heart of him, there was passion and fire, and it was easy enough to spot now.

His eyes blazed as he got rid of his shirt and his hands dropped to the buckle of his belt, undoing it and pulling it off. His movements were slow, deliberate, but his jaw was tight. Tension rolled off him.

He was holding himself back, keeping that fire contained. And perhaps it was a tease for them both, or perhaps he didn't want to hurt her, because it was her first time after all.

But she didn't need him to. She was different now because he'd changed her. He'd turned her into someone else; she wasn't a nun any more. She was the woman who was going to set the fire inside him free.

Anna sat up, running her hands up his powerful thighs as he knelt there, watching him as he undid the fastenings of his trousers.

'Do you like what you see, little nun?' His voice was so deep, so dark. Like the sound of a glacier moving. Except this glacier wasn't cold any more. 'Do you want to touch me?'

'Yes.' She slid her hands over his hips, feeling the smoothness and heat of his bare skin, tracing the hard, chiselled lines of his stomach. 'Yes, so much.' And she did. She loved how powerful and strong he was. Loved how hot his skin was and how hard he felt under her palms.

Yes, he was a mountain. And she wanted to climb him. Not that he gave her any opportunity.

Quickly, he divested himself of the rest of his clothes—far too quickly for her liking—but he didn't listen to her protests, gave her no time to look at him. One minute he was there with his trousers on, the next she was being pushed back on the couch cushions and he was over her again, and this time he was naked.

And he was glorious. A powerful machine of muscle and bone overlain with taut, velvety olive skin. He held himself above her, his biceps flexing with apparently no effort, and his strength excited her for reasons she couldn't explain.

She lifted her hands, ran her fingertips over him, stroking him, watching the piercing blue of his eyes get hotter. Then she glanced down and her breath caught.

He was long and thick, and when he noticed her look, he grabbed one of her hands and pushed it down between them, curling her fingers around him.

Anna gave a little gasp of delight. She'd had no idea that the most masculine part of a man would feel so smooth, like velvet. Or so hot. She'd had no idea he'd feel so hard either—not that she'd ever thought about it. Maybe if she had, she might have been more interested in sex. Certainly, if she'd known he'd feel like this she would have been.

Then again, the thought of touching any other man so intimately didn't have the same effect, so maybe it was just Adonis she wanted to touch.

'You look concerned,' he murmured roughly. 'Are you nervous?'

'No,' she said with absolute truth. 'I was just amazed at how good you feel.' She studied him, watching the lines of his face tighten as she squeezed him experimentally. 'Does that hurt? Or do you like me doing that?'

'No, it doesn't hurt. And yes, I like you doing that.'

'Oh. In that case—'

But he didn't let her finish, giving her a long, hard

kiss, before pulling back again. She opened her mouth to protest, but then from somewhere he produced a silver packet and ripped it open. Contraception, she realised. He dealt with it then stretched himself over her, lazy as the lion he was.

'Now, then,' he said, his voice thick with sensual heat. 'Where were we? Ah, yes…' His hips shifted between her thighs, the head of his sex nudging at hers. Then he slid his hands beneath her, cupping her bottom, tilting her. His gaze held hers, level and intense. 'Are you ready for me, Anna?'

'Yes.' Excitement crowded in her throat, so intense she could barely force the word out.

He didn't wait. As soon as the word had left her lips, his hips flexed and he was pushing into her, a deep, slow thrust that tore another gasp from her throat. But it wasn't painful. No, strangely, despite what she'd heard, there was no pain at all. A vague kind of pull but then nothing but the feeling of her flesh parting for him, stretching around him. And it didn't feel like an invasion so much as a welcoming.

As if she was welcoming him home.

She trembled slightly at the immensity of the feeling that was spreading out through her chest. Of having him so close, inside her, part of her. It made her feel honoured, in a strange way, that he would allow this kind of intimacy.

Especially when you're not worthy of it.

Tears pricked at her eyes, and he stopped, deep inside her, looking down at her. 'Did I hurt you?' His voice sounded raw. 'Upset you?'

She shook her head, for the moment unable to speak, because the strange feeling had closed her throat. Clearly, from the way he was looking at her, this kind of reaction wasn't expected and it made her feel vulnerable in a way she hadn't when he'd first undressed her and touched her.

She didn't understand the feeling, so she reached up to him, took his face between her hands and drew his mouth down on hers, kissing him instead.

And then everything became a whole lot hotter and more desperate.

He began to move inside her, slow, deep thrusts that took hold of her desire and turned it sharper, a bright and intense pleasure moving through her.

She forgot her vulnerability. Forgot about worthiness or deserving. There was only him and the exquisite movement of his hips, the raw heat in his blue eyes, and the deep sounds of masculine pleasure that came from him every time he thrust.

It was amazing. She could barely stand it.

Anna wound her legs around his lean hips, following the rhythm he showed her, taking it and making it her own, lost to the intensity of the pleasure that gripped her.

And when the orgasm came, swelling inside her like a wave, she could only lie there staring up at him as it swept her up and drowned her in pleasure, making her cry his name aloud, holding onto him as if he were her anchor.

She was hardly aware of him moving faster, harder, his breathing as wild and as raw as hers, calling her name in answer, as he turned his face into her neck, and followed her into the tide.

Adonis tried to catch his breath and failed. The orgasm had felt like a cataclysm moving through him, a force of nature he couldn't control. It had broken over his head like a thunderstorm and all he'd been able to do was lie there with his head turned against Anna's skin, inhaling the scent of female arousal, lavender and sex, as pleasure blasted his world apart.

He couldn't move and so he didn't, shifting only so he

wasn't lying directly on top of her because she was small and he didn't want to crush her.

Her own breathing was loud in his ear, a frantic, rushing sound that eventually slowed, the shaking in her body ebbing as the aftershocks faded, the hold she had on his shoulders loosening.

He felt raw and possessive and a little savage, none of which he should be feeling, and he found he'd pulled himself up to look at her, to see whether she was as wrecked as he was.

Her skin had gone a deep pink, curls of hair sticking to her forehead, the sheen of perspiration on her brow and in the hollow of her throat. Her eyes were very dark, her mouth full and red and swollen from his kisses.

Yes, he'd wrecked her. He'd wrecked her utterly.

The savage possessiveness gripped him tighter, along with a fierce satisfaction that absolutely should not have been there.

You cannot let her get to you. Look what she made you do!

His gut lurched, a cold sensation gripping him.

He'd known taking her was wrong and yet he'd done it anyway. All because she'd touched him…all because she'd looked at him with silver burning in her eyes. And he could tell himself all kinds of lies about why he'd changed his mind, but the fact remained that he'd taken her because his control had slipped.

After all these years does your brother's pain still mean nothing?

Her hand came up and touched his mouth, a leisurely, sensual touch, and she smiled one of her luminous smiles. And he could feel something inside him respond, embers in the dead hearth of his heart glowing.

He moved instinctively, pulling away from her, pushing

himself off her and up, beginning to reach for his clothes. The cold sensation was spreading through his blood now, icing the warmth she'd given him.

Because it wasn't true. He hadn't forgotten his brother's pain—the pain their father had put Xerxes through in order to teach Adonis what it truly meant to be a king. How emotion could be a weapon that in the wrong hands could take down a nation.

It had taken Adonis years to learn to get rid of those weaknesses in himself, to tame his own rebellious heart, and his failure to do so earlier had caused his little brother even more hurt. But those lessons had sunk in eventually and he couldn't forget them now. Couldn't throw all those lessons aside just because he wasn't able to resist one sexy little nun.

'Adonis?' Her voice, husky and soft, came from behind him. 'What's wrong?'

'Nothing.' He began to pull his clothes on, ruthlessly crushing the cold sensation in the pit of his stomach.

You put yourself first. That's what you always do.

'I think there's something,' she said. 'Did I do something wrong? Is that the—'

'No,' he interrupted flatly, making his voice hard. 'It isn't you.' He pulled his shirt on and turned around.

She was sitting on the couch, still naked, still pink. Her hair flowed over her shoulders in a pale gold tangle and she looked like any red-blooded man's wet dream, all lush female curves and touchable silky skin. A frown creased her brow and there was a concerned expression in her eyes, though whether that was for herself or for him, he wasn't sure.

'Then what is it?' she asked.

'Other things.' He knew he sounded dismissive, yet made no effort to temper his tone. The best thing for both of them right now was for her to leave. He'd made a mistake, but not one he'd compound by spending any more time with her than he had to.

His detachment might not be as perfect as he'd first thought, but he could fix that. Feeling possessive over one little nun wouldn't break him. He'd patch up his weaknesses, shore up his defences. No one would be able to use his emotions against him, because he simply wouldn't have any.

'Once that crown is on your head you as a person cease to exist,' Xenophon had told him once. *'You're not a brother. Not a son. Not a friend. You* are *Axios. Remember that. You are the king and there is no room for you to have or to be anything else.'*

He wasn't anything else. Once, he had been. But he wasn't now and he couldn't forget that.

'Do you need help finding your way back to your room?' he asked expressionlessly.

Disappointment flickered over her face. 'Adonis,' she began.

But the sound of his name made that tight sensation grip him again and he knew he couldn't allow her to use it. 'You may address me as sire.'

A spark of silver gleamed in her eyes.

You're hurting her.

It shouldn't matter. She had to be merely a woman with whom he'd spent a pleasant half-hour, nothing more. He couldn't afford for her to be anything else. His detachment was everything and right now she compromised it.

Still, she *was* his godmother's charge and he owed her more than a cold dismissal.

Gritting his teeth, he forced himself over to where she sat and crouched down in front of her. Not a good move when that brought him close to her naked body and he could feel the pull of desire rising inside him again, making him hard. Making him want to push her back down onto the cushions and teach her a few more new things.

But he only reached out and took her hands in his, holding them. 'We only had this moment,' he said, consciously keeping his voice gentle. 'I did tell you that.'

She stared at him a moment and then pulled her fingers from his. 'Yes, thank you, I know that,' she said coolly. 'There's no need to treat me like a child.'

He narrowed his gaze. 'Then don't look at me like one.'

'I'm not looking at you like anything.' She rose to her feet and moved past him, enveloping him in a wave of lavender, musk and sex, making him inexplicably want to reach out and grab her, to put his hands all over that beautiful body.

But he was strong and so he didn't. He rose to his feet too and watched her as she went to grab her clothes, beginning to pull them on in a series of small, deliberate movements.

That was a mistake.

Yes, obviously.

'You looked disappointed,' he said, again not sure why he was bothering to explain himself.

'You said nothing was wrong and that's clearly a lie.' She smoothed her dress. 'I was only disappointed you didn't want to share what it was with me.'

'I don't have to tell you. I'm not your boyfriend, Anna.'

She opened her mouth, probably to say something sharp. But then she must have thought better of it, because she closed it again, bending to pick up the tie for her hair instead. 'Yes,' she said in that cool voice, as she tied back her hair 'I'm well aware of that.'

'Anna—'

'You got up suddenly and all I wanted to know was whether there was anything bothering you. I wasn't asking you for a rundown of your entire life up to this point or for you to get down on your knees and declare your undying love. I only asked because it seemed like something was wrong, but if you didn't want to answer, you could have just said. You didn't need to treat me like some fragile flower who doesn't know the difference between casual sex and true love.'

His jaw tightened. This was not how he'd thought this would end.

How did you think it would end?

The question annoyed him. The whole situation annoyed him. Her feelings shouldn't touch him yet they had and he didn't know why.

He couldn't even tell himself that it wasn't his fault. Not when it was his control that had slipped. What was he thinking? He was normally much better at handling the women he slept with.

The women you sleep with are not normally nuns.

As if he needed yet another reminder of how he'd forgotten his father's lessons and allowed himself to think that he was a man.

He wasn't. He was a king.

Adonis remembered his crown and straightened. 'Then let us be very clear. That was casual sex. And there will not be another instance. We will go on as if it never happened.'

Her pretty grey eyes were snapping with temper and he thought he detected another flash of hurt. But then it was gone. 'Yes, fine.'

'You are simply my daughter's companion and that is all.'

'Of course, Your Majesty,' she said, and there was an edge to the words, a sarcasm that hadn't been there before. 'We wouldn't want it any other way.'

Your Majesty... You don't want her to call you that.

He ignored the thought, and shoved it hard from his head. 'Then you are dismissed,' he said coldly.

He thought she might argue with him further, but she didn't. She said nothing, simply turning on her heel and walking out.

And he tried to tell himself he wasn't disappointed about that. Not at all.

CHAPTER SEVEN

ANNA SPENT THE following couple of days furious and trying very hard not to be. The nuns had always cautioned against allowing negative emotions such as anger or jealousy to rule her and she'd thought she'd managed to overcome those weaknesses in herself.

But every time she thought of that moment in Adonis's—no, *the king's*—office, where he'd suddenly turned from a passionate man back into the cold, emotionless king, it made her so angry she could hardly stand it.

She might have been a virgin, but she wasn't stupid. And she might be sheltered, but she knew good sex didn't equal love. Even exceptional sex, though she had nothing to compare it to and, for all she knew, sex was like that for everyone every time.

So, she'd felt close to him. So, she'd wanted to know him. So, he'd made her feel things about herself that no one had ever made her feel before. So what?

Those were all feelings that had been prompted by physical pleasure, that was all.

She hadn't fallen magically in love with him. In fact, right now, she didn't even like him.

She tried to do what he'd told her, which was to forget all about what had happened between them and concentrate on Ione instead. But she found that at odd times she'd suddenly find herself remembering his hands on her skin, or the way he'd felt inside her; the pleasure that had bloomed throughout her entire body; the look in his blue eyes and the way her chest had tightened in wonder; the strange sadness that had gripped her as she'd thought about him being a mountain and having no one.

And something whispered to her that there was a reason she'd been so angry with him and so offended in the aftermath. A reason she hadn't protested at his cold dismissal.

It was because she was disappointed—worse, she was hurt. And even worse than that, she knew she had no reason to be. He'd been clear about what the sex would be between them. It was she who hadn't understood how it would affect her.

You were wrong. You are *a fragile flower.*

But she didn't want to think about that, so she didn't. Instead, she pursued her determination to help Ione. Adonis—*the king*—had sent word that her evening reports on Ione's progress would now be given to one of his aides rather than to himself, and he refused all requests for an audience as he was very busy at present.

It was enough to make her think that he was avoiding her, though she couldn't imagine why. Had it been that the passion between them had touched something in him, too? And now he couldn't be around her? But then, why would that be?

Whatever he was doing, it irritated her. So she went to Prince Xerxes instead, laying out her reasons for wanting to take Ione into Itheus without her usual contingent of soldiers.

Xerxes was—unlike his brother—understanding. He was also charming and so ridiculously handsome that he made Anna feel a little like a starstruck teenager. It turned out he had the same fears that Ione wasn't getting the attention she deserved either—he'd become a father six months earlier himself—and promised he'd take the matter to his brother personally.

He must have been far more persuasive than Anna because the next day Anna was granted permission to take Ione into the city with a contingent of two of the palace's most elite soldiers in plain clothes.

The day was beautiful, warm, and sunny, and Anna held fast to the little girl's hand as Ione charged around Itheus's narrow cobbled streets, loudly telling Anna about this thing or that thing. *That's the church where Uncle Xerxes married Aunt Calista. That's where Papa married Mama.*

That caused a small pang of grief in Anna's heart. Ione didn't seem to mind talking about her mother. And after they visited the shop that was renowned throughout Axios, even throughout Europe, for its ice cream, and came outside into the bustling streets, licking melting ice cream from the crisp waffle cones, Anna asked another couple of questions about her.

Ione said very matter-of-factly that something had been wrong with Mama's heart and so she'd died when Ione was still a baby. Was that a playground? Could they go over and play in it?

That the little girl couldn't remember her mother made Anna's heart ache in sympathy. The princess was so very alone. Her father was cold, kept his daughter at a distance, and so she was left to an army of people who looked after her and cared for her. But they wouldn't love her as a mother would. They wouldn't want to get to know her, chat to her, treat her as though she was an ordinary, albeit very special, little girl, and not the heir to the throne.

Resolve settled down through Anna as she wiped the ice cream from Ione's face then let her go and play in the playground. The Reverend Mother had been right to send her to Axios, regardless of whether the old lady thought she was sending Anna to the king or not. Anna wasn't here for him. She was here for this lonely, motherless girl. And she was uniquely qualified to understand Ione, because she'd been a lonely, motherless girl herself. The nuns had given her a home and they'd given her love, but it wasn't a mother's love. It wasn't warm or personal. It was distant and stern and vaguely disapproving.

Like the king.

Anna watched Ione squealing with laughter as she and another girl raced around the playground, the two guards loitering at a discreet distance, and determination settled in her heart.

This little girl needed more than that. She was passionate and giving, with a bright, sparky spirit. And though she might be motherless, she wasn't fatherless. She still had a parent. That was who she needed, not a large contingent of guards and nannies. Not even a stranger like herself to 'manage' her behaviour.

No, she needed her father.

Does he even know how to be one?

Emotion coiled inside her, bittersweet and raw, because she suspected she knew the answer to that. Adonis was a mountain and mountains were distant and icy. They protected and yet they sat apart. They did not bother themselves with the people who lived at their base.

Anna turned away from the children playing and glanced behind her, at the mountains, the ones that reached high above Itheus, all rocky crags and sharp edges. She looked at the palace that had been built into the side of them, as sharp and as dark as the king who ruled it. A medieval fortress, closely guarded and well defended.

Like his heart.

Did he even have one? Well, if he did, he needed to open

it. For his daughter's sake. And there probably wasn't another person in the entire world who would dare demand that he do it. No one but Anna.

Prince Xerxes had his own daughter to look after and the army of servants and guards would never dare challenge the king. But Anna would.

And if it gets you sent home in disgrace?

Then at least she would have tried. Nothing would change if she didn't try.

The day was such a success that the king relented and allowed Anna to take Ione to the playground a number of times in the days following, and even to the swimming pool in Itheus, rather than the palace's own pool. But he still refused all requests for Anna to speak to him directly. He was always in meetings or away from the palace, or undertaking public duties or some other thing that meant she couldn't talk to him.

Even after her 'probation period' of two weeks was up, and nothing further was said about her returning home to England, Anna wasn't granted a personal audience.

So, yes, he *was* avoiding her. Which was ridiculous, not to mention puzzling. Because why would he? Sure, they'd had sex, but he'd told her to pretend it had never happened and that was exactly what she was doing. Could he not do the same? Or was he genuinely busy?

Either way, it annoyed her. She wasn't sure how long she would be kept on here, and, although Ione seemed to be less disruptive whenever Anna was around, she was still prone to inappropriate tantrums and reckless behaviour. And Anna thought that wasn't going to get any better until His Royal Majesty deigned to spend more time with his daughter, though where that would leave Anna herself, she wasn't sure.

One thing she was sure of: Ione had come to trust her and she wasn't going to let the little girl down by not at least making an attempt to talk to the king.

No one else could do this. Only her. And it mattered because she didn't want to see Ione grow up as she had, in the company of distant people who cared for her, but only in a detached way. Who only saw her as a collection of behaviours that needed managing, a future monarch in Ione's case, and not as an actual person.

However, it wasn't until nearly four weeks after she'd first taken Ione to the playground that Anna eventually spotted her opportunity.

The king was giving a special function for dignitaries from various European countries and, since it would be the first time he wouldn't be closeted away and guarded assiduously, she'd have the perfect opportunity to approach him. He could hardly send her away or drag her from the room in front of all his assembled guests—not that she'd interrupt him and demand he speak to her while he was talking to others, of course. She'd somehow get herself into the ball, even though she wouldn't be invited, and then wait for an opportunity. And there would be one, she was certain of it.

Over the past few weeks she'd amassed a few items of clothing, purchased from the salary the king paid her, but a ballgown wasn't one of those things. However, Princess Calista came to her aid, finding her a dress to borrow for the night from one of Axios's most talented designers, while offering her stylist's services to do her hair and make-up. Anna decided not to lie about the reasons for slipping into the ball even though she hadn't been invited, and Calista had been wholeheartedly on Anna and Ione's side.

And so, a week later, Anna found herself standing in front of a small side door—a staff entrance—that led into the grand ballroom of the palace, dressed in a stunning ballgown of ice-blue silk and silver lace, with an overskirt of silver net sewn with crystals, with her hair, golden and gleaming, piled high on her head and perfect make-up, ready to crash the king's reception.

She felt strange, utterly unlike herself, as if she'd put on someone else's clothing. Nerves fluttered in her stomach, making her feel slightly sick. She'd been feeling off-colour the past couple of days, though it hadn't turned into anything more than tiredness and the occasional bout of nausea, so she'd mostly ignored it. Right now, though, it felt worse, making it difficult to find the calm that usually got her through the most trying days in the convent.

This was a move the Reverend Mother wouldn't approve of, that was certain, but then, Anna wasn't doing this for herself, just so she could go to a party and wear a ballgown. Or even to see the king she couldn't stop thinking about.

She was doing this for Ione.

The staff member leaned forward and pushed open the door, and abruptly Anna was thrust into a massive room full of beautiful people wearing beautiful clothes, where the air buzzed with the sound of conversation and the tones of a small orchestra played in one corner.

The vaulted stone ceiling was crisscrossed with heavy beams around which coiled lots of delicate lights. The stone walls had been softened by the inevitable tapestries, along with silken wall hangings. Pots of trees had been placed everywhere as well as enormous tubs of flowers. There were even fountains, giving the illusion of a lovely and elaborate garden that had been brought inside.

It was beautiful, and for a second Anna wanted to simply enjoy it for herself.

But that wasn't why she was here.

Steeling herself, she stepped forward into the crowd.

* * *

Adonis stood next to the wall beside one of the big potted rhododendrons, taking advantage of a minute's gap in the constant round of small talk to scan the crowd, to make sure the evening was proceeding as planned.

The celebration to mark the signing of Axios's latest treaty wasn't something he was particularly enjoying. Unlike his brother, who loved a good party, Adonis did *not* like parties. Nevertheless, many Axians did like to have a fuss made, so he'd ensured the maximum amount of fuss for this particular occasion, opening the royal wine cellars and making sure the royal chefs did not disappoint for the official dinner.

And, indeed, they had not.

A triumph, people were saying, which he took as Axios's due. He might not like parties, but even he could appreciate how a good one could earn respect.

The crowd in the ballroom shifted and turned, the air full of conversation and the sounds of the orchestra. Jewels and sequins sparkled, the light also glinting off medals and cufflinks, while people laughed and talked and drank vintage champagne from the best palace crystal.

Restlessness coiled inside him. A familiar restlessness. It had been rattling around and around inside him like a lion pacing before the bars of his cage, and nothing seemed to get rid of it. He'd been spending long hours in his gym and in the pool, working himself into physical exhaustion, but that hadn't helped. Even rounds in the boxing ring hadn't got rid of it.

He'd tried to fill his days as much as he could with the endless demands of kingship, trying to ignore it, but that hadn't helped either. At the end of each day he lay awake in his bed, that restlessness eating away inside him, and he'd have to get up and walk the corridors just to satisfy it.

As a consequence, he was in a foul mood.

It didn't help that a part of him knew exactly why he was restless, but it was a part he didn't want to acknowledge and so he didn't. Except during the day, when sometimes he could hear the sounds of his daughter's laughter, and along with it the sound of another laugh. Deeper and a little huskier than Ione's clear bell tones, with a warmth that crept through him, touching something inside him. And it made his heart race and his body harden.

And when he walked the palace corridors at night, he sometimes caught the vague scent of lavender and sweetness, and that had the same effect, making desire wrap itself around him, choking him.

Xerxes unfortunately noticed his temper and had asked him what was wrong, but Adonis had ignored him. He didn't want to talk about the real reason he couldn't settle, because it shouldn't have been a problem.

And he didn't know why it was.

You do.

Adonis ignored that thought completely, concentrating his attention on the crowd. He would soon have to resume his tour of the ballroom, talking to all the necessary people...

A glitter caught his eye, his attention drawn to the progress of a woman wending her way through the crowd. The gown she wore was silvery blue and looked as if the voluminous skirts had been scattered all over with tiny diamonds or raindrops, catching the light as she moved. It was strapless, the bodice cupping a pair of the most perfect breasts he'd ever seen and hugging curvaceous hips. Her bare shoulders glowed like pale satin in the light, her blonde hair piled on her head in delicate curls like a fall of winter sunlight. Her face was heart-shaped and delectable, with a mouth made for sin, and she was beautiful, glowing.

His body hardened instantly.

Perhaps after this ridiculous party was over he could make her acquaintance, because the one thing he hadn't tried to stem this restlessness was sex. He hadn't had a woman since Anna. He'd told himself he'd been too busy, that he'd indulge himself later, but later hadn't come so far. He'd found himself...unenthusiastic about the idea of someone else. Yet not now. He watched her come through the crowd, realising with a start that she was making her way very determinedly towards him, and she was familiar in some way. She reminded him of his little nun with her hair and her skin, and those beautiful curves...

Realisation hit him like a lightning strike.

It *was* his little nun, looking like a princess and coming towards him in that single-minded way she had. How he hadn't known her instantly he couldn't fathom, because there was no mistaking those misty grey eyes or the stubborn slant of her chin.

He stared, drinking in the sight of her. It felt like weeks since he'd seen her—it *had* been weeks since he'd seen her—and he hadn't realised how hungry he was for the sight of her until now.

It was wrong, of course, but he couldn't drag his gaze away.

What was she doing here? He hadn't invited her. This wasn't the kind of event she should be attending. And yet here she was, making straight for him, dressed in a magnificent gown with her hair and make-up perfect... If he hadn't noticed that her hands were clasped tightly in front of her and that even under the make-up she was slightly pale, he would have said she belonged here. The most beautiful jewel in the crown.

His guards loitering a discreet distance away instantly came to attention as she approached, but he shook his head slightly and they relaxed again. He could have had them usher her from the room before she even reached him, but it was clear she was determined to talk to him and he couldn't think of a reason why she shouldn't.

You've thought of plenty of reasons for weeks.

It was true he'd refused all her requests for a meeting, but that was because he'd been extremely busy. And yes, he'd delegated her nightly reports on Ione's progress to an assistant, but again, he'd been extremely busy. It had nothing to do with how she threatened his detachment. Nothing at all.

However, it had been weeks since he'd seen her and surely he was master of himself enough that meeting her wouldn't be a problem. He could spare her a couple of minutes.

Yet his heart beat strangely fast as she approached, his body was hard, and the man who was somehow still alive inside him, the man who should have been displaced entirely by the king, wanted to take her in his arms and find somewhere quiet, somewhere dark, and resume what they'd started in his office weeks ago.

But that could not happen, not again. Nothing had changed.

He was still a king and distance was still required. He would not take her again, no matter what the man inside him wanted.

So he watched her approach, remaining unmoving. People would be looking at him because a king was always under scrutiny, but, since he was relatively hidden by the rhododendrons, he wouldn't be visible to that many people. And neither would she.

'Your Majesty,' she said formally, coming to a stop in front of him and sweeping into a low and graceful curtsey. 'Do you have a moment?'

He eyed her. It really was a magnificent gown, the light glittering off the crystals sewn into her skirts. Where had she got it?

'I do not recall inviting you to this party, Anna.' He kept his tone flat. 'And yet here you are, in a couture gown, with your hair and make-up done…'

She rose from her curtsey, her colour high, her eyes glittering silver, much like her gown. 'No, I know I wasn't invited. Princess Calista helped me with the gown and her stylist did my make-up and hair. I wasn't going to turn up at something like this wearing my grey dress, if that's what you were wondering.'

'What I was wondering was why you are here at all. Especially when, as I said, I did not invite you.'

She gave him a narrow look, her hands clasped tightly in front of her. 'Since you refused all requests for a meeting, I had to find some way of talking to you directly. This seemed the perfect opportunity.'

She was enterprising, his little nun.

Yours?

Just a figure of speech. Of course she wasn't his.

'I've been busy,' he said shortly. 'What is this about?' He very much hoped it wasn't going to be about what had gone on in his office, yet what else could it be?

She was very cool and collected, but he could see the familiar little spark that spoke of her temper all the same, which meant he had to be careful. He found her bright sparks of emotion altogether too fascinating, though at least now he was aware of where his weaknesses lay.

'What do you think this is about?' She seemed annoyed that he didn't know.

'If you're here to talk about what happened in my office—'

'Of course I'm not here to talk about that,' she interrupted, apparently feeling that she could interrupt a king at will. 'I'm here to talk about Ione.'

Surprise rippled through him, closely followed by disappointment, which made no sense. He hadn't wanted to talk about what had happened between them, and Ione was far more of an important subject.

'What about her?' he asked. 'My assistant has been keeping me updated with her progress and I'm pleased with what you've been doing with her.' And he was. Ione had been doing very well by all accounts, though he hadn't seen much of an improvement in her behaviour the few times he'd glimpsed her.

Perhaps she's only good with other people.

It was a thought that did nothing for his own temper.

'She is doing well and has been enjoying the outings I take her on,' Anna said. 'And thank you for granting permission, by the way.'

Ah, yes. The outings. Xerxes had plagued him about that for hours, presenting argument after argument. But it hadn't been until Xerxes had mentioned his being too like their father for comfort that he'd changed his mind. Xenophon had been brutal, but Adonis wasn't, and so he'd given in.

'You can thank my brother for that,' he said coolly.

'And I did.' Anna gave him a stern look. 'But outings aside, Ione's behaviour probably won't get any better until she spends more time with her father.'

He stiffened at the inescapable hint of judgment in her tone. 'Are you questioning me?'

'Yes, actually, I am.' Anna took a step towards him. 'I know you're very busy, that being a king is time-consuming. But the truth is that she needs more of you, Adonis. And she doesn't get it.'

Heat lanced through him at her casual use of his name,

as though she had a right to it. As though he was simply a man and she a woman, naked in his arms.

'I did not give you leave to use my name,' he said coldly, trying to lock down the anger at his own reaction to her. 'You forget yourself, Sister.'

But of course she wasn't cowed by him. She never had been. And instead of inclining her head and accepting her chastisement, she took another step, so she was right in front of him, determination and anger glowing bright in her eyes. 'I don't care. You might be a king, *sire,* but you're also a father. And your little girl needs you.'

She's right. And you know it too.

Hot anger and a smothering sense of guilt tore through him, though he tried to fight it. Because deep inside the heart he tried to tell himself he didn't have, he *did* know it.

But being a father would always come second to being a king, and Ione had to learn that. Because one day she would have to make the same choices that he had.

'Choose, Adonis,' his father had demanded, the day after Adonis had successfully rescued his brother from captivity in the desert, risking the entire succession of Axios to do so. *'I have told you again and again that you cannot be my heir and a brother at the same time, that there will always be an enemy who will use someone you love against you. So you must choose. Your brother or your throne? Which is it to be?'*

Of course he'd chosen the throne. Every time his father had made him choose, he'd always chosen the throne. And not for the power, but because that was his duty.

Ione would have to learn that too when she was old enough. He wouldn't teach her the way his own father had taught him, of course, but when it came time for her to become the Lioness of Axios, he would sit her down and explain why detachment in a monarch was important.

Are you so sure that's true? Do you really want her to turn into what you've become?

Adonis crushed the thought. He had become a king. What was so terrible about that?

'Ione is not more important than my subjects,' he snapped, some of the anger that gripped him leaking out in his voice no matter how hard he tried to stop it. 'I am responsible for millions—including at least a million children—so please forgive me if they take precedence over the needs of one already happy child.'

Anna's expression flickered, something entering her eyes that he didn't like the look of one bit. Her gaze narrowed and she took another step, her skirts brushing closer to him, and he was suddenly surrounded by the scent of musk and lavender, by the warmth of her. Making the breath catch in his throat.

'But she's not happy, Adonis,' she said quietly, her voice very level. 'And neither, I think, are you.'

Happy. What did he know about being happy? Happiness was just another useless emotion he couldn't allow himself to have.

And your daughter? You want that for her?

He ignored the thought. 'Happiness is irrelevant. Rulers do not need to be happy in order to rule.'

Anna's gaze searched his. 'No, but happiness is necessary for children, don't you think?'

'No,' he said before he could stop himself. 'My childhood was unhappy and I survived.'

Concern flickered over her face and she began to lift one of her hands, as if she'd been going to touch him before remembering where she was.

It was a good thing she stopped herself. Touching him would have been a bad idea.

'Oh?' There was concern in her voice now, too. 'What happened?'

And, looking into her steady grey eyes, he felt the strangest urge fill him, almost as if he wanted to tell her.

To tell her about how, when he was seven, he and his mother had been carjacked on the way back to the palace from a function. How their enemies had been expecting the king to be riding with them and were disappointed, demanding to know where he was. And how his mother had refused to give away her husband's location and so they'd hurt her. And because he'd loved her and because he was desperate to save her, Adonis had told them what she wouldn't. She'd tried to grab one of their guns after that, to stop them, but they shot her.

About how his father's bodyguards had managed to hold off the resulting attack, though Xenophon had been injured. And how afterwards his father had told him that her death was his fault, that if Adonis had only been strong in the face of her pain, the palace guards might have been able to rescue them and her death might have been avoided.

'Choose,' his father had said after her funeral. *'You must choose, Adonis. The throne must come before everything. Even before your own mother. You can be my son or you can be my heir, but you cannot be both.'*

He had chosen the throne, of course he had. His younger brother had been too little to take over and Adonis had always been the responsible one. And once his mother had gone, he'd only had his father left.

Yes, he could tell her that.

Or he could tell her how Xenophon had been extra-vigilant after his mother had died, making it his mission to 'harden up' his oldest son. He'd given Adonis a puppy and then, when the dog had grown, had given Adonis a gun and told him to kill it.

Adonis hadn't been able to. He'd been twelve and furious, weeping with rage at himself and his inability to do what his father had asked and shoot his beloved pet. He'd tried, but his heart had got in the way. Again, he'd been weak. In the end he'd had to give the dog to someone else—his father would only have killed the animal himself if Adonis hadn't got rid of it—and hoped that that would be enough for his father.

It wasn't enough. Xenophon had punished him, told him that the lessons in detachment would continue until Adonis learned how to put his feelings completely to the side, because their enemies would show no mercy and so neither could Xenophon.

Or he could tell her about how Xenophon had kidnapped Xerxes, hiding his own identity to test Xerxes's strength and will, torturing him in a cell beneath the palace. He'd ensured that Adonis had been present behind a locked door, with instructions that he absolutely must not interfere. Adonis had had to sit there, listening to his brother's cries, knowing that the moment he tried to get to Xerxes, Xenophon would only redouble his efforts. The only way to end Xerxes's suffering was to do what his father wanted, to lock those feelings away, to endure.

So he had. He'd turned his heart into a block of ice, into stone. A dead hearth in which nothing burned. It had been hard, because his emotions had always been fierce, raw things and he'd found it difficult to contain them.

But he'd had to. For his mother's sake. For his brother's. For his country's.

Yes, he could tell her all those things. But he wouldn't. They weren't her burdens to bear; they were his.

'No,' he repeated, icily. 'I'm afraid that's none of your business, little nun.'

That expression was in her eyes again, the one that made his chest hurt. And it made him angry for no good reason. Her hand was rising again and he knew she'd forget herself this time, and that couldn't happen.

'Anna.' He kept his voice hard. 'Don't forget where we are.'

She took a small, audible breath, her half-lifted hand dropping again. But the expression in her eyes didn't change. 'I'm sorry.'

Her voice sounded small and he had the impression that she wasn't apologising for forgetting herself, but for something else. Something deeper. It made him want to ask what she meant, but already he'd stood here too long. Already he'd spent too much time with her, especially when he had dozens of other people he had to talk to before the night was out.

'Is that all?' he asked without inflection. 'Forgive me, I have many other commitments tonight.'

It was a dismissal and he made sure it sounded like one, and he could see a bolt of hurt dart through her eyes. He didn't like it, but there wasn't any other way to handle this. Besides, she was the one who'd cornered him, not the other way around.

He waited for her to curtsey and leave, but it took her a moment to realise that was what he was expecting. Finally she did, and dutifully sank down. Yet as she was rising he caught the sudden drain of colour in her pretty pink cheeks. And he saw her sway. And when her hand came out as if to grab hold of something he was there.

And when she fell he caught her, holding her close as she fainted away in his arms.

CHAPTER EIGHT

ANNA CAME SLOWLY back to consciousness to the sound of a man talking quietly. He had a very deep voice that she found inexplicably soothing, and so she didn't open her eyes immediately. She was lying on something hard and yet incredibly warm, that deep, gravelly voice was all around her, and she didn't want to move. She felt safe and protected in a way she hadn't for years, if ever, and, since she was tired, more tired than she'd ever felt in her life, she saw no reason to open her eyes.

His voice continued and she drifted for a moment, content to be exactly where she was. Then he stopped talking and silence enveloped her. It was so warm and she was being held, and she didn't want to wake up, so she didn't, drifting back into unconsciousness for a little while longer.

When she came to again, strong arms were still around her, and she was still warm, though a fresh breeze was playing around her ankles and moving over her face. There was movement too, as if she was being carried somewhere. She didn't like it, so she turned her face into the hard warmth she was being held against, and determinedly kept her eyes closed.

Some more time passed, and then a very loud noise rattled through her head, and it sounded so much like a helicopter starting up that she cracked open her eyes just to check.

And then she blinked.

Because it was true. She was being held tightly in someone's lap and she was in a helicopter. A helicopter that was rising up into the night sky and soaring like a bird over the mountains, the lights of Itheus and the palace disappearing beneath it.

Itheus…the palace…

The king….

The breath rushed into her lungs, memory swamping her.

Of walking into the glittering crowds to find him, and then spotting him on his own at last, so tall and broad in black evening clothes, his position only given away by the aura of power that surrounded him. That and the discreet crowned lion fashioned in gold that was pinned to his lapel.

He'd let her approach, watching her with those icy blue eyes, and she could feel something intense and strong pull inside her, something she'd been ignoring for weeks. And she'd known in that instant that it wasn't just for Ione's sake that she'd been trying to get a meeting with him. It was for herself as well.

Because it wasn't until he was right in front of her, the sheer magnetism of his presence drawing her, tugging at her, that she'd realised how much she'd been longing to see him again. Just once. Just to be near him.

That longing had gripped her so hard she'd had to clasp her hands together to stop them from reaching for him. And it had taken everything she had not to ask him for another night. Or even five minutes and only to talk. But she had her pride and he'd been very clear, and besides, it was Ione that mattered, not herself.

But it had been obvious that he neither wanted her, nor had the time to give his daughter.

'Happiness is irrelevant. A ruler doesn't need to be happy in order to rule...'

He'd said that before mentioning his own unhappy childhood, and her heart had twisted. And, given that bleak statement, she might have called her mission a failure.

Yet when she'd asked him to tell her about what had made that childhood so unhappy, she'd had the impression that he'd wanted to. Something had flickered deep in his eyes, a momentary glimpse of something more human. Something that had looked like pain.

And that sense had assailed her once again, of his isolation. His loneliness. The mountain who had no one.

It had made her heart twist in helpless sympathy.

And she'd been desperate to know more. But then he'd dismissed her and the nausea she'd been fighting all day had turned over inside her and blackness had crawled along the edges of her vision. And then...nothing.

Until she'd come to in someone's arms.

You know whose arms.

She moved, her heartbeat racing, but a warm hand rested lightly on her head and a deep rumble of sound vibrated against her ear. The noise of the rotors prevented her from hearing what it was that he said, but his touch calmed her almost instantly.

Of course it was him. His distinctive scent was around her, his heat soaking through the material of her gown, the steady, strong beat of his heart against her ear.

She had no idea where she was going or why, but somehow that didn't matter. And she wasn't afraid. The king might be ice-cold, but he'd never hurt her.

Anna relaxed against him and closed her eyes. She didn't sleep, only let herself enjoy this endless moment, with the noise of the helicopter flying through the night somewhere mysterious, held in the strong arms of a king.

But it ended far too soon.

Anna's eyes opened as the helicopter landed, the rotors slowing, and then cold air was washing around her, bringing the scent of the sea, and she was being carried in darkness along a lighted path.

'I can walk,' she protested, her voice sounding husky. She could hear waves crashing against a distant shore and smell salt in the air.

'No,' the king said. And, since there was no loosening of his hold on her and because she was actually quite happy where she was, she didn't fight him.

She did allow herself to look up though. The lights of the path illuminated his harsh, handsome features. They were set in hard lines, brutal as stone and just as unyielding, and she felt, for the first time, a little quiver of fear.

Whatever had happened and wherever they were, it was because of something serious.

Yet his hold was gentle, and he carried her effortlessly, and, even though there was that fear there, she kept herself relaxed.

The path wound its way through a rocky garden to a small house constructed of white stone with lots of windows. It was lit with hidden lighting, making the place glow like alabaster, warm and inviting.

So. Definitely not a prison, then. Not that she'd done anything wrong, but being transported in the dead of night was always a worry.

A woman opened the double front doors as they approached, potted olive trees standing on either side, and then they were in a pretty tiled entranceway with plain whitewashed walls.

The king said something Anna didn't catch to the woman

and then she stepped outside, shutting the doors behind her. Anna found herself carried down a short, wide hallway and through into a lounge area.

Again, the floor was tiled, the walls whitewashed. Big windows faced the darkness, while luxurious low couches and chairs carved from heavy dark wood and covered in plain white linen were arranged around them. Thick cushions in jewel tones brought colour to the room, while on the floor was a cheerful rag-rolled rug in what looked like bright silks. The king walked to the couch and gently deposited her on it, but he didn't sit. He only stood there, looking down at her, tall and forbidding in his black evening clothes, the golden lion pin gleaming on his breast.

'I suppose you're wondering why you're here,' he said at last. 'Anna, why didn't you tell me you were pregnant?'

Anna blinked, not understanding. 'Excuse me?'

'You fainted in my arms. I had my own personal doctor attend you and he was able to run a number of blood tests. This included a pregnancy test to eliminate the possibility.' The king's face remained hard as granite. 'It was not eliminated and is no longer a possibility. It is a reality.'

She opened her mouth but nothing came out. A cold feeling moved through her, starting at her extremities, making her fingers and toes go numb. Shock. But then, she could only be shocked if it was true, surely. And it couldn't be true. This was all a terrible joke that he was playing on her…

But his hard expression didn't change and his beautiful mouth looked as far from smiling as it ever had.

It's not a joke.

The tiredness that had been dogging her, the nausea that had come and gone, making her feel so awful…

Her lips were now numb and she couldn't feel her hands either, or her feet. 'But we used protection,' she said faintly.

'Protection that apparently failed.' His gaze was so sharp it felt as if it could cut. 'You didn't know?'

Anna shook her head. The possibility had never occurred to her, not once. And now... 'I can't be.' Her voice sounded strange and distant. 'My vows... Oh...' Her heart was beating far too fast and she couldn't breathe. All she could think about was the Reverend Mother and what she'd say, and this last, perhaps greatest mistake. There would be no place in the convent for her now...

Helpless tears filled her eyes, loss gripping her. The convent had been the only home she'd ever known, the nuns the only people who'd ever wanted her, and she'd tried so hard to be good. To be the kind of nun they wanted her to be. But there was no hope of that now.

Pull yourself together. This isn't about you.

Anna swallowed and found she'd put a hand on her stomach, as if to protect the tiny germ of life inside her from her own thoughts. And underneath the shock and the numbness was a small thread of wonder with strands of steely determination woven through it.

She'd been abandoned as a baby; her mother hadn't wanted her then and she hadn't wanted her years later, either. But Anna wouldn't make the same decisions her mother had. Her child would be wanted. Her child would be loved.

She looked up to find the king very close, having taken a couple of steps towards her, obviously to provide some support. But already the shock and self-pitying thoughts that had assailed her were fading away, crushed by the growing strength of her determination.

Anna pushed herself to her feet and met his blue gaze, watching in some satisfaction as surprise rippled across his roughly handsome features. 'I don't care what you say.' Her voice this time was heavy with certainty and almost as hard as his. 'I'm keeping this baby. And I will never get rid of it. This baby is mine.'

A deep blue glow sparked in his gaze. 'I haven't said anything, and if you think I'm going to order you to get rid of it, then you're sadly mistaken. This baby is mine also and of course you will be keeping it.'

Somewhere inside her something instinctive and old as time warmed in approval and satisfaction, but she ignored it. A wave of emotion was building in her, part shock, part anger, part joy and a few other things that she couldn't untangle. It made her heart race. The numbness had receded and so had the light-headedness and nausea, leaving behind it nothing but flames. She was on fire, burning up with reaction and nowhere to direct it.

Nowhere but at him.

'Are you sure about that?' she shot back heedlessly. 'When you don't have time for the child you already have?'

The blue spark in his eyes became a flame, joining the ones already burning inside her, the intense tangle of emotion coalescing into something much hotter and much more definite.

He was so close and his scent was around her, his big, hard body right in front of her. And she could feel the heat of him, the fire that burned inside of him despite his icy exterior. The same fire that burned inside of her, and suddenly she was hungry. It had been weeks since she'd touched him, weeks since she'd been anywhere near him, and it felt like too much. She was so lonely and here he was, his heat burning away the dark.

The baby wasn't real, not in this moment, and the future impossible to contemplate, but he was real and he was hot. He was strong and powerful, and he filled up her entire world.

She lifted her hands to touch him but he caught her

wrists, his fingers like manacles of fire on her delicate skin, his strength overwhelming.

'Adonis.' His name came out, part prayer, part plea, part command.

And the blue flame in his eyes leapt high.

'Please,' she said.

His fingers tightened, and that was the only warning she got as he lowered his head and took her mouth.

There was no thought, only action. Only the fierceness of the anger he couldn't control, no matter how hard he tried, and it came thick and hot, leaping high as she challenged him, flinging a truth at him that he didn't want to hear. And then when her silver gaze had caught fire, that anger had exploded into a deep and instinctive desire.

He didn't know what had changed, whether it was simply their chemistry reacting in proximity to one another, needing only a spark to ignite it, weeks of denial turning into wildfire, or whether it was something deeper.

Something to do with her carrying his child and the decision he'd made as he held her in his arms on the flight through the darkness to his island, his mind already sorting through possibilities and plans after the doctor's shock revelation. He could have laid her on the seat next to him, but the strong sense of possessiveness that had gripped him on hearing the news, the same possessiveness he'd felt the night he'd first taken her, wouldn't leave him. This time he didn't resist it and kept hold of her instead.

He had been angry—no, more like furious—with himself. Because it was no one's fault but his that this had happened. He was the one with the experience and he was the one who knew that even with condoms there was a small failure rate. And there was nothing to be done about it. It had happened and the fierce protectiveness that had rushed through him, as strong as the possessiveness, wouldn't be denied, no matter what justifications he gave himself.

He knew what he must do. Nothing was certain until after the twelve-week mark and it was still early days, but that didn't matter. There was Ione to consider, and what Anna had said to him at the celebration, about how Ione wasn't happy, had stuck in his head.

Happiness was a feeling he didn't need, but, no matter his father's training, he found he couldn't bear the thought that his daughter didn't need it either. He knew what the expectations were of an heir and how heavily they had sat on his shoulders. How sometimes he'd wanted his parents to be normal parents, who put him first and not the crown. Yet they never had. Even in those last moments, his mother had been acting to protect her husband, not him.

He could do that for Ione, though. He could give her someone who would put her first. Someone loving and loyal, someone who could perhaps provide him with some physical relief too. A wife, in other words. He hadn't planned on marrying again, not wanting to put a potential partner through the misery Sophia had endured. But perhaps it would be different this time with Anna. He would set it out plainly for her, like a job. And she could also choose to view it that way if that was preferable to her.

She wasn't from an aristocratic family, but his kingship was secure. It didn't matter who he married, and Anna was the logical choice, even if her pregnancy didn't go ahead.

After all, it wasn't as if she loved him.

You thought that about Sophia. And Anna is passionate; she feels things deeply. You can't possibly expect her to remain unengaged.

But he refused that thought, just as he'd refused it as she'd flung her accusation about the lack of attention he gave the one child he already had. She'd stood straight and tall, blazing, not like a little nun, but like steel tempered in fire, becoming stronger and sharper.

He hadn't been able to stop himself as she'd spoken his name, the blaze in her eyes changing into passion as he felt his own desire rise. He didn't want to stop though. He'd been dreaming of her, of her mouth under his, of the sweet heat between her thighs and the soft curves of her breasts, for weeks, and he was hungry. So very, very hungry. And it was a sharp, raw thing that clawed at his insides with a deep, insistent ache.

He shouldn't give in to the intensity of his need and he knew it. He knew, too, that his detachment was already compromised from their previous encounter.

But he hadn't been able to resist.

She'd awoken the lion and this lion was ravenous.

His grip tightened on her wrists and, though she made an attempt to pull away, he didn't let her, pushing her wrists behind her back and holding them there. She groaned as her mouth opened beneath his and he tasted her, the hot sweetness of her like summer wine.

And just like that night in his office, there was no shyness in her and she held nothing back, her kiss that of a starving woman and he a feast brought before her.

She made an insistent, demanding sound, pushing herself against him, her soft curves pressed to his body, and his hunger sharpened further, gaining a possessive edge which was choking in its intensity.

He should have resisted that too, but he didn't. Because as her teeth sank into his lower lip, the lion escaped its cage entirely.

Adonis growled, gripping her wrists hard in one hand and jerking down the bodice of her gown with the other, baring her to the waist. Then he cupped one breast, squeezing gently, testing the weight of it. Her skin was silky and warm in his palm, and she gasped against his mouth, arching into him.

He kissed her harder, deeper, teasing her hard nipple with his thumb, then pinching it lightly. She shuddered, a low moan escaping her. Her soft curves were crushed against him, the heat of her skin burning through the black wool of his tuxedo, and suddenly the clothing separating them was too much.

He wanted her naked, wanted skin on skin with nothing between them.

She is yours now.

Yes, she was.

He let go of her straining wrists, found her zip and tugged it down. Then he peeled the gown away from her, leaving her naked but for her plain white knickers.

'Adonis,' she gasped, reaching for him, but he pushed her down onto the couch.

'Stay there,' he ordered harshly as she tried to get up, shrugging off his jacket and dropping it carelessly onto the floor.

She stilled, watching him, her breasts rising and falling fast and hard with her quickened breathing. She was a beautiful sight, all white skin and luscious curves and rosy nipples. Her pretty hair was still piled on top of her head, but he would take that down. He would ruin it. He would ruin her for anyone but him.

Ripping open the buttons of his shirt, he tore it off, then reached for his belt.

She moved on the couch as if to go to him, but he shook his head. She ignored him, lioness that she was, coming to stand before him then dropping to her knees.

'Please,' she said hoarsely, tipping her head back and looking up at him. 'Let me.'

His hunger turned savage. 'Are you sure you want to do

that?' He didn't bother to hide the growl in his voice. 'I am in no mood to be kind.'

Silver gleamed in her eyes, as though the sharp edge of the blade she had become was glinting. 'Neither am I.'

This woman was dangerous. She would make a good match for him.

He bared his teeth in a lion's smile. 'Are you hungry for me, little nun? Are you desperate for a taste?'

'Yes.' She lifted her hands, shaking, to his belt buckle. 'So much.'

Dimly, he could feel the king inside him try to take back some control, try to put some distance between him and his hunger. But the king wasn't in charge now.

He was a man and he would have what he wanted.

So he stood there while she undid his belt and then the fastenings of his trousers, pulling down the zip and opening the two sides. And when she reached inside his boxers to grip the hard length of his shaft, he didn't stop her. Sensation rippled through him as her fingers circled him. She drew him out, sparks of pleasure igniting along all his nerve endings, and another growl was torn from him.

She looked up at him, stroking him, her eyes like moonlight. 'I don't know how to do this. Show me.'

He didn't need to be asked twice. Reaching down, he speared his fingers into the delicate confection of curls on her head, destroying its perfection, and her gasp intensified the pleasure inside him.

'Take me in your mouth,' he ordered.

And she did.

Heat exploded through him, the catch of his breath echoing through the room, fire leaping in her eyes in response. Oh, she liked that. She liked giving him pleasure.

It made him even harder and as her lips closed around him, heat enveloping him, he was trapped by the intensity of her silver gaze, caught in an endless loop of pleasure. She gave him pleasure, and his reaction sparked pleasure in her, which then gave it back to him; it was a constant cycle, an unbreakable current.

She wasn't a nun any longer. She was a lioness, a sword. A goddess kneeling at his feet. And he wanted more, which made his decision to take her for himself the best decision. The only decision.

The man cannot have anything, you know this.

But he discarded that thought as he'd discarded the golden lion pin on his jacket. Tonight, the king was forgotten. There was only the man, and the man had been denied too long.

He told her what to do, but soon she didn't need much in the way of guidance, finding her own way, licking him, tasting him, exploring him, giving little hums of satisfaction every time she drew a growl of pleasure from him, driving him to the brink of insanity.

He pulled her head away from him, ignoring her cry of protest. 'On the couch,' he ordered. And as she did what she was told, he got rid of the rest of his clothes. Then, finally naked, he joined her on the cushions, pushing her rounded thighs wide apart so he could kneel between them.

She was panting, her eyes dark, her skin like silk as he ran his hands all over it.

'Oh… Adonis…please…'

'Beg for me, little nun,' he murmured, his voice nothing but gravel and sand. 'Again.'

And she did, and when he buried his face between her legs, she begged again and again as he tasted her, licking her, exploring all her hidden valleys, all the places she was most sensitive, all the places that gave her the most pleasure, using her cries and sobs as his guide.

Then, when he felt her muscles lock, he slid his hands

beneath her bottom and lifted her higher, drinking from her, using his tongue to drive her straight to the edge and then over it.

She arched, convulsing, a cry of ecstasy breaking from her, but he didn't stop, tasting the wild, sweet flavour of her orgasm. Then he slipped one hand between her thighs, stroking through her slippery folds, driving her straight towards another. A choked gasp escaped her, and he shifted, pushing himself up and leaning over her, bending to take one stiff pink nipple in his mouth, sucking hard as he eased one finger inside her, then another, setting up an insistent rhythm of sensation that had her twisting on the sheets and screaming his name yet again as another climax hit her.

He eased her down after that, stroking her as she shuddered through the aftershocks. Strands of hair clung to her damp forehead, her skin gleaming with perspiration, and she looked thoroughly ruined.

But he wasn't done.

You'll never be done.

The thought whispered through his head as he picked her up from the couch cushions, heading for the stairs and the upstairs bedroom, the truth of it settling down into him. No, possibly he wouldn't. But that didn't matter.

She was his now and he'd have all the time in the world to test that theory.

The bed upstairs that faced the windows with the dark sea beyond was wide, the sheets cool, and when he laid her down on it he scanned her face, looking for any signs that she'd had enough.

But when he settled himself between her thighs, her warmth and softness beneath him, she slid her hand into his hair and pulled his head down, her mouth hot and sweet and open under his.

She was so generous. She would never turn him away

and he felt the truth of that deep inside him. He could come to her and she would take him in, and she would hold him. He could pour himself into her and she would take it all.

She will put you first.

Something in his chest shifted, something tight. Something he wasn't comfortable with. The embers in the dead hearth of his heart glowed as if someone had breathed air on them.

He ignored it. Instead, he embraced the pleasure as he lifted his head from her mouth and looked into her eyes, thrusting inside her, sheathing himself in her slick heat.

She gasped, his name a prayer on her lips. And when he drew back and thrust again she cried out, her legs closing around his waist, her hips rising to meet his.

And he kept on staring into the silver darkness of her eyes as he drove them both to the edge of oblivion.

And over it.

CHAPTER NINE

ANNA WOKE TO sunlight pressing against her closed lids. She sighed and shifted, conscious that her body ached as if she'd had a hard workout, which was strange, since she wasn't a fan of exercise at the best of times.

Perhaps she'd done too much running around with Ione yesterday?

She shifted again, only to have the large, heavy arm wrapped around her waist tighten, drawing her against something hard and very, very hot.

Her breath caught, shock rippling through her, closely followed by flickers of memory.

Memories of fainting at a ball. Of the king catching her. The king kissing her.

The king inside her, moving with a savage, relentless rhythm, and the cries he'd drawn from her. The pleasure that had coursed through her.

Of looking up into blue eyes gone the colour of midnight, his gaze fierce as it held hers. Moonlight had caught his brutally handsome features, limning them in silver, and her heart had kicked hard in her chest.

He'd been strong and beautiful and hungry. And he'd kept her awake, demanding more and more of her as the night had gone on. But she hadn't cared. She'd given him everything she had and more, because she was hungry too.

For him and only him.

She kept her eyes closed for a second longer, not wanting to move because there were other memories there apart from pleasure: him telling her that she was pregnant and the future she'd always imagined for herself burning to ashes.

They hadn't discussed anything last night, too caught up in sating the desire that had blazed so intensely between them. She still didn't even know where he'd taken her or why.

Cautiously, she opened her eyes.

They were lying in a big, wide bed, white sheets tumbled and tangled all around them. The bed faced big windows that looked out onto a deep blue ocean, flooding the room with bright sunlight that made the whitewashed stone walls glow.

The dark wood of the floor was covered in bright silk rugs, another rug pinned to the wall above the bed. It was a simple, bare room, the only furniture the bed, two bedside tables in heavy, dark wood and a carved wooden dresser against one wall.

Clearly, it was the king's house but…where was it? And why had he brought her here?

Moving slowly, she managed to wiggle out from underneath his arm and sat up, turning to look down at him. He was still asleep, the hard lines of his face relaxed, making him seem younger. She stared at the way his mouth curled slightly, as if he was on the verge of a smile.

That would never happen. Adonis didn't smile, or if he did, she'd never seen it.

Her heartbeat gave another kick. She wanted to see it. And she wanted to be the one who made him smile, too, wanted that very much. In fact, there were a lot of things she wanted when it came to him, and it wasn't all about sex, either.

She reached out to touch one heavily muscled shoulder, loving the velvety feel of his warm skin. The lines of his royal tattoo, a crowned lion, stalked across his back, the colours deep and rich, red and gold and black. It was beautiful. She traced the lion's roaring mouth and the edges of its mane, yet another sign that it wasn't just a man lying next to her, but a king.

A king who won't let himself be a man.

'You like that?' The sound of his voice, roughened by the night they'd spent together, took her by surprise, sending a pleasant shock through her.

She almost snatched her hand away, unsure whether she should be taking such liberties. Then again, after last night, surely everything was allowed?

'Yes, it's beautiful.' She touched the gold crown on the lion's head. 'Is it only kings who are allowed the tattoo?'

'Only the crowned lion. Xerxes has one, but his lion doesn't have a crown.'

'When did you get it?'

'When I was eighteen. The royal tattooist is the only one permitted to use this design and only on the royal family. The inks are special too.'

'Will Ione have one?' she asked, curious. 'Or is it only men who have it?'

'Not only men. Ione will have hers when she turns eighteen.' His gaze was clear and cold as a winter sky, focusing intently on her. 'Don't you want to know where we are and why?'

She slid a finger along one of the lion's big paws. 'Tell me.'

'This was my mother's house. My father gave her this island as a wedding present.'

A dark current of emotion threaded through the words

and Anna paused in her tracing of the lion on his shoulder, glancing down into his eyes.

His mother. Who'd died in a car accident, according to the history books.

'It seems lovely,' she said carefully.

'It is. She didn't come here much.' He reached suddenly for her hand and took it in his, turning her palm over and studying it intently. 'She preferred the palace. I had a nanny who used to bring me here for holidays.'

Anna shivered as he ran a finger lightly over the centre of her palm, her whole body reacting to his touch. 'A nanny?'

'I didn't spend much time with my parents.' He circled her palm gently, his attention on her hand. 'They were always busy.'

Again there was a dark edge threading through his tone, and it made her throat close in sudden foreboding. The queen had died when he was young… Was this part of his unhappy childhood?

'Your mother died in a car accident, didn't she?' Anna asked hesitantly.

'No,' he said without any discernible emotion. 'It was not a car accident.'

'But wasn't that—'

'A story the media were told. There was no accident. Our car was ambushed by an enemy faction when I was seven. They wanted my father, but he never rode in the same car with us for safety reasons. They overcame our guards, dragged us from the car, and tried to make my mother tell them where he was. But she wouldn't, so they hurt her.'

Anna stared at him, shocked. 'Hurt her?'

'They tortured her, but she wouldn't give away my father's position.' He paused, the icy blue of his eyes fathomless. 'I was desperate to stop them hurting her, so I told them instead.'

Anna's breath caught. 'Oh, Adonis...'

'Even after I'd betrayed the king, she tried to stop them, grabbing one of their guns. But they shot her. My father was injured in the subsequent attack, but luckily his body-guards were able to save him. My mother died of her in-juries.' His voice was so cold, as if it were someone else's mother who'd died, and not his own.

Horror and a terrible sympathy flooded through her. This was the source of the pain she'd seen in his eyes back at the ball, wasn't it? And no wonder. His mother had been tortured right in front of him.

'I'm so sorry,' she whispered. It seemed so empty and inadequate, but it was all she could think of to say.

'My father was furious. He blamed me. Told me that if I'd stayed strong and hadn't given away his position, she wouldn't have grabbed the gun. That the palace guards would have found us and rescued us.'

Anna's throat constricted. 'But you were just a little boy. How could you—'

'It doesn't matter how old I was,' he interrupted harshly. 'I shouldn't have broken. I shouldn't have told them where my father was. I put my feelings for my mother before my duty to protect the throne.' His gaze glittered. 'And she died.'

The look in his eyes made her heart hurt. It was so bleak. So...cold. As if he felt nothing. Which was a lie, because he did, she knew he did. Last night had proved that, though the mountain might appear icy and remote, inside he was molten. Inside, he was a volcano.

'Adonis...' she began softly.

But he went on, implacable. 'My father was determined to teach me a lesson. He thought I was far too emotional and that enemies would be able to use those emotions against me, so he made it his mission to excise that weakness from me.'

The foreboding that hadn't quite gone away tightened its grip on her.

She didn't want to ask, but then, she didn't need to, because he went on anyway,

'Xenophon kidnapped Xerxes and interrogated him, tortured him. He pretended to be an enemy, using my voice as a way to break my little brother. I was put in the next room and ordered not to intervene. I had to listen to him scream. My will had to be strong enough to withstand him being used as a weapon against me. My first duty was to my throne, not to him.'

Shock washed through her, a bucket of ice water dumped over her head.

This was the reason he was so hard and so cold. She didn't know much about King Xenophon, only that he'd been an old-style king, harsh and militaristic in his ways. But this brutal? Torturing his own sons? Because that was what Adonis was describing. Actual torture. And not only the torture of his brother, but the torture of himself too.

'That's terrible,' she said, an instant and fierce protectiveness rising inside her. Because of what he'd suffered. Because of what his father had put him through. Because of what he'd become. 'That's abuse.'

'It was necessary,' his voice was even icier now, 'because to break would have been to prolong Xerxes's pain.'

'What about your pain?' She knew she sounded demanding, but she was angry and couldn't hide it. 'What kind of father would do that to his own children?'

'He wasn't a father,' Adonis said relentlessly, 'he was a king. Just as I ceased to be his son, only his heir. Emotion can be used as a weapon and so I had to rid myself of it.'

'So that was his excuse?' She couldn't shut herself up. 'That was his justification for hurting you? The fact that emotions can be used against you?'

'He said that our enemies would have no mercy and so he couldn't have any.' Adonis's thick black lashes were a stark contrast to the blue of his eyes. 'He wasn't wrong. Our enemies had no mercy. They tortured my mother because they knew I would break.'

'But that was years ago—'

'Xerxes was captured while on a mission with his platoon,' he interrupted in the same cold tone. 'Our father refused a rescue mission. He was certain Xerxes had been captured in order to draw me out.' A muscle jumped in Adonis's hard jaw. 'I knew I should have put my duty as heir first, but I couldn't let them have my little brother. So I disobeyed my father's orders and mounted a rescue mission. I was successful, but Xenophon wouldn't have any of it. He made me choose once and for all—the throne or exile. He would make Xerxes his heir instead.'

Anna took a shaken breath, fury making it difficult to speak. 'He would have disowned you? Because you rescued your brother?'

Adonis's face remained granite, his eyes hard jewels. There was no softness in him anywhere. 'A king has to put his country before his feelings. Before his family. Before everything. Besides, exile was kinder to Xerxes than the throne would have been. The lessons my father would have taught him would have destroyed him. I was born for this. It is my duty. I chose to remain his heir.' Adonis paused. 'Xerxes didn't know, but it was that decision that got him banished. My father put him out of my reach once and for all.'

Cold wound through the heat of her anger like a slow-moving frost, cold as the wintry blue of his eyes.

Dear God, the horror of it. No wonder this man was so icy, so hard. He hadn't just learned his father's lessons, he'd become them. They'd turned him to stone.

'I am telling you all of this so that you understand,' Adonis went on, his tone utterly flat. 'A king cannot allow himself to be a man. To feel as a man would. To love as a man would. A king must put his country before everything, even his own family.'

His harshness felt like an arrow to her chest, piercing her. Was that what he was trying to say? That he could have nothing for himself? Nothing for the man? He could have all the power and authority, but there could be no friendship. No laughter. No love.

The nuns might have been distant, but even they had smiled and laughed. Even they had shown her what peace looked like and given her a taste of happiness.

But he hadn't tasted it. He didn't even know what it looked like. How could he? When his father had stripped him of all emotion? His childhood ripped away, a boy tortured for the sake of a throne, and all because of one mistake…

Her eyes pricked with tears, the ferocity of her anger at what had been done to him choking her. 'You know you've been brainwashed, don't you?' she said hoarsely. 'That everything you've been told is a lie?'

An expression rippled across his face, gone too fast for her to tell what it was. 'I brought you here, Anna,' he went on as if she hadn't spoken, 'because first, you are pregnant with my child, and until that resolves itself one way or the other I want you out of harm's way. And second… Ione needs a mother.'

Anna stared at him, her anger forgotten for a moment. 'What?'

His hold on her hand tightened. 'Ione knows you. She

likes you, too, which makes you perfect. I want you to be my wife, Anna. Be my queen. Be the mother Ione needs.'

Another wave of shock hit her, stealing any breath remaining in her lungs. 'But…you can't want to marry me. I'm just a nun. I have vows I want to take.'

'You're pregnant. And you can't take your vows if you have a child, most certainly not if that child is mine.' His thumb brushed over the centre of her palm in a sensual stroke that, despite the shock, set all her nerve endings alight. 'And you were right about Ione. She does need more than I can give. You care about her, you put her first.' His gaze was focused, relentless. 'She needs you more than the convent does. More than the Reverend Mother.' Something hotter glittered abruptly in his eyes. 'A convent is not the place for a woman like you, anyway. You're passionate, intense. And I can give you everything you need to satisfy that passion.'

Sex, he was talking about sex. He didn't mean any other kind of passion.

But you want more than that.

Yet the thought was a dim one, hazy, lost under the stunning surprise of his proposal and the vision of a different life that it had conjured up. A life she'd never thought she'd have and yet always wanted.

She could see it now: a husband and child; a family; a place where she belonged.

She'd thought she'd found that in the convent, with God as her husband and her family the church. But now that she considered it, there had always been something…passionless and detached about that vision. Something distant. There was no immediacy to it, no heat. No desire. No laughter and no joy. At least not for her.

There will be no joy with him either, you realise.

Anna stared into his blue eyes, pain winding tight. His

childhood had been so bleak, abusive even. He wouldn't even know what joy was. But if there was ever someone who needed to learn, it was him. His father had brainwashed him into thinking his emotions were the enemy, but if he could learn how to isolate himself, he could also unlearn it. He'd already given in to the passion inside him, so perhaps he could also allow himself other things. Such as happiness and warmth. Joy and laughter.

Love.

And why not love? Who loved him? His brother did, but that was a sibling's love. His daughter loved her father, yes, and his people loved the king, but who loved the man?

You can.

The thought had sharp edges, cutting her in places that were far too vulnerable and exposed, but she ignored them. Yes, she could love him. That was possible. No, it was necessary. He hadn't had enough love in his life from the sounds of it, and he needed it. And so did his little girl. He had no one else to give it to him. No one but her.

And the convent? Your vows?

He was right; the convent didn't need her. She'd never fitted in there anyway. And the Reverend Mother had been right, too, to send her to Axios, to a king desperate for what she had so much of to give: love.

And what about you? Don't you need it?

The warning was loud in her head because if he couldn't put his daughter before his country, then he would never put *her* first. He would never give her in return what she could give him.

But maybe that didn't matter. She'd gone years without it, and he had passion at least. Maybe in time that would change. And there was Ione to think about as well…

Was it even a choice?

'Yes,' she said, her voice only a little rough, staring

into those cold, implacable blue eyes. 'Yes, I will be your wife.'

The fire in his gaze leapt high. He let go of her hand, his arms coming around her, drawing her in against him, into his heat. Then he turned them both and she found herself lying beneath him, caged by heat, hard muscle, and smooth, velvety skin.

He was above her, his piercing gaze holding her captive. 'Then you'll be mine, little nun. And in return you will be queen, your nights full of all the pleasure I can give you, and your days spent with a little girl who desperately needs you. You have a home with me at the palace, I swear it.'

You will be his. But he will never be yours.

A shudder moved through her, a fault line inside her reminding her that there were cracks in her heart. Cracks that hadn't healed and perhaps never would.

But it didn't matter. Her heart, cracked or not, was big enough for all of them.

Conviction settled down inside her as she looked up into his strong face. Yes, she was here for a reason and that reason wasn't just a small, excitable girl, but a man. A king. A lonely mountain who needed someone, even if that mountain didn't know it yet himself.

And she knew that the vows she was meant to take were never supposed to be ones of chastity and sacrifice, and her vocation wasn't to be part of the church. Her vows were those of marriage, and her vocation was to be with him. He was her church and she was meant to worship him.

She didn't speak.

Instead she reached up and pulled him down, taking her first communion from his mouth.

Adonis decided not to return to the palace that day. Or indeed the next. Or even the one after that. Instructing Xerxes to take over for a couple of days, he didn't bother with an explanation, merely telling his surprised brother that he was taking some time off. He also issued another order for Ione to be brought to the island after a couple of days, allowing himself and Anna to have some time together before they broke the news of their impending wedding to the little girl.

He told himself that keeping Anna with him was necessary because they needed to discuss how a marriage between them would work, nothing at all to do with the raw possessiveness that gripped him, making it impossible to keep his hands off her.

They spent that first day in bed, disturbed only by palace staff arriving with clothing and personal items for them both, not to mention stocking the place with food. And then the staff left, leaving them entirely alone.

So he indulged himself with her. Indulged himself utterly. She'd left his detachment in ruins the night she'd fainted in his arms, and since it had shattered so completely there wasn't any point in rebuilding it. Not yet at least.

There would be plenty of time for that later, when they returned to the palace, and in the meantime he might as well let himself be a man for a little while. It was temporary. He'd rebuilt himself once before; he could do so again. And besides, if he gave his hunger for her free rein, perhaps it would ease their intense physical chemistry.

She certainly took delight in the lessons he gave her on how to please him, taking to them with relish and enthusiasm, cementing his opinion that the convent was not and had never been the place for her. She had far too much passion to lead the quiet life of celibacy required of a nun, and it made him rethink his position on the Reverend Mother sending her to him.

Perhaps his godmother knew more than he'd initially thought.

While he demanded her passion during the day, in the evenings he decided to cement their relationship further by cooking for her, much to her shock, which amused him. In fact, shocking her for his own amusement was getting to be moderately addictive, and, since she was getting harder to shock in bed, he found he had to demonstrate his talents elsewhere.

Cooking was one of those talents. His nanny had taught him right here in this very kitchen, with the scrubbed wooden table and herbs, and pots and pans hanging from a wooden frame above it. She'd been of the opinion that a man needed a few practical skills and being able to feed himself was one of the most basic. Xenophon hadn't approved, but Adonis had learned all the same, and discovered he had quite the talent for it.

Since ascending the throne, he never got a chance to cook, and rather to his own surprise he found himself appreciating the opportunity to do so now. Especially with Anna sitting at the table opposite him, watching him chop onions with wide eyes, making him want to show off like a thirteen-year-old boy in front of a girl he had a crush on.

'I can't believe you can cook,' she said in awed tones.

'My nanny taught me. She was a firm believer in a man being able to look after himself.'

Anna took a sip of the orange juice he'd poured for her, leaning her chin in one hand, watching him. 'You enjoy it, don't you?'

Did he? He never did anything for his own enjoyment, because his own enjoyment was never paramount. Yet... there was something about creating sustenance for her that pleased him.

'There is something meditative about working with your hands,' he admitted.

Her eyes gleamed. 'I know how you can work with your hands.'

He smiled. Her fledgling attempts at flirtation were adorable. 'What a naughty nun you are. Perhaps after dinner I can show you a few other things I can do with my hands.'

She flushed beautifully, her mouth turning up. 'Perhaps I'll even let you.' Her gaze flickered to the flash of his knife on the chopping board and her smile faded. 'I never learned how to cook. The nuns wouldn't let me near the kitchen.'

There was a wistful note in her voice, making him pause in his chopping to stare at her lovely face. 'You sound unhappy about that.'

'Oh?' She looked a little surprised. 'Do I?'

'Yes.'

'I don't mean to. I suppose I was only thinking about how lovely it was that you had someone to teach you.' She let out a breath, but didn't offer more.

He put the knife down, unable to tear his gaze from the flicker of sadness in her grey eyes. She'd been fostered with the nuns, or so she'd told him that night in his office, which meant that she wouldn't have had a family. And it was clear from the look on her face now that she felt the lack acutely.

It made his chest tighten with sympathy.

You feel the lack of yours too.

But how could he? He'd never had a family. All he'd had was a training regime.

'You've been brainwashed... Everything you've been told is a lie...'

'I know you were fostered by the nuns,' he said, shoving that memory aside, 'but did you ever make contact with your parents?'

Her smile vanished, her gaze dropping to the table top. 'I couldn't find my father. But I tracked my mother down a couple of years ago and yes, I made contact with her. I emailed her a few times, talked to her on the phone.' Anna traced a small line in the condensation on the sides of her glass. 'She seemed nice enough.'

He frowned, caught by the edge in her tone. 'And?'

Her head tilted, her concentration on the glass. 'I wanted to meet her and she told me she wanted to meet me too. So I tried to organise a few meetings, but when the time came she would always cancel. I asked her why and she told that me that she already had a family and didn't want to rake up the past again. Then she broke off all contact.' Her voice grew tight. 'I understood. It was hard for her.'

His own muscles tightened too because, while Anna might have said she understood, it was clear the rejection had struck her somewhere vulnerable deep inside. And he disliked the thought of her in pain. He disliked it intensely.

'But you were hurt nonetheless,' he said, not making it a question.

Anna lifted a shoulder as if that wasn't relevant. 'She'd had a hard life. It made sense that she didn't want to have it all brought back to her.'

He noted the tension around her mouth and jaw. 'Except you wanted to meet her, didn't you?' He wasn't sure why he was pushing for information, especially since it was obviously an old wound and he didn't want to reopen it, not to mention that her pain made him uncomfortable. But he couldn't ignore it, either.

She gave another small sigh. 'I would have liked to. I just…wanted to make contact with someone who was related to me, to see where I came from, that kind of thing. I felt out of place in the convent, so I wanted to know if I perhaps belonged elsewhere.' She made a dismissive gesture. 'But my mother was uncomfortable with that and so I let it go. It's fine.'

But it wasn't fine and he could see that.

'Your mother might have had her reasons for not wanting to keep in contact with you, Anna, but that doesn't make it any less a rejection. Especially one you didn't deserve.'

'That's the issue though. Perhaps I did deserve it. I wasn't very nice to her, you see. I told her that she owed me a meeting after getting rid of me and then she got upset and hung up on me.' Anna sat back, her hands in her lap, and her shoulders hunched. 'I shouldn't have got so angry with her. It was the wrong thing to do.'

He could hear the bitterness in her tone, saw the hurt radiating from her. And he'd moved around the table towards her before he was even conscious of doing so.

She lifted her head as he approached, resisting slightly as he pulled her from the chair she was sitting in. But as soon as he put his arms around her, she melted utterly against him and put her forehead on his chest.

'I made a stupid mistake, Adonis,' she said, her voice muffled in his T-shirt. 'I shouldn't have got so angry. I just wanted so badly to talk to her, to have some kind of connection with her. To know where I came from and who my family was. And why she didn't want me. What was so wrong with me that...' Anna broke off, her small body shivering.

And he felt that shift in his chest again, a tight sensation that wouldn't let up, and he didn't like it. He didn't know where the impulse to take her in his arms had come from either. But he didn't release her. She was upset and in pain and it felt wrong to leave her to deal with it alone. She was also warm and holding on to him, clinging to him, calling to the deep protectiveness that had woken when he'd found out about her pregnancy.

'There's nothing wrong with you.' He put a comforting hand on the back of her head, letting his palm rest against her pale, silky hair. 'You know that, don't you?'

'Mum didn't want me, not even years later. And I was

always such a trial to the nuns. I don't think they wanted me either—'

He reached for her chin, forcing her head back so she had to look up at him. Her eyes were full of hurt and a bitterness that he hated to see there. 'It's not you. How could it be? Your mother didn't even know the woman you grew up to be.' He let her see the conviction burning in his eyes. 'And as for the nuns, the Reverend Mother knew your worth. Why else did she send you to help Ione? You're unselfish and generous. Warm and passionate. You're exactly what Ione needs.'

Anna's eyes gleamed with tears, but there was something else in the look she gave him that made the tightness in his chest contract even further. 'And you?' she asked. 'What about what you need?'

You need her.

The thought was bright and burning, making longing curl through him. Anna, warm and generous and giving. Anna, who'd braved his disapproval in order to help Ione.

Anna, who'd never put a throne before a person.

The way your parents did?

'You shouldn't ask me questions like that, little nun. Not when you know the answer already,' he said, his voice unaccountably rough, ignoring that thought. Of course his parents had put the throne before their son. They'd *had* to.

She didn't look away, and he had the disturbing impression that she could see inside him, see all the thoughts in his head.

'I wasn't asking the king,' she said quietly. 'I was asking you.'

He lifted his hands and cupped her face between them, keeping his touch gentle, because his words would not be. 'Anna. You know this already. I can't be anything other than the king. And a king can't need anyone.'

Her gaze searched his face and the strange, tight feeling inside him grew. 'I know that's what your father made you believe. But it's not true.'

'Anna—'

'Do you think I can only be a nun? That I can't be a friend as well? Or that Xerxes can only be a prince and not a father?'

It felt as if she'd found a vulnerability in his armour and had slid a knife inside it, cutting him. 'It's different for you. Different for him,' he said flatly, not wanting to discuss it.

'Why?' She threw the question at him like a stone. 'How? You're a man like Xerxes is. You're also a father.'

'A king has to protect millions—'

'Stop spouting the lies your father taught you, Adonis,' she interrupted, suddenly fierce. 'Because that's what they are. Lies. Not having emotion doesn't make you a king, it makes you a robot.' Her eyes glittered. 'It makes you him.'

He dropped his hands from her face and took a step back, his heart beating far too fast and he wasn't sure why. He wasn't his father, of course he wasn't. Xenophon had been brutal, yes, but everything he'd done had been to help Adonis be a better king.

It had been for Axios's sake.

It's always about Axios. Never about you.

'I'm not him,' he growled. 'If I were, do you think I would have asked you to marry me? I would not do to Ione what was done to me.'

'And yet you hold her at a distance. You tell her you have no time. And you tell yourself that the throne comes first.' Concern flooded her lovely face along with a sympathy that cut him open. 'Is that what your father told you, too? That he couldn't put you first? That the throne came before everything?'

Pain throbbed inside him, a crack running through his soul.

His mother had held out despite how those men had tortured her, but not to protect him. It had been for her husband. To protect the king. Then she'd taken that gun, bringing about her own death, and it had all been to protect the throne. Not to save her son.

And his father hadn't seemed to care how the blame he'd laid on his oldest son for his mother's death had crushed him. How the torture of his little brother had torn him apart.

The throne was more important. It was always about the throne.

But how could it be about anything else? A country and the lives of millions were always going to be more important than he was.

'He was right,' Adonis forced out, hearing his own father's voice in the words and hating the sound of it. Hating himself for saying it. 'The throne has to come first.'

She lifted her hand and cupped his cheek before he could pull away, her touch warm as sunlight. 'You can't believe that.'

But he did. The love he'd once had for his father had died a death the day Xerxes had been banished, yet he still carried the spirit of Xenophon's teachings.

'You don't understand,' he said roughly. 'I *have* to believe it. Otherwise everything that was done to me, to Xerxes, would have been for nothing.'

There was such sadness in her eyes. 'That's the bleakest thing I've ever heard.'

He could feel tension crawling through every part of him and he had to concentrate to hold himself still. 'What do you want from me, Anna?'

She stared at him and he didn't know what she was looking for. 'I don't want anything from you. I just want you to know that you're not alone.'

He couldn't have said why that felt like a knife twisting inside him, cutting him deeper, but it did, a sharp, insistent pain.

He didn't like it. And he didn't want to talk about this any more. So he kissed her hard instead, ending the conversation.

CHAPTER TEN

ANNA SAT ON the end of the small jetty that projected out from the rocky beach of the island and into the deep blue water. The sun was warm on her back and she had her feet dangling in the cool water.

In the small, sheltered cove, a little sailboat tacked back and forth, its white sail shining in the sun. She could hear Ione's shrieks of delight echo across the water as her father guided the small boat, and a bittersweet feeling collected inside her.

Ione had arrived a couple of days earlier and had greeted the news that her father was going to marry Anna with a great deal of satisfaction.

'Good,' Ione had said. 'I didn't want you to leave. Marrying Papa means you have to stay.'

They'd spent the past few days adjusting to the new state of things, not that Ione seemed to require much adjustment. Not when she'd spent most of the time basking in the attention from not just one, but two adults.

When Ione had first arrived, Adonis had been stiff and unbending, as if he didn't quite know how to treat her, not helped by the fact that Ione had been a bit manic to start off with. But then, when she realised that her father wasn't suddenly going to send her away as he did in the palace, she settled down and relaxed, and little by little so did he.

Anna didn't know what had changed, whether it was being away from the palace and his duties, or whether it had something to do with the conversation she'd tried to have with him about his father, or perhaps it was simply having some time with his daughter, but Adonis seemed different.

He became less expressionless, less cold. A granite statue became warm, living flesh. A king slowly turned back into a man.

He joined in the activities Anna had organised: picnics and swimming and fishing off the end of the jetty, then stories and games in the evenings, and walking along the beach finding seashells during the day.

One night he'd smiled at her and it had taken her breath away. Then the next, he'd laughed at something Ione had said and the sound had made her heart squeeze tight in her chest.

Today he'd readied the small boat kept in a little shed by the water, deciding to take Ione for a sail. Sailing was something he'd learned from his nanny and, considering the casual competence with which he handled the boat, it was obvious he'd once spent a lot of time out on the water.

But watching him with his daughter made Anna ache.

Did he know he was a different man out here, on the island? Was he aware at all?

He was so unbelievably handsome when he became human. So charismatic. A king anyone would follow. A king anyone would die for.

'You don't understand, I have to believe it...'

Her throat contracted at the memory of his voice and the ferocity in his eyes as she'd confronted him about his father, about those lessons Xenophon had taught him. Lessons in torture and pain. Lessons in abuse.

She could only guess at his father's motives, and she had no idea whether Xenophon had truly believed that he was helping Adonis be a better king or whether he had been punishing his son for his mother's death—or perhaps even punishing himself for failing to save his wife. But maybe that didn't matter. What mattered was that Adonis felt he had to believe his father.

She put her hand up over her eyes to shield them from the sun as she looked out over the sea to where the little boat sailed. It was the sun that made her eyes water, surely, not the memory of him looking down into her eyes and cupping her face between his hands, telling her that there was nothing wrong with her, that she was a great many wonderful things. And that she was needed.

He wasn't detached, no matter what he said. And he didn't believe what his father had taught him, not deep down, she was sure of it. Why else would he hold her so gently? And give her such reassurance?

Why else would he be worrying so much about his brother, even now?

'Everything Xerxes went through would have been for nothing...'

He carried guilt for his brother's torture at their father's hands; she'd seen it in his eyes. Guilt for his mother's death, too, and no doubt guilt for his own treatment of his daughter as well. No wonder he clung to his father's lies and detached himself so completely from his own emotions. They must have caused him such agony.

Anna blinked the moisture from her eyes, a ghost of that agony echoing inside herself.

Knowing all of this didn't change anything, though. She'd wanted him to know that he wasn't alone, and that was still true.

But what you feel for him...

She knew what she felt for him. She'd known it for days.

Perhaps she'd even known it for weeks, ever since the night he'd made love to her in his office.

The decision she'd made the first morning here had taken hold: she'd fallen for him completely and utterly, and with no hope of return.

Not that falling for him changed anything either. No, it only made her even more certain that what she was doing was the right thing.

He was a lonely man with deep wounds and he needed healing, but they hadn't talked about his father again, and the only connection with her he'd allowed was in bed, in that room overlooking the sea.

It was a start. She only hoped it would be enough of one.

Anna's throat felt sore as the little boat turned towards the jetty, the waves glittering in the afternoon sun, and began to make its way back to shore.

Ten minutes later the boat was tied up, and Ione had leapt off, chattering at Anna about how she was going to be a pirate queen when she grew up and make people walk the plank. Adonis, leaping off after her, laughed and in a completely natural movement reached down to swing her up onto his shoulders, telling her that she would make a superb pirate, though he wasn't sure about the plank-walking.

The pain in Anna's throat worsened at the show of spontaneous physical affection, and not only that, but there was also laughter in his voice and in his eyes, his beautiful mouth turning up into a smile that took her breath away.

This was the man he should be. A man who looked as though he knew happiness. Who was relaxed and smiling, warmth radiating from him as he reached out his hand to her, and they all walked up the path to the house above the sea.

Not the hard, granite-faced king, but this charming,

charismatic man. The man he would never allow himself to be.

It won't happen. He won't let it.

No, it had to happen. And if she loved him enough, he might…

They spent another couple of magical days on the island, Anna shoving aside her growing trepidation at returning to the mainland, trying to remain optimistic that the happiness they'd discovered as a small family would remain even after they'd returned to the palace.

Yet when the day came that they had to leave, and they were all in the helicopter flying back to Itheus, the trip was a silent one; even Ione was quiet. And the closer they got to the palace, the more Anna felt Adonis withdrawing. His features hardened, his powerful body tensing, those blue eyes becoming sharper, cutting. The smile vanished and his mouth became hard and unyielding.

The man he'd been on the island disappeared so completely it was as if he'd never existed.

She had no time to speak with him when they landed. The instant he got out of the helicopter he was surrounded by people, and he didn't look at her or Ione once as they exited behind him. He didn't glance around to see if they were coming; he simply strode along the path to the palace, deep in conversation with his aides.

Anna had hoped some sign of the man would remain, but it hadn't.

The man was gone. All that was left was the king.

It felt like a knife in her heart.

More palace staff surrounded her, and as Ione was led off Anna was taken back not to the little room she'd once occupied, and not to the king's personal suite either, but to another suite of rooms in the wing where the royal family lived.

The bedroom was large and airy, with big windows that looked out over Itheus and a stone balcony to take advantage of the magnificent view. A huge four-poster bed, hung with gauzy white curtains, stood against one wall, angled towards the windows, while other carved, heavy furniture was scattered about.

It was luxurious and beautiful, but a chill had settled down inside her and she couldn't get rid of it. She didn't know why she'd been put here. Surely, she would now be sleeping with Adonis? Then again, maybe not. Maybe he was trying to keep a sense of propriety.

She tried to ignore the cold feeling, busying herself with settling in and then going to see if Ione was okay. The little girl had been fractious and tired, only wanting to watch TV and not do anything else, which was unusual, since she was normally very active. Her nannies were puzzled by this behaviour, but Anna wasn't. She knew that Ione was feeling exactly the way she was feeling too because she wouldn't see her father again, not the way he had been back on the island.

Anna did what she could for her, and later that evening tucked her into bed with a story, but Adonis didn't come to say goodnight the way he'd done every night in that house by the sea, and he didn't send a message.

And when she went back to her own rooms she found a meal had been laid out for her on the coffee table, but it hadn't been made by him and he wasn't sitting there waiting for her, smiling. There was no one there at all.

He had become the mountain again: icy, remote and completely inaccessible.

She told herself that it was okay, that, now he'd experienced what it was like to have a real family, he would start to let down his guard again. It would just take some time.

But, deep down, a part of her doubted.

The next couple of days were the same. She didn't see him, and when she asked where he was she was told that the king was catching up on work and was very busy.

Of course he was busy. He was always busy. Not that she had nothing to do herself. Wedding preparations were happening and there were dress-designer appointments and make-up consultations, plans for her hair and for the flowers she would carry, a meeting with the Archbishop of Axios, who would conduct the ceremony in Itheus's big cathedral.

But no Adonis. And no message from him either.

She tried not to let that bother her. Tried to tell herself that of course there would be a period of adjustment. That he would find his way back to her and to the man he'd been on the island again in time, she just had to be patient. In the meantime, she flung herself into caring for Ione to distract herself from the insistent, dragging doubt that the little family she'd been part of so briefly would always be missing one of its most vital components.

Him.

Five days later, alone in the luxurious rooms he'd set aside for her, Anna pushed wide the doors to the balcony and stumbled outside, feeling inexplicably as if she couldn't breathe.

She'd had a day of dress fittings and Ione being difficult, and there was a sadness inside her that she couldn't escape. It dragged at her, pulled at her, made her bad tempered, and the brittle calm she'd been trying to maintain had broken. She'd spoken too sharply to Ione, making the little girl run from her in tears, and making herself feel as if she were right back in the convent, desperate for something she couldn't name.

The night was deep and warm and velvety, the lights of the city beneath the palace glittering, the mountains looming on either side. The air was cool on her skin, but not too cold, carrying with it the memory of the hot noonday sun.

It was a beautiful night, but Anna couldn't enjoy it, unable to shake the sense that she'd only swapped one empty place for another, and both of those places were missing something vital. Something that could have made them home. Something she could never have.

She stood at the parapet and put her hands on the cool stone, taking breath after breath. Perhaps it was simply panic about the wedding and becoming queen. An attack of bridal nerves…

It's him you're missing. It's him you'll never have.

Cold iced the blood in her veins, doubt hooking its claws into her, and she had to take yet another breath to get control of it.

Yes, she was missing him. But she had to be patient. Had to believe that he would eventually come to see that what he'd found on the island he could have here too.

Ione was only tired and so was she. Tomorrow would be better. Perhaps she might even see him. That would help. She didn't need much, just his presence somewhere close by.

Behind her came the sound of her bedroom door shutting, and when she turned it felt as if her heart had stopped beating and was seizing in her chest.

Adonis was striding towards her, tall and powerful, shrugging out of his suit jacket and discarding it on the couch as he came. Pulling at the grey tie around his neck and jerking that off too, he tossed it negligently onto the floor, leaving him wearing a black business shirt and charcoal suit trousers that highlighted his strength and dark, masculine power, making every feminine sense she had sit up and take notice. His expression was stony, but the blue of his eyes burned like a gas flame.

Had he remembered their time on the island? Was he coming to tell her that was what he wanted? Was he coming to tell her that he needed her?

But he didn't say a word and he didn't look anywhere else but at her, coming across the room and through the double doors that led out onto the balcony. And he didn't stop. He reached for her and pulled her into his arms. He lifted his hands, sliding his fingers into her hair, tipping her head back and covering her mouth, hard and demanding.

It was a hungry, frantic kiss, echoing the hunger and demand in her own heart, crushing the doubt, melting the ice.

That man was still there. Her lover of the island. She could taste the desperation in his kiss, the longing for something more, the need for a connection.

It was there and perhaps it would take a long time for him to say it, or perhaps he never would, but that didn't mean he didn't feel it. That didn't mean he didn't want it.

She couldn't doubt him or put her own fears before what was in her heart.

His parents might not have put him first, but she would.

He needed her to and so she'd give him everything. Whatever he wanted, anything at all. She would give him all of it. Her mind. Her heart. Her soul.

Anna melted against him the way he'd been dreaming of for days now. Her mouth was open and hot under his, her lush curves pressed to every inch of him.

Since getting back from the island, he'd had a mountain of work to get through, because, although Xerxes had handled most of it, there was always more, and there were some things he alone had to do.

Adonis had informed Xerxes of his intention to marry and had installed Anna in new rooms in the family wing of the palace. To say Xerxes had been surprised was an understatement. But Adonis hadn't been in the mood to discuss that, or the child Anna was carrying, and so he'd sent his brother away and buried himself in his work.

Or, at least, he'd tried, starting with rebuilding the detachment he'd left in ruins back on the island.

Yet for some reason he couldn't. Because every time he attempted to detach himself from his emotions, all he could think about was walking along the beach and the leap of joy in his heart as Ione had put her hand in his; the tenderness that had filled him as Anna lay against him in the dark; the satisfaction of cooking for her; the happiness as he'd tacked across the bay in the little yacht, with Ione laughing in the sun...

The happiness that had ruined him.

That was why it was impossible to put his emotions aside, why he couldn't shake the coiling, tangling need that had clawed at him ever since he'd returned to the palace.

He'd tasted happiness and now he wanted more.

He'd thought denial would work, that his will would be strong enough, that if he stayed away from Anna, he would be able to hold out. But all those years of his father's training apparently hadn't been enough, because the instant he'd had an evening free he'd left his office and made straight for her rooms.

He was weak, the way his father had always told him he was.

Adonis kissed her deeper, harder, the hunger inside him seeming to get more intense with every passing second. And there was no point resisting it now, so he didn't.

Anna shuddered against him, her arms around his neck, letting him devour her, letting him ravage her mouth like a conqueror.

She tasted like heaven and he was so hard he couldn't think, let alone resist.

Picking her up in his arms, he turned from the balcony, striding back into the room. He laid her down on the bed, pulling off the silky white nightgown she wore and exposing all that beautiful soft pale skin. He got rid of his own clothes in seconds flat and then he was on the bed with her, pushing apart her thighs. She gasped as he slid a hand between them, stroking the hot, silky flesh he found there, making her writhe, readying her for him. But only when she was slick and trembling did he settle himself between her legs.

She reached for him without hesitation, and when he thrust hard into her she groaned and closed her legs around him, holding him tight to her in welcome. And then there was nothing but the building hunger, the feel of her around him, slippery and soft, her pulse beating fast and frantic in the hollow of her throat.

This is it. This is happiness. With her.

Her eyes were very dark as they looked up into his, pleasure glittering there, and the truth caught at his heart, fierce and bright, like embers exploding into flames.

Yes, *this* was happiness. *She* was happiness. She was what he'd wanted all this time. What he'd needed and never known.

What you can never have.

But he couldn't deal with that thought, not now, so he tried to drown it with pleasure, taking her to the brink of climax over and over again, keeping her hovering, almost but not quite tipping over.

She trembled and shook beneath him, her nails digging into his shoulders, his name a ragged prayer. The bright, fierce heat he felt in his own heart glowed in her eyes, and, when he drove her over the edge and ecstasy rippled over her lovely face, it flared, making her gaze glitter as brightly as stars, illuminating her from within.

He couldn't look at her, so he kissed her savagely instead as he took his own pleasure in hard, deep thrusts, letting the orgasm take him, letting the ecstasy annihilate him.

But there was no escape. Even when he closed his eyes the truth was still there, the fire burning hot in the hearth of his heart—the hearth that was supposed to stay dead and cold, but hadn't.

This is what your father was protecting you from.

Yes, he understood now. Of course his father hadn't shown mercy. Of course he'd been brutal and hard. Because happiness was a drug, and once you'd had a taste, all you wanted was more.

Xenophon had known his son too well, had known how hot Adonis's emotions burned. How he'd always wanted more. He'd wanted his mother to protect him, not his father's position, not the throne. And he'd wanted his father to comfort him after she'd died, not blame him. And when his father had made him choose between being a son and being an heir, he'd wanted to be a son. But how could he choose that when Xenophon had only wanted an heir?

His emotions were the problem. His need to be put before everything, his need for love. Because Xenophon had known, even if Adonis hadn't, that his son would always put that need before everything else.

And he had. He could have stopped Xerxes's torture, could have protected him, but he'd let it go on, because he'd wanted his father's approval. He'd wanted his love. Perhaps he'd even betrayed his parents all those years ago out of anger. Because he'd wanted to be put first, and he never had been…

His heartbeat was far too fast, the heat of his orgasm dissipating, leaving behind it a creeping, icy sensation.

Love was the problem. Love was the mistake. And he could feel it burning in his chest—love for the woman lying under him, so deep and intense and fierce. And he knew if he gave in to it, he would end up doing anything for her.

Even betraying a nation the way he'd done years ago.

He couldn't do that. He couldn't give in. Which meant there was only one option, only one choice. The same choice his father had always given him.

Son or heir? Brother or crown? Love or country?

He chose the throne. He always chose the throne.

Adonis shoved himself away from the woman on the bed, rolling off it and getting to his feet. His blood rushed through his veins, his pulse loud in his head. He couldn't get enough air.

'Adonis?' Her voice was soft and he could hear concern in it. Concern for him.

He turned and there she was, sitting up on the bed, completely naked, her hair around her shoulders and gleaming softly in the dim light of the room. Concern shone in her face, because that was the kind of woman she was. Unselfish and giving. Honest and open.

A woman he couldn't allow himself to have, no matter how badly he wanted her.

His emotions could put an entire nation in danger and he couldn't allow that. And, since he hadn't been able to resist her, the only thing he could do was send her away.

As his brother had been sent away.

There were tears in her eyes. 'You're going to send me away, aren't you?'

Of course she knew. She could read him like no one else. She could read every thought in his head.

'I have to,' he said, because there was no point in denial.

'Are you going to tell me why?' Her chin took on a determined slant. 'But don't feed me the same lies your father told you. I don't believe them.'

Pain crawled through him, aching and raw, his need for

her tightening his fists and eating at his heart. 'Because I love you.' The words weren't a blessing. They were a curse.

Shock flickered over her lovely face and then came joy, lighting her up like a Roman candle. She threw aside the sheet, sliding from the bed, apparently not caring that she was naked. Her skin glowed like pearls, her eyes like fine silver, glittering and precious as she came to him.

But he threw up a hand, stopping her in her tracks. He couldn't let her get close, otherwise he would break. And he wasn't going to break, not again. 'But I can't love you, Anna,' he said harshly. 'That's why you have to go.'

A fierce expression shone in her face. 'If you can't love me, then don't. I didn't ask you to. Just don't send me away.'

Of course his little nun would protest. Except this was the best decision for her too. He could cut out this love he felt; he could survive its loss. But she wouldn't. She was an orchid, in need of heat and light and care, and there was only darkness and coldness where he was. She would end up withering and dying, and she deserved more than that.

'No,' he said, his voice icy. 'Regardless of whether you asked for love or not, you need it, Anna. You cannot survive without it.'

'That's not true—'

'Tell me I'm wrong, then. Tell me you haven't been searching your whole life for someone who will love you the way your mother didn't. The way the nuns in your convent couldn't.'

She flushed, her eyes glittering. 'What does that matter? I don't have to get that love from you.'

'Then where will you get it? From whom? From Ione? That's a child's love. What about at night, when you want someone to hold you—'

'Don't make this about me,' she interrupted fiercely.

'This is about you. You want love, Adonis. You want it
so badly, but you won't let yourself have it. You won't let
yourself take it.' Her eyes glowed so bright, like stars. 'I
love you. And I'll wait for you. I'll wait as long as it takes
for you to realise that you can have what you want: joy,
laughter, happiness… Everything you never had, everything you want, it's yours.'

He did want it. He wanted it so badly that if he moved,
even a step, it would be to take her in his arms.

She will fail you in the end. They all fail you…

And that was true, wasn't it? His mother had put her
husband first and his father his throne. They hadn't cared
about what happened to him. No one had.

He'd told himself Xenophon had only been trying to
make him into a better king, helping him to protect his
country, and that maybe, deep down, his father was doing
it because he cared.

But those were lies, just as Anna had said.

His father hadn't cared about him. He'd just wanted him
to do what he was told.

And now here was Anna, telling him she loved him,
that she'd give him everything he ever wanted. But…how
could he trust that? How could he trust that one day something or someone else wouldn't become more important
to her than he was?

He couldn't. He wouldn't. Detachment was better than
that pain any day.

Besides, when there was a choice, he chose the throne.
That at least was familiar.

'No,' he said coldly, surrounding himself in ice and
stone. 'I'm sorry, Anna. It's you or the crown and the crown
always wins.'

The pretty flush that had stained her skin slowly dissipated, the joy leaving her eyes. She looked hollowed out

and far too pale. 'You're not going to change your mind, are you?' Her voice was only a whisper. 'You'll never change your mind. He did his work far too well.'

A crack opened up inside him, yawning wide, pain pressing at the edges.

He ignored it, turning away and picking up his shirt from where he'd thrown it, anything to distract himself, to get himself under control.

'And Ione?' Anna asked huskily when he didn't speak. 'If you can't love me, then you can't love her. Will you send her away too?'

'I'll find someone else to fulfil your role.' He kept his voice hard as he pulled on the shirt and then the rest of his clothes.

'Will you bring her up to be like you?' Anna went on implacably. 'Will you crush her spirit? Torture people she cares about so she learns to detach herself as well? Make sure she never knows joy or happiness or love?'

He whirled back to face her, shirt still open, his heart racing. 'Enough!'

But somehow Anna had come closer and she was standing in front of him, small and beautiful and naked. And her hands reached for him, cupping his face. 'Don't become him,' she said hoarsely. 'Don't become your father. If not for my sake, at least for hers.'

Her touch burned, fire against his skin, the pain in her eyes reaching into his soul and wrenching him apart.

Isn't she right? Isn't that what you've become?

Perhaps she was right. Perhaps this had been his destiny all along.

He took her wrists gently in his fingers, pulling her hands from his face even as he buried the pain in his heart. 'I won't hurt her, I swear it.'

'That's not what I asked.' Her gaze searched his, a sharp,

bright grief in her eyes. 'He failed you, Adonis. And he failed your brother too.'

A thread of agony crawled through him, despite the ice, but it was the agony of the man and so he crushed it. Crushed it utterly.

He didn't want to be the man any longer.

He needed to be the king.

'No, Anna,' he said without expression, getting rid of his emotions once and for all. 'Don't you see? He saved me. Without him, I would never have had the strength to send you away.'

Tears tracked down her cheeks in shiny silver trails, but she didn't look away from him. 'That's not strength, that's fear,' she said, her voice broken and yet firm. 'But I suppose you'll never understand that, will you?'

'No, little nun,' he said gently. 'I won't.'

More tears slid down her face, but she didn't bother wiping them away. 'Fine. But what happens to our baby?'

A whisper of pain echoed through him, a ghost of that possessiveness, so faint he could hardly feel it.

'You will be monitored,' he said. 'The child will be provided for, whatever happens.'

She remained standing there, her back straight, her chin lifted. 'I meant what I said. I'll always love you, Adonis Nikolaides. And if one day you wake up and realise that you do want me after all, I'll be waiting for you.'

Deep down, where the man lay buried beneath the rock and ice of the king, a tremor shook him.

But he'd made his choice. And he wouldn't choose again.

'Don't wait,' he said coldly. 'Never is a long time.'

Then he turned on his heel and walked out.

CHAPTER ELEVEN

ANNA THOUGHT ABOUT going to bed, but she knew she wouldn't sleep. It felt as though her heart had broken into a thousand jagged pieces in her chest and she couldn't stop the tears from streaming down her cheeks.

But they weren't tears for herself. They were for him. For the man she'd watched slowly and relentlessly become encased in stone and ice. For the burning flame in his blue eyes that was snuffed out, to be replaced by a cold, jewel-bright glitter.

He was becoming the king. Becoming his father.

And she'd been wrong. He hadn't come to his senses at all. He'd told her he loved her and, far from that being the thing that brought him to her, it had only driven him away.

He was afraid; she could see that now. Afraid of what he felt for her. And maybe he was afraid of what she felt for him too, because telling him she loved him hadn't changed things, either. She didn't know why.

He did love and he loved passionately, but he'd spent so many years fighting it there was clearly nothing she could do to change his mind.

Just like when her mother had cut off all contact, Anna hadn't been able to change her mind either.

You're not enough for him. You'll never be enough and you know it.

The thought was so painful that she eventually took herself into the shower, ending up sitting on the floor weeping for a lonely man who couldn't acknowledge his own need for comfort and love. A cold and unyielding mountain.

Eventually, she hauled herself out and dressed, just as someone knocked on her door. Her heart leapt and fluttered like a bird inside her chest, but when she pulled it open it wasn't Adonis, but his brother.

The disappointment was so bitter she could hardly bear it.

She wiped ineffectually at her cheeks, but was too tired to pretend she hadn't been weeping. 'What do you want?' she asked, not bothering with any proper form of address, despite his being a royal prince and she nothing but a banished nun.

Prince Xerxes was tall and ridiculously handsome, his dark eyes glinting with gold as they surveyed her. 'Are you going to invite me in?' he asked eventually, his tone neutral. 'Or are we going to have this conversation in the hallway? I am a prince, you know.'

Anna sighed and gestured for him to enter, since it didn't look as if he was going to go away.

'Why are you here?' she asked, closing the door after him, her voice raw and scratchy.

He gave her a long, considering look, then without a word vanished into the bathroom, coming back a minute later with a box of tissues. 'Here,' he said, handing it to her. 'You look like you need these.'

Not in the mood to argue, Anna took the box and sat down on the edge of the bed, blowing her nose determinedly and wiping her face.

'So,' Xerxes said slowly, 'my brother stormed out of here a little while ago looking like he wanted to chew through a palace wall with his teeth. And, since he told me earlier that apparently you were going to marry him, I thought I'd better come and see what all the fuss was about.' His gaze settled on her, concern in his dark eyes. 'What's happened, Anna?'

Her throat closed at the gentleness in his tone. 'There is no wedding. He just told me he's going to send me away.'

Xerxes frowned, muttering something very rude under his breath. 'I see. Did he say why?'

She could feel her eyes getting sore, more tears beginning to gather. 'He made the mistake of falling in love with me and apparently that's a cardinal sin.'

'Ah,' Xerxes murmured, as if that explained everything. 'I expect he mentioned that emotions are bad.'

'Yes.' Anna wiped away another tear. 'I told him it didn't matter that he couldn't love me back. That I didn't need it. I just wanted to love him, because he needs it so badly...' She stopped, because there was no point going on. 'It doesn't matter now. He won't change his mind; I know that much.'

Xerxes was quiet a long moment. Then he muttered, 'My brother is a fool. He's taken on too many of our father's lessons, that's the issue. And he's so damn stubborn.'

'I know.' She blew her nose again, debating whether to tell him that she was pregnant and then decided not to, since Adonis obviously hadn't mentioned it to him. 'He wants me to leave tomorrow morning.'

Xerxes frowned. 'Do you want to go?'

She thought about it. She thought about insisting on staying, on fighting for the man she loved, crushed beneath the crown he wore. But she'd tried that before and it hadn't worked, so why would it work now? She'd thought her love would be enough to move him, but it wasn't.

Which left her with only one option.

'Yes,' she said thickly. 'I need to go home. Back to the convent.'

The prince's face was expressionless, but something shifted in his dark eyes. 'If you would prefer to leave earlier and not at His Majesty's pleasure, I can arrange that for you.'

Yes, she could go tonight. She didn't have to wait until he got rid of her.

It wasn't much of a power move, but it was better than nothing.

Anna took a deep breath, wiping the remaining tears from her face, and met Xerxes's steady gaze. 'Yes, I think I'd like that.'

He nodded. 'You'd better start packing, then.'

Then she remembered something. 'Xerxes, I need Ione to know that I'm not leaving because of her. That I would have stayed if I could.'

'I'll tell her.'

Tears threatened again, but she fought them down. 'She's a special little girl. Adonis needs her so much.'

'Oh, I know. And don't worry.' There was a fierce glint in Xerxes's gaze all of a sudden. 'I'll make sure he's made aware of that.'

The next morning, Adonis made preparations to fly Anna back home to England, only to discover that she'd already gone. Apparently, she'd left in the depths of the night in one of the royal jets, courtesy of his brother.

He wasn't upset. Any pain he'd felt earlier was gone. He felt nothing, only a sense of…heaviness. As if something weighty had descended on his shoulders, something that would be there for ever.

But that was fine. He was carrying the heavy burden of his country anyway, so what was a little more weight?

He adjusted his arrangements, sending one of his aides to England instead to keep him up to date with the progress of her pregnancy. A decision needed to be made about that, but he had a few weeks yet; he'd make it closer to the time.

Right now, though, there was a wedding to be cancelled, not to mention other decisions to make, including finding a new companion for Ione.

He was in the middle of working through a stack of papers that afternoon, when the doors of his office flew open and his daughter came racing in, tears staining her face.

He frowned at her, a pang of something echoing inside him that he reflexively ignored. 'What's wrong?' he asked, putting his pen down. 'Where is your—'

'Where's Anna?' Ione demanded. 'I want Anna!'

Another something in his chest shifted, making it tighten. 'She had to go home to England, little one.'

'No!' Ione shouted. 'You told me she was going to be my *mama*. You said we would be a family.'

A sense of pressure increased in his chest, like someone pressing a hand down directly above his heart. 'That's not going to happen now,' he said firmly. 'She had to—'

'I hate you!' Ione's bright blue eyes, so like his own, were burning with rage. 'I hate you, Papa!' Then she turned and ran out of the room, weeping.

Adonis's jaw tightened, the pressure on his chest intensifying. He ignored it. She would learn, as he had, what it meant to sacrifice everything for the throne.

'Don't become him...if not for my sake, at least for hers.'

Anna's voice wound through his head, but he had no time to dwell on it, because Xerxes was suddenly strolling in, his dark eyes far too sharp for Adonis's liking. 'Ione is not happy with you, apparently,' he said casually.

'Get out,' Adonis ordered. 'I have work to do.'

'Or perhaps a high horse to sit on.' Xerxes ignored him, coming up to his desk. 'Tell me, is it cold up there, Your

Majesty? Is it comfortable? Does it matter that you've broken a woman's heart, not to mention your daughter's?'

Adonis didn't think that relentless pressure inside him could get any worse, but apparently that wasn't the case. It felt as if he was suffocating.

He kept himself very still, because if he moved he *would* suffocate. Either that or he'd explode and Xerxes would get caught in the fallout. 'I don't recall asking for your opinion, Xerxes. What I would like you to do is get out…'

His brother leaned over his desk and casually knocked his stack of papers over, scattering them on the floor. 'Look up and pay attention,' he snapped. 'The best thing to come into your life since Ione has gone and all you can think about is your work? Are you as blind as you are stupid?'

Adonis wasn't sure if it was the papers that broke him or Xerxes's insolent tone. Or that after Anna his detachment was irreparably damaged and nothing could fix it.

Whatever it was, right in that moment, fury rose, thick and hot, and he was out of his seat, coming around the side of his desk. He took his brother by the shoulders and flung him up against the wall before slamming an arm across his throat. 'Don't you *dare* speak to me like that.' He wanted his voice to be cold, but it wasn't. It was hot, gravelly, and full of rage. *'I am the king.'*

Xerxes didn't fight him and didn't move, but gold gleamed in his eyes. 'You're not a king. You're an idiot. You love her.'

'I can't love her,' Adonis ground out. 'Love can be used—'

'Why did you send her away?' Xerxes interrupted, as if his brother's arm wasn't pressing against his throat. 'She loves you, brother. Her tears broke my heart.'

He'd thought that after facing Anna the night before he'd

got rid of his emotions. That he would never feel anything again. Yet here he was with fury eating him up inside and guilt following on behind, along with grief and pain, and all those other emotions he'd been struggling his whole life to ignore.

They were cracks in his detachment, in his soul, fracturing him like veins of magma in a volcano, weaknesses undermining the strength of the whole. And they were getting wider, spidering out, making him feel as though he was going to break apart.

'I had to send her away,' he said roughly. 'A king cannot—'

'A king can do whatever the hell he pleases.'

'No.' He forced his arm harder against his brother's throat, his heart beating hard in the cage of his ribs. The cracks widened and he tried to stop them, tried to keep himself together. 'You of all people should know what love does to someone. What it did to me.' He was breathing faster now, the tangled wave of emotion boiling up inside him making those cracks turn into fissures, great chasms that would swallow him whole. 'What it did to you, Xerxes. What our father did to you. And all because of me!'

Strangely, the look in his brother's eyes softened. 'I know, Adonis.'

'I could have saved you.' The failure of it choked him, guilt strangling him. 'If only I'd stood up to him. But I didn't. Because I wanted his approval. I was desperate for it.' He could hardly breathe. 'I put my need ahead of your pain, ahead—'

'Adonis,' Xerxes said quietly. 'Let it go.'

'How can I do that? After what you suffered? After how I failed you?'

'You were just as much a victim as I was.' Xerxes's gaze was very direct, very steady. 'And my suffering led me to Calista. Believe me, brother, I would go through it all again, every second twice over, if it meant I got to have her in my life.'

His jaw was tight, his body ached. 'I can't let it go. It's not that easy.'

'I know it's not,' Xerxes said. 'But if I found the strength to step away from Xenophon's shadow, then so can you.'

'How?' He searched his brother's face. 'I don't understand how it's possible.'

'Look into your heart, Adonis. That's where your answer is. That's where your true strength lies.' A fierce light burned suddenly in Xerxes's eyes. 'That's where I found mine. In my wife and in my daughter. In my love for them.'

Every muscle in his body was tense. He felt as if he was in the middle of a battlefield.

How could love be a strength when it had been nothing but failure and pain for him?

Anna knows how.

Something surged through him, something that felt like rage and yet wasn't.

His little nun. His brave little nun. Who loved without fear and without reservation. Who didn't cut herself off or detach herself. Who threw herself passionately into everything she did, including caring for his daughter.

Including loving him.

She is so strong. How could you think she would fail you?

He went utterly still, frozen rigid where he stood as the thought hit him. She'd told him she loved him and he'd ignored it. Dismissed it. All the important people in his life had failed him, so why wouldn't she?

'That's not strength. That's fear...'

He'd dismissed that too, because he wasn't afraid.

Or was he? Was that the real truth? That deep down he *was* afraid? Afraid of all those emotions burning inside him. Afraid to let himself feel. Afraid to let himself trust. 'How do you know?' he asked in a voice that didn't sound like his. 'How can you ever believe someone when they tell you they love you?'

Xerxes stared at him a moment longer. Then he shrugged. 'It's called trust, Adonis. You can only trust them.'

'I don't know…' His voice was cracked and broken. 'I don't know if I can ever trust anyone.'

'You can trust her, though,' his brother said quietly. 'Her heart is big enough for both of you.'

And he was right, wasn't he? His little brother was wiser than he was. Because if there was one person in all the world he could trust, it was his indomitable little nun who'd told him she would wait for ever for him.

She won't fail you. You cannot fail her.

He could feel it then, the cracks running through him, but they weren't fissures or chasms after all. They weren't going to swallow him. They were letting the light in, pouring all over him, engulfing him in warmth. In strength. In certainty. A certainty he hadn't felt for years. And this time he didn't fight it, he embraced it.

It didn't matter if one day she might feel differently. It didn't matter if one day she changed her mind or found someone else more important to her than he was.

What mattered was that *she* was important to *him*. She was more important than anything in his entire life, except possibly Ione.

She was certainly more important than his throne.

And this was a choice, his last choice.

So Adonis Nikolaides chose.

'You're right.' He looked at his little brother, his heart

thundering in his chest. 'I need her back, Xerxes. I need her back right now.'

'Of course you do.' Xerxes smiled. 'And I have a very good idea how to go about it.'

CHAPTER TWELVE

THE FLIGHT TO England was interminable, the journey back to the convent deep in the rolling green hills of the English countryside even longer.

But Anna didn't care. She found she didn't care about much at all.

It was late and the Reverend Mother received her with little fanfare, apparently not requiring much of an explanation. She showed Anna back to her little room without comment, which was good because Anna didn't want to talk and was pathetically grateful she didn't have to, falling into a restless sleep the moment her head touched the pillow.

The next day she didn't feel any better, gritty-eyed and hollow inside. Some of the other nuns wanted to hear about Axios, but she didn't have the heart for conversation, staying in her room instead, lying on the bed with her arms wrapped around herself, trying not to think of Adonis or Ione.

Trying not to think of what she'd left behind.

She didn't know what time it was when there was a quiet knock on her door and it opened to reveal the Reverend Mother. She looked at Anna for a moment, then said quietly, 'You have a visitor.'

Anna shook her head. 'I'm sorry, Mother. I'm not up for visitors today.'

'Nevertheless, I think you'll want to see this one.' The Reverend Mother's lined face softened. 'He's waiting in the garden and he said he'd wait there all day if he had to.'

Everything inside Anna went still.

No. It couldn't be...

She didn't want to hold on to hope, so she tried not to as she walked the convent's echoing halls and out into the tiny walled garden with the roses climbing up the walls.

Yet hope burst out of her all the same, opening its wings and flying straight into the sky when she saw the tall, powerful figure waiting beside the fountain.

She froze, unable to move, her heart shuddering in her chest.

And then the figure turned and her heart plummeted.

It wasn't Adonis. It was Xerxes.

'What are you doing here?' Anna demanded, agony crawling through her.

Xerxes, against all odds, smiled. 'I'm here on behalf of my brother. He's been unavoidably detained, so he sent me to ask you if you'd like to attend a wedding.'

Anna blinked. 'A wedding? What wedding?'

Xerxes's smile grew even warmer. 'Your wedding.'

Shock moved through her and for a minute she had no idea what to say. 'Mine?' she eventually forced out. 'What do you mean?'

'The king wants to know if it's still true. If you're still waiting.'

She shuddered.

'Yes,' she said hoarsely, before she'd had time to think. 'I am.'

'In that case, he told me to tell you that "never" came sooner than he thought and that you're stronger and braver than he'll ever be. And that he loves you more than he'd ever thought possible.'

Anna felt unsteady, the world upending under her feet. 'I don't...'

'But don't take my word for it,' Xerxes said. 'If you come with me he can tell you himself.'

Everything was the same. Nothing had changed. She still loved a lonely mountain of a man who'd cut her out of his life. Who'd told her that he would never wake up one day and realise that he wanted her love.

But it seemed as if never was here. And she had nothing better to do. The convent was still a prison. And there was a wedding. *Her* wedding.

'Anna,' Xerxes said gently when she didn't move. 'Please. He needs you.'

She didn't know what that meant, and Xerxes wouldn't explain, but in the end she went with him, shocked when she was taken from the convent to a private airfield and the royal jet took off up into the sky.

On the plane, Xerxes showed her a room where a simple, long, white, silky dress was hanging, plus a raft of feminine beauty products, hairbrushes and pins and make-up.

A wedding, Xerxes had said. Her wedding.

Anna's heart thumped hard, and after Xerxes had closed the door behind her she stared at the dress on the hanger. Her wedding dress.

With shaking hands, she took it off the hanger and put it on. It fitted perfectly.

She paused over the make-up and then settled for her hair loose over her shoulders and a bit of lipstick. She didn't need blusher. Her cheeks were already glowing.

And when she came out of the room, Xerxes's smile filled the entire cabin.

Then there was nothing to do but wait.

Eventually, the jet touched down in Axios and she expected to be taken to the cathedral. Instead she was taken to a helicopter and bundled inside, and then they were fly-ing over the mountains and across the sea, to a small, fa-miliar island.

Anna's eyes filled with tears as the helicopter touched down and the doors were opened, and then Xerxes was guiding her out of the machine and along a rocky path strewn with white rose petals that led to the sea.

And there on the pure white sand, with the blue of the ocean beyond, stood a man.

Just a man.

He was tall and broad and powerful, and he wore a sim-ple white shirt with black trousers. His feet were bare, and pinned to his breast was a gold crowned lion.

He was looking at her and his eyes weren't cold; they were a fierce bright blue, full of heat, full of the passion that burned in his soul. The mountain had become a volcano.

Anna's throat closed and the tears threatened to spill, but when a little girl with bright red curls dressed in a sparkly white dress rushed up to her and thrust a bouquet of sea lilies into one of her hands while taking the other, Anna held on tight. And together they walked towards the man waiting on the beach.

There were only three others watching, Xerxes and his wife, Calista, and the priest standing with Adonis.

And when Anna arrived at last by his side he held out his hand to her, and the love and fierce possession that shone in his face made her heart tremble in her chest.

'You came,' he said, his deep voice hoarse as he took her hand in his. 'I wasn't sure if you would.'

'I told you I'd wait.' She took no notice of the tears on her cheeks. 'And I would have waited even longer.'

'I didn't want you to.' He brought her hand to his mouth, kissing the back of it, passion blazing in his eyes. 'You already waited too long for me to come to my senses. Forgive me, little nun. I've caused you such pain.'

Anna's tears fell and she didn't wipe them away. 'There's nothing to forgive. You were just afraid and I understood that.'

'But I never meant to hurt you.' He turned her hand over and kissed her palm, keeping his gaze on hers all the while. 'I should have trusted you and I didn't. All I ever wanted was someone to put me first, to be more important to someone than a throne. But when you gave me that... I couldn't take it. Because you were right, I was afraid. I told myself I was afraid that you would fail me somehow, but it wasn't that. It was the pain I was afraid of.'

Her throat closed in helpless sympathy. 'Oh, Adonis...'

His eyes gleamed hotter, fiercer. 'I thought my detachment would save me from that, but it didn't. There was too much inside me, all those feelings I'd been denying. I couldn't shut them off. Then someone I know pulled me aside and told me what a fool I was.' He glanced over to where Xerxes stood and smiled. 'He told me where to find the strength I needed to step away from my father's lessons. To overcome my fear.' Adonis glanced back at her, the fierce love of the man shining in the king's eyes. 'It was you, little nun. You're my strength. You showed me how to love without fear, how to love with passion and bravery. You would never fail anyone. And so I don't want to fail you. I want you to teach me new lessons, better lessons. I want you to bring happiness into my life and I want so much to bring it into yours too.'

Anna couldn't stop her tears and she could barely speak, her throat was so tight. 'I want that,' she forced out, her voice husky and raw. 'That's all I ever wanted.'

His smile was like the dawn after a long, dark, lonely night. 'Then marry me, Anna. I should have come for you myself, but I wanted this to be a surprise for you. And I wanted to give you a choice too.'

Anna took a shuddering breath. 'My choice will always be you, Adonis.'

His gaze was bluer than the sea behind him. 'I always chose my crown before. But not today, little nun. Today, I choose happiness. Today, I choose you.'

And so they were married on the beach, with no fanfare, only family and a priest.

Not a nun and a king.

Just a man and a woman.

And after the ceremony Adonis took her into his arms and kissed her passionately and for a long time, much to Ione's disgust.

Then much, *much* later, after celebrations with their family and after Xerxes, Calista and the priest had got into the helicopter and gone, Adonis and Anna let their little girl put Anna's bouquet into the sea as an offering for Ione's mother.

'Will she get it?' Ione asked her father as it floated in the waves.

'Yes,' he said quietly. 'She will.'

Then, as Ione scampered down to the water's edge to play, Anna leaned back in her husband's arms, his body tall and powerful against her back, a mountain protecting her, sheltering her. Loving her.

'You haven't said it, you know,' Anna murmured, watching the moonlight on the waves, and listening to Ione's laughter.

'Said what?' Adonis's breath was warm against her neck.

He was teasing her, of course he was. 'Xerxes told me to come with him so I could hear it from you myself.'

'You're mine.' His lips brushed against her skin, making her shiver. 'Is that enough?'

Anna turned in his arms and looked up into his strong face, meeting blue eyes gone dark as midnight. 'And are you mine, Lion of Axios?'

He smiled just for her, lighting up her heart. 'Of course, Anna Nikolaides. Who else's would I be?'

Her new name made her happiness overflow inside her. 'Say it.'

His expression intensified, blazing into hers. 'I love you, little nun. I love you, my wife, my lioness, my strength. I love you, Anna.'

'And I love you, my husband,' she whispered back.

He kissed her under the moonlight, there on the beach, with Ione's laughter in their ears. He was a king and a lion. A mountain and a man.

But most importantly of all, he was her love. He was her heart.

He was her home.

He was hers.

EPILOGUE

XERXES LOOKED INTO the crib and pulled a face. 'Twins? Really, Adonis? You always have to go one better, don't you?'

Adonis, feeling very smug indeed as he looked down at his two sons, laughed. 'What did you expect? I am a king.'

Ione stood on the other side of the crib, looking as smug as he felt. 'Achilles and Hector,' she pronounced. 'Those are their names, Papa. And they're my Defenders of the Throne, aren't they?'

'They are,' Adonis agreed. 'Both of them.'

'God help them,' Xerxes muttered. 'She's been reading too many myths.'

But Adonis wasn't listening. He was already turning back to the bed where his beautiful wife lay, resting on the mound of pillows he'd arranged behind her head.

He sat down and snuggled her into his arms, every muscle in his body relaxing as she turned her radiant smile on him. 'We should keep those names,' she said.

'Really? You like them?'

'Yes.' Her smile deepened. 'They're heroes. Just like their father.'

'Next time, I want heroines,' he said and kissed her. 'Just like their mother.'

Anna gave a long-suffering sigh. 'There won't be a next time. Not after that.'

But there was. And another. And then again.

Because, though the Lion of Axios was a stern and regal king, Adonis Nikolaides was a man who turned out to have an unlimited appetite for laughter and joy and happiness. For his wife.

And for love.

Always love.

* * * * *

COMING SOON!

We really hope you enjoyed reading this book. If you're looking for more romance, be sure to head to the shops when new books are available on

Thursday 17th September

MILLS & BOON

Coming next month

CHRISTMAS IN THE KING'S BED
Caitlin Crews

"Your Majesty. Really." Calista moistened her lip and he found himself drawn to that, too. What was the matter with him? "You can't possibly think that we would suit for anything more than a temporary arrangement to appease my father's worst impulses."

"I need to marry, Lady Calista. I need to produce heirs, and quickly, to prove to my people the kingdom is at last in safe hands. There will be no divorce." Orion smiled more than he should have, perhaps, when she looked stricken. "We are stuck. In each other's pockets, it seems."

She blanched at that, but he had no pity for her. Or nothing so simple as pity, anyway.

He moved toward her, taking stock of the way she lifted her head too quickly—very much as if she was beating back the urge to leap backward. To scramble away from him, as if he was some kind of predator.

The truth was, something in him roared its approval at that notion. He, who had always prided himself on how civilized he was, did not dislike the idea that here, with her, he was as much a man as any other.

Surely that had to be a good sign for their marriage.

Whether it was or wasn't, he stopped when he reached her. Then he stood before her and took her hand in his.

And the contact, skin on skin, floored him.

It was so...*tactile*.

It made him remember the images that had been dancing in his head ever since he'd brought up sex in her presence. It made him imagine it all in intricate detail.

It made him hard and needy, but better yet, it made her tremble.

Very solemnly, he took the ring—the glorious ring that in many ways was Idylla's standard to wave proudly before the world—and slid it onto one of her slender fingers.

And because he was a gentleman and a king, did not point out that she was shaking while he did it.

"And now," he said, in a low voice that should have been smooth, or less harshly possessive, but wasn't, "you are truly my betrothed. The woman who will be my bride. My queen. Your name will be bound to mine for eternity."

Continue reading
CHRISTMAS IN THE KING'S BED
Caitlin Crews

Available next month
www.millsandboon.co.uk

LET'S TALK
Romance

For exclusive extracts, competitions
and special offers, find us online:

 facebook.com/millsandboon
 @MillsandBoon
 @MillsandBoonUK

Get in touch on 01413 063232

For all the latest titles coming soon, visit
millsandboon.co.uk/nextmonth

MILLS & BOON

THE HEART OF ROMANCE

A ROMANCE FOR EVERY KIND OF READER

MODERN

Prepare to be swept off your feet by sophisticated, sexy and seductive heroes, in some of the world's most glamourous and romantic locations, where power and passion collide.
8 stories per month.

HISTORICAL

Escape with historical heroes from time gone by. Whether your passion is for wicked Regency Rakes, muscled Vikings or rugged Highlanders, awaken the romance of the past.
6 stories per month.

MEDICAL

Set your pulse racing with dedicated, delectable doctors in the high-pressure world of medicine, where emotions run high and passion, comfort and love are the best medicine.
6 stories per month.

True Love

Celebrate true love with tender stories of heartfelt romance, from the rush of falling in love to the joy a new baby can bring, and a focus on the emotional heart of a relationship.
8 stories per month.

Desire

Indulge in secrets and scandal, intense drama and plenty of sizzling hot action with powerful and passionate heroes who have it all: wealth, status, good looks…everything but the right woman.
6 stories per month.

HEROES

Experience all the excitement of a gripping thriller, with an intense romance at its heart. Resourceful, true-to-life women and strong, fearless men face danger and desire - a killer combination!
8 stories per month.

DARE

Sensual love stories featuring smart, sassy heroines you'd want as a best friend, and compelling intense heroes who are worthy of them.
4 stories per month.

To see which titles are coming soon, please visit

millsandboon.co.uk/nextmonth

JOIN US ON SOCIAL MEDIA!

Stay up to date with our latest releases, author
news and gossip, special offers and discounts, and
all the behind-the-scenes action
from Mills & Boon...

 millsandboon

 millsandboonuk

 millsandboon

It might just be true love...